*for Mylo; the
beginning of a series
we hope you will*

*—Dexter
#2 of*

Scout

*The Secret
of the Swamp*

Enjoy the adventure!

*love,
Opa & Oma*

The small door of the little hut slowly swung open and a young-looking man came out, stooping to get through the low doorway. He was wearing the uniform of the British air force. His eyes were fixed on the boy and the dog. He studied them a moment, and then he smiled. He pointed to Tom's wet clothes. — Pg. 40

Scout

The Secret
of the Swamp

by Piet Prins

INHERITANCE PUBLICATIONS
NEERLANDIA, ALBERTA, CANADA
PELLA, IOWA, U.S.A.

Canadian Cataloguing in Publication Data
Prins, Piet, 1909-1985
  Scout : the secret of the swamp

  Translation of: Snuf de hond.
  ISBN 0-921100-50-7

  I. Title.
  PT5866.P75S3613 1997 j839.3'13'64 C97-910372-X

Library of Congress Cataloging-in-Publication Data
Prins, Piet, 1909-1985.
  [Snuf de hond. English]
  Scout : the secret of the swamp / by Piet Prins.
    p. cm.
  "Including 10th anniversary catalogue of Inheritance Publications."
  Summary: During the Nazi occupation of the Netherlands, a young Dutch
boy's German shepherd proves himself invaluable when his tracking ability saves
his young owner's life.
  ISBN 0-921100-50-7 (pbk.)
  1. Netherlands — History — German occupation, 1940-1945 — Juvenile fiction.
[1. Netherlands — History — German occupation, 1940-1945
2. German shepherd dogs — Fiction. 3. Christian life — Fiction.] I. Title.
PZ7.P9366Sn 1997
[Fic] — dc21   97-19929
                                                     CIP
                                                     AC

First published in Dutch as *Snuf de hond*, © Uitgeverij De Vuurbaak b.v.,
Groningen, The Netherlands,

Translated by Harry der Nederlanden
Cover Painting and Illustrations by Jaap Kramer

6th Pinting 2020

Contents

Books by Piet Prins

Scout Series:
The Secret of the Swamp
The Haunted Castle
The Flying Phantom
The Sailing Sleuths
The Treasure of Rodensteyn Castle
The Mystery of the Abandoned Mill
Scout's Distant Journey

Inheritance Readers Series
#1 Rob and Roland
#2 Rob and Roland on the Farm
#9 Anak, the Eskimo Boy

The Four Adventurers - The Evil Professor
Four Adventurers - The Mystery of the Three Fingered Villain

Run Kevin, Run!

Shadow 1 - The Lonely Sentinel
Shadow 2 - Hideout in the Swamp
Shadow 3 - The Grim Reaper
Shadow 4 - The Partisans
Shadow 5 - Sabotage

Sheltie 1 - The Curse of Urumbu
Sheltie 2 -The Search for Sheltie

Stefan Derksen's Polar Adventure

Struggle 1 - When the Morning Came
Struggle 2 - Dispelling the Tyranny
Struggle 3 - The Beggars' Victory
Struggle 4 - For the Heart of Holland

Wambu 1 - The Chieftain's Son
Wambu 2 - In the Valley of Death
Wambu 3 - Journey to Manhood

Chapter 1

The Stranger

The pet shop was alive with noise and movement. Songbirds fluted, parakeets squawked, and a brightly coloured parrot fluttered his eyelids and screeched. In one large cage a spider monkey was swinging on the branch of a dead tree.

There were also dogs: big ones and little ones, each in his own pen. There were yappy little whelps and calm, noble beasts; expensive, pedigreed dogs and cheap, friendly mongrels.

In one cage, staring through the wire mesh, sat a German shepherd puppy with a beautifully marked head. His intelligent eyes stared sadly out into the world. He was lonesome. The puppy had been born two months earlier on a big farm and was used to open fields. For the last three days he had been locked up in the strange surroundings of the crowded pet store.

The sudden change was very hard on the puppy. He was well-cared for, but no one ever petted him or took him outside for a run.

On the street in front of the pet shop a small station wagon pulled up. Out of it stepped a man and a boy about ten years old.

"I want a puppy for my son," said the man.

The storekeeper opened several cages and showed the boy a number of puppies, but each time the boy shook his head, and so did the father.

Then the storekeeper lifted the German shepherd puppy from his cage and set him on the floor. Happy to regain his freedom, the puppy wagged his tail joyfully and began sniffing about in the store.

"Oh, Father, isn't he beautiful! Can I have that one? I've already thought of a name for him. See the way he's sniffing around? He must be a good tracker. So I'll call him Scout!"

"Well, all right, Tom," said the boy's father. "If you're sure you want him. He's going to grow up into a big dog, you know, and you'll have to take care of him."

A few minutes later, when the car pulled away from the pet store, Scout was sitting in the front seat between Tom and his father.

Soon they were leaving the city. They drove through country that Scout had never seen before, but Scout felt the hand of his new master stroking his head and he was happy.

After about an hour's drive, the car turned up a long driveway to a large remodeled farmhouse. On the fence hung a sign: *Heathview*. The station wagon stopped by the side door. Scout was led into the house. First he came into a large porch where his nails clicked on the linoleum. Then he was coaxed down a carpeted hallway to the living room. A tall, handsome woman jumped to her feet and opened her mouth in happy surprise.

"Look, Mom! Isn't he beautiful!"

"Oh, he is! And he'll make a fine watchdog too!" exclaimed Mother.

Everyone admired Scout, including the housekeeper and the gardener; they all petted him and spoke to him in friendly voices. Then Tom took the puppy into another room — a light, airy bedroom where a young girl lay in bed. She was Tom's sister, Ina. She had been ill for a long time and was slowly starting to recover, but she would have to remain in bed for some time yet.

Ina, too, thought Tom had made a good choice. "When you're in school, he can come into my room and play with me," she said.

That was all right with Tom. And with Scout too. He barked and wagged his tail happily.

The days that followed were very happy ones for Scout. Every day he played and romped with Tom, and chased around the large yard with him. Sometimes he spent hours in Ina's bedroom learning funny little tricks and listening to her friendly voice.

At night he slept in his own basket in the kitchen.

At mealtimes he was spoiled by everyone, and he quickly grew into a strong, young dog.

One day as Scout was wandering about in the back yard enjoying the sun and exploring, he put his head through the hedge. Suddenly he started. Right beside him were the legs and tattered boots of an evil-smelling man who was standing on the other side of the hedge studying the house.

The man was startled too when the German shepherd's head came poking through the hedge. He aimed a hard kick at the dog's nose, but Scout was too quick for him.

Scout wasn't afraid of the man; he bared his teeth and growled.

Then the man suddenly changed his behaviour. He bent forward toward Scout, clucking his tongue and patting his leg. "Here, boy! Come here. Good boy! Look what I've got for you." From his pocket he pulled a chunk of meat and held it out to Scout.

The meat smelled delicious, but Scout sensed that the man was not a friend. The man's evil smell mingled with that of the meat. The dog ignored the outstretched hand and fixed his eyes on the man's face, growling deeply.

The gardener came walking into the back yard, whistling. The man mumbled a few curses and, dropping the meat back into his pocket, he hurried off, still crouching behind the hedge.

Several days later in the middle of the night, as he lay sleeping in his box in the kitchen, Scout was suddenly awakened. Had he heard a strange noise in his sleep? He pricked up his ears and listened but heard nothing. Nevertheless, something was amiss. He sniffed. There was a strange smell in the house. A stranger? The fur on his neck bristled. He remembered that evil smell. Growling softly, he rose to his feet. Now he also heard noises.

The door to the study was partly open. When Scout peered into the room, he saw a man with a bright torch burning a hole in a large black cabinet. A second man was bending over him, but Scout paid no attention to him, for he recognized the man with the torch. It was the man at the hedge who had tried to kick him.

Scout shot through the doorway like an arrow and was on the man in an instant. With a smothered cry, the safecracker dropped the torch, but at the same time the other man brought a steel pipe down on Scout's head, and the dog sank to the floor without uttering a sound.

"There! He's dead," whispered the man. "He won't bother us again."

But he was wrong.

Several hours later, Scout regained consciousness. Daylight was streaming in through the windows. The safe stood wide open and empty. The burglars had escaped with everything.

Coby, the young housekeeper, bent over him, crying. She was usually the first one to be up and around in the morning, and she had discovered the robbery.

"Oh! Oh, how awful!" she wailed. "And just when Mr. and Mrs. Sanders are away! Those burglars must have known. Oh, oh! They've stolen everything and nearly killed poor Scout."

Scout wagged his tail a little to show that, in spite of the roaring in his ears, he was far from dead. But when he tried to get up, he toppled over again and lapsed back into unconsciousness.

When he came to for the second time, a veterinarian was bandaging the gaping wound in his head. Tom hovered over him with tears in his eyes. Also in the room were two policemen, one of whom was busily writing in a small notebook.

"Poor Scout," said Tom. "If only you could talk, then you could tell the police what happened."

But it was too late anyway; the robbers were long gone.

Chapter 2

On the Trail

That afternoon Scout was already feeling much better. When Coby put his favourite dog food before him, he ate hungrily, and later he began roaming about the house again. Tom had stayed home from school. He was sitting in Ina's room talking about what had happened.

"I wish Dad and Mom were home," said Tom. "They should have the telegram by now, I think. Maybe they'll come home tonight."

Scout was sniffing about out in the back yard. The two policemen had left, and everything seemed to be back to normal, but the clever dog sensed that something was still amiss.

A little later Tom joined him in the back yard. Tom was feeling somewhat tense and tried to unwind by playing a little with his dog. But Scout didn't feel much like playing.

They ended up near the back of the large yard, close to the hedge. Suddenly Scout stood still and growled. There was the opening that he had put his head through when the burglar had been spying on the house. It seemed to be much larger now. The tangled branches of the hedge had been bent back and broken. Scout sniffed at the spot excitedly. He smelled that strange, evil smell.

Tom looked at him. What was Scout doing? Then he too saw the opening in the hedge. From one of the branches dangled a small shred of cloth. It must have been ripped from the clothes of whoever had come through the hedge. Suddenly Tom understood. The burglars must have come through here.

Tom had an idea. He took the shred of cloth from the branch and held it in front of Scout's nose.

"Find him, Scout. Fetch!" he said.

Scout sniffed and immediately headed for the hole in the hedge and squeezed through. Tom was right behind him.

The dog trotted away into the dusk, his nose close to the ground. Tom had a hard time keeping up to his tracking dog. For a short distance, they followed the dirt road that passed behind their property, but soon Scout turned off on a trail that led out onto the wide heath. It was almost dark when they reached the trail. Tom was becoming a little uneasy, but he decided to go on anyway.

The darkness didn't bother Scout, but for Tom it was rough going. The moon was almost full, however, and as it rose higher in the sky, Tom could pick his way over the rough terrain more easily. There were no farms or houses of any kind to be seen. In every direction that he looked Tom could see only the low brush and the spiky grass clumps of the heath. He and Scout seemed to be the only creatures moving for many kilometres around. The path had petered out, and once in a while Scout seemed to lose the trail, for he would go sniffing round and round in circles. Sometimes, too, he would go back a short way, but each time he picked up the trail again.

At last they reached the other side of the heath. It was becoming very late, and Tom was exhausted. He tried to call Scout back to head home, but the dog went on, his nose still to the ground. They were now on the edge of a large forest, and Scout pushed his way through the underbrush. Reluctantly Tom followed. The branches lashed at him and snagged his clothes. This was worse than the heath. He was almost sobbing with effort and anxiety.

Just as he was thinking about turning back, without Scout if necessary, he saw a faint glow of light between the trees. It was just for a moment and then the woods were dark again. Tom found himself on a winding path. Suddenly it widened into a clearing. Against the blackness of the dense woods, he could just make out the shape of a sagging old shack. A narrow strip of light showed under the door.

"This must be where the light came from," thought Tom. "Someone must have opened and closed the door."

Scout was standing in front of the shack. A low, threatening growl rose from deep in his throat.

"Shhh! Here Scout!" whispered Tom. He cautiously circled the shack. It seemed to be divided into two rooms. There was light in the front room, but the only window had been covered with a piece of cardboard. Near the bottom of the cardboard, however, was a small slit. Tom sneaked up to the window, and by standing on his toes, he could peek through the slit into the room. Two men were sitting at a wobbly old table. Between them stood a big bottle and three glasses, and also a metal money box. Tom started in surprise. He recognized the box. He had seen Father taking it out of the safe many times. The men were talking. Tom held his ear against the window and listened attentively. He was so absorbed in what the men were saying, he didn't notice that Scout was acting restlessly and growling angrily. Tom could catch only snatches of the conversation. The men were talking about someone called Max and about a car, but much more than that he couldn't understand.

Suddenly strong fingers seized him by the neck and jerked him away from the window. At the same moment, Scout launched himself at Tom's attacker, barking furiously. Tom struggled wildly to get out of the man's grasp, but without success. The man's companions inside the shack immediately came storming outside in response to his cries for help. One of them wielded a big club. Tom thought he was done for, but then his attacker uttered a scream of pain as Scout sank his teeth into the man's arm. In trying to shake off the dog, he let go of Tom with one hand, and Tom tore himself loose.

But now the other two men had also arrived. Tom saw one of them bringing down his club hard on Scout's wounded head. The dog dropped like a sack of grain. The other man made a grab for Tom, but Tom dodged him and then dove into the trees.

The moon was hiding behind the clouds, so Tom could hardly see where he was going. Wild with panic he ran through the trees and bushes. A branch whipped his face, hurting him badly, but he ran on. Faster and faster! Away from those angry voices behind him.

He stepped on a slippery tree root and skidded sideways falling headlong to the ground. He scrambled up to run on, but a stabbing pain in his ankle stopped him. He tried again, but the ankle wouldn't support his weight. He must have sprained it! He stumbled ahead a few steps, wincing with pain, but his pursuers were catching up. Not knowing what else to do, he quickly crawled into a thick clump of bushes.

One of the men walked right by his hiding place and stopped to peer into the tangled growth. Tom held his breath, but the man saw nothing. The voices faded away and Tom began to breathe easier. His foot, however, ached terribly.

Listen, the men were coming back! One of them was carrying a flashlight this time.

"He's got to be hiding around here somewhere. He can't have gotten away so quickly," Tom heard one of them say.

His heart pounded with terror. "Lord, help me," he prayed silently.

The beam of the flashlight came closer.

"Look," said the same voice, "here are the boy's tracks. They stop here. Let's look over there."

The burglar pushed into the bushes, shining his flashlight ahead of him. The light caught Tom full in the face.

"Okay, boy! Come on out!" said the man, with a nasty laugh. "We've got a much better spot for you."

When Tom made no move to get up from where he was sitting, the man grabbed Tom by his jacket and dragged him out of the bushes.

Tom was on the verge of tears, but he bit his lip and forced back the tears. The men asked him his name and demanded to know what he had heard at the window, but Tom said nothing. They shoved him ahead of them back to the shack. He limped forward on his sprained ankle, dizzy with pain.

When he got to the shack, the bottle was still standing on the table, but the money box was gone.

"You won't be running off again with that sprained ankle," said the man who had found him. "In an hour or so it will be so swollen, you won't be able to take a single step. But just to make sure, I'm going to tie your hands behind your back."

With the help of one of the other burglars, he tied Tom's hands tightly behind his back. Then he opened the door to the other, unlit room and shoved Tom inside, adding in a threatening tone, "One peep out of you, and we'll fix you like your dog."

Tom was left standing alone in the blackness of the small room. His foot was burning and throbbing, his shoe was beginning to pinch, and the rope was biting painfully into his wrists. He lowered himself to the floor and sat there thinking.

Although he was in poor shape himself, he had not forgotten his faithful friend Scout. He was very worried about him. Had he been killed by the man with the club? Was he lying outside the shack, dead?

With some difficulty, Tom managed to get back on his feet. His eyes were beginning to get used to the darkness, and he had decided to explore the room a little. With his hands tied on his back that wasn't easy, but he didn't give up.

He found nothing in the room except built into one wall was an old-fashioned closet-bed with a smelly old mattress lying in it. When he shuffled farther into the room, he suddenly got an awful scare. In the far corner his foot bumped into something soft, something alive.

Tom's heart pounded in his throat. He hardly dared to hope. Forgetting to be careful, he dropped to his knees and turned his back toward the object on the floor, groping at it with his tied hands. He felt something furry and warm. It was Scout. He was lying on the floor, motionless.

Tom could have shouted with joy, but at the same time he became aware of his own utter helplessness. Carefully he groped farther until he found Scout's head. He felt something sticky — blood! The dog moaned quietly. Fear flashed through Tom's body. Scout could be lying there slowly bleeding to death, and Tom was unable to help him. He had to get his hands free to take care of Scout's wound!

Feverishly he tried to think of something. Might there be a sharp nail or something jutting from the wall on which he could cut the rope from his wrists? He stood up once more and went around the entire room searching the wall. Nothing.

Then he had another idea. In his right pants pocket was a jackknife, but with his hands tied he couldn't reach it. Lying down flat on the floor, he wriggled and squirmed until his pants twisted around his body, so that he could just reach the edge of his pocket with his fingers. He seized the edge and tugged until the side seam of his pants gave with a sudden rip. After that, it was only a matter of working the bottom of the pocket upward until the knife slid out onto the floor.

Ah, there it was! Quickly he sat up, and a moment later he had the knife in his hands. Getting it open, however, was no easy matter. It cost him a couple of broken fingernails. And to cut the rope with the open knife was even more of a problem. He just couldn't get enough leverage.

But Tom had already thought of something else. When he had searched the walls for a nail, in one place he had found a wide crack between two boards. He shuffled over toward the spot and managed to wedge the handle of the knife into the crack. Then he carefully rubbed the ropes binding his wrists along the knife-blade. It was a tricky business. Twice the handle slipped out of the crack, and once he received a nasty cut in the side of his palm, but finally the ropes began to give. He wrenched hard and the ropes snapped.

Loud laughter sounded in the other room. The three burglars seemed to be in a good mood.

As he started crawling back across the room toward his wounded dog, suddenly a wet nose was snuffling at him. Scout had revived and sought out his master.

Again loud voices sounded from the room next to Tom's prison.

"I'm telling you, Max must have had car trouble! Otherwise he'd have been here long ago. And I'll bet you he shows up before daybreak," someone argued.

"He'd better! Because I want to put a good distance between myself and this place before morning," growled another voice.

"But what are we going to do with that boy?"

"Shut up!" said the third man, who seemed more sober than the other two. "Wait a minute."

Tom heard his chair grate across the floor. Immediately he grasped what the man was doing.

"Scout! Play dead, Scout!" he whispered right by the dog's ear. It was a trick he and Ina had taught Scout when he was still a puppy. The dog lay flat on the floor, his legs extended and his eyes closed. Tom lay down next to him, his hands behind his back as though they were still tied.

He was just in time! The door opened and one of his captors shone a flashlight into the room. Tom and Scout both lay motionless, and after a few moments, the door closed again.

"It's okay. I think the dog is finished this time, and that boy has fallen asleep," the man said, satisfied. "When we leave, we'll tie our little snooper so he can't move, and we'll put a gag over his mouth. Someone should find him in a couple of days, but then we'll be long gone. And if that blasted dog isn't already dead, I'll cut his throat before we leave."

Tom shuddered. He and Scout had bought a little time, but if they didn't get out of their prison soon, his future looked bleak. What if he had to lie

in the shack for days, gagged and tied up so he couldn't move? If he wasn't found in time, he might die of starvation and Scout would be killed for sure.

The men went on talking. Tom was beginning to understand what was going on. Max was the fourth burglar, who was supposed to come and pick up the others with a car. When Tom had arrived at the shack and sneaked up to the window, one of the men had been out by the road looking for Max. That had been Tom's undoing.

His thoughts went back to Scout. The dog was still bleeding and sometimes he moaned quietly. Tom had to do something for him. He took off his shirt and cut it into strips with his jackknife. Then he bandaged Scout's head as well as he could. The dog didn't resist in the least.

Suddenly Tom noticed that the room seemed to be getting lighter. He could now see Scout's head. Where was the light coming from?

When he looked up, he found out. In the roof was a gaping hole! As long as it had been dark outside, the hole had been invisible. But now the moon had broken through the thick cloud cover and was shining into the hole. One of the boards in the roof was broken and a couple of roof tiles were missing. The sky was clearly visible. Looking up into the sky, Tom suddenly felt very calm. The Lord could see him down here in this dark shack. He closed his eyes and asked God to save him.

As he opened his eyes, another idea came to him. The hole in the roof was directly over the built-in bed. Maybe he could climb out through the hole! He stood up and started to walk toward the bed; immediately a stabbing pain reminded him of his ankle. It was now so swollen, he could hardly bend it at all. He couldn't take a single step without doubling up with pain. He sat down on the floor again and removed his shoe. Then he wound the remaining strips of cloth that he had cut from his shirt tightly around his ankle. That helped, but not enough that he could walk.

Still, he didn't want to give up on his idea. Suddenly he thought, "What if Scout could get out through the hole and bring help!" The dog had been badly hurt, but he was again sniffing about the room. Scout was unusually smart. Maybe Tom could make him understand.

Tom limped to the bed and carefully climbed up on it. Now he could just reach the hole with his hands. The opening wasn't wide enough, but the boards were extremely rotten. If he pulled hard, he was sure he could make the hole bigger. He would also have to push aside some of the roof tiles, but then the men in the next room would certainly hear it.

He stood still and listened for many minutes, his hand on the rotten board. The three burglars must have drained the bottle by now, for they were becoming quite noisy. One of them told a joke and the room echoed with loud laughter.

Crack went the board. It broke off as Tom tugged with all his might, but the laughter drowned out the noise, and it went unnoticed by the three men, as did Tom's cry of pain. One of the roof tiles had come tumbling in through the hole and had fallen right on his sore foot. Tom fought back the tears at the intense pain that shot through his ankle. Fortunately it soon let up.

Now the hole was large enough, but he couldn't very well climb through it himself and try to escape on his sore ankle. Tom felt Scout's nose against his knee. The dog had also jumped up on the bed.

The moon was shining brightly through the jagged hole, and Tom could see the bloody, bandaged head of his dog quite clearly. The bandage seemed to have helped, for Scout was steady on his feet again and looked quite alert.

"I've got to risk it," thought Tom. "I can't make it myself, so Scout will have to go for help."

He pointed to the hole and tried to lift the German shepherd, but that was out of the question. Scout had put on a lot of weight in the past year

and had become a heavy dog — too heavy for Tom to lift. He'd have to find some other way.

He stood and thought a moment. Then he had an idea. He stooped down, lifted Scout's face upward and pointed to the hole. "Through there, Scout. Jump, boy! Up, up! Run home. Home, boy!"

He repeated this once more, pointing up at the hole. Scout wagged his tail and whined softly, as if he wanted to say, "I understand, but it's too high." But Tom had thought of that. He listened to the sounds in the next room for a moment. The burglars were still talking loudly.

Then Tom stooped forward, putting his hands on his knees, and whispered, "Jump, Scout! Jump!"

The dog understood. With his first jump, he landed on Tom's back. Tom swayed momentarily as a sharp pain shot up his leg because of the heavy weight on his back, but he caught himself. Then Scout jumped again and disappeared through the hole.

Tom heard him landing on the roof tiles; then followed a muffled thump. The dog had jumped to the ground. Tom listened with bated breath whether the men inside had heard the noise, but the talk in the other room went on uninterrupted.

Closing his eyes, Tom thanked God that the plan had worked, and he prayed that Scout might make it home safely and quickly return with help. After he had prayed, his fear ebbed.

Chapter 3

The Search

At *Heathview*, the home of the Sanders, there was no rest and peace that night. Tom's parents had come home from their trip that evening. They already knew about the burglary, but a new shock awaited them upon their return. Tom had disappeared!

The anxious parents forgot all about the robbery. All they could think of was their boy.

Tom's two best friends were contacted immediately, but neither of them had seen him.

Coby discovered that Scout, too, was gone. Then a frightening thought came to Mr. Sanders' mind: what if the boy and the dog had gone off on the trail of the burglars! Perhaps they had been caught by the crooks.

Mr. Sanders immediately called the police, and it wasn't long before a motorcycle with a sidecar came driving up to the house. Two policemen came to the door.

Everyone in the house was questioned about when they had last seen Tom, including Ina. Ina, who still had to get plenty of rest, had seen Tom and Scout playing in the back yard from her bedroom window. She had seen them disappear through the hedge. That was not long before sundown.

"Well, Sir," said the older of the two policemen. "I'm sorry, but it wouldn't do much good for us to start searching tonight. Tomorrow we'll get us a good tracking dog from the city police, then we can pick up your boy's trail, and we might even find the thieves."

"But by then our boy may have been murdered!" sobbed Tom's mother.

The policeman turned up his palms and shrugged. "We can't do much now, Madam. Tomorrow we'll broadcast your son's description over the radio and look for him with a dog. There may be nothing to worry about."

*   *   *

Outside, the pale light of the moon shone on the woods and fields. Across the wide heath plodded a dog, his head wrapped in blood-soaked bandages. He swayed on his feet and made his way forward very slowly. The dog's powerful body was burning with fever, sapping almost all his strength. But he dragged himself on, for he knew that Tom was in great danger and that he had to fetch help. Once he stopped at a large puddle and drank greedily.

*   *   *

The two policemen were ready to leave. Mr. Sanders escorted them to the door. One of the men climbed into the sidecar and the other straddled the saddle and kicked over the engine. He waved to Mr. Sanders and started to drive away.

At that moment the figure of a dog passed through the beam of the headlight, wobbled up to the steps and collapsed at Mr. Sanders' feet.

It was Scout. Mr. Sanders was seized with fear when he saw the bloody, bedraggled animal.

"Stop!" he shouted after the departing policemen.

The motorcycle stopped.

Scout lay motionless as if dead. The men carried him into the house. When they took the bandages from his head, Tom's mother, who was also hovering over the dog, cried out, "Those strips were torn from Tom's shirt!"

It was obvious that something very serious had happened to the dog and that Tom, too, was involved. Tom's parents were more frightened than ever.

Mr. Sanders went to the telephone and called the vet. It was some time before anyone answered the phone, because the man was already in bed.

18

But when Tom's father told him what had happened, he promised to come immediately.

Scout revived and looked about him restlessly. When he saw Tom's father, he wagged his tail a little and then tottered toward the door. When Mr. Sanders opened the door, Scout walked straight down the hall to the front door, looking back to see if the others were following.

"He wants us to follow him!" cried Mr. Sanders. "Tom must be in danger."

Although the dog tried to resist, Mr. Sanders led him back into the room, for he was still much too weak.

Then the vet arrived. He examined the dog and said, "He's lost a lot of blood and has been badly weakened, but he has no dangerous injuries."

"Do you think you can fix him up well enough so that he can lead us to the boy tonight?" asked one of the policemen.

The vet frowned doubtfully. "That's asking a lot," he said. "But the dog looks exceptionally strong and tough. If you give him a piece of raw meat to eat, I'll give him a shot that will pick him up. It's a risk, but I understand the boy's life may be in danger."

When Scout had received his shot and something to eat, he perked up considerably. He was still restless, however, repeatedly going to the door, scratching at it, and looking questioningly at Mr. Sanders.

"Come on," Tom's father said at last. "We'll just have to try it. Every minute might be precious, and the dog seems to be feeling much better."

Mr. Sanders got a long, thin leash from the closet and fastened it to Scout's collar. The vet had already left, but the gardener insisted on going along to search for Tom. He armed himself with a hatchet, while Mr. Sanders selected a heavy cane. The policemen each carried a revolver and a billy club.

When the front door was opened, Scout lunged ahead so hard that Mr. Sanders almost lost his grip on the leash. They crossed the moonlit yard and Scout started to go through the hole in the hedge, but the gardener unlocked the back gate, and they emerged on the dirt road behind the house. Following the road to the heath, they were soon in the middle of the wide, empty grasslands. All the men were tense and apprehensive about what lay ahead. Scout never hesitated a moment, but went straight on. He seemed to know exactly where he was going.

Across the heath ran an old road, used only occasionally by farmers hauling something by horse and wagon. As the search party cut across this road, they suddenly saw a car approaching from the left, running without lights.

"That man must be nuts," muttered one of the policemen. "We don't have much time, but I better give him a warning."

19

He stood in the middle of the road and, with his flashlight, signaled the car to stop. Suddenly the headlights of the car blazed on and the driver stepped on the gas. He aimed straight for the policeman, who jumped aside at the last second. The car disappeared, roaring away at full speed into the night.

"Why that reckless . . . !" exclaimed the officer. "Did anybody get his license number?"

No, no one had. The license plate light of the car hadn't been working, and the incident had happened so fast no one had had the chance to get a close look. They were sure, however, that there had been only one person in the vehicle.

"Then let's keep moving," said Mr. Sanders, who was very anxious about his son, and the foursome, led by Scout, continued on its way across the heath. None of them suspected that the man in the car was very intimately involved in the burglary and with Tom.

Chapter 4

The Fight

After Scout had disappeared through the hole in the roof, Tom sat down to wait, full of suspense. He knew that it would be some time before help arrived; nevertheless, his heart beat faster at every sound from outside.

His biggest worry, however, was that one of the men might check the room and find Scout missing. Then they might carry him off to another hideout, or perhaps even kill him. The time passed very slowly, maddeningly slowly, and gradually fear began to return to Tom's heart. Had Scout reached home? Perhaps he was lying somewhere in the woods dying. It seemed as if hours had passed. The waiting seemed endless. Tom was getting cold. His foot was throbbing painfully and he felt miserable. He tried to fight back the tears, but he was too tired. He crawled into a corner of the built-in bed and sat down on the rotting mattress as his body shook with sobs. Slowly he calmed down, and finally he fell asleep, utterly exhausted.

He was wakened by the sound of an engine. How long had he slept? He had no idea. It was still dark. There was the sound again. A car was coming!

Tom's heart leaped with joy. Help was coming! He clambered out of the closet-bed and waited in suspense.

He heard the car stop close to the shack and the door slam.

The burglars had apparently also noticed the arrival of the automobile, for Tom heard them getting up and going outside.

Then suddenly there was the sound of loud, bickering voices. The men entered the shack, and Tom heard an unfamiliar voice saying, "It wasn't my fault! The car broke down. Why don't you quit your bellyaching and pack up and get moving. There are two cops and two other men with a big dog headed this way. They're going to be here any minute."

Tom's heart seemed to leap into his throat.

"What?" shouted one of the burglars. "With a dog, did you say? Did that nasty dog . . ."

The door to Tom's room burst open, and the four men pushed inside, cursing and bickering. Tom had shrunk down into a corner, so at first the men didn't see him.

"He's escaped!" shouted the first man. But the new man was carrying a flashlight and, shining the light around the room, he quickly discovered Tom in the closet-bed.

Rushing at Tom, one of the men grabbed him by the shoulders and shook him violently. "What did you do, you little spy?" he shouted. "Where's the dog?"

Tom said nothing, but one of the other men had already discovered the hole in the roof and pointed it out to the others. This was a bad moment for Tom. One of the men struck him in the face so hard that his nose began to bleed.

But the man who had just arrived in the car said, "There's no time for that. We've got to hurry or we'll get caught. What are you planning to do with that boy? Should I . . ." He whispered the rest to one of the other men, who seemed to be the leader of the group.

"No," said the man. "No killing. I don't want a murder sentence hanging over my head if I get nabbed. But we can't leave him behind either. We'll have to take him along and decide what to do with him later."

Tom felt himself to be a wretched mess. His nose had stopped bleeding, but his face and clothes were covered with blood. Although he knew his life was in danger, however, he felt very calm. The Lord was watching over him, he knew. He also knew that help was on the way and resolved to do everything he could to delay their getaway. To this point, he had said nothing, but now he began to talk. He turned to the leader and begged, "Please let me go. I can't do you any harm."

"So!" sneered the man. "Did your tongue come loose at last? Too late, buddy. No way am I going to let you go! You can put the finger on all of us. Move!" He gave Tom a hard shove in the back. Tom let himself go tumbling forward, screaming in pain as he put his weight on his ankle.

"Get up!" screamed the hoodlum.

"I can't walk!" moaned Tom. "My ankle is sprained."

It was the truth, but Tom didn't want to get up either. The men quickly lost their patience, however, and two of them grabbed him and dragged him to the car. Tom resisted, kicking and thrashing, but the only thing he achieved was another beating.

The other two burglars meanwhile hurried back into the shack for the money box and other things they had stashed there and came running back to the car. The driver jumped behind the wheel and started the engine. At that moment, a bright beam of light suddenly shot out of the dark woods. It darted around briefly and then fastened on the car.

"Halt! Police!" someone shouted.

Tom heard the shout. He was already in the car and one of the hoodlums had a firm hold on him. "Help!" he shouted, struggling to break free, but the man clamped one arm around Tom's neck and put his other hand over Tom's mouth. The car doors slammed shut and the engine roared.

Two shots rang out. Seeing the burglars escaping, the two policemen shot at the tires as the car pulled away. But the night was very dark and the policemen were still in the woods, so they didn't get a clear shot at the moving wheels. They missed.

Tom struggled furiously, striking out with all his strength, but two men threw themselves on top of him to subdue him.

Suddenly a pale shape came shooting through the open window on the driver's side. The driver cursed and then screamed in pain. It was Scout! He had sunk his teeth into the driver's arm. The man tried to shake off the enraged dog, but Scout did not let go. The car swerved down the narrow forest road. It smashed through some bushes and then stopped against a tree. The two policemen, Tom's father, and the gardener came running after the car.

The burglars kicked open the door on the other side of the car and tried to make a run for it, but Scout still had hold of the driver, so he didn't get a chance to do anything. He was grabbed by one of the policemen.

The other policeman and Tom's father jumped another man, a tall, strong fellow, who put up a good fight. The gardener was sparring with one of the other burglars.

The fourth, the man who had been holding Tom, remained in the car a few seconds longer, watching for a chance to make his getaway. Suddenly he clubbed Tom against the side of the head with his fist, grabbed the money box, and made a run for it.

He was a tall, wiry fellow and could run fast, so he got a good headstart, especially because Tom's liberators had their hands full with the other three. But he had not reckoned on the German shepherd. No sooner did Scout notice that one of the hoodlums was escaping, than he dashed after him.

The fleeing burglar was just beginning to think he had made good his escape, when the dog broke out of the undergrowth and leaped at his throat. Warding off the dog's first charge, the man slipped a knife out of his pocket and slashed at Scout's throat.

But Scout wasn't eliminated so easily. He dodged the knife and again leaped at the man. It became a furious struggle between man and beast. Finally the hoodlum managed to grab the dog's collar with his left hand. His right hand held the knife, and he raised it high to dispatch the dog once and for all. Suddenly someone else seized his upraised arm.

It was Tom. He had been stunned only temporarily by the blow dealt to him in the car. Shaking off his dizziness, he had seen the man fleeing with the money box and had also seen Scout taking off after him. Although his head was still spinning, he had jumped out of the car and gone after them, hopping and limping on his sprained ankle.

He had reached the place of the fight precisely at the critical moment, and he was able to throw himself at the hoodlum just in time to keep him from killing Scout. Catching him unawares, Tom succeeded in wresting the knife from his hand and tossing it into the bushes. The man was rabid with fury.

"You!" he hissed. "You and that dog! You've loused me up for the last time. I'll fix you both for good!"

He tried to grab Tom by the throat. Hampered by his sprained ankle, Tom was hard put to defend himself and went tumbling over backwards. But when the man tried to throw himself on the boy, Scout attacked him so viciously, he had to turn all his attention to the dog. Meanwhile, Tom again broke free.

Still, the fight might not have turned out well for Tom, if help had not arrived. The first to arrive was one of the policemen, and right on his heels was Tom's father. After overpowering the other three burglars, the rescue party had tied their hands behind them and left them under the supervision of the other policeman and the gardener. The first policeman and Tom's father had rushed off after Tom and the escaping prisoner. The two men had been led to the right spot by Scout's barking and growling. Seeing himself so outnumbered, the hoodlum quickly surrendered. His hands, too, were tied behind him and he was led back to the car.

Scout was panting heavily and seemed a little unsteady on his legs. The bandages around his head had come loose and his head wound was bleeding again. Tom wasn't in very good shape either. He could hardly stand up. He had carried himself courageously during the fight, but now that everything was over, he suddenly burst into tears.

Mr. Sanders took Tom on his back and carried him to the car. Tom was rather ashamed that he had cried. Fortunately the policeman, who had gone ahead with the captured burglar, had not seen him, and by the time they got to the car Tom was again in control of himself.

First of all the prisoners were herded back into the shack. One of the policemen lit the lamp, and Mr. Sanders put the recovered money box on the table. The burglars had broken the lock, but the contents, mostly bank notes and stocks, were all still there. The policemen searched the burglars and found two knives, burglar tools, and several pieces of jewelry.

Everything that had been stolen had thus been recovered. Mr. Sanders was very happy. "You did a very courageous thing, my boy," he said to Tom, who was sitting on a chair, still pale from all the excitement. "But it was rather foolhardy of you to start tracking those burglars by yourself. God spared you this time, but you might have been killed. I'm happy we got back everything that was stolen, but I'm happiest of all to get my foolhardy little boy back."

"If Scout hadn't been with me, you'd never have found me."

"Yes, Sanders," said one of the policemen, "that's a smart dog. He'd make a good police dog. You wouldn't want to sell him, would you?"

"Are you kidding?" Mr. Sanders said, laughing. "Tom and Scout are inseparable companions — now more than ever."

The policemen decided to take their captives into town two at a time. One policeman and the gardener would remain in the shack with two of the burglars. The second policeman, Mr. Sanders, Tom, and Scout would drive the two other men into town, and then the policeman would return for the remaining two. Mr. Sanders took the wheel, and Tom and Scout took the seat beside him, while the policeman sat in the back between the two bound prisoners.

For Tom the trip back went much faster than the trip to the old shack; this time he didn't go across the heath but along the dirt road.

At *Heathview* everyone had been up all night waiting anxiously for the return of the rescue party, and they raised a loud cheer when they saw Tom and Scout getting out of the car with Mr. Sanders. Tom's mother wept with relief, and so did Ina, his little sister.

The policeman shook hands with Tom and his father. "You're a brave fellow," the policeman told Tom. "I think we made quite a catch in this foursome. This wasn't their first job. We'll let you know what happens."

In the east the sky was beginning to turn red. The sun would soon be up. After Tom had eaten a little and washed up, his mother sent him straight to bed, where he fell asleep immediately.

Scout, too, received special care: after the bandage had been changed on his injured head, he joined Tom in the bedroom and curled up in his corner, close to Tom's bed.

A few days later, Tom found out that the capture of the four burglars had indeed been a big catch. Over the past several months they had pulled numerous break-ins around the area. They were all sentenced to several years in prison.

Tom was soon his old self and won great admiration from his friends for his role in the capture of the burglars. Scout, too, quickly recovered from his injuries, and he was spoiled more than he had ever been. Tom and he were now together constantly. Tom often thought back to the anxious hours he had spent in the dark room of the shack. His friends admired him, but he knew all too well how afraid he had been. It had been God who had rescued him in answer to his prayer. He would never forget that. Not even later, when he and Scout were caught up in even more frightening adventures as they faced an enemy much more dangerous than the burglars.

For suddenly the armies of Hitler invaded the Netherlands, and in a few days the country was occupied by German soldiers. A time filled with fear and danger lay ahead for the small nation bordering Germany — and also for Tom and his dog.

Chapter 5

The Strange Farmhand

It was a windy, sunny autumn day. Ina, Tom, and Scout were romping in the large back yard behind the house. Tom and his sister were tossing a ball, and Scout went dashing after it so wildly that leaves went swirling up on every side. He snapped at the bouncing ball, and when he caught it, he triumphantly brought it back to Tom and Ina. The threesome had endless fun together now that Ina had completely recovered from her illness.

But just as he was about to throw the ball again, Tom lowered his arm. On the dirt road that passed behind the hedge a platoon of marching soldiers suddenly appeared. Tom's face clouded over.

Listen, they were singing:

> *Heute gehört uns Deutschland*
> *Und morgen die ganze Welt!*
> (Today Germany is ours,
> And tomorrow the entire world.)

The two children listened, quiet and pale. They knew very well what the German soldiers were singing. The Germans had been occupying the Netherlands for more than four years already, and Hitler had ambitions to conquer the whole world.

Even Scout seemed to understand that these soldiers weren't friends. He growled angrily. Tom quickly grabbed him by the collar and hushed him, for he looked ready to go dashing through the hedge to bark at the intruders.

Just then Mrs. Sanders called Tom and Ina inside for lunch. Scout ran for the house along with the two children, since he was also allowed inside. He had been taught good table manners so he was permitted to walk around the table as the family ate and to beg for tidbits. Not that there were very many tidbits nowadays, with the Germans demanding everything for the war effort.

"We're fortunate to be living out in the country," Tom's father often said, "for food is much scarcer in the cities."

During lunch Tom told of the platoon of soldiers, with their deep helmets and heavy boots, and of the song they had been singing. "I wish those lousy Krauts would all go hang!" he said. "They're ruining everything here and all over the world. I hope the English bomb Germany all to pieces so there isn't a single one of those Krauts left!"

"That's enough, Tom!" interrupted Father. "That's no way to talk. What the Germans are doing is bad, true enough, but we must pray and work to put an end to it. There's no need to add to it with bitter words and curses. Maybe we've deserved this trial."

Tom blushed and kept quiet. Father was right, he knew, but he couldn't stand the sight of those arrogant German soldiers.

He was now going to junior high, but the school had been seized by the German army. Classes were being held in a huge abandoned barracks, but they would soon have to be closed because the weather was turning colder and there was no fuel available. Tom expected classes to be cancelled any day now. Many students had already dropped out; some because they had to come too far and their bicycles had broken down, and others because they were weak or sick from starvation.

After lunch Tom's friend, Carl Van Doorn, came to see if Tom could come with him for a walk. Carl was about a year younger than Tom and was still in grade school. When they had both been in grade school they had always been together, along with a third companion, Bert Verhoef, who lived some distance from town on a farm along the river. Tom asked his father if he could go, and soon the two boys were hiking across the fields, accompanied by Scout.

"Should we go to the mill?" asked Carl. "Or should we visit Bert?"

Carl's father owned a mill which milled grain as well as lumber, so there was always something going on there. Tom thought a moment. He liked to play high in the top of the large windmill, but he hadn't seen Bert for almost two weeks. Bert had dropped out of school to help his father on the farm, but today was Saturday and Tom was sure Bert's father would let him go.

"Let's go see Bert," he decided. "Then the three of us can do something together."

"You mean the four of us," said Carl, laughing. "Scout is one of us too."

It was a long hike to the farm, but the boys knew a shortcut across the fields that made it much shorter. Scout was elated that he could come along and went leaping and darting around them.

"You'd better be careful with Scout," Carl said. "I hear the Germans are impounding all big, strong dogs to be trained as army dogs. Yesterday they took away our neighbour's dog."

Tom paled at the idea. Might the Germans come and take away Scout too? "I'll never turn in Scout!" he said determinedly. "He's a smart dog. I'll have to train him to hide whenever there are Germans around."

"Good idea," said Carl. "Let's train Scout like an army dog ourselves. You can train a clever dog like him to do almost anything. It might come in handy."

Enthusiastically they talked on, making all kinds of fantastic plans. But suddenly Tom looked glum again.

"But we can't do it ourselves," he sighed. "We could teach him a few little tricks, but to really train a dog takes a lot of know-how, which we haven't got."

"Maybe we can get a book on how to train dogs," suggested Carl. "We could ask the man in the bookstore."

By this time, the two boys were almost at the Verhoef farm. Scout dashed ahead barking happily; he tore through the middle of a flock of chickens which scattered in all directions, squawking and cackling. But they settled down again in a hurry when they noticed the dog was not about to hurt them.

Bert was just coming into the yard leading a horse. He was happy to see his two best friends. Tom watched him come, amazed at how much muscle Bert had been putting on since he had quit school. He looked like a strapping big farmer already and could ride a horse and drive a team as well as any farmer. "Can you get this afternoon off?" they asked him. "We thought we'd go somewhere."

"I'll ask my dad," said Bert. "I think it's okay. There's not much going on anyway. Come on."

They walked with him to the horse's stall where Bert put away the horse. Mr. Verhoef was in the barn too. He readily gave Bert permission to go with his friends.

As they were crossing the threshing floor, Carl saw a man working there whom he had never seen around the farm before. Apparently he was a new hand, for he was sweeping the threshing floor with a large broom. Carl nudged Bert.

"Is that a new hand?" he asked softly.

"No . . . I mean, yes," stammered Bert, blushing. "He just started working here. His name is Mr. . . . I mean, that's Haaksma, our new hand."

Carl and Tom looked at each other questioningly. Why was Bert acting so strangely?

Haaksma swept some straw into a heap, and, playful as he was, Scout dove right into the middle of it. The new hand suddenly stopped sweeping and stood still, studying the beautiful German shepherd with obvious appreciation.

"Is that your dog?" he asked the two boys.

"He's mine," said Tom. "His name is Scout."

Tom noticed that Haaksma spoke differently from the other farm people in this area. He sounded more educated, and his hands didn't look like those of a farm labourer either. "I see," he said. "He's a beautiful animal." He thumped Scout on the back and examined him closely, as if he knew what he was doing.

"Do you know about dogs, Sir?" asked Tom. He didn't know why he addressed him so formally.

Haaksma smiled at him. "No need to call me Sir; I'm only a farmhand. Where I come from everyone talks like me. Know about dogs? Well, yes, a little. I've trained a few dogs in the past. Just for fun, of course."

Tom could hardly hide his delight. "Could . . . would you teach Scout something?" he stammered eagerly. "I'm . . . I'm afraid . . . you see, the Germans . . . I don't want them to get their hands on him."

Haaksma laughed. "Tell me what you have in mind."

Tom told him that Scout was the best and the most loyal dog in the whole world and that he had saved Tom's life once and that now he was afraid the Germans were going to impound him. So he wanted to teach Scout to hide when any German soldiers came around. Could Haaksma train him to do that?

The farmhand stood and thought a moment. "If that dog is as smart as you say, it should be possible to teach him all kinds of things. Let's try him out now."

They spent an unusual, exciting afternoon out in the field behind the farm. Haaksma seemed to have a magical control over the dog. Scout took to him right away and willingly did everything the man told him. If the dog did not catch on immediately, Haaksma did not get impatient, and he never struck him. He just kept trying until Scout understood what he was supposed to do. After about two hours of this, Haaksma turned to Tom and said, "This is enough for the time being. He's a first rate animal. I've never before trained a dog that caught on so quickly. I'd be glad to work with him some more. If you come back again soon, we'll continue where we left off."

When Tom and Carl were on their way home some time later, they were still excited about what they had seen.

"That Haaksma is quite a man!" said Tom. "Did you see the way he commanded Scout? He didn't sound like a farmhand at all." Suddenly it came to him. Of course, Haaksma wasn't a farmhand. He was at the Verhoef farm hiding from the Germans. He was a diver, as such people were called. Maybe he had even been an officer in the Dutch army. Tom looked at Carl, and at the same time Carl's eyes met his. They both had the same thought at the same time, but they left it unspoken.

"This is our secret," Carl said quietly. "No one may know. Especially not the Germans."

A few days later, as he had expected, Tom's school was closed. Tom stayed home and spent a lot of time with Scout running through the training exercises he had seen Haaksma do.

His biggest worry was that some day the Germans might come to pick up Scout. So far they had left the Sanders' place alone.

Every Saturday afternoon Tom and Scout went to the Verhoef farm. Usually Carl came too. Then Haaksma continued Scout's training. Haaksma was just as excited about the progress made by the dog as were the boys.

Scout could now crawl across a field on his belly so that he could hardly be seen. He used every little hillock and dip in the terrain to keep himself hidden, and he reacted immediately to the whispered commands of either Haaksma or Tom. When Haaksma fired off a starter pistol, the dog would play dead, not moving a muscle until he was called.

Scout learned to make long trips with heavy weights strapped to his neck, during which he had to swim the river without letting the package get wet. Above all, Haaksma taught him to do everything he had been taught without barking or making noise of any kind.

In a few months Scout was a well-trained dog, of which Tom was justifiably proud. Tom himself still didn't know what use this might be, but he had the feeling that the more Scout learned, the better.

He would soon be proven right.

Chapter 6

In the Windmill

Recently large squadrons of planes had been passing over the village every night — English planes on their way to bomb Germany. Often they were shot at by German antiaircraft guns that had been set up in the vicinity of the village. The people had gradually grown used to the drone of the planes and the clatter of the guns, and Tom, who had always been a sound sleeper, usually heard little or nothing of the nightly fireworks.

But one night something suddenly woke him up. At first he didn't know what had wakened him. It had been something unusual. Listen, there it was again. The German antiaircraft guns were firing and one of the airplanes sounded very close. Something seemed to be wrong with the engine, for it was labouring and missing.

Tom jumped out of bed, went to the window and opened the curtain. Scout, who always slept beside his bed, came and stood beside him.

Outside in the night sky a spell-binding drama was being played out. Huge searchlights swept the dark sky. At first the airplane was nowhere to be seen, but then it was suddenly caught in one of the beams of light and stood out pale and gleaming against the darkness. Again the antiaircraft guns chattered, and suddenly flames burst from the low-flying bomber.

Tom shrank back in horror. Were all the men in the plane going to be burnt alive?

The plane was quickly losing altitude. Then it banked steeply to the right and disappeared into the darkness. Tom listened, and, sure enough, a few minutes later he heard a muffled explosion in the distance. The bomber must have hit the ground.

He was trembling with emotion. Oh, how he'd like to . . . Like to what? What could he do?

He was about to go back to bed, when out of the corner of his eye, he saw something pale against the sky, just on the edge of one of the searchlight beams. Underneath it dangled a dark figure. Then the searchlight moved on and the pale blotch blended into the darkness, but Tom's heart leaped with joy. He had seen it for less than a second, but he knew what it was: a parachute with a man hanging from it! He stared and stared into the darkness in the hope that he might catch another glimpse of it, but no, the searchlight was turned off. Good! That meant the Germans hadn't seen it.

Oh, if only he could help the English flier! Or maybe it was one of his own countrymen, for many men had crossed the English channel to join the Allied forces in England.

"Listen, Scout," he whispered, "tomorrow we'll go out and search for that man. I'm counting on your help. Okay?"

The dog pushed his nose into Tom's hand as if to say, "You can count on me!"

The next morning Tom was downstairs earlier than usual. There was a lot of talk around the breakfast table about last night's events. The bedroom of Tom's parents, however, was on the other side of the house, so they hadn't seen the airplane at all.

Coby, the housekeeper, said the plane had crashed somewhere about three kilometres from the village. The milkman had told her. The Germans had been the first to arrive at the scene and were keeping everyone else out of the area.

Excitedly Tom joined in the conversation. He was about to tell everyone about the parachute he had seen in the glow of the searchlights, when he caught himself. Maybe it was better if not everyone knew about it. After breakfast he would tell Father when they were alone. But he didn't immediately get the chance.

After praying, Father got up from the table and said, "Tom, would you please run over to Van Doorn's a minute? I need a saw to cut down a couple of those big, old trees in the back. We'll need some firewood this winter, and it's almost impossible to get it elsewhere."

There was nothing Tom liked better than to hang around the Van Doorn mill. If there wasn't something going on at the flour mill, there was sure to be action at the sawmill. Maybe Carl would still be home. Although the grade school had not been closed, it didn't start until nine o'clock. Tom called Scout, and they trotted off across the fields.

The last few weeks, whenever he went out with Scout, Tom stayed off the roads. He stuck to the fields where he had less chance of unexpectedly running into German soldiers, and where Scout could hide more easily in case something did happen. Cutting across the fields, it took them about twenty minutes to reach Van Doorn's mill.

Van Doorn was just coming out of the sawmill where a tall tree was being cut into beams by a huge circular saw. Van Doorn was covered with sawdust. When he saw Tom and Scout coming, he smiled.

"Hey, you two are up and around early this morning! What can I do for you?"

Tom delivered his message, and Van Doorn said, "I'll tell you what. I'll send over a couple of men this afternoon. They can chop down those trees and then haul them over here to be cut into pieces."

Meanwhile, Carl had also come outside. "Hey," he shouted, "did you see that plane last night? An English bomber came down not far from here. Should we go up to the top of the mill? Maybe we can see where it crashed from there."

That was a terrific idea, thought Tom. Together they hurried into the mill and began climbing a long ladder. Climbing to the top of the ladder, they came to a small attic from which another, smaller ladder led straight up to the very top of the windmill. From two little windows they could scout the countryside for many kilometres around. The sun was shining brightly, but the air was a little hazy in the distance.

After a few moments, Carl said, "See that dark spot over there? That must be it. See? I think there are people walking around it. I know what, my father has a pair of binoculars. He won't mind if we borrow them. You wait here; I'll go get them."

It wasn't long before Carl was back with his father's binoculars. They took turns studying the dark spot in the distance. As they had suspected, the binoculars showed them the fragments of the crashed bomber. A few German soldiers were searching the wreckage, while others were deployed around the area to keep sightseers away. Off to one side there was something that looked like stretchers covered with sheets.

"Look," said Tom, "those must be the English fliers." He did not tell his companion about what he had seen last night: that at least one of the crew had parachuted from the plane. For the time being it was his secret.

"Well," said Carl. "Adios! I've got to go to school. But you can stay longer if you want. I wish they would close down our school too. Then I could stay home like you."

"Oh," shrugged Tom, "you can't see much anyway without binoculars."

"That's all right. You can keep the binoculars for awhile. My dad won't mind. As long as you're careful."

Tom thought that was great. Now he could look things over at his leisure. Carl disappeared and Tom refocused the binoculars as clearly as possible. Maybe he could sight the man who had jumped out of the plane last night.

He scanned the horizon with the binoculars. Suddenly his heart skipped a beat. Two German soldiers had come into his field of vision. They were searching a clump of bushes. About half a kilometre farther an entire patrol was scouring the countryside. Soon Tom found even more soldiers hunting elsewhere.

Had the Germans gotten wind of the fact that one or more of the crew had escaped the crash? They must have, if they were searching for survivors.

Again, like last night, Tom felt the urge to go help the fugitive, to save him from the Germans. He just had to try — he and Scout, who was waiting for him downstairs.

It would be dangerous, he knew. For a moment he hesitated. Was it right to take such risks? Was it being foolhardy? But then he thought again of the man, the small, dark figure that had hung up in the huge night sky between heaven and earth. Maybe he, Tom, was the only one who had seen him. That was surely no accident. And the fact that he had the smartest dog in the district, didn't that mean something? Now he also had the binoculars so he could see the Germans long before they saw him.

He had thought long enough. He hurried down the ladder.

Downstairs Scout came bounding up to him, barking a happy welcome. Tom seized the dog's head between his hands and whispered, "You've got to help me, Scout. We're going to do something very dangerous. I'm counting on you."

Scout wagged his tail as if he understood.

Together they struck off across the fields, both solemn in the face of the danger that lay ahead.

Chapter 7

Tom's Search

Tom really had no detailed plan in mind. He had only a vague idea where the flier had come down, so he simply headed in the general direction where he had seen the parachute.

According to his calculations, the parachutist had landed somewhere near the river. That was where he decided to begin his search. It was extremely dangerous, for the Germans were also working their way in that direction.

They made good time. The route they were following was bordered by low underbrush; Tom trotted along bent low so that he wouldn't be seen. He had told Scout to stay close on his heels so he wouldn't stray beyond the cover of the bushes.

After they had followed the river for about a quarter of an hour, the ridge of bushes suddenly quit. The path continued across open fields. Tom stopped behind the last cluster of shrubs. He carefully edged forward to study the terrain ahead. What he saw gave him a terrible fright!

Less than two hundred metres down the path stood a German soldier, his back toward them. Apparently he was guarding the path so that no one could use it.

What should they do now? Make a big detour? But when he looked around further, he saw that there were also guards to the right and to the left at intervals of several hundred metres. When he had been up in the windmill, he had seen no soldiers in this area. The Germans were probably searching the countryside very systematically and had divided it into sections. They must have cordoned off another section in order to flush out the fugitive flier.

Tom was worried. After what he had seen last night, he was almost sure that the Englishman had landed somewhere in this area, unless he had come down on the other side of the river.

He studied the surrounding terrain. To the left of the path, about ten metres away, ran a deep, wide canal. In all likelihood it didn't have much water in it, for the summer had been unusually dry. If he and Scout could reach the canal, they could slip past the guard and could probably make it all the way to the reeds along the river.

Should he take the risk? His mind told him, "Don't do it, Tom; it's much too dangerous. You probably won't find the flier anyway, and if you do find him, you may not be able to help him."

But Tom's urge to try it was too strong. He couldn't resist. Suppose the Englishman was hiding in the reeds along the river, then Tom could lead him out by the same route. After that, it shouldn't be too hard to find a hiding place for him.

Tom now kept a close eye on the movements of the guard closest to him. The man was pacing back and forth a little. He seemed to be bored.

Not far from where Tom was hiding a large flock of crows was pecking around in the grass. He had a sudden idea. He picked up a rock from the path, stood up a little, and tossed the rock at the birds. Cawing loudly, the birds exploded into the air, swooping past the soldier in a dense flutter of wings.

The soldier watched the flight of the birds, playfully aiming his rifle at them as if to shoot. As he did so, he turned his back to Tom.

This was the moment Tom had been waiting for. "Follow, Scout! Stay low," he whispered. They covered the distance to the canal in two seconds. Tom slid down the bank on the seat of his pants.

Good. He had made it. He lay absolutely still at the bottom of the bank, listening to every sound, but all he heard was the wild pounding of his own heart.

The canal was almost dry. Only a dirty little stream trickled down the centre. Tom waited for about a minute, which seemed to last for an hour, before he dared to move. Then he slowly began crawling along the canal, with Scout quietly stalking along behind him. Metre by metre they made their way forward.

They must be just about even with the guard now. Slowly they went on, crawling and squirming along the ground. The canal took a sharp turn. When they were around the corner, Tom felt much safer.

He wanted to peek over the bank of the canal to see where the guard was, but he knew that would be awfully risky. Then he had a sudden idea. Growing along the canal were lots of reeds. Tom dug his jackknife out of his pocket and cut off a number of the long, tough stalks. Then he quickly wove them together to fit around his head. He stuck in a few loose leaves and his headgear was complete.

"There!" he said to himself. "Now they won't see me so easily."

Carefully he crept up the bank and lifted his head over the edge.

The guard closest to him was still pacing back and forth. He hadn't noticed a thing. The other guards were far enough away not to be an immediate threat.

It made Tom bolder and he decided to move a little faster. In a low crouch he ran along the partly dry canal bed toward the reeds lining the river. This went all right for quite aways, but gradually the canal became deeper and wider, and the stream of water in the middle broadened, coming ever closer to the bank. His progress grew more and more difficult and finally he could go no farther along the canal. What should he do now?

Wade on through the slimy water at the edge? But then he would get sopping wet. Besides, even from where he stood now, he could see that even then he couldn't go much farther.

Again he crept up the bank. He looked around. The soldiers were quite far away by now and the beckoning reeds were close. The river made a sharp bend here. If he cut diagonally across the field from where he was, it was only fifty metres or so to the cover of the reeds. Then no one could find him.

Should he risk it? How should he do it? Crawl? Or simply make a mad dash? He decided on the latter.

"Come, Scout," he whispered. "Be very quiet, but fast."

They darted across the field side by side, like two arrows shot from a bow. It was going well. Only twenty metres to go . . . ten . . .

Then suddenly a loud, hoarse shout sounded behind them. "Halt!" shouted the German soldier. They had been seen!

Tom only ran faster.

Then a bullet whistled overhead and a shot rang out.

Tom's heart leaped into his throat. A few more steps. Ah, he had reached the reeds. He dove forward into them, crawled forward several metres, and then lay still, panting hard. Scout lay down beside him.

His fear almost got the better of him. But after about half a minute, he cautiously crawled back to peer out between the reeds. His worst fears were confirmed. German soldiers were coming from all directions. The shot had brought them running, and the fact that the fleeing figure had been partly camouflaged with reeds made them sure something suspicious was going on.

Tom lay back in the reeds, overcome by despair. Escape was impossible; he was trapped. A host of thoughts crowded into his brain as he lay among the reeds. He had been foolhardy and wrong in exposing himself so recklessly to danger. Maybe the Germans would shoot him or ship him off to a concentration camp. Maybe his mother and father would never find out what had happened to him; they would keep looking for him and never find him. He fought back the tears that burned in his eyes.

A wet nose nudged his face. Scout seemed to sense his despair and was trying to comfort him.

It made him think of another time, a long time ago, when he had been in a similar desperate situation. He had been locked up in a shack by a group of burglars. Then he had prayed and he had been rescued. God could also rescue him now, he knew. Again he folded his hands and he pleaded for forgiveness for his recklessness and begged the Lord to help him once more.

When he looked again, the soldiers approaching across the fields were much closer. They formed a huge semi-circle as they neared the reeds. Tom retreated farther between the tall, slippery stalks.

Should he try to swim the river? He could swim fairly well, but the water was very swift here. It would be too dangerous, and Scout couldn't pull him in such a current. The dog might make it alone, but with Tom clinging to him, they would both drown.

But what should they do then? They had to get out of here, for the Germans were coming closer and closer.

Frantically he pushed farther into the reeds to the river's edge.

Suddenly he squealed in surprise. Anchored among the reeds lay a small rowboat. It was a battered old thing, but to Tom it was an answer to prayer.

He fumbled at the rope by which the boat was anchored, but in his nervousness he only made the knot tighter. Finally he gave a hard jerk on the rotten old rope and it snapped. There was water in the bottom. It must have been lying here for some time, for it looked as if it hadn't been used recently.

As Tom stepped into the boat, it rocked and creaked, but he was in too big a rush to be careful.

"Come, Scout!" he whispered.

The dog, too, jumped into the boat. Tom grabbed an oar and pushed off. He slipped the oars into the oarlocks and started rowing quietly. The beating of his heart seemed louder than the splash of the oars. Would he make it?

He rowed as fast as he could, for if he were discovered, the Germans would open fire.

In the middle of the river, he hit a strong current. He was making very poor headway. The boat felt as heavy as lead. He threw all his strength and weight into the oars, all the while keeping his eyes fixed on the reeds, watching for the Germans.

Suddenly he noticed that his feet were getting wet. Startled, he looked down. The boat was almost half full. The water was pouring in through small cracks in the bottom of the boat. Panicking, he tried to row even faster. Crack! went one of the oars. It snapped off.

The boat now spun around helplessly in the middle of the current. The water was rising higher and higher. Tom tried to bail with his bare hands, but he couldn't keep up. The boat sank underneath him.

He struck out with his arms and started swimming for the far shore. But the current was too strong and he was quickly being swept downstream. Looking around, he spotted an island about a hundred metres down the river. He had been there before with his friends. They called it Willow Island because it was almost completely overgrown with willows. If he could reach the island by swimming with the current, he'd be safe for the time being. It was his only chance.

But the weight of the water in his clothes was pulling him down, and his shoes made his legs feel leaden. Swimming became harder and harder. He was getting closer to the island, but his strength was almost spent. Was he going to drown only a few metres from the island?

Then suddenly something was beside him in the water. It was Scout. Tom seized his collar just as the water was about to pull him down. Paddling strongly, the big dog pulled his master the last few metres to the island. Several seconds later Tom felt ground under his feet. He staggered forward a couple of steps and collapsed into the dense undergrowth on the shore.

He was just in the nick of time, for at precisely the same moment his pursuers appeared among the reeds on the other riverbank. They looked around but saw nothing. They searched the reeds for some time, shouting and cursing, but finally they withdrew, hollering insults at the guard who had seen Tom.

Tom listened to their loud voices carrying over the water. He lay still between the tall weeds until the Germans had been gone for some time.

Then he closed his eyes and thanked God.

Chapter 8

Danger on Willow Island

Tom knew that his troubles were far from over. His clothes were wet and he was thoroughly chilled. And how was he going to get off the island without a boat?

He decided that first of all he would move farther to the middle of the island. Last summer he and his two friends had built a small hut there. They had often rowed out to the island. The hut was made of willow branches woven together. It leaked like a sieve when it rained, but in dry weather it served quite well. A thick layer of straw covered the floor. The hut was low enough so that it couldn't be seen above the willows.

In the hut Tom could at least take off his clothes and wring them out. After that, he would make further plans. Cautiously he made his way through the dense mass of willows, until he found what he was looking for: a small path that snaked through the undergrowth to the middle of the island. A few minutes later he was approaching the open space in the centre of the island where the hut had been built.

Scout had run ahead, but suddenly he stopped, hesitating. A deep growl rumbled in his throat. Tom was just pushing his way through the last of the undergrowth, which was especially thick here. Scout's growl brought him up short. Had the Germans come to the island?

His eyes traveled over the clearing in front of him. He saw nothing . . . Yes, there was something! Beside the hut. It looked like a piece of cloth — a piece of silk folded repeatedly. And there was also rope.

Tom's heart raced. Of course! It was a parachute!

That was it. The missing flier had landed on the island. Was Scout growling because the man was hiding inside the hut?

Tom stood still a moment, not knowing what to do. How should he announce himself to the Englishman? Maybe the man would think he was helping the Germans. He had to call out to the man. In school he always got good grades in English, but now he had trouble thinking of even one sentence.

"Hello!" he cried. When there was no answer, he tried again, "Hello! I'm a friend!" He waited in suspense.

The small door of the little hut slowly swung open and a young-looking man came out, stooping to get through the low doorway. He was wearing the uniform of the British air force. His eyes were fixed on the boy and the dog. He studied them a moment, and then he smiled. He pointed to Tom's wet clothes.

"How did you get so wet?" he asked.

Tom blushed. Stammering with excitement, he began to tell the man about seeing him jump from the plane last night and about his attempt to find him and about his run-in with the Germans. As he talked, the Englishman took his arm and led him into the hut, where he wrapped his coat around Tom's shoulders. Tom went on with his story. It was quite a chore for him; he had to stop frequently to find the right word, but the pilot seemed to understand, nodding sometimes as Tom acted something out to make his meaning clear.

The English pilot — John was his name — listened attentively and laughed every now and then. Finally he eyed Tom anxiously and said, "We've got to get you out of those wet clothes, or you'll get sick."

Tom knew the man was right. He was shivering from the cold, but how was he going to dry his clothes here? The sun was still shining brightly, but it didn't give a lot of warmth this late in the season.

John knew what to do, however. He had spent the morning gathering firewood on the island. Clearing away some of the straw, he built a small pile of twigs and branches in the middle of the hut, and held a match to it. Soon they had a nice little fire warming the hut.

"Isn't that dangerous?" Tom asked worriedly. "If the Germans see the smoke, they might come to the island."

The Englishman laughed and shook his head, "Don't worry. There's not enough smoke here for anyone to notice." Actually John, too, was worried about the smoke being spotted, but he didn't want his young rescuer to catch pneumonia.

Tom took off his clothes and hung them by the fire to dry. Then he huddled close to the fire himself with the heavy overcoat of the pilot wrapped around him. He was already starting to feel better. Slowly the chill was starting to leave his body, and he stopped shivering.

John produced a few crisp, white biscuits from one of his pockets. He gave two to Tom, who eagerly devoured them. Scout, too, got a few pieces.

It was almost noon by now. Tom suddenly thought of his parents: they would be worrying about him because he hadn't come home. What could he do?

His clothes were fairly dry by now, so he put them back on. The binoculars! He had forgotten all about them. What if they had been spoiled by the water? He hadn't even asked Mr. Van Doorn's permission to take them along. He opened the leather case in which the binoculars were stored and poured out a little water. Good. They didn't look too bad. He wiped off the binoculars and took them outside. Carefully he scanned both riverbanks to see whether the Germans were still in the area, but he saw nothing to worry him.

He went back into the hut and sat down with John to plan their next move. John had planned to swim the river during the coming night and then look for help. But he knew full well that he ran a great risk of being caught by the Germans if he started wandering about.

Suddenly a penetrating scream sounded on the river. They both jumped, then broke into laughter. A boat passing by on the river had just sounded its steam whistle.

This gave Tom an idea. Boats were constantly going by on the river. They could wave one down and ask for a ride. But, that would be dangerous. The boatmen would immediately see who John was, and it would take only one loose tongue to betray them. Besides, the Germans might still be keeping an eye on the river, and if Tom began yelling at boats, he would give away their hiding place.

Still turning it over in his mind, Tom stared out over the river. In the distance he could see the thatched roof of the Verhoef farm. If he could send them a message, then Bert or Mr. Verhoef or Haaksma would figure some way to get them off the island.

Tom's mind began working feverishly. Scout could swim the river and deliver a message to the Verhoefs. The dog would have to carry a note, so it would have to be fastened to him somehow. What if the Germans stopped him? It was dangerous, but they had to try it.

"Do you have something to write on?" he asked John.

John ripped a page out of a small address book. Tom dug a pencil stub out of his pocket and started to write. It took some thought, for he wanted to write the note in such a way that Bert would understand it, but not the Germans, in case Scout was caught. He wrote:

Dear Bert,
I'm with a friend who dropped in on us out of the blue. We're in the hut we built last year. Can you come and pick us up? Maybe Scout's trainer can help.
Tom

He folded the note and put it in the binocular case. Then he fastened the case to the top of Scout's collar.

Taking the dog to a place where he could clearly see the Verhoef farm, Tom pointed to it.

"Go, Scout. Go to Bert. And no barking. Quiet!"

First Tom looked around once more to see if it was safe. There were no Germans in sight and no boats to be seen on the river.

Once more he repeated his instructions to the dog. Then he pointed to the water. The dog looked at him once, his eyes full of trust, and then he waded into the water and paddled across to the other side. He disappeared into the willows that lined the river. With butterflies in his stomach, Tom watched him go. He was afraid a German might come popping out of the bushes at any time. But nothing happened. Nevertheless, he stood listening for shouting or shooting until Scout was far out of earshot. When he had still not heard anything, he turned to John, who was sitting in the grass beside him, and said, "If Scout gets through, it won't be long before someone shows up to help us."

Together they walked back to the hut. John told Tom about some of his adventures as a bomber pilot. He also told him what had happened the night his plane had been brought down by German antiaircraft fire. His plane had already been hit over Germany, and he was desperately trying to make it back to England when he had again been hit over the Netherlands. He thought that he was the only one of the crew who had had the time to jump before the plane crashed.

Suddenly they heard the chug of a small boat on the river. Tom stalked to the water's edge. Was help arriving already? Verhoef could hardly be here this soon.

A small motorboat was heading straight for the island. In it were two German soldiers and an officer.

Tom felt the blood draining from his face in sudden fright. To hide on the small island was impossible. When the Germans found the hut and the parachute, they would search the whole island.

The boat was very close. Suddenly the soldier who was steering turned the craft sharply upriver. The boat passed Willow Island and headed for a heavily loaded cargo boat slowly coming down the river.

Still dizzy with fright, Tom looked on. The Germans shouted at the boat, and the officer and one of the soldiers climbed aboard, while the other stayed with the small motorboat. They asked some questions of the skipper and the crew, and then they disappeared below deck. They were gone for some time.

They must be searching the ship, thought Tom. Maybe the search for the English flier had been widened to include ships.

After a while the Germans appeared back on deck, clambered back into the small motorboat, and chugged off. Apparently they had found nothing. They continued to cruise the river, however, looking for other boats.

Carefully Tom crept back to the middle of the island. He knew they were in great danger now.

Fortunately the fire had been put out some time ago, otherwise the Germans would surely have spotted the smoke. Still, they might at any time take it into their heads to check out the island. Tom and John hurried to wipe out all traces of their presence. They buried the ashes from the fire and stashed the parachute under a pile of leaves between some bushes.

When they had removed all signs of their stay as well as they could, they concealed themselves in a dense growth of willows on the edge of the island, where they could also keep an eye on the German river patrol. They lay there waiting in great suspense. Every now and again a boat came by and was stopped and searched by the Germans. Whenever the soldiers weren't occupied by boats, Tom was in a constant dither lest they should take it into their heads to look on the island.

The hours went by very, very slowly. Tom looked forward to the coming of Verhoef and Haaksma with both hope and fear. As long as the Germans were around, Verhoef couldn't very well help the two fugitives. Still, Tom couldn't resist focusing his binoculars on the Verhoef farm every so often.

Suddenly he heard voices. Coming toward them in the distance, floating down the river in a small flat-bottomed boat, were a man and a boy. They seemed to be in a jolly mood, for they were singing loudly, "Row, row, row your boat gently down the stream . . ."

"Look!" Tom whispered excitedly to his English companion. "It's my friend Bert and Haaksma. They're coming from the opposite direction I expected them to. What do you think they're doing?"

The Germans must have asked themselves the same question, for they steered over to the small scow. "*Wohin?*" (Where are you going?) shouted the officer.

Haaksma, dressed like a farmhand, pointed to the bottom of the scow, which was covered with willow twigs, and answered, "What's it look like? Gathering willow twigs, of course."

The Germans peered into the boat. There wasn't much to see and no one could be hiding under the small load of twigs. They waved the little scow on.

The flat-bottomed boat floated along the island. Coming to shore, Bert and Haaksma jumped out and began cutting willow twigs.

The two fugitives watched from their hiding place, dying a thousand deaths. Haaksma's plan seemed awfully bold, thought Tom. How were they ever going to get aboard the scow without being seen? Moreover, the Germans might come to watch the willow cutters out of mere curiosity.

But Haaksma had laid his plans very carefully, selecting the time of his arrival very deliberately. Just then a long row of boats came down the river, so that the Germans were kept busy stopping and searching them.

Meanwhile, Haaksma and Bert tossed a few bundles of twigs into the boat and then moved down-river a little and cut more twigs. In this way, they gradually moved to the other side of the island, until they were out of sight of the Germans.

Then Bert whistled softly. It was the whistle that the three friends always used to signal to each other.

"Let's go," whispered Tom. "This is our chance."

They quickly crept through the undergrowth, the willows lashing their faces. Ahead lay the boat. Haaksma and Bert were busy cutting twigs, but they kept looking up to see whether the two fugitives were coming. When Haaksma saw them, he hissed, "Quick, get in the bottom of the boat."

No sooner had Tom and John scrambled inside, than they were being buried under bundles of willow twigs. Bert jumped into the boat and rearranged the load so all that could be seen was the load of willows. Haaksma untied the boat and they began moving down-river toward the Verhoef farm.

Underneath the load of willows Tom and John lay anxiously listening for the chug of the German motorboat. Haaksma and Bert were just as anxious, but they didn't show it. They moved very unhurriedly and again took up their rowing song.

Fortunately the Germans were still occupied with the other boats, so the small scow was hardly given a second glance. A bend in the river soon carried them out of sight of the Germans. About ten minutes later Haaksma was steering the boat to shore on Verhoef farmland.

After looking around carefully to see that the coast was clear, he and Bert quickly pushed aside the bundles of twigs and helped their two stowaways up. Haaksma told John in fluent English, "Have no fear. You're among friends and we'll help you. First we're going to the farm."

The two rescued fugitives jumped ashore and hurried to the large farmhouse not far away. Halfway they were greeted by the joyous barking of Scout, who gave his master an enthusiastic welcome.

Mr. Verhoef met them too. He held out his hand to each of them. "You did all right there, Tom," he said.

He took John upstairs to get him a change of clothes. Tom went to the kitchen. He was famished. Bert's mother was already slicing up a loaf of bread and had a pan of soup on the stove. Tom hadn't eaten so hungrily in a long time, and John also attacked his food with an appetite.

Tom laughed every time he looked at the English pilot. He looked so completely different in the farmer's clothing Verhoef had given him.

Haaksma was also sitting by the table talking with John. They talked so fast Tom had difficulty following the conversation. Suddenly it entered his mind that it was very unlikely that a simple farmhand would be able to speak English so well. He smiled to himself. He had long suspected that Haaksma was no mere farmhand, and now he was sure.

When Tom had eaten his fill, Mr. Verhoef sat down at the table opposite him and said, "Tom, I'd like to talk with you a minute. Would you come with me?"

He led Tom into the living room. Tom was feeling very uneasy. Mr. Verhoef looked very serious. What did he want? The farmer came right to the point.

"Tell me, Tom, how did you happen to run into that pilot?"

Tom told him everything, from his sighting of the man in the sky last night to the time they were rescued. When he was finished, Verhoef said, "My boy, you can thank God everything turned out as well as it did. For you were very reckless and took tremendous risks."

Tom blushed and looked at the floor. He knew all too well how right Mr. Verhoef was.

"Still," the farmer continued in another tone, "I'll repeat what I said when I first met you two: you did all right. Although you took great risks, you acted courageously when the chips were down. But now, about the pilot. I'm sure you know that what we're doing is extremely dangerous to all of us. If the Germans find out, we'll all be shot. So promise me one thing. We'll see to it that John is taken care of, and after the war I'll tell you all about it. But before then, promise me that you'll never say or ask me anything about him. Tell no one what happened today. No one at all! Will you shake hands on that?"

Tom's blush grew even deeper, but he didn't take the hand offered him. Stammering, he said, "B-b-but my parents don't know where I've been, and when I get home, they'll ask me what happened. What do I say then?"

Mr. Verhoef smiled, "You're right," he said. "You'll have to tell your father, but also tell him what you promised me here. He'll understand."

Then Tom put his youthful hand in the rough, calloused hand of the farmer. Together they walked back to the kitchen, where Tom said goodbye to John. John thanked him for his help, pounding his shoulder repeatedly, and he promised to look Tom up after the war and bring him a souvenir from England.

Scout danced excitedly around Tom, as he stepped outside to head for home. They made a big detour to make sure they didn't run into any Germans who might still be out searching. Dusk was not far off when they finally reached home again.

Father was pacing about in the yard, looking anxiously over the fields. His relief was written all over his face when he saw them coming up the path.

"Where have you two been all day?" he cried. "We've been worried sick!"

"Oh . . . we went . . . the pilot . . . ," began Tom confusedly. But then he stopped. The yard was no place to tell his story. What if he were overheard! Father noticed his hesitation and had also caught the word "pilot."

"Let's go to the study," he said.

Tom followed him, relieved to hear that Father wasn't angry. In the security of Father's study, he told everything that had happened since that morning. When he was finished, Father looked at him very seriously.

"Your little adventure could have been the end of you," he said. "Do you realize how much worry you've caused us? Your mother is lying in bed with a splitting headache. I was ready to go to the police. The only reason I didn't was because I was afraid you were up to something involving the Germans, and I figured raising an alarm might make more trouble. You should have used your head. You should have told me."

Tom nodded. He wanted to swallow, but he couldn't. Had he brought on one of Mother's migraine headaches?

"Wait here," said Father. "I'll go tell Mother you're back."

Tom sat in his chair, quiet and dejected. When they had arrived at the Verhoef farm, he had felt like a hero. Still, Father was right: he had acted unwisely.

The door opened. Mother came rushing in. She was pale, but she was beaming. She ran to Tom and hugged him in her arms.

"Thank God! Thank God!" she whispered. "The Lord has spared you again."

Then Tom was reminded of his prayer in the reeds. Yes, he had been miraculously saved. Later that evening, before he went to sleep, he thanked God for having saved him and the English pilot. He also asked God to protect them in the coming days. He had a vague premonition that the future held more danger in store for them all. He was not mistaken.

Chapter 9

Flight Through the Forest

One late afternoon about two months later, Tom and Scout were roaming about in the woods. Because it was the latter part of November, the light

46

was beginning to fade between the tall trees. A recent storm had matted the forest floor with a thick layer of leaves and branches.

Nothing unusual had happened during the last two months. For several days after his adventure with the English pilot, Tom had lived in considerable suspense. Whenever he saw German soldiers in the neighbourhood, he was seized by the fear that they had discovered who had helped the Englishman escape, and that they were coming to pick him up. He made sure that Scout stayed inside the house as much as possible. But when nothing happened for several days, he began to relax. He went back to the Verhoef farm a few times without Scout, but saw nothing of John. Although he was very curious, he restrained himself from asking any questions.

Then the school had been opened again. Every day he had pedalled to town on his bicycle. He had to study hard and had little time to play with Scout. But yesterday the school had been closed again, probably for the rest of the winter. The school's fuel was all gone, and the students had been sitting in their desks shivering in unheated classrooms.

So once again Tom was home all day. In the afternoon he had decided to take Scout for a good run. Tom hadn't seen any Germans in this area for a long time, so he felt safe. Scout was enjoying the outing and so was Tom. They had roamed some distance from home, and Tom had just decided to turn back, when he heard shouting and a commotion not far away.

What could that be? He headed in the direction of the noise. The woods were less dense here. Now he knew where he was. A few hundred metres beyond the edge of the forest stood the farmhouse of Jeremiah Sap. Jeremiah Sap was a strange man, a bachelor of about fifty years old, who lived alone on his small farm. He did all his own cooking, and also farmed his land and milked his cows without any help. He seemed to like being alone and was seldom seen in the village.

The shouting was coming from his yard. What was going on there? Tom went ahead very cautiously, but suddenly Scout stopped. The fur on his neck bristled and he growled threateningly. Something was amiss at the farm. The loud voices sounded very close. Despite Scout's warning, Tom crept forward through the trees and bushes. He soon reached the edge of the forest, where he had a clear view of the yard of the small farm. He turned pale at what he saw.

A group of German soldiers and a few local Nazis, members of the National Guard, were looting the farmhouse. They were smashing furniture, tossing dishes through the windows, and gorging themselves on ham and sausages that they had found in the house. Others were busy in the barn. They cut loose the horses and cows and chased them outside into the yard.

Tom looked on, his heart thumping violently. Scout, who was lying beside him, bared his teeth and growled softly.

Then Tom got another shock. In one corner of the yard stood a group of people, which he hadn't noticed at first. He knew one of them — Jeremiah Sap. The farmer stared at his house, his mouth a hard line in his pale face. His hands were tied behind him. Beside him stood two elderly people, a man and a woman. The man had a long, gray beard, a large nose, and dark eyes. The woman's hair was a silvery white. She seemed to be very tired and weak, for she was having trouble standing up.

Now Tom understood. These strange people were Jews. Jeremiah Sap must have been hiding Jews, and the Germans had found out.

What shocked Tom most, however, was the little girl standing beside the old woman. She looked about six or seven years old and had long, black braids. She clung to the old woman, weeping uncontrollably. The woman was talking to her, trying to console her, but she couldn't even hug the child, for her hands were also bound behind her. Only the little girl had not been tied. In front of the miserable little group stood a German soldier, his rifle at the ready, to see that the prisoners didn't escape.

Rage swept through Tom. Those bullying beasts! Why didn't they leave those harmless, innocent people alone! The captives were sure to be sent to some prison camp, Tom knew. He had overheard his father and mother talking about the Nazi treatment of the Jews often enough to know that these people had nothing but suffering ahead of them. If only he could help!

Numerous fantastic plans flashed through his mind, but his reason told him there was nothing he could do here. If he tried to rescue them, he would only be throwing away his own freedom. So he lay in the carpet of dead leaves grinding his teeth in frustration.

The Germans and National Guardsmen were still dragging out whatever caught their fancy and smashing the rest. The guard with the little group of prisoners was watching the goings-on in the house with great interest.

A movement caught Tom's eye. He shuddered with excitement. Jeremiah Sap, who was standing with his back to Tom, was slowly trying to work his hands free of the ropes. A little more . . . and one hand came free. The farmer kept his hands behind his back. The guard hadn't noticed a thing.

Suddenly a cheer went up from the gang of looters at the house. They had stacked a pile of broken furniture, wood, and old newspapers against the house and sprinkled it with gasoline. Now they were lighting it. Two others were trying to light the thatched roof at another corner of the house.

"Wicked Krauts!" Tom scolded under his breath. They weren't satisfied with arresting those poor people; they had to burn down the house too. Maybe the woods would go up in smoke with it.

But the looters gave no thought to that possibility.

They had found a jug of liquor and were passing it around, as they watched the flames leaping upward along the roof. The soldier guarding the prisoners was apparently feeling left out. He shouted to one of his companions to bring the jug to him. When no one paid any attention, he went to help himself.

This was the moment Jeremiah Sap had been waiting for. He spun around and leaped into the bushes.

Tom almost whooped with joy. No one in the area knew the woods and swamps better than Jeremiah Sap. The Germans would never catch him now.

The celebrating soldiers didn't immediately notice his escape. Tom saw the two old people whispering nervously to each other. With their bound hands and stiff old legs, they had no chance to escape. They both bent forward whispering to the little girl. The child shook her head. Again the two old people talked to her, in obvious desperation. The girl again hugged the old woman. All three of them were weeping now.

Tom found he had difficulty swallowing; his throat was taut and dry.

The two old people kissed the little girl and, obeying the older people, she turned and ran into the woods. She disappeared into the undergrowth only a few metres from where Tom was hiding.

She was just in time, for a few seconds later the guard came running back, having discovered the disappearance of the farmer.

"Where's the farmer?" he screamed at the old couple, and when they didn't answer right away, he shook and cuffed the old man, but neither of the two prisoners said anything. The soldier began ranting furiously and shouted to his companions for help. Cursing and hollering, they turned toward the woods.

Tom realized that it was high time for him to make himself scarce, too. Jeremiah Sap had run the other way. He had a good headstart on the Germans and would have no trouble staying out of their hands. But he himself was in great danger now, and so was the little girl, who was still quite close. He carefully turned around and, keeping low, ran back into the forest, Scout following on his heels.

Only now did he notice that it was almost completely dark in the woods. He had been staring so hard at the burning house, that he hadn't noticed the darkness creeping up on him. He had to watch out where he was going. Branches kept reaching out at him, and a few times he was tripped up by tree roots.

His progress was slower than he had counted on. He had told himself that, unfamiliar as they were with the woods, the Germans wouldn't make very fast time in the woods either. But when he looked back, he saw lights coming through the trees not far behind him. The soldiers had flashlights with them, and the Dutch Nazis with them probably knew these woods as well as he did.

Suddenly he came onto a narrow path. Now he could make better time. Scout trotted ahead of him. Tom counted on the dog's eyes to pick up anything in the dark, and he ran behind him as fast as he could go. He could tell that he was outdistancing the Germans now, because their shouts were becoming fainter and fainter behind him.

A few minutes later the path divided. Scout stopped, and so did Tom, not sure which path to take. As he stood there, he suddenly heard muffled sobbing nearby. It came from the path on the left. The little girl! Was she here? He ran down the path.

Now the sobbing stopped.

As he went down the path a few more metres, Tom saw something moving between the trees. Now he was sure: it had to be the little girl. She was trying to run away from him. But something seemed to be wrong for she wasn't making much headway. "Wait!" Tom hissed loudly. "I want to help you! I'm a friend!"

The little girl, however, seemed to be so upset, that the sound of his voice only made her even more frantic. She scrambled around a bend in the path and disappeared behind some trees.

Then Scout sprang into action. He dashed ahead of Tom and caught up to the girl in a few bounding strides. He didn't touch her, he just ran past her and blocked her path. The poor child was terrified by the dog. She threw herself face down on the ground, covered her face, and wailed. Soon Tom was beside her.

"Shhh! It's all right!" he said. "The dog won't hurt you, and I won't either. I saw you getting away from the Germans, and I want to help you."

She kept her face hidden against the ground, sobbing and cringing in terror. At first nothing Tom said seemed to get through to her, but as he kept on talking, she slowly calmed down. Finally she sat up.

"What's your name?" asked Tom.

"Miriam," the little girl answered very quietly.

"The two old people with you — were they your parents?"

"No, my parents are gone. I was staying with my grandma and grandpa in Amsterdam. We've been hiding in Mr. Sap's house for a long time. Until the soldiers came today. Somebody must have told on us."

Tom was about to ask another question, but just then he heard a loud voice barking orders not far behind them.

"Come on," Tom said anxiously. "We've got to get going, or else they'll catch us here."

The girl stood up and tried to follow him, but she winced as she stepped forward.

"What's the matter?" Tom asked.

"I fell and hurt my knee," she said. "But I think it's getting better. I can walk."

She bit her lip to keep from crying. Although it was very dark where they were, Tom could see that she couldn't walk very well. The Germans were catching up; his heart raced with fear as he heard the German voices drawing closer.

He took the girl on his back and hurried on after Scout. Miriam was small and thin, but after Tom had carried her for about five minutes, he was panting with effort. She kept sliding down his back, and he kept stumbling over his own feet.

Again they heard voices. The Germans were right behind them now. Miriam began sobbing again. Tom had to put her down a minute to rest.

"Run!" she sobbed. "Run, or else they'll catch you too!"

But Tom was determined not to leave the little girl alone. He racked his brain to think of something. Scout stood beside him and nuzzled his hand.

Suddenly he had an idea. Scout had grown into a big, strong animal; he had often surprised Tom with his strength.

"I know what!" Tom said to the little girl. "My dog can carry you, and I'll walk alongside and hold you."

He lifted her up and gently put her on Scout's broad back. So the threesome went on. Scout seemed to understand that the girl couldn't walk and that they were in danger. Carefully he carried his heavy load down the forest path.

Chapter 10

A Close Call

Now they could move much faster, especially because the woods were becoming less dense.

When Scout began stumbling under his load, Tom carried Miriam on his back for a while, and then it was the dog's turn again. The night had now become so dark, Tom could hardly see his hand in front of his face. Scout showed the way, but Tom, who was walking beside him to support Miriam, kept running into branches and tree trunks. The dog was becoming extremely tired. Tom had no idea at all where they were and how soon they would get out of the forest. Exhaustion and anxiety had him close to tears, but he put on a confident front for the girl. They stumbled on through the trees and tangled undergrowth. Suddenly the forest opened up into a clearing. A dark shape rose up out of the darkness in front of them. With a glad shock of recognition, he realized that the dark shape was the wooden shack where the burglars had kept him imprisoned.

Now he knew the way home. They were close to the edge of the forest. Beyond that was the open heath and on the other side, home.

Tom was very tired, and Scout, too, was on his last legs. And the little girl was shivering with cold. Why not rest a while in the shelter of the shack?

He tried the door. It was unlocked. The old, sagging little house was still uninhabited. The threesome went inside. Although it was dark, having four walls around them gave them a feeling of security. Miriam and Tom each plopped down on a wobbly old chair, and Scout stretched out on the floor close to the door.

Tom didn't dare to stay too long, for their pursuers were probably still looking for them. But they simply couldn't go on without a short rest.

Miriam began sobbing quietly. Tom started talking with her in order to take her mind off her situation. She told him about when she had lived in Amsterdam and about the time she had spent hiding on Mr. Sap's farm, where she had lived in constant fear of the Germans.

"Don't worry," said Tom. "Pretty soon we'll be at my house, and my parents will find you a good hiding place. I guess we better get moving again."

"I think I can walk now," said Miriam, sliding off the chair.

Tom opened the door. He froze with fright. Through the trees a bright light came speeding toward the shack. Quickly Tom shut the door again. The light had looked like it was coming straight toward them. He hurried to the window and peered outside. Miriam came to look, too.

The light swayed back and forth through the trees. It was coming from the same direction they had come from.

"It must be someone on a bicycle," Tom said after a moment. "He's following the path and it leads straight to this shack."

"Do you think it's a German?" Miriam asked, frightened.

Tom didn't answer. After all, he didn't have the faintest idea. Scout had also noticed the light. He, too, was looking outside with his forepaws on the windowsill. A threatening growl rose from his throat.

Now the cyclist reached the clearing surrounding the shack. Suddenly the old shack must have come into the light, for he grunted and his headlight swung around as he went tumbling to the ground with his bicycle. Several loud German curses echoed in the stillness of the night.

"It's a German," whispered Tom. "I think he's drunk: he's really slurring his words."

The light had disappeared. It must have been powered by a wheel-driven generator and gone out when the bicycle tipped. The soldier was scrambling to his feet, muttering drunkenly to himself. He left the bicycle in the grass, turned on a flashlight, and came stumbling toward the door. Everything had happened so fast, Tom hadn't had time to make a plan. Miriam clutched his hand, trembling in terror.

Scout was the only one not frightened out of his wits. Even in the dark Tom could tell that he was furious. He felt the dog bristling and trembling with anger.

"If he comes inside, we'll run outside," Tom whispered to Miriam. "He won't see us in the dark."

He made himself sound confident for Miriam, but inwardly he wasn't at all sure about his plan.

As the soldier stepped into the shack, however, Tom got unexpected help. With a lightning leap, Scout was on the German. The man uttered a hoarse scream of terror, stumbled backwards and then crashed to the floor

under the weight of the big German shepherd. His flashlight clattered across the floor.

"Quick!" shouted Tom.

He pushed Miriam out through the door. She dashed out into the darkness, spurred on by terror. Tom tripped over something and fell hard. His arm was gouged by something sharp, but he hardly felt it. Frantically he scrambled back to his feet.

Then he realized what it was he had tripped over. It was the soldier's bicycle. Immediately an idea flashed into his mind. In his panic to get away, he started down the path, but then he stopped. It was a good idea. Miriam wouldn't be able to walk very far with her sore knee, the woods were full of Germans, and it was still a long way across the heath. They might easily be overtaken there, and then there would be no place to hide. The bicycle was a Godsend!

He picked up the bicycle and went running down the path after Miriam. "Miriam, Miriam!" he called softly. "Over here!"

She was waiting a few metres into the woods. She was delighted to hear Tom's voice, for she had begun to think the soldier had grabbed him.

"I'll walk the bike for a ways, because we can't ride here," whispered Tom. "Just hold on to the rear carrier. I know how to get out of here. When we get clear of this brush, I'll pedal and you sit on the carrier."

Hurriedly he pushed the bicycle through the undergrowth in the direction of the heath.

Behind them, they could still hear the furious barking and growling of Scout and the screaming and cursing of the soldier as he fought to get free of the dog.

Suddenly Tom was brought to a halt by the sound of two muffled shots. The German must have managed to get his hands on his gun. Had he shot Scout?

Tom cupped his hands around his mouth and shouted, "Scout! Scout! Here, boy!"

They waited, suspended in fear. Again Tom called. Then suddenly they heard panting as the dog came running after them.

"He must have missed," said Miriam. "Otherwise the dog wouldn't be able to run so fast."

Quickly they hurried on again, hearing the soldier shouting behind them in the clearing. His flashlight beam flitted faintly through the trees and he fired a few shots at random in their general direction. Tom and Miriam struggled on with the bicycle. Driven by fear, they forgot all about their weariness and pain.

Here was the edge of the forest. The large expanse of heath that lay ahead of them was just barely visible under the twinkling stars. Across it was a narrow path that Tom had often travelled by bike during the day, but then it had been light; now it was dark — very dark. Tom didn't dare to use the light on the bicycle for fear they might be seen. They had to risk riding along the path in total darkness.

The angry shouting of the German soldier, who seemed just to have discovered the theft of his bicycle, rang through the woods behind them.

Tom straddled the bicycle and Miriam climbed on the rear carrier. Tom pushed off, and away they went. Keeping the bicycle on the path was very tricky. Tom kept swerving into the tall grass and every so often he was stopped by a dip or a clump of grass that caught the wheel. Then they had to dismount to get back on the path. Still they were making better time than if they had walked.

The dark woods dropped far behind them and they no longer heard the pursuing German, but Tom was far from easy. At any moment lights might appear on the heath behind them, so he toiled on, perspiring with fear and effort. By the time they reached the dirt road that also ran behind Tom's house, they still had detected no signs that they were being followed.

But then Tom was faced with a new problem. He realized that the bicycle might bring him into great danger if he didn't get rid of it. If the Germans found the bicycle on their property, he and his family were in deep trouble. He hadn't intended to keep it in the first place. He had only grabbed it to help them get away.

Stopping on the road, he stood and thought a moment. Yes, he knew what he had to do. He didn't turn right, in the direction of the house, but he turned left. In that direction the road turned and led to the canal, where there was a small bridge.

When they reached the bridge, Tom and Miriam got off the bicycle. Although it was very dark here, Tom's heart pounded with fear. Carefully he walked the bicycle to the middle of the bridge. Scout started coming with him, but when Tom said, "Stay, Scout. Stay with Miriam!" he sat down next to the girl. In the middle of the bridge, Tom leaned the bicycle against the railing and then stopped and listened a moment whether anyone was coming. He heard nothing. Then he took hold of the bicycle and heaved it over the railing. It disappeared over the side with a loud splash.

"There!" mumbled Tom. "That's taken care of."

But the next moment, he was seized by fright, for a beam of light suddenly pierced the darkness and a loud voice cried, "Halt! Who's there?"

The voice came from the other side of the canal. Tom sprinted off the bridge and, taking Miriam by the hand, he panted, "Come on! Run!" They ran as fast as they could, Scout bounding ahead of them.

"Blockhead!" Tom scolded himself. How could he have forgotten that the Germans had recently stationed a guard by the bridge to protect it against sabotage? Were they still going to be caught after coming all this way? Behind them a noisy motor sprang into life. A motorcycle! A minute later a big headlight came sweeping down the road.

"This way!" panted Tom. "Into this yard."

He pulled Miriam with him off the road toward a big, old house that stood a short distance from the road. He dashed through the gate and pulled Miriam down behind a clump of shrubs in the front yard.

They flattened themselves behind the bushes just in time, Scout between them. The bright light was already terrifyingly close. They stretched out on the chilly ground and didn't move a muscle.

A motorcycle carrying two German soldiers slowly came riding down the road, playing the headlight over both sides of the road. The beam also passed over the shrubs where the children were hiding. Momentarily Scout's eyes lit up like two bright coals, and Tom's heart raced in fear that the Germans had seen them. But no. The motorcycle continued down the road and disappeared around the bend. They sighed with relief. Tom felt limp, and he could feel Miriam trembling from head to foot.

Tom's only thought was to get home as quickly as possible. But he didn't dare to use the road. The motorcycle might return any minute, and maybe more soldiers were coming to take up the search. When the group that had burned down Jeremiah Sap's place got back to town, things were going to be even more dangerous.

What should they do? Should they awaken the people in the old house and ask if they could come in? He knew the people that lived there, but not very well. He didn't dare ask them for help in hiding a Jewish girl. The only thing to do was to head for home by cutting across the rugged countryside and through back yards.

"Follow me," he whispered to Miriam. "I know this area very well, and I'll find another way to get us home safely."

They crept past the house through the back yard. The house was completely dark. "It must be close to midnight," thought Tom. "Father and Mother must be worried sick."

They found an opening in the hedge that divided the yard from the neighbouring fields. They slipped through it and trudged on. It was a very black night. Tom led Miriam by the hand, but sometimes he had little or no idea where they were. Twice they had to climb a fence. Then suddenly they were on the edge of a canal.

Tom tried to figure out where they were. Ah, now he knew. On the other side of the canal was a large nursery for shrubs and trees. If they could get across the canal and across the land of the nursery, Tom knew where there was a path that led straight to his back door. Unfortunately the canal was deep, and he knew of no bridges across it in this neighbourhood. It was too wide to jump across; besides, Miriam couldn't jump anyway.

"If only we had a big board," thought Tom. They were close to someone's back yard, and Tom looked around to see what he could find. His eyes had grown quite used to the dark by now. In the back of the yard stood a shed, and stacked against it was a pile of old lumber. Tom groped around in the pile until he found a thick board. When he tugged at it, suddenly a dog started barking by the house. Scout growled threateningly.

"Shhh, Scout! Go to Miriam!" whispered Tom.

He pulled at the board with all his might. It was stuck in the pile. The dog began barking furiously. Lights came on in the house. A new fear shot through Tom. The people next to the nursery were said to be friendly to the Germans!

In his fear, he tugged at the board with renewed strength. The pile of wood tumbled over with a loud clatter, but the board was loose. Tom fell over backwards, but he was right back on his feet again.

"Quick!" said Tom. "This board should be long enough to reach the other side. Let's go!"

As they hurried to the edge of the canal, the back door of the house opened.

"Quiet, Nero!" a gruff voice shouted.

A tall, husky man came outside and walked toward the shed. He almost tripped over the lumber that had rolled off the stack, and he uttered a few curses.

"Lousy thieves! Steal my wood, will you!"

In the meantime, Tom had dragged the board to the edge of the canal, and now, with the help of Miriam, he dropped it across the water. The man heard the noise of the board hitting the other bank and came striding toward the sound. The board was in place.

"Quick!" Tom whispered to Miriam. "You first!"

She was trembling with fear, but step by step she made her way across.

"Okay, Scout, go!" commanded Tom. He was afraid the dog might attack the rapidly approaching man. But Scout didn't need the board. He took a run and jumped across to the other side. He made it without any difficulty.

The angry man was almost upon Tom now. He lunged at Tom, but Tom ducked under his outstretched arms and ran across the board. His pursuer followed him. When Tom was almost on the other side, his foot slipped off the board and he went sprawling forward. Happily, he landed on the bank of the canal and didn't even get a wet foot. But his fall knocked the board sideways so that the man, who was on the middle of the board, lost his balance and toppled into the canal. He hollered and screamed as if he were being murdered.

The nursery was quite large. The two children went running and stumbling across the rough ground, but Tom soon found a path along which they could make good their escape.

The hollering behind them had stopped. Tom and Miriam were still afraid that the big man would suddenly appear out of the darkness, but nothing happened. The man seemed to have been scared off by his sudden dunking. Soon they came to a barbed wire fence and carefully crawled underneath it. On the other side was a narrow path that wound along the edges of the fields.

"We don't have to be afraid anymore," Tom whispered to the frightened little girl. "We're almost there."

They followed this path for about five minutes. Then suddenly a high hedge blocked their way. A few metres to one side of the path, Tom found the spot he was looking for. Close to the ground there was a small opening in the hedge, big enough for them to slip through. They crawled through one at a time. Tom took Miriam by the shoulder and in a voice filled with relief, he said, "We're safe. This is *Heathview*, my home. See, there's the house."

Against the starry night sky they could just make out the shape of the big farmhouse. They walked through the large yard toward the house. Inside, lights were still burning. When Tom rang the doorbell, his father opened the door. Because of the blackout regulations, which forbade the showing of light outside at night, he had not switched on the hall light, so at first he didn't notice Tom's guest.

"Tom!" he exclaimed. "What on earth are you doing, coming home so late! Your mother and I have been . . ."

Then he saw there was someone else with Tom.

"Who's that?" he blurted in surprise.

"A little girl, Father. I found her in the woods. She escaped from the Germans," Tom whispered, still cautious in case there were Germans in the neighbourhood.

Mr. Sanders said nothing, but he quickly closed the door behind the threesome. "Come on, let's go into the living room and you can tell me what happened."

They went down the hall and Tom's mother came hurrying to meet them. In the glow of light from the living room Tom could see that her eyes were red from weeping.

Now that the pressure was off, Tom felt how exhausted he was. Miriam was in an even worse condition. She was as pale as a corpse, and she looked as if she were ready to collapse. Tom's mother quickly set her down on the sofa and ran to fetch her a glass of milk.

Then Tom sat down and told his parents everything that had happened. They listened attentively. When he was finished there was a moment of silence, and then his father said, "You did well, Tom, I'm proud of you. The Lord has entrusted Miriam to us and we'll take care of her."

Tom's mother stroked the little girl's dark hair. That was enough to trigger a flood of tears, as all the pent-up fear came pouring out. Sobbing violently, Miriam clung to Mrs. Sanders who put her arms around her and let her cry herself out.

Tom stood by, a little bashful now. He felt very sorry for Miriam, but he didn't know what to say or do.

"Why don't you go to bed, Tom," his father suggested. "You must be dead tired." Tom was glad to take the suggestion. He climbed the stairs to his room. Scout followed him, and lay down on the rug beside the bed, where he always slept. Tom quickly dressed for bed, but before he slid under the covers, he thanked the Lord for having protected him, and he also asked Him to be with the poor little girl he had brought home.

The next morning, Ina, Tom's sister, was surprised to find a strange girl at the breakfast table. Father told her that Miriam would be staying with them for a while, but that she would have to stay indoors, at least for the next few days, and that no one was to know she was living with them.

Ina didn't understand it all, but she promised to do everything Father said. She was overjoyed to have a friend staying with her. It would be almost like having a sister.

Miriam was much calmer today. She was even able to laugh and was very happy for Ina's company. She hadn't played with anyone of her own age for many months.

Tom was still somewhat uneasy. Had the Germans really lost his trail? Would they keep searching? He couldn't stand being cooped up in the house all day, and after a while he carefully scouted the street in front of the house to see whether the neighbourhood was safe.

When he walked past the house beside the nursery, he saw that the man was just angrily restacking the lumber that had been scattered about last night. Tom grinned to himself. He thought of the splash and the hollering he had heard as he and Miriam were escaping. The man looked up at him, and Tom quickly walked on. What if the man recognized him?

A little farther on he came to the bend in the road. Coming around the bend, he could see the bridge in the distance. A small group of men and boys had gathered by the bridge. They were being held back by a German soldier. Two other soldiers were dragging the water beside the bridge. They seemed to have snagged something heavy.

Fear seized Tom's heart. He knew what they had snagged. He hid behind a tree and waited. After a little while he saw the soldiers hauling up the bicycle which he had tossed off the bridge last night.

He paled and quickly turned back home. This was dangerous. The Germans would quickly figure out that the boy who had taken the bicycle was from around here, and that the little girl had to be hiding here, too. They would probably organize a house to house search, or perhaps punish the whole village. If only he hadn't been so careless as to forget about the guards at the bridge!

At home he told Father what he had seen. Father did not seem to become too worried and tried to put Tom's mind at ease.

"Don't get too anxious, Tom. Things might not be as bad as all that. You told me the soldier who found you in the shack was drunk. He probably remembers very little of what happened."

"Yes," said Tom, "but what if he does remember. If the Germans start asking around about a boy and a big dog, won't that lead them right here?"

Father put a hand on Tom's shoulder. "Listen, Tom. What you did was good. You may well have saved that little girl's life. The Lord has entrusted Miriam to our care, so there's no need for us to fear. He'll take care of us. If they pick up your trail, we'll take you and Miriam and Scout to a place where you'll be safe."

Tom knew his father was right. He had to learn to trust in the Lord Jesus who could protect him from all dangers. He didn't tell Miriam about his fears. The girl quickly fit into the life of the family and seemed quite happy, especially when she was playing with Ina. The two girls became fast friends.

Sometimes when Miriam was alone, she thought of her grandparents and everything that had happened to her. Then Mrs. Sanders occasionally found her hiding somewhere and crying. But everyone in the family did their best to make her forget the past as much as possible.

When Father told Bible stories every Sunday, Miriam also came to listen. She listened very attentively. She knew most of the stories from the Old Testament, but she knew nothing at all about the New Testament and the Lord Jesus. Father told her that Jesus was the Messiah promised in the Old Testament, whom the Jews had always looked forward to.

When, after a week, the Germans still hadn't been seen or heard from, Miriam was sometimes allowed to go and play in the large back yard with Ina and Tom. Scout always joined in, too. He seemed to feel responsible for the girl's safety. He always kept an eye on her. If any Germans appeared in the neighbourhood, he would immediately growl a warning. Then the children wasted no time getting into the house, for they were still afraid Miriam might be recognized and seized.

Chapter 11

On the Verhoef Farm

The dark days of winter had come. The days were short and gray and sunless. Famine held many parts of the country in its awful grip. In the village where Tom lived, people were still getting by, but the farmers in the area were continually hounded by starved, wretched-looking people from the big cities who came to their doors searching for food. Sometimes a few of these hungry wanderers spent the night at Tom's house, telling their hosts of the terrible suffering in the cities.

Everyone hoped for a speedy end to the war. They had been sadly disappointed this past autumn when the English had been stopped at Arnhem. Now the liberating armies of the Allies wouldn't begin to move again until spring.

Ina, Miriam, and Tom had always had enough to eat. But the terrors of war did not entirely pass them by. Every night large squadrons of planes passed over the village, and once several bombs had been dropped, destroying one of the homes in town.

*   *   *

It was the week between Christmas and New Year.

Tom, Ina, and Miriam, had been invited to spend a few days on the Verhoef farm with Bert. Carl was coming too, and, of course, so was Scout.

The children sent up a loud cheer when the invitation arrived. There was so much to see and do on the Verhoef farm. They left for the farm at dusk. The evening shadows would make it safer for Miriam.

This was the first time that Miriam was venturing outside of the Sanders' yard. The three children would cut across the fields so they wouldn't run much danger of being stopped. Mr. Verhoef knew that Miriam was Jewish and had assured Mr. Sanders that the girl would be safe on the farm. Carl and Bert had also been told the secret, and they had promised to mention her to no one.

Mrs. Sanders had dressed Ina and Miriam warmly and packed extra clothes for them. She had insisted that they leave their best clothes at home, for she knew that their clothes would take quite a beating as the children played around the farm.

Tom, Scout, and the two girls set out in high spirits. First they went to the windmill to pick up Carl. Carl was already waiting for them, and waved happily when he saw them coming. Together they walked to the Verhoef farm.

It was quite a walk, so darkness had fallen when they arrived at the farm. A warm reception awaited them. Haaksma also came to the door and Scout jumped up against his trainer, barking happily. Mr. Verhoef, Haaksma, and Bert were just going out to do the milking, so the three children went along to the barn, where the cows were waiting in a long row. It was warm and cosy in the barn.

Tom asked if he could help. In the past, he had occasionally helped to milk and had caught on quite well. Grabbing a pail, Tom sat down beside a cow.

Everyone looked up in surprise, however, when Miriam shyly asked, "Shall I help, too?"

Mr. Verhoef laughed. "So my pretty little blossom, do you think it looks so easy?"

"Oh," said Miriam, "but I know how. I learned it at . . . I mean, I . . ." Then she blushed and kept quiet.

But Tom understood. She must have learned how to milk while she and her grandparents were hiding at Jeremiah Sap's place. Mr. Verhoef asked no more questions. He gave Miriam a pail and she joined the men between the cows. She handled herself like an experienced farmhand.

After supper everyone gathered around the fireplace in the large living room of the farmhouse. Mrs. Verhoef had fixed a kettle full of anise milk, and Mr. Verhoef brought in a big bag of chestnuts, so the children sat around the fireplace drinking anise milk and roasting chestnuts. After burning their fingers a few times, they were soon munching eagerly on the roasted nuts.

Meanwhile, Haaksma told them one story after another. He seemed to know not only the Netherlands, but many other countries as well, and he had quite a few adventures to tell. The children listened very closely. Tom smiled to himself when he thought of Haaksma passing himself off as an ordinary farmhand.

In this way, the first evening flew by, and they had to stifle a murmur of disappointment when Mr. Verhoef said it was time for bed. They all fell asleep dreaming of the wonderful places Haaksma had described to them.

*   *   *

It was the middle of the night. Tom turned restlessly in his bed. The moon shone brightly through the window of the bedroom where Tom was sleeping. He opened his eyes and blinked in the silvery light; then he yawned and sat up. Strange, he seemed to be rested, but it was far from morning.

Scout was sleeping curled up on a mat at the foot of the bed. Carl and Bert were sleeping in the next room. Ina and Miriam shared a room downstairs. They had all been at the Verhoef farm for two whole days now and were enjoying themselves immensely. They helped a little with the work, rode horseback, and invented many different games together. The farm was a wonderful place to play hide-and-seek, because there were so many places to hide.

Yesterday they had thought of a new game. Bert and Carl played the role of German soldiers, while Tom, Ina, and Miriam pretended they were "divers." "Divers" was the name given to people hiding from the Germans for any one of a number of reasons. The divers used Scout as a messenger. When Scout came to the hiding place of one of the divers wearing a red cord about his neck, this meant danger, then that person had to find a new place to hide. If Scout was wearing a blue cord, everything was safe. It was a very exciting game. Even Haaksma had stopped to watch the game with great interest.

The children's Christmas vacation on the farm had turned out even better than they had expected. They had a marvelous time playing together, and Mr. and Mrs. Verhoef spoiled them terribly. Tom and the two girls had never gone hungry at home, but they had gone without many things. Mrs. Verhoef made them all kinds of good things to eat.

A movement from Scout brought Tom out of his thoughts. The dog had suddenly raised his head with his ears pointed straight up. Tom listened closely, but he heard nothing. Still, Scout must have heard something, for he stood up and walked to the window.

Tom was very curious now. Quietly he slid out of bed and tiptoed to the window, not wanting to waken his two friends in the next room. The farmyard was bathed in moonlight. At first Tom noticed nothing peculiar, but suddenly something moved in the shadow of one of the sheds. It was too dark for Tom to see what it was. Were two men standing over there? Carefully, noiselessly, Tom opened his window. The cold night air quickly cooled off the room, but Tom hardly noticed. His eyes were beginning to grow used to the darkness. Now he could just make out the shape of a man in the shadow of the shed.

Then Tom heard a noise coming from the direction of the river. It sounded like the soft splashing of oars. Then followed a scraping sound and a few thumps. The boat must have been hauled ashore.

The waiting man stepped out of the shadows. Tom was not really surprised to see that it was Haaksma. Two other figures approached from the river. They were carrying a big crate between them, and they set it down beside the shed.

Tom felt a pang of guilt. Should he be watching? First he had thought there were strangers prowling about, but now that he knew Haaksma was involved, it was really none of his business. However, Tom's curiosity won out, and he stayed at the window.

The three men stood close together whispering. Tom couldn't hear a thing, but from the motions they were making with their hands, Tom could tell that Haaksma was the leader and was telling the others what to do. One of the strangers looked like a young man, not much older than Tom himself, but Tom didn't recognize him. The other struck Tom as familiar, but he hadn't been able to see the man's face. Suddenly the man turned around, so that for a moment the moon lit up his features. Tom almost spoke aloud in surprise. It was Jeremiah Sap, the escaped farmer.

Now the men carried the crate into the shed. Shortly they came back out carrying two full potato sacks, which they carried to the river. A few moments after they had disappeared into the darkness, Tom once again heard the soft splash of oars. The two men were apparently leaving. Haaksma soon returned by himself and slipped back into the shed.

Not until then did Tom realize how cold he was getting. He was shivering in the chilly night air. Scout was still standing beside him with his forepaws on the windowsill. He hadn't made a single sound while watching the men in the yard. Tom quietly closed the window. He hurried back under the covers, where it was some time before he was warm again.

Scout had once more curled up on his rug and was soon back to sleep, but Tom couldn't get back to sleep so easily. He was too busy thinking about what he had seen. Was Jeremiah Sap hiding somewhere close to the farm? Had there been food supplies in the two sacks? Who was the third man? What was in the big crate?

Tom thought and thought, but he got no answers. He told himself he would never tell anyone what he had seen tonight. With this in mind, he fell asleep.

The next morning was gray and gloomy. Nevertheless, the children were in a holiday mood, because tomorrow was New Year's Day. This afternoon they were going to help Mrs. Verhoef fix a special New Year's treat. Mrs. Verhoef would bake little waffles which the children would roll up on a stick while they were still steaming hot. They looked forward to this because they knew there would be lots of fun and lots of tasting in the process. Although they couldn't make all the goodies they usually made because of the food shortage, Mrs. Verhoef had decided to make this one treat anyway, since the children always looked forward to it so eagerly. That night Tom, Ina, Miriam, and Carl would all go home again.

But now it was still morning. The two girls were in the kitchen helping Mrs. Verhoef. The boys had other plans. Yesterday each of them had made a bow for himself and several arrows. They had spent the day practicing. Today they wanted to go hunting in the marshlands along the river with Scout. They could always dream up some game there.

They left after breakfast, in high spirits. The sun had finally broken through the clouds and stood low in the steel-gray sky. The grass in the fields was still wet and here and there the ground was covered with water because the river was so high.

Tom and Carl had both borrowed wooden shoes. Carl was wearing Haaksma's and Tom an extra pair of Bert's. Thus they didn't have to worry about getting their feet wet. They still had to make detours around the biggest puddles, however. Especially among the reeds they had to be careful that they didn't suddenly step into a hole full of water.

The reeds rustled in the wind as the boys stalked through them with their bows ready like primitive hunters. Whenever they saw something moving in the reeds, they let an arrow fly. The game grew more and more exciting.

Suddenly Scout stopped, sniffing the ground. The boys looked on excitedly. Had he found the trail of some animal? Sniffing the ground, the dog swiftly pushed his way through the dense reeds. He turned this way and that, so the boys had a hard time following him. Several times they had to jump waterholes or ditches, but they didn't give up. Scout seemed to be on the trail of something.

Now they reached an area that was so wet and marshy that their wooden shoes almost stuck in the mud. They communicated with hand signals so that they wouldn't spook off the animal they were tracking. Suddenly Bert poked his two companions and pointed to the ground.

In the muddy soil the animal's tracks were clearly visible.

"Do you know what kind of animal that is?" Carl whispered to Bert.

Bert shrugged his shoulders.

Suddenly the tracks turned again and headed straight toward the river. Scout bristled with eagerness and went bounding ahead into the reeds, out of sight. The boys scrambled after him to see what he was after. They heard some loud hissing and angry growls from the dog. Then followed a splash. They just caught a glimpse of a shiny, brown animal diving into the water and swimming away under the surface.

"A big otter!" exclaimed Bert.

Cheeks aglow from the chase, they stared down into the rippling water. Teeth bared, Scout waited on the river bank, but the otter had disappeared without a trace.

Suddenly Carl looked down at his feet in disgust. In the heat of the chase, he had stepped into a hole and now the water was pouring into his wooden shoes. He jumped away to dry ground, but it was too late. His socks were soaking wet. He pulled them off and wrung them out as well as he could, but they were far from dry.

"Sometimes we put straw in our wooden shoes at home," said Bert. "That keeps your feet warm and dry. Let's pick leaves off some of these dry reeds. They should work just as well."

Carl thought it a great idea, for none of the three wished to interrupt their adventure in order to go home and get dry socks for Carl. They hadn't been paying any attention to Scout, but Tom suddenly noticed that he was acting strangely. An angry, threatening glint had come into his eyes. The hair on his back rose and a low growl rumbled in his throat as he stalked toward the edge of the reeds and the neighbouring meadow.

"Hey, boys!" hissed Tom. "Look at Scout. Something is wrong."

Stooping, the boys crept to the edge of the reeds after Scout. Like a well-trained scout, Scout had edged forward on his stomach. Only his curled upper lip, showing his sharp teeth, revealed the dog's anger. Now the boys, too, could see what disturbed him. The sun had again disappeared behind a gray haze of clouds, and in the gloom of the morning a small troop of German soldiers was marching across the meadow only a few hundred yards from where the boys were hiding. They were marching straight toward the Verhoef farm.

The boys turned pale with fear at the sight and looked at each other in consternation.

"They're heading for our house," said Bert, his lips trembling. "It must be a raid, and Miriam and Haaksma are there!"

In his fright he mentioned Haaksma, who was supposedly nothing more than a farmhand, but no one noticed. They were all seized by the same fear.

"Couldn't we run and warn them?" asked Carl.

But all three of them could see that that was impossible. As soon as they came out of the reeds, the Germans would see them and stop them, and if they stuck to the reeds, they would have to make such a long detour that they would never reach the house in time.

"Maybe someone in the house will see them coming," said Tom.

"No," explained Bert. "The way the Germans are approaching the farm, no one will see them until they're on the yard. There's a big stand of trees between them and the house."

They huddled together, staring numbly after the group of soldiers. The soldiers moved forward purposefully, seeming to have a goal in mind. That goal could only be the Verhoef farm, for there were no other homes in the area.

Bert looked at Scout. "Couldn't Scout deliver a message?" he asked Tom.

Tom jumped up. "Of course!" he exclaimed. "Scout delivered a message when I was stuck on Willow Island with . . ." He almost dropped the name of the English flier, which he had sworn not to mention until the end of the war. Carl knew nothing of the story. "Quick! We've got to write a note," continued Tom. "Then we'll tie it to Scout's collar."

They all searched their pockets, but none of them had a pen or pencil or even a small scrap of paper. They looked at each other helplessly.

Meanwhile the Germans were marching on, closer and closer to the farmhouse. If they didn't do something quickly, it would be too late.

"We've got to do something!" Bert blurted anxiously. "Maybe if we all started screaming, they'd come after us and then one of us could circle around and run for the house." His voice trailed off. He knew it wouldn't work.

Once more Tom searched his pockets. Wasn't there something he could use to send a message? Suppose he just sent Scout. Would Mr. Verhoef guess that something was wrong? Unconsciously his fingers toyed with a piece of cord in his pocket. Suddenly he yanked it out and barely managed to stifle a cry of triumph.

"Bert! Carl! Look!"

But the boys didn't catch on right away. "It's from the game we were playing yesterday. This is the red cord. It means danger. Haaksma knows what it means, and so do the girls."

"That's it!" Bert cried eagerly.

"I don't know," said Carl. "What if they think we're still just playing?"

"We've got to try!" whispered Tom, tying the cord around Scout's neck with trembling fingers. Then he pointed in the direction of the farmhouse. "Go, Scout! To Haaksma. Bring! And be careful!"

Once more he repeated his orders. Scout looked at him trustingly, wagged his tail, and leaped away out of the reeds.

Pale with worry and suspense, the boys watched him go. The Germans would be sure to see him. What would they do?

Scout was making a big circle around them. A few of the soldiers spotted him running across the fields, for they turned their heads in his direction. One of them unslung his rifle, but the commander of the group motioned to him not to shoot. He obviously didn't suspect that Scout was acting as a messenger, and a shot would, of course, have warned the people in the farmhouse that they were near.

The boys watched Scout until he disappeared over a ridge. Then they looked at each other once more.

"He'll make it," Tom said confidently. "He's way ahead of the Germans."

"Yes," said Carl. "But what if no one notices the cord around Scout's neck?"

They all knew that it was a matter of a few minutes one way or the other. Even if the message were understood in time, they couldn't be sure that it would help. The Germans weren't fooled so easily.

Bert wiped tears of anxiety from his eyes. "God will take care of my parents and the others," he said simply.

The other two boys nodded. Everything was in God's hands.

Chapter 12

Scout Captured

Meanwhile, in the Verhoef house everyone was very busy. Mrs. Verhoef was in the kitchen making preparations for the waffle-making party, and the girls were helping her. Miriam had never experienced this New Year's treat, but she was looking forward to it even more eagerly than the others. Her cheeks were flushed with excitement. She had fetched a couple of fresh eggs from the chicken coop and was just going into the shed attached to the house, when Scout came dashing across the yard and lunged through the half-open door. He had such a momentum, he collided with Miriam and sent the eggs flying out of her hands onto the floor.

Miriam broke into tears, for eggs were very precious during these times of famine. Mrs. Verhoef had said that they might not use any more than two. Ina and Mrs. Verhoef came running from the kitchen to see what had happened. Mrs. Verhoef tried to soothe the weeping little girl, "Don't cry. You couldn't help it. It was the dog's fault."

Ina looked accusingly at Scout. She was ashamed at his behaviour. Scout seemed to have gone berserk. He was barking, and he kept leaping up against Ina and nervously running back and forth.

Haaksma came walking in from the barn. "What's the matter?" he asked. "Is Scout back alone? Where are . . ." Suddenly he stopped and stared at the dog, who was becoming more and more frantic. In two long strides he was beside the dog. He seized him by the collar and pulled him to the window.

"There's something wrong," he said urgently. "Scout is wearing a red cord. Either the boys are in danger or we are."

Quickly Haaksma scaled a ladder to the loft to look out of an upstairs window. He was back in a few seconds, pale with shock.

"There's a troop of German soldiers heading for the house! They're almost here!" he cried.

He rushed to the corner of the shed where blocks of peat called turves were stacked for fuel. Haaksma pushed against the large stack of blocks at a certain spot, and a section of turves gave way. He quickly tossed a few loose turves aside. A wooden panel became visible behind the stack. Haaksma jammed his fingers into a crack between two boards and slid something back. Then he tugged, and suddenly a dark opening appeared, one big enough to crawl through.

"Quick!" he said to Miriam. "They must not find you here."

He lifted her through the opening and then crawled in himself. He closed the panel from the inside.

The tramp of soldiers' feet in the yard could already be heard. Mrs. Verhoef and Ina quickly pushed the turves back into place as best they could, but they wouldn't have had enough time if Scout hadn't been there. He slipped outside and suddenly attacked the officer commanding the German troop. He struck the officer with such force, the man fell over backwards, fighting to keep the snarling dog away from his throat.

The other soldiers rushed in to help their commander. One of them aimed his rifle at the dog, but the officer shouted, "Don't shoot him! We're taking him along." But that was easier said than done. Three, then four soldiers rolled around in the yard trying to pin Scout down, but the dog defended himself valiantly. One of the other soldiers, however, waited for an opening and then clubbed the dog with his rifle butt. This momentarily stunned Scout, and the soldiers seized the opportunity to tie him up.

At that moment Mr. Verhoef came walking from behind the house. He had been working elsewhere and had not seen the soldiers arrive, but Scout's

furious barking and snarling and the shouts of the soldiers had warned him that something was amiss.

The sight of the Germans in the yard gave him a terrible fright, but he managed to put on a calm exterior. Right away he understood that he had to keep the soldiers talking as long as possible in order to give those inside the house time to hide. Scout had revived and was growling angrily, but he couldn't do much, because the soldiers had muzzled him and tied a strong piece of rope around his neck.

"What are you doing with the dog?" demanded Mr. Verhoef. "Why do you have him tied up like that?"

"Because that vicious beast tried to grab me by the throat!" barked the officer. "Look what he did to me and my men." He pointed to his own bloody hand and to the torn uniforms of two soldiers who had also felt the strength of Scout's jaws.

"Strange," said Mr. Verhoef. "You must have stirred him up in some way. He's never attacked anyone before. I'll pump you some water so you can wash your hand." He picked up a pail from beside the house and strolled over to the pump.

His slow, calm manner infuriated the officer. Perhaps he sensed that the farmer was putting him on. "First we'll search this place!" he bellowed. "You stay right here, and two of my men will keep an eye on you. That dog is going with us. We can use him on the eastern front, and if we find anything suspicious around here, you're coming too. I don't like your face."

"The feeling is mutual," Mr. Verhoef almost retorted, but he just caught himself in time. That would have been foolish.

Two soldiers stayed outside to guard Mr. Verhoef and also to hold Scout and keep an eye on the side door. Two others were dispatched to the front door and the back door. The rest went inside, led by the officer.

The shed attached to the house was in semi-darkness and deserted. A soldier pushed open the kitchen door. Mrs. Verhoef was kneading dough on the table. Ina stood beside her. Looking the officer unflinchingly in the eye, Mrs. Verhoef asked him what she could do for him.

"We've come to search the place," he barked. "Something is fishy around here."

"Go ahead," said Mrs. Verhoef. "But please don't wreck my furniture. It has lasted me a long time and I hope to use it many more years."

The gang of soldiers spread out through all the rooms. In spite of what Mrs. Verhoef had said, they began upsetting furniture and messing up the whole house. The bedding was yanked off the beds, the cellar was thoroughly searched, as were all the other farm buildings and the loft over the shed. But the Germans found nothing suspicious.

The officer seemed to be extremely humiliated by this and was ranting and raving. Seeing the large pile of turves in the shed, he ordered his men to search them, too. The soldiers seemed very reluctant to do so and went to work rather slowly. Their commander stood by, shouting at them to hurry. He soon saw that it would take far too long to move the whole stack, so he ordered them to make a hole in the middle of the pile to see whether anything was hidden behind it.

Ina came into the shed. She could not keep as calm as Mrs. Verhoef. She had to see what was happening. When she saw the soldiers digging in the turves, her eyes widened in alarm. The soldiers had made a deep hole in the large stack of peat blocks already. The fuming officer grabbed a rifle, fixed a bayonet on it, and waded into the opening. He raised the rifle to bayonet the back wall of the shed to check it for secret panels. At just that moment, however, the stack began to sway and suddenly the turves collapsed into the opening where the officer stood.

The soldiers had to dig their commander out from under the fallen turves. Cursing and sputtering, he was pulled out by his legs, covered with dark brown peat. His face was scratched and his eyes were full of peat dust. He had had enough. He stormed outside to wash himself at the pump.

Mr. Verhoef saw him come bursting out of the door and had to fight to keep a straight face. He almost said, "I like your face even less now," but he restrained himself.

After he had washed up and uttered a few threats to Mr. Verhoef, the officer led his men away from the farm.

They dragged Scout along with them. The dog braced himself and resisted with all his strength, but it did no good. The rope around his neck choked him, and the soldiers kicked him until he gave in.

Mr. Verhoef watched them go until they were gone from sight. He breathed a sigh of relief and hurried into the house to see how those inside had fared. Mrs. Verhoef met him in the shed. Now that the danger had passed, her composure had also left her. She was pale and trembling, and her knees were so weak, she could hardly stand. Ina too was very upset. She was sobbing.

"You can relax," said Mr. Verhoef. "They're gone. God has spared us. What did they do inside?"

Mrs. Verhoef told him the whole story. After checking once more to make sure the soldiers were really gone, Mr. Verhoef went to the collapsed pile of turves and cleared away a passage in front of the secret panel. He tapped on the wall, and a few seconds later, the wooden panel was opened.

The grinning face of Haaksma appeared in the opening. He lifted Miriam out, then he climbed out himself and carefully closed the wall behind him.

"There!" he said, beginning to stack the turves back in place. "That was touch and go for a while, but all's well that ends well."

"That was more touch and go than you perhaps realize," said Mrs. Verhoef. "That officer didn't give up easily. He had his men clear a passage through the turves to the back wall, and then he was going to bayonet the wall to see whether it was hollow. He might have found you if those turves hadn't fallen at just the right moment."

"Yes, I know," said Haaksma chortling with delight. "I tipped those turves on him. I had left a small crack beside the panel so that I could see what was happening. When I saw what he was about to do, I put my arm out through the opening and gave those turves a good shove so that they went tumbling down on top of him. While everyone was watching the officer getting buried under the turves, I quickly closed the panel again. It was a bit risky, but I had to do something."

Meanwhile Ina was talking with Miriam. "How was it behind the wall?" she asked.

"Oh, the space behind the wall is really narrow," she said. "But then it goes down, and underneath the floor is a little room. It was very dark, but there were some boxes to sit on. I stayed down there, while Mr. Haaksma went back up to see what was happening."

"Weren't you scared?" asked Ina.

"Yes," Miriam said softly, "I was, but I prayed to Jesus to protect us."

Ina blushed. Miriam was Jewish and hadn't heard about Jesus until recently. She had been in much greater danger than Ina, but she had showed more trust in Jesus than Ina had.

"It's too bad the soldiers took Scout along," said Haaksma. "But better a dog than a human being. Besides, he'll probably get better treatment than we would have."

Ina and Miriam looked at each other in dismay. They hadn't thought of it until now: Scout was gone.

Chapter 13

Homeward

Meanwhile the three boys had been awaiting the return of the German soldiers in great suspense. They had made their way through the reeds closer to the farm and were now watching from a spot where they would be able to see the soldiers leave. They had been waiting a long time.

"Should we sneak up on the house?" asked Tom. "If we're real careful, the Germans won't see us."

But Bert and Carl thought that would be too dangerous, and Tom had to agree that the risk wasn't worth taking.

They were still asking themselves whether Scout had made it in time and whether the others had understood the message. The fact that the troop of soldiers was staying away so long could be a bad sign.

As they huddled in the reeds, the damp chill began to penetrate their clothes. They began to shiver, and tried to keep warm by stamping their feet and swinging their arms.

Then suddenly Bert said, "Hey, they're coming!" The threesome hid deeper in the reeds and, filled with suspense, watched the soldiers coming.

In the hazy morning it was hard for the boys to see from that far off whether the group of soldiers included any prisoners.

"No," Carl said happily. "I don't think they have anyone with them."

The boys grinned at each other, their faces beaming with joy. Scout had done his work well.

Tom peered through the reeds again. Then the joy faded from his face and he grew pale. He pointed to the last soldier in the group.

"Look! He's pulling along a dog on a rope. It's Scout. He's got Scout!"

Now the other two boys saw him too. Scout was being led away by a soldier at the end of the column. Now that the troop was coming closer, the boys could see that the dog was not going willingly, but kept struggling against the rope.

Tears sprang to Tom's eyes. "Those bullies! Those mean, sneaking thieves! They're taking my dog!" He had to fight to keep from breaking into tears.

Carl and Bert were also fuming with indignation. With their fists clenching and unclenching helplessly, they watched their faithful friend being led away.

Now the soldiers were close to the reeds, and Scout seemed to sense that the boys were nearby. He was still muzzled, but he turned his head in their direction and suddenly made a desperate, but vain, lunge toward them.

Tom needed all his self-control to keep from leaping out of the reeds and running to Scout's aid, but he knew that would be very foolish. When the Germans and their prisoner had disappeared across the fields, Tom wept silently.

Shattered, the three friends slowly made their way back to the farm. Not until they came in sight of the house did their sorrow over Scout give way to anxiety about how the others had come through the ordeal. What did the house look like inside? What if the soldiers had murdered Haaksma and the others?

"I didn't hear any shots," said Carl. "We would have heard them from where we were."

"I don't know," said Tom. "The wind was blowing the other way. Besides, they didn't have to shoot. There's plenty they can do without shooting."

The suspense hurried them on. As they walked onto the yard, the three boys heaved a sigh of relief, for Haaksma was just coming out of the house carrying a couple of pails. He looked as cheerful and calm as always. When he saw the boys, he put down the pails and hurried toward them with a big smile.

"Well, boys, thanks for the warning. Miriam and I managed to hide just in time. We're a little shy about visitors, you see. Our guests searched everywhere, but they didn't find a thing. Did you see them leave?"

"Yes," said Tom, "and they had Scout with them."

Haaksma looked serious. "Yes, Tom. And I know that's hard to take, but much worse could have happened. Perhaps we can get him back somehow. Miriam and I owe him our freedom and maybe our lives. We won't just abandon him, if we can help it."

Cheered a little by Haaksma's words, the three boys filed into the house. Questions and stories filled the air until both sides had heard the whole story. Although they knew they ought to be thankful that everything had turned out so well, the children remained downcast because they missed Scout. Tom especially racked his brain trying to come up with some way to free his dog, but he could think of nothing.

That afternoon the waffle-making party went on as planned. The children eagerly joined in making the waffles. They enjoyed the brittle, golden rolls tremendously and even joked and laughed, but the absence of Scout put a damper on the celebration.

Soon evening drew near. After supper all the guests would return to their own home.

After what had happened that morning, Mr. and Mrs. Verhoef thought it would be safer if the children didn't go home by the usual route. They decided that Haaksma and Bert would take the children down-river in the rowboat and drop them off where they could take a safer, more direct route home.

After supper, Tom, Carl, Ina, and Miriam said goodbye to their hosts and thanked them for their hospitality, then they walked down to the river and the boat. Haaksma pushed off and soon they were in the middle of the river. He let Tom and Carl row while he steered.

It was very dark on the water. Haaksma hadn't put a light on the boat, because he didn't want them to be seen, so they all had to keep their eyes open to avoid running into something or being run over by another boat.

Haaksma and Bert, however, seemed to know the river like the back of their hands and anticipated every obstacle.

The trip went well, and after about fifteen minutes, Haaksma nosed the boat into shore. The four children climbed out. From here, Carl could be home in about ten minutes and it was only a little farther to the Sanders' place.

After cautioning them all to be very careful, Haaksma and Bert turned the boat back upriver. It was a dark night, but fortunately the children knew the terrain very well. They carefully made their way down the un-lighted streets until they reached the Van Doorn windmill, where they said goodbye to Carl.

Tom and the two girls went on around the outskirts of the village. Tom was filled with a sense of uncertainty and loss, but he didn't show his grief to the girls. At other times, Scout had always been with him on such night-time outings, but now his dog was gone — probably for good. Even Haaksma wouldn't be able to rescue the dog from the hands of the Germans.

Suddenly Tom stopped. He heard whispering in the dark and saw a faint shape moving off to one side. Were there Germans lying in wait here? After all that had happened that day, they were all still a little shaky, so they immediately dove behind some bushes along the path. Not far away the children could just make out the dark mass of a couple of houses in the night.

Again they heard whispering. Then a tiny flame flared up and . . . BLAM! A loud explosion rang out.

Terrified, the three children flattened themselves on the ground. Their hearts raced with fear. Someone was shooting.

Then the back door of one of the houses burst open, and an angry male voice shouted into the night, "Listen, you rascals, scram or I'll take a stick to your hides!"

From nearby came the sound of muffled giggles, and then running foot-steps as several young boys retreated into the night. Laughing nervously, Tom stood up. Now he knew what was going on. "We let ourselves be scared for nothing," Tom said to the two girls. "It's New Year's Eve. There are boys pulling stunts and setting off firecrackers everywhere."

The threesome walked on, feeling a little silly at their own fright. They were happy when they finally reached home. Mrs. Sanders opened the door for them. She was very relieved to see them, for their late return had her a little worried.

Together they went into the living room where they told Father and Mother everything that had happened that day.

Their parents listened very attentively. They had, of course, been completely unaware that their children had been exposed to such danger while they were gone, and they sympathized very deeply with Tom at the loss of his faithful dog. But all other feelings were secondary to their feeling of thankfulness that their children had been spared.

Tonight the children were permitted to stay up later than usual because it was New Year's Eve. They discussed the bygone year: their high hopes when the British had tried to seize Arnhem and their deep disappointment when the Allied advance had been stopped. How long, they asked themselves, would it be before they were liberated? In the western part of the country, many people were suffering severe hunger. In their own locality most people still had enough to eat, but they too were beginning to feel the pinch of shortages caused by the occupation and the war.

Before they went to bed, Mr. Sanders prayed with the whole family. He asked the Lord to put a speedy end to the war and to keep His church faithful in the struggle. Tom crawled into bed, but he was still wide awake. Other nights Scout would always be lying curled up on the rug by his bed. Where was Scout now? Had the Germans fed him? Did the Germans beat their dogs? He asked the Lord to bring Scout back to him. Finally he fell asleep.

High over the village huge bombers droned eastward through the night sky, but Tom did not hear them. Occasionally he moaned in his sleep and thrashed wildly with his arms. He was fighting German soldiers who were going to kill his dog, but no matter how hard he fought, the Germans dragged Scout away, his dark, brown eyes fixed on Tom.

Chapter 14

The Chase

What had happened to Scout? Unwillingly he had been pulled along by the rope that kept tightening about his neck, threatening to choke him.

The troop of soldiers had a long way to go yet. They didn't head straight back to the village, for the officer wanted to stage another raid elsewhere. They marched across fields for over an hour. Scout kept looking for a chance to escape, but without success. The rag tied around his jaws as a muzzle made it impossible for him to use his teeth.

Finally the soldiers came to a wide canal. Across it was an earthen dam blocked by a gate. The officer opened the gate and everyone filed through. Scout and his keeper were the last in line. As the soldier turned to close the gate, Scout tried again. With a desperate lunge, he hurled himself against the man. In trying to keep his balance, the man let go of the rope. With a quick leap, the big German shepherd was back over the gate flying home-ward.

But escape wasn't going to be that easy. The other soldiers had turned when the soldier in charge of Scout had uttered a yell. "After him!" the officer shouted angrily. They kicked open the gate and came running after the dog, but he could easily outdistance them all.

When the officer noticed that the dog was getting away, he became furious and, taking out his pistol, opened fire on Scout. Now things looked very bad for him, for the other soldiers also raised their rifles and began firing. If he hadn't been so well trained by Haaksma, he would certainly have been hit, but Scout used every trick and dodge that he had been taught. Instead of running in a beeline, he zigzagged, ducked behind ridges, crawled along gullies, dropped down on his belly as if he had been hit and then jumped up again and ran on. Shouting and shooting, the soldiers came after him. A bullet burned across his back, but it did no injury other than removing a tuft of fur.

His pursuers managed to cut off his way back to the farm. They spread out in a huge semicircle and slowly but surely drove the dog toward the river. There was no way he could break through the semicircle without being shot.

He made a last desperate effort to escape through the reeds along the river's edge, but it was too late. The soldiers had already reached the reeds and cut off that avenue of escape, too. Slowly the circle was closing in on him.

"Take him alive!" shouted the officer. "Don't shoot unless he gets away."

But before they could close in on him, Scout took a powerful leap and dove into the cold water of the river.

Paddling furiously, he was quickly swept downstream. The soldiers appeared on the riverbank and watched the dog escaping down river with a mixture of admiration and frustration.

Scout had almost reached the middle of the river. The current was very strong, but the dog paddled bravely for the other bank. Cursing, the officer snatched a rifle from one of his men, dropped to one knee, and took careful aim. He fired. The German was a skilled sharpshooter. The bullet hit the water only a few centimetres from Scout's head. The dog ducked and swam on.

Again the man fired. Scout felt a burning pain in his back and every-thing turned red before his eyes. His powerful legs stopped paddling and hung limp in the water. The current swept him away. The officer stood up and spat into the water.

"That's how you shoot," he said to his men. He looked out over the eddying stream once more, as if in regret. A few of the soldiers looked at the ground, not meeting the eyes of their commander. They felt not at all proud at hunting down and killing the brave, beautiful dog, but then the officer barked an order, and they threw back their shoulders and clicked their heels together. Soon they were marching on again to their next destination.

The gray waters of the river had carried Scout away.

*   *   *

The skipper of the boat *Reliable* was a tough old man. He stood in the prow of his old boat smoking a pipe full of smelly, imitation tobacco. Jesse, his only crewman, was at the rudder.

Old man Sikkema was in a good mood. The trip had gone well. He had a good wind in his sails and was making good time. He ought to be able to drop off his load before dark, and if all went well, he would be home in time to spend New Year's Eve with his family.

He was a calm, impassive man, but he looked up startled when the boat came around a bend in the river and he suddenly saw a small troop of German soldiers marching away from the river bank. His face darkened. "I wonder what those filthy Krauts were doing over there," he muttered to himself. He took the pipe from his mouth and spat in the water. "Maybe they shot someone along the riverbank and dropped him into the river. Those snakes are capable of anything."

Sikkema could see nothing on shore, but the boat was still far away. He scanned the water. His face froze. Not far from the boat a red stain floated on the water. The old skipper's heart plummeted. Perhaps someone had been fleeing from the Germans and had been shot swimming the river. "Bloody murderers!" he muttered angrily.

Without thinking, he bent down and picked up a boathook that lay at his feet. Meanwhile, he kept a sharp eye on the river for the victim. A little farther on was another red spot, and a piece of rope drifting on the water. Was someone tied to it, floating just under the surface of the water?

"Hard to port!" the old man shouted to the man who was steering.

Jesse looked up in surprise. He knew this river like his own home and was sure he was on course, but he was used to following the old man's orders and hesitated only a moment before turning the rudder. The boat swerved toward the rope. Sikkema reached forward as far as he could with the boathook. The rope wouldn't stay on the hook, but as he reached farther into the water with the long pole, it hooked on something below the surface. Carefully he pulled it up. Was it a body?

His eyebrows raised in surprise as the head of a German shepherd broke the surface. The dog seemed to be dead. His mouth was tied shut.

So this was what the Germans had been after. Strange! The old man was going to release the hook and leave the dog in the river, but he was seized by curiosity and compassion. Maybe the dog was still alive. He had heard the shots that must have hit the dog. That was only a couple of minutes ago.

Carefully he pulled his find toward the boat. When the dog was alongside, he reached down and caught him by the collar, where the pole was hooked. He tried to lift the dog aboard, but the dog was too heavy, so he told Jesse to tie down the rudder and give him a hand.

Jesse had been watching the skipper, mystified; he had no idea what the old man was doing. Now he came hurrying toward the prow to see what was going on. Together the two men hoisted the limp body aboard.

The dog lay motionless on the deck. A slight trickle of blood seeped from a wound over his left foreleg. The dog had apparently been hit from the back and the bullet had passed through his body, making another hole by his front shoulder.

"Sadists!" Sikkema spat out. He carefully untied the muzzle from the dog's mouth and then, with the help of Jesse, carried him forward to the cabin. The cabin was heated by a small stove. They put the bedraggled dog down on some old sacks beside the stove, and Sikkema bound the wounds as best he knew how.

"He's still alive," he said to Jesse. "See, he's already moving his head a little. Better get back topside or else we'll be stuck on a sandbar pretty soon."

Jesse dashed back to the rudder. The old skipper lit his smelly pipe again and sat down beside his patient. He rubbed the dog dry with an old towel and stoked up the stove a little. Several spasms passed through the dog's body, and after a little while he raised his head and looked at the old man. Then his head sank down again.

"He'll make it," Sikkema told himself, pleased. He threw an old blanket over the dog and went back up on deck.

Meanwhile, old *Reliable* had been making good headway. They reached their destination before nightfall. By this time, Scout had revived considerably. When the old skipper came down into the cabin to check on him, he wagged his tail. With a little effort, he even managed to struggle to his feet, but he had obviously been badly weakened by his loss of blood. Nevertheless, the bullet had apparently hit no vital organs. When they arrived at the dock, Sikkema and Jesse carried the dog topside and put him in a wheelbarrow.

The skipper's house wasn't far from the harbour, so he took the dog home with him. His wife looked a bit startled to see her husband come home with a big dog riding in a wheelbarrow. But when she heard the skipper's story, she was filled with compassion for the wounded animal and treated him like an ailing child. She immediately fetched him something to eat and then fixed a place for him to lie down.

The next day Scout was feeling much better. His left shoulder was still very stiff, but he was able to limp about the house. Both the skipper and his wife were already becoming attached to the beautiful dog.

"He can stay home with me," said Mrs. Sikkema. "Then I'll have a little company when you're gone with the boat."

But the skipper wouldn't hear of it. "I fished him out of the river," he said, "and when he's all better he'll come with me."

They argued back and forth, but it was all done good-naturedly. The two were very close. Scout showed his appreciation for the care the man and wife were giving him, but he was very restless.

That evening Sikkema and his wife went for a walk along the harbour. They left the back door standing open just a crack. When they returned, to their surprise, the dog was gone. The old man went outside and whistled for him, but his foundling was nowhere to be seen. He went back into the house, and with a grin he told his wife, "We can stop arguing about that dog. I think he went back home. It's too bad, he was such a nice-looking animal."

"Still, I'm glad that you pulled him out of the river, and that we took care of him," answered his wife. "I only hope he gets home safely and that the Germans don't catch him again."

Then she went to bed.

Chapter 15

Tom's Dream

At the Sanders' home, the children spent a sad New Year's Day together. Usually this was an especially happy day, but this time they were all grieved about losing Scout. That morning the family went to church, but in the afternoon Tom had to get out of the house for a while. He went out to see if he could find any trace of his dog. The German officer who had led the raid on the Verhoef farm lived just on the outskirts of the village in a huge mansion that had been commandeered by the German army. The buildings behind the mansion had been converted into barracks for the soldiers.

Keeping a careful lookout, Tom approached the large house. The Germans must not notice that he was spying on them, otherwise he was in for trouble.

At the heavy iron gate to the grounds of the mansion stood a single guard. Tom got a sudden fright when he saw the guard. Was it the same man who had tried to seize him and Miriam in the old shack? Tom didn't dare go any closer. If it was the same man, he might also recognize Tom. Tom's heart sank to a new low point. Scout's future looked grim indeed. What would happen if this soldier discovered that Scout was the same dog who had attacked him that night?

When he thought it over further, Tom grew even more frightened. Once they placed Scout on the scene of Miriam's escape, it wouldn't take them long to trace the dog to him. All they had to do was release the dog and see where he went.

Tom didn't dare stay where he was any longer, but neither did he want to give up his search for Scout. He made a big circle through the surrounding fields until he came to the rear of the mansion, where he could view the barracks and the back yard. But no matter how he looked, he saw nothing of his dog.

Discouraged, he finally turned back home. He went up to his room and wept as he hadn't wept in a long time. He didn't even hear Coby calling him down for supper. When he didn't show up at the table, Mother came upstairs to see what was keeping him.

Tom quickly wiped away his tears, but Mother could tell he had been crying. She put her hand on his shoulder.

"What's the matter, Tom? Are you crying about Scout?"

Tom nodded silently. He had to fight to keep from bursting into tears all over again.

"I know it's very sad to lose a friend like Scout," she said. "I loved him very much, too. But at the same time, I'm glad none of you were taken away by the Germans. It would have been much worse if the Germans had found Miriam, for instance. A human life means much more than that of an animal, no matter how much you may like him."

Tom nodded again. He knew Mother was right, but it didn't make the loss of Scout any easier. Mother went on, "Just think, Tom, how many people have lost everything. How many boys and men have died in concentration camps or been executed by the Germans. How many people haven't been made homeless by the Germans, and in the western provinces many people are starving this winter. We are being sorely tried as a people. We in this part of the country really haven't been much affected by the occupation. It isn't right to become so disheartened just because you lost your dog, Tom. Scout saved Miriam's life and perhaps also the lives of others. That's wonderful, that's something to be thankful for, isn't it?"

Mother's words helped him put his grief in perspective. When he went downstairs with Mother a few minutes later, he felt much calmer.

*   *   *

That night Tom dreamt. He saw Scout being dragged away by a troop of German soldiers. The dog looked back at him with pleading eyes, as if to say, "I've helped you so often, aren't you going to help me?" But when Tom tried to go to his aid, an invisible hand held him back. He fought and struggled to break loose, but it did no good.

Suddenly one of the soldiers went up to Scout. Tom recognized him. It was the soldier who had almost captured them in the shack, the one guarding the mansion yesterday. The soldier looked at Scout with fury in his eyes and he said, "Now I'll settle accounts with you."

He was holding a big club in his hand, and he lifted it over his head to strike the dog down. Scout dodged the blow, and suddenly he was free. The rope dropped from his neck and the rag muzzling him also disappeared. Barking triumphantly, Scout jumped up against the soldier and knocked him to the ground.

Now the setting changed. Scout still held the soldier pinned. But they were back in the dark shack where Scout had originally fought with the soldier. Tom took Miriam by the hand and they ran into the woods.

Lying across the path, he found the German's bicycle. He picked it up, and fled with it. He could still hear the dog barking and snarling in the shack.

The dream was so realistic, in his sleep Tom cried, "Here, Scout! Come, boy!" The dog answered, barking loudly. Again Tom called him. Scout was coming; he was somewhere nearby, for the barking was very close.

Then Tom woke up. He looked around, confused. Although it was almost morning, it was still dark in the bedroom. For a moment, he thought he was actually in the woods.

Scout was barking again. Tom groped around in the darkness. Where was Miriam? Then he touched the blankets and realized he had been dreaming. He was home in bed, but the barking still went on. Tossing back the covers, Tom leaped out of bed. He dashed to the window and yanked it open. A cold blast of air struck him, but he hardly noticed it.

"Scout! Scout! Is that you?" he cried into the night.

A triumphant bark sounded from below, just like the one he had heard in his dream, but he knew it was real this time. Scout was outside under his window!

He dashed down the stairs, down the hall, and threw open the front door. There came Scout.

Tom closed the door behind him and turned on the hall light. It really was Scout, but he was limping badly. Over his left shoulder was a dirty bandage that was almost coming off. The dog, however, was wildly happy to see Tom. He wagged his tail furiously, yelping and licking at Tom's face as Tom hugged him, weeping with joy.

"Dad! Mom!" he shouted. "It's Scout! He's back!"

The next minute, Father and Mother as well as Ina and Miriam came thumping down the stairs in their pyjamas. They were all overjoyed to see their lost friend back home.

First Father was afraid it might be a German trick to discover the owner of the dog, but he quickly dismissed the idea. They wouldn't have released him at night, and he could see no one following the dog.

When Mother removed the bandage, she could see that he had been shot, but the wound was already starting to heal. She put a new bandage on the leg and quickly found something for the dog to eat, but Scout didn't seem to be unusually hungry.

The whole family wondered what had happened. They assumed that he must have escaped from the Germans and that he had been shot while fleeing, but someone must have bandaged his wound and given him something to eat.

"We won't get anywhere puzzling over it," Mr. Sanders said finally. "We'll probably never find out what really happened, but the Lord brought Scout back to us, and for that we must be very thankful."

They all nodded. Tom especially said a fervent prayer of thanks to God that morning for having spared and safely returned his dog.

Scout's wound was treated very carefully the next day. They all went out of their way to spoil him. His shoulder wound healed quickly, and soon he was running and jumping as well as he ever did.

Tom didn't dare take Scout outdoors for a long time afterwards. He was afraid he might be seen by the Germans, and that might prove very dangerous. For the first few days, he lived in constant fear that German soldiers might appear at the door any time for Scout. But when nothing happened for several days, he began to relax.

After a couple of weeks he again took Scout out into the back yard. Scout was elated to be outside once more. Thereafter, the children went out to romp with him for a while every day. However, when they went into town, Scout stayed home. They didn't want to lose their dog again — not for all the money in the world.

Chapter 16

The Canadians Are Coming!

The winter passed very slowly — a sad, sombre winter. Starvation threatened many, especially in the large cities in the western provinces. The food shortage didn't hit Tom's village nearly as hard; everyone could at least get enough food to still his hunger. Not that they escaped suffering completely. The Germans were persecuting people for a host of reasons, and not a week went by without arrests.

The children of the Sanders household rarely left the yard. Especially not Miriam, for Mr. and Mrs. Sanders were afraid she would be spotted as being Jewish. Despite all this, however, the family was in a hopeful frame of mind. There were signs that the Allied offensive would soon be renewed. The whole country was looking forward to the final defeat of Hitler's army, and in the Sanders' home daily prayers went up for peace and freedom.

One day Carl Van Doorn came bursting through the gate all excited. He dashed into the yard, shouting, "Have you heard?"

"Heard what?" asked Tom.

First Carl looked around. "The Americans took one of the bridges across the Rhine. It's in Germany. Now the Germans won't be able to stop them."

Tom hurried into the house to pass the news on to his father. Mr. Sanders smiled. "I know, Tom," he said. "But you've got to be careful you don't blast it around too much. I don't think it has been reported by the German-controlled radio stations yet. If the Germans heard you talking about it, they would know we have been listening to radio broadcasts from England, and people have been arrested for much less."

The days that followed were filled with suspense. Every day new reports circulated about Allied advances. Even the Germans were forced to admit that the English and American armies were making gains. The village was astir with excitement as it became known that the Canadians were preparing to liberate the eastern and northern provinces.

Tom and his two friends were now able to visit each other more frequently. They made all kinds of fantastic plans about how they could help their liberators when they arrived. For the present, however, they had to keep their eyes open and tread very carefully, for the closer the day of liberation approached, the more hysterical the German reign of terror became. The occupation forces were becoming extremely nervous. Fortifications were built on all the roads leading into town and trenches were being dug everywhere. The men of the village were forced to help construct the German defenses.

Many managed to avoid the forced labour, but many others were rounded up and set to work on the trenches.

Here and there artillery was set up around the village. The Germans seemed determined to put up strong resistance here. Many villagers shook their heads anxiously. They were afraid that the worst part of the war and occupation was yet to come. When the Allies came to liberate them, perhaps the whole town would go up in flames and everyone would be killed.

Over against these prophets of doom, were those who were full of optimism and hope. They were sure that, despite all their fortifications, the Germans would pull up stakes and run when the Canadian army got close.

Tom was very curious about the fortifications being put up by the Germans. In his fantasies, he saw himself informing the Canadians where the German defenses were located and describing the best route for the advancing army to follow. But when he began poking around the areas where the trenches and barricades were being constructed, his father gave him strict orders to stay away. Tom was very disappointed, although he knew his father was right. It was too dangerous for him to draw attention to himself; he must not expose himself to danger needlessly. Besides, there was little or no chance for him to pass on whatever information he might gather.

Spring had finally come. New grass was sprouting up everywhere; here and there flowers were beginning to blossom, and hope once again blossomed in the hearts of a depressed people.

The Canadians had launched their attack on the German positions in the eastern and northern provinces. Every day the English radio broadcasts brought news of new Allied successes. Bursting with excitement, Tom followed the course of the Allied advance over the radio. Then he rushed to meet his two friends and discuss the latest news. He even neglected Scout, who jumped up against Tom as he went out, trying to get him to play with him, but for the first time in his life, Scout got the feeling that Tom had no time for him. Tom was interested only in how the war was going. He was already dreaming about the triumphant arrival of the liberating armies. He had little or no idea of the tense and dangerous times that still lay ahead for him and his family.

A few days later a muffled thumping could be heard in the distance. It sounded like artillery fire. It seemed the Allies weren't very far away.

Wild rumours circulated in the village. Paratroopers were supposed to have been dropped in the north to seize the rail road lines. The milkman claimed that the Canadians had already penetrated to within twenty kilometres of the town. Others whispered that an Allied tank had been spotted not far away, but had turned around when the soldiers had noticed how heavily fortified the town was.

No one knew what was true and what wasn't, but the muffled shocks continued, and fighters were seen wheeling about in the sky. It was obvious that heavy fighting was going on somewhere in the vicinity. The village lived in anxious suspense. Many people hardly dared stir from their homes. The Germans had forbidden all gatherings. During the past night, several people had been snatched out of bed by the Germans and dragged off, nobody knew where.

The German officer in command of the local forces seemed to have made the decision to defend his position to the very end. Barricades were erected everywhere and machine gun nests planted along all the main roads.

Tom found it impossible to just sit at home and wait. He chatted with Ina and Miriam a while, and then he tried reading a book, but his mind kept racing elsewhere. Finally he climbed up into the attic and sat at the attic window staring across the countryside looking for a sign of the advancing Allies. It was a beautiful, sunny day, genuine spring weather. In the back yard, the trees were already beginning to open their buds to the sun.

86

"Too bad I don't have a better vantage point," thought Tom. "I wish I were up in the windmill at Carl's place. Then he and I could climb all the way to the top and look around with the binoculars."

He went back downstairs, where Father was pacing back and forth with a worried look on his face. When he saw Tom, he began to say something, but then he seemed to change his mind and went on pacing. Tom could tell that something was bothering Father.

"Can I do something for you, Dad?" he asked.

"Yes," said Father, "but I don't know whether I should ask you to do it. Van Doorn has promised me some flour, and I'd like to pick it up today. The road to the mill might be blocked at any time, and we're almost out of bread. If there's any fighting around here, no one will be allowed out on the streets, and then who knows how long it will be before we can get out again. But I can't go myself right now. Could you go and pick it up on your bike? You could take the trail across the fields, but promise me you'll watch out and be very careful!"

Tom, of course, was delighted at the chance to get out. Now he could go to the mill! He immediately promised to be careful and to keep his eyes wide open. Then he ran to the hall to get his jacket, for the weather was still a bit chilly for cycling.

Scout came dashing after him. When he saw Tom getting ready to go out, he eagerly jumped up against him.

"No, Scout," said Tom. "You can't come along. It's too dangerous for you, old boy."

The dog understood. His ears flattened against his head and his brown eyes looked so sad and pleading, that Tom's heart melted with compassion. He stopped and thought it over. Scout hadn't been outdoors for several days. Would it really be dangerous to take the dog along? Scout would be a help keeping an eye out for danger, for he sensed danger before Tom did. Tom made up his mind.

"Okay, Scout, you can come too."

The German shepherd danced around Tom, wild with joy, and went flying out ahead of him when he opened the door. The dog headed straight for the shed where Tom kept his bike and impatiently waited for him to take it out. They went out through the back gate and turned down the narrow dirt road in the direction of the windmill. Tom pedalled along slowly, keeping a constant watch.

Scout had no trouble keeping up; he even ran out ahead of Tom every now and then. He was obviously elated at this unexpected outing.

The trail led around the outskirts of the village. About halfway to the mill, it curved. The stretch just before the bend was lined with dense bushes. As Tom approached the bend, he suddenly heard singing. It was a German marching song! Tom was seized with fear. A troop of German soldiers was coming up the road.

What should he do? His first impulse was to turn and speed back the way he had come, but the soldiers would round the bend any moment and would see him riding away. Perhaps they might recognize Scout and open fire on them.

Tom jumped off his bike. Frantically he looked around. Was there no place to hide? He had no time to look; the singing seemed to be coming right from the bend. Behind the bushes ran a small canal. It was quite deep, but he had no choice.

"Come, Scout," he whispered. "Quick! And no barking!"

He pushed his bicycle through the bushes and lowered it into the water. It almost disappeared before it struck bottom. Then he lowered himself on top of it, supporting himself on the handlebars and the seat. He hung only a few centimetres above the water and pressed himself against the grass growing on the bank.

Scout also flattened himself against the low bank. The bushes between the canal and the little road were already covered with tiny new leaves, so there was a good chance they wouldn't be seen. But Tom was afraid that at any moment his bike might slide out from under him and send him splashing into the cold water. Then not only would he get a dunking, but the soldiers would capture him for sure.

The singing was very close now and he could hear the tramp of the soldiers' boots. Heart pounding with suspense, Tom waited to see what would happen.

The tramp, tramp, tramp was right above him now, and the singing seemed to be right in his ear. He tried to duck down even farther.

No one seemed to notice him. The soldiers took perhaps half a minute to pass by, but it felt more like a half hour to Tom. He lay still for another minute or so. Then he carefully lifted his head to peek through the bushes after the departing soldiers.

At that moment, a loud laugh exploded right over his head. It frightened him so badly, he almost lost his balance. Quickly he flattened himself again. The bicycle rocked, and slowly the front wheel started sliding away in the muddy bottom of the canal. He felt giddy. Never before had he had such a terrible scare. He expected to be seized any moment, but nothing happened. After cringing for several endless seconds, he realized that he hadn't been discovered after all. Two men were walking along the road on the other side of the bushes. One of them had cackled at something the other man had said.

They were still talking. They were talking in German, but one of them spoke with an accent. He sounded like a Dutchman.

"If they come down this road, they're in for a nasty surprise," Tom heard the man say. "Now all that's left to do is to lead them into the trap."

"And that, my dear Sir, we will leave in your capable hands," answered the German.

"Yes, Captain," responded the other, with what sounded like forced enthusiasm.

As the two men walked on, Tom could no longer hear what they were saying. They moved out of earshot not a moment too soon, for Tom's bicycle was sinking away farther and farther. In another moment he would be swimming.

Moving very carefully, Tom managed to squirm ashore without getting very wet. He peered between the bushes. The troop of soldiers was far down the trail. Walking some distance behind them was the same German officer who had captured Scout.

When Tom saw him, he took a quick glance at his dog, who was lying beside him on the bank of the canal. The hair on Scout's neck stood on end, and his upper lip was curled back from his teeth. Never before had Tom seen such fury in Scout's eyes. The dog had recognized his old enemy.

Then Tom studied the other man walking beside the officer. He was dressed in civilian clothes. He had to be the Dutchman. Who could he be?

Of course! It was the man from whom he had borrowed the board the night he had helped Miriam escape from the Germans, the man who had chased them! Everyone knew he was pro-German. Many of the others who had been helping the Germans had already fled to Germany, but not "Van der Nazi," as everyone called him behind his back. He was going to stick it out to the end. His real name was Van der Nat, but he had received his nickname when his Nazi sympathies became known.

Tom did not spend long thinking about what he had heard. As soon as the soldiers were out of sight, he hoisted his bicycle out of the canal and continued on his way to Van Doorn's mill. He felt a little queasy as he rode on. The suspense had almost been too much for him. He felt so weak, he was afraid that if any more Germans showed up, he wouldn't have the strength to even attempt an escape.

Fortunately, the rest of the trip went well, and slowly Tom got over his reaction. He took his time, and Scout cavorted alongside him. By the time they reached the windmill, he was feeling much better.

Mr. Van Doorn, nevertheless, noticed that something unusual had happened to him. "Hi, Tom," he said. "What's the matter? How come you're looking so pale?"

"Oh, I got a bit of a scare on my way over here."

He told Van Doorn what had happened. Carl's father looked very grave. "So, that was a close call! You can thank God it turned out all right. No wonder you're upset. Better sit down and rest a while, or better yet, go talk to Carl. He's not doing much of anything. I have to get your flour ready anyhow."

Tom started toward the house to find Carl, but then Mr. Van Doorn called him back.

"I just wondered, did you hear what Van der Nat and that German officer were talking about?" he asked Tom.

"Not much," said Tom. He told Van Doorn what he had overheard.

"Hmm," pondered Van Doorn. "That doesn't sound good. I'd give a pretty penny to know what that means. That Van der Nat is capable of anything."

Tom had given little thought to the words of the two men who had given him such a terrible fright. But now he began to suspect that perhaps he had overheard something very important, although he had no idea what the words meant.

Tom found Carl in the sawmill. He was standing by a large circular saw, his clothes covered with sawdust. He was very happy to see Tom and to be told that his father had given him some time off. The two boys went outside together and spent a little while roughhousing with Scout. Tom told Carl what had happened to him on the way to the mill.

"And to think I was so happy when Father asked me to go!" he said. "I had climbed up into the attic of our house to see if I could catch sight of the Canadians, but there are too many trees around our house. So I thought, 'How I'd love to be able to climb to the top of the windmill.' What do you say? Should we climb up and take a look? We should be able to see a long way from up there."

Carl was quick to agree. "I'll go and get my father's binoculars," he said.

Tom flushed a little. He hadn't dared to mention the binoculars; last time he had unthinkingly run off with them. Fortunately, Van Doorn had asked no questions when he brought them back the following day.

Carl ran into the house, and a few moments later he reappeared with the binoculars. Together they went to the mill and made the long climb to the top. Climbing all those ladders was always a heady sensation for Tom. By the time he reached the top, his knees felt rubbery, but he was thrilled each time anew by the magnificent view from the two small windows in the windmill's crown.

When they reached the top this time, however, a disappointment awaited them. From the ground they had not noticed the fine mist that was settling over the fields, but now the mist was very obvious. The surrounding countryside was being hidden by a gray shroud. The woods to the right were barely visible in the haze. They stared through the binoculars for a while in the hope that they might spy something anyway. A few times they thought they heard gunfire.

Their imaginations helped them see all kinds of shapes in the gathering fog. Sometimes they saw figures of soldiers advancing across the fields, and once they thought they heard the clatter of tank treads, but they soon discovered that they were fooling themselves. Disappointed, they turned away from the window.

Carl went to the other window, which looked out over the village. "Hey, this is much better," he cried. "The fog hasn't reached the village yet."

Tom hurried over to take a look, too. The windmill stood by itself some distance from town, but it gave them a perfect vantage point from which to view the whole village.

"Look!" exclaimed Carl. "There goes Linus, our hired man."

He handed the binoculars to Tom, but Tom had already seen him without the binoculars, for Linus wasn't very far down the road. With the binoculars, however, he could view the man and the wagon up close.

"Nice!" said Tom. "I can almost read the words on the flour sacks. Linus is smoking. I can see the smoke rising from his pipe."

"Better hold your nose," said Carl, laughing. "Linus smokes the smelliest home-made tobacco I've ever smelled. He mixes all kinds of leaves and junk with it so he has enough tobacco to keep his pipe going all day."

Tom kept the binoculars fixed on the wagon. The horse was moving at an easy trot. Soon Linus would be on the outskirts of the village.

Suddenly Tom cried out in surprise, "Look! Look what's happening! Linus has just been stopped by German soldiers hiding along the road."

"Let me see!" Carl demanded excitedly, reaching for the binoculars. Yes, Tom was right. One soldier was holding the horse and the other was talking to Linus. Now Linus was pointing to town. He must be telling them where he had to deliver his load, but the German was shaking his head, and when Linus gave him an argument, he made a threatening motion with his rifle. Then the wagon turned around on the road and headed back toward the mill.

Tom and Carl watched until they were sure that Linus was actually coming back; then they quickly climbed down the ladder to tell Carl's father what had happened.

Mr. Van Doorn looked surprised and puzzled when the two excited boys blurted out the story. "What on earth are they up to now?" he grumbled. "Can't we even go into town anymore? What's the matter with those Krauts? Are they trying to make things miserable for us while they've still got the chance?"

He went outside, followed by the two boys. A few minutes later Linus came driving back into the yard. "It's no good," he cried. "We're cut off from town. I was stopped by a couple of German soldiers, and they refused to let me pass. I thought the one soldier was going to shoot me when I insisted that I had to get through. He said that all the roads into town are closed. He told me that this area is now part of the front."

Carl's father uttered a low whistle. "That doesn't look good," he said. "The Krauts must know more about where the Canadians are than we do. They must be expecting the Canadians to attack from this side at any time. I'm afraid we might be caught smack-dab in the middle. I hope no one gets the idea of putting a few soldiers up in the windmill. It would make a great lookout post for the Germans."

Tom stood and listened, his face puckered with worry. "How do I get home?" he asked. "I promised my dad I'd be home soon. He wanted to have the flour before the fighting started here."

"Sorry, Tom," said Van Doorn. "But there's nothing much we can do about it. If you try to get home now you're taking an awful risk. I'm sure the Germans are extremely on edge now, so they won't flinch from shooting a boy. You'd better make yourself at home here. For the time being we're quite safe, and if there's any fighting around here, we'll just have to entrust ourselves to God's hands. We are in His safekeeping."

The two boys didn't feel much like playing after that. The suspense about what was coming was far too great.

Soon it was time for lunch. Carl's mother called everyone into the kitchen. Van Doorn's three hired hands, who usually went home for lunch, also joined them at the table, because they, too, were cut off from the village. A place had also been set for Tom. When Mrs. Van Doorn had heard about the blockade, she had quickly baked a batch of rolls. She seemed to take the whole matter calmly. "We've got plenty of flour," she said cheerfully, "so we're not going to starve."

The guests fell to hungrily. Despite his concern that his parents would be worried, Tom discovered that he too had a good appetite. Mrs. Van Doorn saw to it that Scout also got something to eat.

After lunch Tom and Carl climbed up to the top of the windmill again. The fog had lifted, so now they could see much farther. It was very busy in town. Apparently German reinforcements had arrived, for the boys could see many more soldiers marching through the streets than they had ever seen in the village before. Two columns marched by only a few blocks from the mill. They were heading for the barricades that had been erected on the highway, spreading out across the surrounding fields, where long trenches had been dug. Mr. Van Doorn also came climbing up the ladder to have a look.

"Better be careful up here, boys," he said with a frown. "If the Germans noticed you up here with those binoculars, we'd be in for it."

"Oh, Dad, please let us stay," begged Carl. "We'll be careful, I promise."

"Well, all right," said Mr. Van Doorn. "You may stay, for now anyway, but as soon as you see any Germans heading this way, you come scooting downstairs and into the house. Agreed?"

Tom and Carl promised.

Mr. Van Doorn went back down the ladder while the two boys watched the preparations in town. Suddenly they heard shooting in the distance. It came from the direction where the Canadians were expected to attack.

Quickly they rushed to the other window. In the distance lay the neighbouring village, clearly visible now the mist had disappeared.

"Look!" Carl cried excitedly. "Something is burning. It must be a farmhouse."

Smoke and flames were belching from a farm on the edge of the next town. Fighting seemed to be going on right in the village.

Now Tom had the binoculars. Suddenly he uttered a loud cheer. He shoved the binoculars back at Carl. "Look over there!" he cried exuberantly. "See it? They're putting up the flag. It's the red, white, and blue! And other people are hanging out flags too. They've already been liberated over there!"

The boys danced about with excitement in the small attic. Then Carl quickly scrambled down the ladder to tell his father.

A few minutes later everyone came clambering up the ladder — Carl's father, his mother, the three hired hands, and the maid. There was hardly room to turn around in the small space.

They took turns staring at the neighbouring village through the binoculars. Sure enough, the Dutch flag was sprouting all over the village. Every now and then a shot rang out, but the fighting seemed to be virtually over.

Carl's father had tears in his eyes. "We're going to be liberated, wife!" he cried jubilantly. "We've been praying for it these five years, and now it has finally come. One or two days at the most and then we'll be hanging our flag from the windmill."

Chapter 17

The German Plot

After they had each taken another look, Carl's parents, the hired men and the maid went back down. The boys were permitted to stay, but only after promising once more to be careful and to keep an eye out for Germans approaching the windmill.

Tom and Carl were enthralled by their magnificent view. They resolved to stay up in the windmill all afternoon so they wouldn't miss anything. For the next hour or so they saw nothing unusual. The flames gradually died down at the farm as it was reduced to cinders. Finally only a smoking pile of rubble was left.

Suddenly, however, Carl poked Tom. "Look," he said, "there are two Canadian tanks coming from the town. They're coming this way. I think they're going ahead to see if the road is safe."

The boys followed the progress of the advancing tank with intense excitement. "They'll never make it," whispered Tom. "The Germans have put up strong barricades across the road, and the whole area around there is full of trenches, bunkers, and machine-gun nests."

Tom's words were soon borne out. When the tanks were a few hundred metres from the barricades, the Germans opened up on the two tanks with a furious barrage. The Canadians fired back, but the German firepower was vastly superior.

Suddenly smoke and flames burst from the lead tank. The Germans had scored a hit. Three soldiers leaped from the machine and sprinted for the one that came rolling along right behind. One of them fell and didn't get back up. The other two were hauled aboard the undamaged tank. It turned around and headed back toward the liberated village.

Tom and Carl had been totally absorbed in the drama before them, gasping in horror when the tank burst into fire and holding their breaths as the soldiers made their escape. They had been so absorbed, that they hadn't noticed a small troop of German soldiers marching straight toward the mill from the other side. They jumped with fright when suddenly right below them they heard a harsh voice barking orders in German.

They looked at one another in consternation. Carl slid over to the trapdoor on his stomach to hear what was being said. They heard Van Doorn's voice carrying upward, "I can't permit it! A lot of people depend on this mill and it's my livelihood. If you use it as a military lookout, it might be destroyed."

Again the boys heard the German voice. This time Tom recognized it. It was the same officer he had heard on the road that morning! He was really fuming, calling Carl's father a saboteur and a spy, and threatening to arrest him if he continued to protest.

The boys were pale with fright. They knew very well why Carl's father was giving the officer a hard time. Not only didn't he want to help the enemy, he also wanted to give Tom and Carl time to escape. If they were discovered in the mill with the binoculars, they would probably be shot as spies.

Again Van Doorn raised an objection. "You can't make this mill into a military object. It's vital to this area's food production. I forbid you to enter my mill!"

The German officer began ranting and cursing at Carl's father. He called him every name he could think of, and then he said to his men, "Arrest this scoundrel and take him away. I'll deal with him later."

Carl, who heard it all, was almost beside himself. He wanted to go storming down the ladder to help his father, but he knew this would only make things worse. Downstairs there was a sudden commotion. The soldiers had seized Van Doorn and were leading him away. Mrs. Van Doorn came running from the house weeping and said an emotional farewell to her husband. Tears were also rolling down Carl's cheeks, and Tom had a huge lump in his throat.

Van Doorn himself remained very calm. He hoped that the soldiers would be temporarily diverted from the mill so that the boys would have a chance to escape. For a moment, Tom and Carl thought it had worked, and they stepped toward the ladder, but then the voice of the German officer again sounded downstairs in the windmill.

"That fool's taken care of," he said to someone with him. "Now let's go up and take a look at the terrain. We should run through the plan once more."

The boys heard the ladder creaking. Two men were climbing up to the crown. The boys looked at each other in panic.

"We've got to hide the binoculars!" whispered Tom. "That's the most dangerous thing."

Frantically they looked around. Suddenly a flicker of hope entered Carl's eyes. "I know what!" he hissed. "Quick! They'll be here any minute!" In one corner stood a large wooden box that looked like a window seat without a backrest. Before this, Tom had paid no attention to it, but now he discovered that the top was loose as Carl lifted one end.

"Quick, inside!" whispered Carl. "It'll just hold both of us."

"Won't we suffocate in there?" asked Tom.

"No. See, there are holes in the sides for handles. They'll let in plenty of air. Get down!" Tom lay down in the bottom of the box, and Carl joined him, lowering the lid after him. It was a tight squeeze, but they could just lie side by side. Less than a minute later, they heard the German officer and his companion climbing through the trapdoor and stepping onto the attic floor.

The boys didn't move a muscle. They hardly dared to breathe. Would they be discovered?

It soon became clear to the boys that the two men didn't suspect a thing. Apparently they had gone straight to one of the little windows to look at the burning tank on the road. The officer seemed to have a pair of binoculars with him to study the situation. He chuckled mirthlessly as he saw the second tank fleeing back to the liberated village.

"Did you think we were going to give up so easily?" the German said in the direction of the Canadians. "You'll not take this town without a fight. We'll make you wish you stayed home before we pull back from this position. We're much stronger here than you may think."

Then, for the first time, the boys heard the other man speak. They almost snorted in surprise. It was the voice of "Van der Nazi," the Dutch traitor. He sounded very anxious. "I can count on you to take me and my family with you when you pull back, can't I, Captain?" he asked.

"Of course!" snapped the officer. "I've given you my word, haven't I? If you serve our cause well, we will not abandon you. We'll take you back to Germany with us, if necessary. We'll see that nothing happens to you, as long as you carry out your end of the deal. You know what happens to traitors!"

"You can count on me, Captain," answered Van der Nat fawningly. "You know my loyalty to the Führer and to the great German Empire."

Then the boys heard the rustling of paper. The officer must have taken out a map, for he began giving Van der Nat instructions. "Look, these are the Canadian lines, and this is the village they just took. They won't break through our lines here; we're strong enough to hold them here for quite a

33rd Anniversary Catalogue

INHERITANCE PUBLICATIONS
(Church Music & Records)
3317 Twp Rd 624
County of Barrhead, Alberta
T0G 1R1 CANADA
All Prices are in U.S. dollars
e-mail: orders@inhpubl.net
Website: inhpubl.net

Bible History for Children

BIBLE STORIES For Our Little Ones
by W.G. VAN DE HULST
Illustrated by J.H. Isings

Bible Stories
For Our Little Ones

W.G. VAN DE HULST

This book is intended to be a book for mothers. A book to be read in quiet hours, to little ones of four to seven or eight years old who sit at Mother's knee. A book to be read slowly, yes, especially slowly; very clearly with warm, loving reverence and awe which creates in little children's heart a pious reverence and a joy filled awe. It desires to be a BIBLE FOR THE LITTLE ONES, reaching out to all areas of a child's understanding. A child does not comprehend everything, yet understands a great deal. This story bible wishes to tell about the holy things in plain, clear, almost simple language, which still must never profane the consecrated happenings. It is not meant to be complete. Completeness would hinder children. This book is not meant to be anything but a modest, reverent endeavour to lead the little ones into the holy sphere of Godly things. The interest of the little ones will be the test to see whether this endeavour is accomplished. May God give our little ones His wonderful blessings in the quiet hours, listening to His voice at Mother's knee.

— The Author

Subject: Bible
ISBN 1-894666-69-0

Age: 7-10
US$29.95

The Word of the King Series

by Cor Van Rijswijk

The Word of the King Series

Abraham's
Sacrifice

Cor Van Rijswijk
Illustrated by Rino Visser

The Word of the King Series

Gideon
Blows the Trumpet

Cor Van Rijswijk
Illustrated by Rino Visser

The Word of the King Series

David
and Goliath

Cor Van Rijswijk
Illustrated by Rino Visser

These hard cover Bible story books are wonderful. Children just learning to read can use them as little readers, either reading them on their own, reading them aloud, or reading them along with the narration on CD. Yet what every child enjoys most is being read to. Here are Bible stories written in a language which is simple and reverent. These are stories which edify both adults and children. The drawings must also be given due attention: they are simply beautiful. Real to life, they are a great contrast to the modern concept of Bible cartoon characters. There is a great need for good reading for children. Here is a good beginning.

Rev. J. Visscher in *Clarion*: "These books are usually about 40 pages long, are well-illustrated by Rino Visser and are faithful, biblical renderings. They make for good birthday presents to four and five year olds."

Abraham's Sacrifice	ISBN 1-894666-21-6	US$9.95
Gideon Blows the Trumpet	ISBN 1-894666-22-4	US$9.95
David and Goliath	ISBN 1-894666-23-2	US$9.95

FREE with an order of three W.K. books:
CD Bible Stories from The Word of the King Series
read by Theresa Janssen
CD 1-894666-24-0
Reg.US$9.95

Frederika Pronk in *The Messenger* about *Abraham's Sacrifice*: "The focus of this Bible story, Abraham offering Isaac, his only son, is told reverently and with deep feeling. Woven throughout is the theme that Abraham knew by implication and believed that the animal sacrifices he offered pointed to the perfect sacrifice of the Son of God. Psalm quotations from the *Book of Praise* illustrate this theme. The tension of Abraham's struggle to obey is made very clear. It was not only his love for Isaac, but especially the knowledge that the Lamb of God would come through his heir, that caused Abraham the agony of soul when the command came to offer His son Isaac. This Bible story is told from the redemptive-historical viewpoint — redemption stands central. We gladly recommend this book for children approximately 6 to 10 years old."

Theresa Janssen Reads Bible Stories from The Word of the King Series

by Cor Van Rijswijk

My Bible Story Book by Dena Korfker

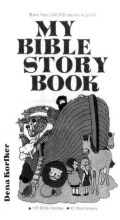

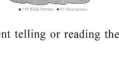

• 270 exciting Bible stories
• Simply written on the level of the child's understanding
• Attention-getting questions with every story
• A book children everywhere will love

"A Bible story book which is excellent in its simplicity, accuracy, appeal, and unity . . . stories are short enough to be read in one sitting and the vocabulary is so simple that even pre-school children will listen and easily understand . . . parents and teachers will find in it a great help in bringing the Bible to their children." — THE BANNER

"The Bible becomes a living, meaningful book, and the characters become alive and understandable . . . ." — THE MENNONITE

"The whole Bible historical record from the creation to the Lord's appearance, to John on Patmos, told in 270 simple stories. Should be a delight to the child, and helpful to the parent telling or reading the Bible story to children." — THE BAPTIST RECORD

• 62 Illustrations
More than 230,000 copies in print!

Subject: Bible   Age: 7-10
ISBN 978-1-928136-23-4   US$24.90

Marian's Big Book of BIBLE STORIES
by Marian M. Schoolland

To retell the stories from the Bible so that the very young will understand is an art that requires much skill and experience. The author of this volume has gained a wide reputation as a successful writer of children's stories, and her books have delighted many thousands of youngsters.

"Miss Schoolland possesses keen imaginative skill. She places herself in the young child's world and then presents the material in a manner which makes it real to the child."
— THE BANNER

"Does more than make the Bible come alive for children. That the author is a trained teacher of little children is evidenced by the perfect simplicity of her modern English."
— THE SUNDAY SCHOOL TIMES

"The purpose of this book is to capture the interest as well as the heart of the child and to lead him to know and love God. She has succeeded gloriously in accomplishing that."
— CHURCH HERALD

"God is always at the center, so that the child gets not only a story, but sees God in the story " — LUTHERAN COMPANION

"Captivating titles . . . words carefully chosen . . . sentences and paragraphs are short . . . repetition has been used with splendid effect . . . print is large and clear."
— THE FREE METHODIST

"Beginning with creation and following through to Revelation, the stories are told with a clarity and simplicity unusual in Bible story books." — THE MOODY MONTHLY

"A very well written and pleasing Bible story book for very small children."
— THE CHRISTIAN HOME AND SCHOOL

"(It is) easier to hold the attention of a four-year-old child with this version of the Bible stories than with any other . . ." — THE CALVIN FORUM

Subject: Bible   Age: 5-10
ISBN 978-1-77298-006-6   US$19.90

"... was sorting through old pictures today and found this one. It was taken eleven years ago ... on my son's birthday party. See all those party boys listening to a beautifully told Bible story by Anne DeVries! We have read these books over and over and they are now falling apart. I would love to buy a big stack to equip my grown up children (we have nine — all busy growing) [with] these two bible story books so they can read them to their children. They are written precisely to Scripture, by a man who clearly understood God's redemption plan and portrays it in a faith-building way. I have bought and read other Bible stories but none so able to build a child's faith. My Mom read these books to me and my siblings in Dutch and how I loved them. So I am pleading with you to republish them." — MvV at Q, BC

Story Bible for Older Children
by Anne De Vries

This story Bible is a classic in which Anne DeVries touches on the episodes recorded in Scripture one by one, bringing them to life for children through dramatic dialogue, imaginative description, and careful attention to narrative structure. The exquisitely detailed and unique illustrations by Cornelis Jetses reinforce the story of God's dealings with His people in a beautiful way.

For Age: 7-12

Old Testament	ISBN 978-0921100-96-6	US$29.95
New Testament	ISBN 978-0921100-97-3	US$29.95
SET OF OLD & NEW TESTAMENT 0921100-96-6/97-3		US$55.95

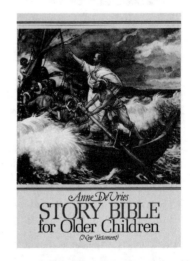

I Am the LORD Your God by **Wolf Meesters**
The Bible Narrated For Young Adults, Vol. 1

Wolf Meesters

The many children's Bibles available today are aimed at *young children*. In contrast to those children's Bibles, this book relates the stories of the Bible at a level intended to appeal to adolescents. It provides a wealth of Scriptural information in a very readable, story-like form. The style makes for light reading, yet the book is both instructive and spiritually rewarding.

Author Wolf Meesters enriches the young reader's insight by showing the Christ-centered line that runs like a golden thread through the Bible. This volume deals with God's redemptive work from creation to the death of Joseph in the land of Egypt.

Subject: Genesis & Job　　　　　　　　**Age: 12-99**
Cat. Nr. IP 3127　　　　　　　　　　**US$29.90**

And You Shall Be My People by **Wolf Meesters**
The Bible Narrated For Young Adults, Vol. 2

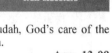

Wolf Meesters

This volume deals with Israel in slavery in Egypt, their journey out of slavery to the Promised Land, through the time of the judges and King Saul, and the beginning of the reign of King David.
Subject: Exodus - 2 Samuel　　　　　　**Age: 12-99**
Cat. Nr. IP 9824　　　　　　　　　　**US$29.90**

Your King is Coming by **Wolf Meesters**
The Bible Narrated for Young Adults, Vol. 3

Wolf Meesters

The end of the reign of King David through the time of the kings and prophets, the events leading to the exile of Israel and Judah, God's care of the exiles, and their return to rebuild Jerusalem.
Subject: 2 Samuel - Malachi　　　　　　**Age: 12-99**
Cat. Nr. IP 10226　　　　　　　　　　**US$29.90**

Behold the Lamb of God by **Wolf Meesters**
The Bible Narrated for Young Adults, Vol. 4

W. Meesters

New Testament: The birth of Christ and the start of His ministry. The most reliable, most trustworthy, and most Christ-centered story Bible available. In his preface to the first edition (1948), the author writes that he has in mind those who are at an age between childhood and maturity — that is, adolescents.
Subject: Beginning of the N.T. Gospels　　**Age: 12-99**
Cat. Nr. IP 0155　　　　　　　　　　**US$29.90**

I Will Be With You Always by **Wolf Meesters**
The Bible Narrated For Young Adults, Vol. 5

Wolf Meesters

The end of Jesus Christ's earthly ministry and the continuation of His work through His apostles to establish the New Testament Church.
Subject: New Testament　　　　　　　**Age: 12-99**
Cat. Nr. IP 7512　　　　　　　　　　**US$29.90**

Quintus by R. Weerstand
A Story About the Persecution of Christians
at the Time of Emperor Nero

The history of the Church in A.D. 64 is written with blood and tears. This book, based on historical facts, relates what happened in Rome in the summer of that year. It is a gripping chronicle. In the story we meet Quintus, the central character. He is a typical Roman boy, who through a number of ordeals experiences the grace of God.

Time: A.D. 64   Age: 12-99
ISBN 1-894666-70-4   US$10.90

AUGUSTINE
THE FARMER'S BOY OF TAGASTE
P. DE ZEEUW, J.Gzn

Augustine,
The Farmer's Boy of Tagaste
by P. De Zeeuw

C. MacDonald in *The Banner of Truth*: Augustine was one of the great teachers of the Christian Church, defending it against many heretics. This interesting publication should stimulate and motivate all readers to extend their knowledge of Augustine and his works.

J. Sawyer in *Trowel & Sword*: . . . It is informative, accurate historically and theologically, and very readable. My daughter loved it (and I enjoyed it myself). An excellent choice for home and church libraries.

Time: A.D. 354-430   Age: 9-99
ISBN 0-921100-05-1   US$7.95

Martin Shows the Way by Cor Van Rijswijk
Series: In Father's Footsteps

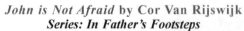

It was cold and dark outside. Yet there were some boys walking in the streets.
They were going from one house to an other. Do you know what they were doing? Listen! They were singing. Suddenly a door was opened. A kind woman gave the boys something to eat. How happy they were.

Time: 1483-1546   Age: 4-9
ISBN 1-894666-80-1   US$9.95

John is Not Afraid

The books in the Series: In Father's Footsteps *are independent stories written by Cor Van Rijswijk about important people in Church History.*
Read them to your four or five-year-old, and let your six or seven-year-old use them as readers.

John is Not Afraid by Cor Van Rijswijk
Series: In Father's Footsteps

John Knox was smart. He could study very well and learn quickly. Father and Mother really liked that. One day, John was called to go to his father. "John," he said, "you are a big boy now. You must either work, or keep going to school."

Time: 1513?-1572   Age: 4-9
ISBN 1-894666-81-X   US$9.95

The Carpenter of Zerbst by P de Zeeuw, J.Gzn
A Story from the Time of the Great Reformation

Johan Tetzel, the indulgence pedlar, was coming to the town of Zerbst. However, Otto Maehler was forbidden to join the procession to meet this distorter of God's truth. Father Maehler called Tetzel a blasphemer and after going to the church to tell the people so, he lost favour with the town magistrates. Despite the fury of the magistrates, Father Maehler offered Martin Luther the cup of honour. But the consequences were harsh. Their lives were spared, but . . . Where had Martin Luther gone?

Join Otto's family as they cling to God's promises through all their grief and tension. Witness with joy the work of God in the lives of His children as well as in the lives of the enemies of the cross.

Another historical novel by P. de Zeeuw. Written in a fascinating way for children to learn church history. It will encourage them to remain steadfast in the faith and to confess with Martin Luther:

Here I stand!
I cannot do otherwise.
May God help me! Amen.

Time: 1517-1522   Age: 9-99
ISBN 978-1-894666-34-8   US$9.95

The Farrier of Buda by P. De Zeeuw
Based on a story about the Reformation in Hungary

Kapotsky Andreas is the court farrier to the King. He helps to have one of the most famous Reformers thrown into prison, but soon after the arrest the Lord lets their paths cross again, with remarkable consequences.

Time: 1523-1586   Age: 10-99
Cat. Nr. 0000005632   US$9.95

For the Heart of Holland by Piet Prins
Struggle for Freedom Series 4

General Valdez had mercilessly surrounded Leiden with his Spanish troops. Rather than attacking the city, he let a different weapon do the work. This weapon was

hunger. Hardly anyone could get into the city or out of it, and the hunger, together with the black death wreaked death and sickness among the citizens.

Elisabeth Govaerts was having trouble keeping her father and brother as well as their lodger Boudewyn fed and in good shape. It was therefore a feast when Martin Meulenberg managed to creep through the Spanish fortifications and bring Elisabeth food. But the time was short since Martin wanted to join the Sea Beggars again. He left the city with reports of starving people. Even so, the Prince of Orange was doing his best to free Leiden. But even after the dykes had been breached by the Sea Beggars the water would not rise, and thus the Sea Beggars could not sail into Leiden to liberate it. Help seemed impossible.

Time: 1573   Age: 10-99
ISBN 978-1-894666-20-6   US$12.95

The Five Books on this page are among the very best ever published. These are the books that FATHERS find HARD TO STOP READING.

William of Orange - The Silent Prince
by W.G. Van de Hulst

Whether you are old or young you will enjoy this biography on the life of William of Orange. Read it and give it as a birthday present to your children or grandchildren. A fascinating true story about one of the greatest princes who ever lived and already by his contemporaries justly compared to King David.

Time: 1533-1584   Age: 7-99
ISBN 0-921100-15-9   US$11.95

Struggle for Freedom Series by Piet Prins

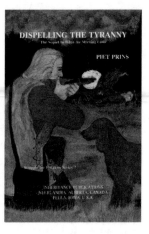

David Engelsma in the *Standard Bearer*: This is reading for Reformed children, young people, and (if I am any indication) their parents. It is the story of 12-year-old Martin Meulenberg and his family during the Roman Catholic persecution of the Reformed Christians in The Netherlands about the year 1600. A peddlar, secretly distributing Reformed books from village to village, drops a copy of Guido de Brès' *True Christian Confession* — a booklet forbidden by the Roman Catholic authorities. An evil neighbor sees the book and informs . . .

Time: 1568-1573   Age: 10-99

Vol. 1 *When The Morning Came*
ISBN 0-921100-12-4 US$11.95

Vol. 2 *Dispelling the Tyranny*
ISBN 0-921100-40-X US$11.95

Vol. 3 *The Beggars' Victory*
ISBN 0-921100-53-1 US$11.95

Vol. 4 *For the Heart of Holland*
978-1-894666-20-6 US$12.95

SET OF 4 STRUGGLE
for FREEDOM Series
REG. 48.80
Special Set Price
US$41.49

Zarco, the Explorer
by K. Norel

Zarco signs on as mate apprentice aboard the fleet of Bartholomew Diaz who discovers the Cape of Good Hope. Under Vasco da Gama, Zarco later sails to India. Norel was one of Hollands best-loved authors of historical fiction.

Time: 1441 - 1502   Age: 12-99
ISBN 0-88815-877-7   US$10.90

The Sea Beggar's Son (Piet Heyn)
by F.N. Monjo
Illustrated by C. Walter Hodges

Piet Heyn was a Dutchman,
A Dutchman from Delft,
Who braved the blue deeps of the sea,
To sail out, seafaring,
For flounder and herring,
While he dreamed that his land might be free.

Time: 1578-1629   Age: 4-9
ISBN 978-1-928136-24-8   US$8.95

Salt in His Blood — The Life of Michael De Ruyter
by William R. Rang

Liz Buist in *Reformed Perspective*: This book is a fictional account of the life of Michael de Ruyter, who as a schoolboy already preferred life at sea to being at school. De Ruyter is known as the greatest Dutch admiral, who, in spite of his successful career as a sailor captain and pirate hunter, remained humble and faithful to his God who had called him to serve his country. The author brings to life many adventures at sea that keep the reader spellbound, eager to know what the next chapter will bring. . . This book is highly recommended as a novel way to acquiring knowledge of a segment of Dutch history, for avid young readers and adults alike.

Time: 1607-1676   Age: 10-99
ISBN 0-921100-59-0   US$11.95

The Lion of Modderspruit by Lawrence Penning
The Louis Wessels Commando #1

A wonderful historical novel in which Penning has interwoven love, pathos, and loyalty. The conflict the Boers endure with England involves not only a fight to maintain their independence (to which the British agreed in 1881) but also a deep religious significance. Louis Wessels, eldest son of a well-established Transvaal Boer family, is betrothed to Truida, a Boer maiden living in the British colony of Natal, and educated in British-governed schools. When England sends over thousands of troops to invade the independent Boer colony of the Orange Free State, causing the Boers of the Transvaal Colony to prepare to invade Natal, the two lovers are confronted by more than a political conflict — two loyal hearts separated by loyalty to conflicting causes. The horrors of the war drag both Louis and Truida through heights of joy and depths of despair. How can these two hearts, beating strongly for each other but also strongly for their separate causes, ever be reconciled? On which side is justice to be found?

Time: 1899   Age:11-99
ISBN 1-894666-91-7   US$10.95

The Hero of Spionkop by Lawrence Penning
The Louis Wessels Commando #2

A company of twenty-five horsemen with an officer in command galloped into the yard. They jumped down, fastened their horses to the young fig trees which bordered the broad driveway, and in silence awaited orders from their commanding officer.

He carefully scrutinized the terrain and set out five soldiers as watchmen. Five others were ordered to make a thorough search of the barn. Ten were posted at the various exits from the house and with the remaining five the officer entered the livingroom . . .

"Do you have a Boer from the Transvaal hiding here?" asked the officer.

Time: 1900   Age:11-99
ISBN 1-894666-92-5   US$10.95

The Scout of Christiaan de Wet by Lawrence Penning
The Louis Wessels Commando # 3

It is the year 1900 and the Boer War continues to ravage the South African Free State and Transvaal. The English are relentless in their attacks and pernicious in seeking to achieve political power. But the Afrikaners refuse to submit and continue the struggle to maintain their freedom.

Louis Wessels, the young hunter, and the Dutchman Jan Tromp, despite skirting danger, falling into traps, confronting traitors, hiding and escaping, slowly achieve their mission as they transverse the Transvaal as scouts for General Christiaan de Wet. Yet when they are finally trapped with no seeming escape, they meet an old acquaintance.

Even though these dedicated Afrikaners are surrounded by the horrors and ravages of war there is time for laughter at Blikoortje's exploits, and time to receive encouragement from loved ones.

Time: 1900   Age: 11-99
ISBN 978-1-894666-93-0   US$11.95

The Victor of Nooitgedacht
by Lawrence Penning
The Louis Wessels Commando # 4

The commando of Louis Wessels continues to roam the South African countryside, joining whichever division needs them most. But defeat and loss, ruin and devastation seem to be the order of the day. Blikoortje and Jan Potgieter are captured, Wonderfontein is pillaged and ruined, and the church is desecrated. The ravages of this ghastly war are pressing in on all sides and the reality of total defeat looms large in all its starkness. The English Minister Brodrick had declared in the British parliament that "never — but never — had a more civilised war been waged!" Yet all the evidence showed the English army to be full of wantonness, lustful pillaging, savagery, destructiveness, and pitiless cruelty towards women, children, and the defenceless.

Lawrence Penning gives a close up account of some of the events and issues surrounding the Boer War. The English declared they wanted the gold South Africa offered, but was there more at stake? This book, along with the others in the series, are great aids in coming to grips with the South African conflict in a fascinating manner.

Time: 1900   Age: 11-99
ISBN 978-1-894666-94-7   US$11.95

The Colonist of Southwest Africa by Lawrence Penning
The Louis Wessels Commando # 5

After three years of fighting, the Boer War was nearing its bitter end. Even though the Boer armies seemed defeated by the superior British armed forces, many Boer commandoes refused to give up and continued to strike at the English military. The enemy's retaliation was horrible. Systematically the Rednecks combed out the country: farms were burned and the women and children were taken to concentration camps. Malnourished, neglected, and ravaged by Typhus fever, thousands died in those camps.

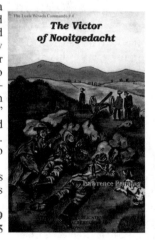

Under the leadership of Louis Wessels, a commando planned a rescue, but with difficulties and traitors abounding, failure and capture were imminent realities. Was escape still possible? Could comfort be found in the words of the field preacher who not only condemned England's insults and scorn heaped on the Boer entreaties for help, but also entreated his fellow Christians to throw dust and ashes on their heads "for we and our fathers — we have sinned grievously! We have erred. We have served alien gods, and now the Lord is visiting us with His scourge." Addressing the Boers, and also the British doctor, the field preacher concluded, "Brothers, let us be silent in this oppression. Let us confess our sins and lift our penitent hearts in prayer to the hills from whence our salvation will come."

This last volume of the Louis Wessels Commando series brings the dark reality of the Boer War into stark focus. May the words of the field preacher never need to be addressed to us.

Time: 1901-1904   Age: 11-99
ISBN 978-1-894666-95-4   US$11.95

Special Price for set of all 5 books
US$49.10

The Man in Bearskin by J. Keuning

A fascinating story about Dutch Settlers in Western Michigan of the Van Raalte colony of 1847

In the middle of the 19th century a band of Dutch immigrants, under the leadership of the Reverend A. C. Van Raalte, came to Michigan to establish their homes in a place now called Holland. Among these early pioneers were Gerrit Kolf, his wife, and four children. Food was scarce those first few months, but the Kolf family were often supplied meat or corn meal by a mysterious, solitary individual who wore a bearskin cloak and who refused conversation with anyone. To read this book is to gain an appreciation of the unconsciously heroic attitude of these people in their new and difficult life. The wildness of the country, the meagreness of their resources, and the lack of medical care make it at first a sheer struggle for survival.

ISBN 978-1-928136-33-0 19th Century   US$9.90

The Man in Bearskin
by J. Keuning

A fascinating story about Dutch Settlers in Western Michigan of the Van Raalte colony of 1847

Life in the Eagle's Nest by Charlotte Maria Tucker (A.L.O.E.)
A Tale of Afghanistan

Afghanistan! To many an uncivilized land of terror and hatred. To others a land of intrigue and adventure. A land where few dare to tread. Go with Walter Gurney, the seventeen-year-old orphan son of a British missionary in India, who, after meeting handsome, boastful Dermot Denis, joined him on a trip into Afghanistan. Negating the danger of such a perilous trip, Walter eased his conscience with the thought of evangelizing. Infected with the exultation of his companion, nothing for the time seemed more enjoyable than this wild foray into a dangerous land. Yet within a few days they were surprised by a brutal group of Pathan Afghans. Despite his companion's ridicule and the danger lurking in his path Walter knew that nothing could separate him from the love of Christ. God's will always comes to pass and as God's child he was safe in the arms of his Saviour. Will Walter be able to hold on to this faith when pressed by a Moslem Holy man? Will Sultána, the daughter of the chief, be able to help him and her people in the Eagle's Nest? Witness with Walter the blessings of God in bringing His Gospel to hungry hearts in ways unimaginable by men.

Subject: Mission / Fiction   Age: 11-99
ISBN 978-1-894666-29-9   US$10.90

The Heroes of Castle Bretten
by Margaret S. Comrie

Eleonore, Lady of Castle Bretten, has been alienated from her friends and allies by false rumours spread by her nephew, General Lucas von Ruprecht, Count of Zamosc. When Guido, a young Protestant, comes to live at the castle, he wins the love and trust of Lady Eleonore and Felix, the General's son. With lots of excitement and action Guido and Felix uncover a plot to gain control of the castle.

Time: 1618-1648   Age: 11-99
ISBN 1-894666-65-8   US$9.90

THE HEROES OF CASTLE BRETTEN

Margaret S. Comrie

INHERITANCE PUBLICATIONS
NEERLANDIA, ALBERTA, CANADA
PELLA, IOWA, U.S.A.

A Fictionalized Biography of Katherine Vastenhout

In an area surrounded by the big woods of Wisconsin, the Mississipi and Missouri Rivers, Walnut Grove and Plum Creek, and the prairies of south Dakota, a new generation of faith, settled in the days of the first automobile, electricity, and gas furnaces (that would explode). Carol Brands has depicted the true story of a country girl, Katherine, in a setting of world wars, by a very accurate account, which will likely cause thousands to visit places such as Rock Rapids in Iowa and Leota and Magnolia in Minnesota in years to come in between exploring De Smet in South Dakota and Walnut Grove in Minnesota.

Living history, so that children (and their parents too) understand times past in order to be a blessing in times present, for the glory of God!

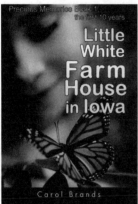

Little White Farm House in Iowa
by Carol Brands
Book 1: The First 10 Years

" . . . a wonderful book . . . spiritually uplifting . . . warm human insight and nostalgia . . . delightful reading as I recovered from hip surgery. I'd like to order four more copies . . ."

"This is no sappy, quasi-Christian literature; this is the real deal. . . the proverbial diamond in the rough . . . I am going to see that the library at Heritage Christian School, where my children are enrolled, has several copies . . ."

"One of the finest Christian books I've read for young people . . ."

Time: 1930-1940	Age: 13-99
978-1-894666-38-1	US$11.95

Little Yellow Farm House in Iowa by Carol Brands
Book 2: Years Eleven through Seventeen: World War II Years

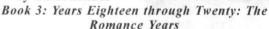

While war loomed in the background, Uncle Bill always on the family's mind, Katherine's farm life continued with a mixture of stories – some humorous, some serious, some full of neighborliness, some with tragedy.

Join the Kroontje family — living daily life on an Iowa farm even while World War II is being fought across the oceans.

Time: 1940-1948	Age: 13-99
978-1-894666-39-8	US$11.95

Strangers in Minnesota by Carol Brands
Book 3: Years Eighteen through Twenty: The Romance Years

When Katherine and her family moved from their tiny home near Rock Rapids, Iowa, to a new home near Magnolia, Minnesota, this is how Katherine felt her first Sunday in a new church.

She felt lost, totally bereft of friends and familiarity.What had she and her family done? They had left everything near and dear behindto start completely over!

Would she ever be able to fit in?
To find friends?
To feel like she belonged . . .?

Time: 1948-1951	Age: 13-99
978-1-894666-40-4	US$11.95

Set of three books US$29.95

109

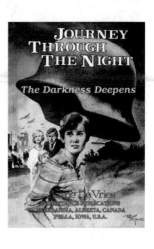

110

The Shadow Series
by Piet Prins

One of the most exciting series of a master story teller about the German occupation of The Netherlands during the emotional time of the Second World War (1940-1945).
K. Bruning in *Una Sancta* about Vol.4 - *The Partisans*, and Vol. 5 - *Sabotage*: . . . the country was occupied by the German military forces. The nation's freedom was destroyed by the foreign men in power. Violence, persecutions and executions were the order of the day, and the main target of the enemy was the destruction of the christian way of life. In that time the resistance movement of underground fighters became very active. People from all ages and levels joined in and tried to defend the Dutch Christian heritage as much as possible. The above mentioned books show us how older and younger people were involved in that dangerous struggle. It often was a life and death battle. Every page of these books is full of tension. The stories give an accurate and very vivid impression of that difficult and painful time. These books should also be in the hands of our young people. They are excellent instruments to understand the history of their own country and to learn the practical value of their own confession and Reformed way of life. What about as presents on birthdays?

Time: 1944-1945		Age: 10-99
Vol. 1 The Lonely Sentinel	ISBN 1-894666-72-0	US$10.90
Vol. 2 Hideout in the Swamp	ISBN 1-894666-73-9	US$10.90
Vol. 3 The Grim Reaper	ISBN 1-894666-74-7	US$10.90
Vol. 4 The Partisans	ISBN 0-921100-07-8	US$10.90
Vol. 5 Sabotage	ISBN 0-921100-08-6	US$10.90

Buy the whole set at 15% discount: US$47.30

It Began With a Parachute
by William R. Rang

Fay S. Lapka in *Christian Week*: [It] . . . is a well-told tale set in Holland near the end of the Second World War. . . The story, although chock-full of details about life in war-inflicted Holland, remains uncluttered, warm, and compelling.
Time: 1940-1945   Age: 9-99
ISBN 0-921100-38-8   US$9.90

Amazing Stories from Times Past
by Christine Farenhorst
Devotions for Children and Families

Is your Bible buried under anything? Is it shared? Can you be an active Christian without humility? How should a Christian define the word *famous*?

Readers will consider these and other thought-provoking questions after reading the amazing stories of people from times past.

Subject: Devotional literature for children Age: 11-99
ISBN 0-87552-823-6 US$9.99

The Children's Morning
Message by Amy Le Feuvre

Dear Little Friend,

Will you try to read a page of this book every morning? I do not want it to take the place of your Bible; but I know that very often schoolboys and schoolgirls are hurried in the morning, and have not time to read their Bible till the evening. This little message will not take you long to read; and I have prayed that God may bless it to you day by day. You will see that we begin the year with the words of Jesus, and we end it with His words. We do not go straight through the Bible, but you will notice that we get our messages from every part of it. Will you try to live out your text every day? Think about it, and act upon it, and ask the Holy Spirit to remind you of it during the day.

Your affectionate friend, —Amy Le Feuvre

ISBN 978-1-928136-61-3 US$17.90

MY FAVORITE STORY BOOK
by W.G. Van de Hulst
Illustrated by W.G. Van de Hulst, Jr.
Translated from the Dutch
by Marian Schooland

1 Two Little Sisters; 2 Dickie and the Little Finch; 3 The Little Wooden Shoe; 4 A Teddy Bear That Grew; 5 The Sick Man; 6 White and Black; 7 Mother and Steven; 8 The Ugly Caterpillar; 9 Grandpa's Watch; 10 Naughty Hector; 11 The Little Man with a Crooked Neck; 12 Little Jack's Vacation; 13 Shiner; 14 Brown Beans, White Beans; 15 In the Little Reed Cradle; 16 Whose Little Goat Are You?; 17 Lettie; 18 The Glass Marble; 19 One Rainy, Rainy Day; 20 The Snowman; 21 My Friend Blackcap and I; 22 The Two Little Lambs; 23 When the Wild Wind Blows; 24 Nibs and the Little Old Man; 25 Tarts ; 26 Who Was Most Kind?; 27 Reta, Meta, and Sofeta; 28 Potatoes for Mother; 29 Donnie's Corner; 30 Hagar and Ishmael; 31 Peeper; 32 Elsa and the Violets.

978-1-928136-22-4 **US$16.95**

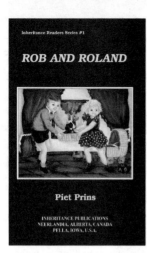

Rob and Roland by Piet Prins
Inheritance Readers Series #1

A little dog walked along the road.
A white dog with brown ears and a brown spot on his head.
It was a puppy.
But he was not happy.
He was hungry and there was nobody to take care of him.

Subject: Fiction   Age: 7-8
ISBN 978-1-894666-32-9   US$7.95

Rob and Roland on the Farm by Piet Prins
Inheritance Readers Series #2

Two storks had built a nest with branches and straw on it.
Mother stork perched on the edge of the nest.
She kept watch over her children.
She also looked around at the wide world.
When you are so high, you can see far over the green pastures.

Subject: Fiction   Age: 7-8
ISBN 978-1-894666-33-6   US$7.95

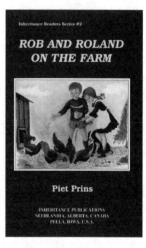

Anak, the Eskimo Boy *by Piet Prins*
Inheritance Readers Series #9

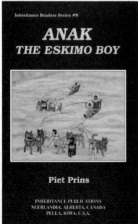

Another captivating story by one of the best-loved authors of juvenile literature in the Netherlands!
Far north, where the sun shines only part of the year, Anak and his family live with the rest of their Eskimo tribe near the Coronation Gulf. Anak experiences both adventure and danger as he learns how to hunt seals, caribou, and walruses; travels to the land of the white man; faces the threat of a bear attack; and accidentally drifts off to sea on an ice floe. As Anak confronts the challenges of Eskimo life, he learns important lessons about responsibility and dependence on God.

Subject: Mission / Fiction   Age: 9-10
ISBN 978-0-921100-11-9   US$8.95

Stories Children Love

A series for boys and girls 4 to 10 years old. To help the reader in a task which is not at all easy — for much beauty is lost through thoughtless reading — the author suggests slow reading in a natural tone of voice, with careful attention to emphasis. The reader must enjoy the story with the child. To taste the full pleasure of reading to a child, the two must roam together hand in hand as it were, through the wonderland of make-believe.

Some things change, and some things stay the same. The world of children has changed dramatically — or has it? In the classroom, in the doctor's office, and on the street, they see things their parents never saw as children. But when they're completely absorbed in play? Or when they're finally tired of playing and they seek out their mother or father at the end of the day? Then you see that their world hasn't changed much at all. A child still loves a story — about a cat that ran away, about a hungry dog waiting for some scraps of meat outside a butcher shop, about an abandoned doll lying in the rain. Each animal, each toy, has its own story. And your child wants to hear that story.

W.G. Vandehulst was a master storyteller. He knew children. And he wrote stories children love. Children have long been enthralled with his tales. That's why more than three million books in this series have been sold in Europe.

SCL01 *Little Wooden Shoe* by W.G. Van De Hulst

A little wooden shoe is found floating on the water, and suddenly Henry's guilty little secret has stirred up the whole village. If only he had told his father! Now the miller, the policeman, the mayor, and the whole village are involved. Henry's whole world seems to be pointing the finger of shame at him. But the mayor, the policeman, and the miller and his wife have a little secret of their own. A day of shame is turned into a day of celebration!

978-1-928136-01-9 US$7.90

SCL02 Through the Thunderstorm by W.G. Van De Hulst

To go to Grandmother's house, Bob, Betsy, and Benjamin have to go through the woods. In the woods there are unseen eyes on the three children — the eyes of the jolly baker, who pulls a trick on them, the eyes of a little bird, which they trap in their basket, and the eyes of a scary old woman, whom they take to be a wicked witch. The children get caught in the woods during a frightful thunderstorm, and they find out about another set of eyes.

978-1-928136-02-6 US$7.90

SCL03 Bruno the Bear *by W.G. Van De Hulst*

Bruno, Rosie's teddy bear, becomes separated from his sick little owner through the thoughtless hi-jinks of Rosie's two rowdy brothers, Jimmy and Joe. Bruno has been endowed with an eye that twinkles merrily with a happy secret. Jimmy and Joe have a secret too, but it isn't a happy one: it keeps them awake at night. In their quest to restore their little sister's happiness, the boys discover that they cannot keep their guilty secret to themselves. What is it that finally puts Rosie and Bruno, the boys and their parents, Bruno and his twinkle back together again?

978-1-928136-03-3 US$7.90

Audio Books on Compact Disc
Ideal fot travelling or to read along!

The Little Wooden Shoe
by W.G. Van De Hulst
AUDIO BOOK CD
Read by Amelie Viersen

A little wooden shoe is found floating on the water, and suddenly Henry's guilty little secret has stirred up the whole village. If only he had told his father! Now the miller, the policeman, the mayor, and the whole village are involved. Henry's whole world seems to be pointing the finger of shame at him. But the mayor, the policeman, and the miller and his wife have a little secret of their own. A day of shame is turned into a day of celebration!

AUDIO BOOK CD SCL01 LITTLE WOODEN SHOE - VAN DE HULST, W.G.
CD SCL01 LITTLE WOODEN SHOE - VAN DE HULST, W.G.
CD 9781928136019 - US$ 8.95

DVD SCL01 LITTLE WOODEN SHOE - VAN DE HULST, W.G.
DVD 9781928136019 - US$ 7.90

A-bk SCL01 LITTLE WOODEN SHOE - VAN DE HULST, W.G.
Audio Book 9781928136019 - US$ 5.98

V-BK SCL01 LITTLE WOODEN SHOE DWNLD - VAN DE HULST, W.G.
Video Book 9781928136019 - US$ 6.97 CD 9781928136019 - US$ 9.90

Through the Thunderstorm by W.G. Van De Hulst
AUDIO BOOK CD
Read by Amelie Viersen

To go to Grandmother's house, Bob, Betsy, and Benjamin have to go through the woods. In the woods there are unseen eyes on the three children — the eyes of the jolly baker, who pulls a trick on them, the eyes of a little bird, which they trap in their basket, and the eyes of a scary old woman, whom they take to be a wicked witch. The children get caught in the woods during a frightful thunderstorm, and they find out about another set of eyes.
AUDIO BOOK CD SCL02 THROUGH THE THUNDERSTORM - VAN DE HULST, W.G.-
CD 9781928136026 - US$ 9.90

All 21 Audio Books and Video Books Available Now on CD, DVD and Downloads

Order the complete download set of all 21 Audio Books or Video Books of the Stories Children Love series by W.G. Van De Hulst and save 15%

VAN DE HULST, W.G. - A-bk SET OF 21 SCL BOOKS DOWNLOAD -
DOWNLOAD SET OF 21 -
US$ 99.90

* * *

Set of 21 download video books - Van de Hulst, W.G. - Set 21SCL VBK DWNL
- US$116.90

CD21 SET OF 21 SCL-VDHULST AU-BOOK - VAN DE HULST, W.G. - CD21
SET OF 21 SCL CDs -
US$159.75

DVD ALL 21 SCL AUDIO BOOKS VANDEHUL - VAN DE HULST, W.G. - 1
DVD OF all 21 SCL DVDs DVD IP17726 -
US$140.95

DVD ALL 21 SLC VIDEO BKS VANDEHULST - VAN DE HULST, W.G. -
DVD IP17727 - US$119.90

DVD ALL 21SCL MP3&MP4 - VAN DE HULST / ROOK -
(only FOR LEGAL OWNERS of all 21 SCL books,
or with an order for all 21 books)
DVD-IP17726 - US$ 29.90

SCL04 The Basket *by W.G. Van De Hulst*

Mother told Julie, Tessa, and Dicky which road to take home from Grandmother's house. But the three children thought they knew a better way, and they got lost in a strange forest guarded by a fierce dog. Grandmother had told Julie, Tessa, and Dicky not to open the big basket with the wonderful gift inside. But the three children just couldn't resist taking a peek, and suddenly they lost something very precious. Out of their fear and confusion came an undeserved happiness. Is it a miracle, or are we just seeing double?

978-1-928136-04-0 US$7.90

SCL05 Lost in the Snow
by W.G. Van De Hulst

Two little boys are lost in the woods. While bringing coffee to their father, they got scared off the path by a hairy black creature. Cold, tired, and lost, they kneel down in the snow and close their eyes. But when they open them again, that scary black creature has become a cold, tired, lost creature like themselves. Can the lost help the lost find their way home?

978-1-928136-05-7 US$7.90

SCL06 Annie and the Goat
by W.G. Van De Hulst

Grandma came into the yard and found the gate open. Annie was gone and so was Billy, the little goat! Off went Grandma to look for her two strays. Then Grandpa came into the yard. Finding everyone gone, he set out as well to look for Grandma, Annie, and Billy. Soon two boys and a policeman join in the search. And then a rainstorm sets in. The policeman finds Annie's ribbon beside the water, and the boys find Billy the goat. But where is Annie?

978-1-928136-06-4

US$7.90

SCL07 The Black Kitten
by W.G. Van De Hulst

Sandy tries to save a little kitten from falling into the water. Instead, she accidentally pushes it under. A passer-by accuses her of trying to drown the kitten. Sandy, the little would-be rescuer, catches a chill and gets seriously ill. Feverishly she dreams of black kittens and that accusing man on the road. In the end the accuser becomes a healer, and the would-be rescuer is in need of rescue herself. As for the victim, the black kitten — it heals a heart and finds a home.

978-1-928136-07-1 US$7.90

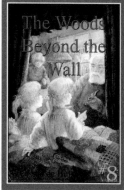

SCL08 Woods Beyond the Wall *by W.G. Van De Hulst*

Grandma wants to protect Carla and Ria, her two little granddaughters, from the dangers of the outside world. Beyond the wall are the woods, the busy highway, and Eddie and Bert—those two little troublemakers. But Grandma and Grandpa discover that they can't wall the dangers out, for the biggest danger comes from within — not from without. Can Carla and Ria scale the wall to friendship?

978-1-928136-08-8 US$7.90

SCL09 My Master and I by W.G. Van De Hulst

My name is Fik. I'm a strong dog. But I'm not very smart. Just listen to my story. My master, John, and I like to spend our time together. Sometimes we do get into trouble though. When there is danger I warm my master. But then my master gets so sick and I cannot help. All I can do is be sad and hope my master will get better.

978-1-928136-09-5   US$7.90

SCL10 Pig under the Pew
by W.G. Van De Hulst

The preacher looks up from his books. The church door bursts open and out tumble three little boys and a girl — his daughter. Over them jumps a little pig. Right behind them, waving his fist angrily, is the church's caretaker. What brings all these together: three little rascals, the preacher's little girl, a curious little pig, and an angry caretaker?

978-1-928136-10-1   US$7.90

SCL11 Three Little Hunters
by W.G. Van De Hulst

Roger, Danny, and Willy are out on a hunt. Very quietly they tiptoe through the woods. Are there any tigers or bears or elephants? With pistols, swords, and bows the three brave hunters are ready for every encounter. Or are they? At once a little kitten in need of compassion is spotted. Was it dying? How will the brave hunters deal with sickness and sadness?

978-1-928136-11-8   US$7.90

SCL12 Search for Christmas
by W.G. Van De Hulst

Looking down from her castle, a little princess sees the Christmas star in the window of a poor little house. Looking up from his poor little house, a little boy sees an angel in the window of the high castle. Both leave their homes to find the newborn Baby in the manger. Although they do not find the baby, they do find Christmas. And so do the parents — through the foolishness of two little children.

978-1-928136-12-5   US$7.90

SCL13 Footprints in the Snow by W.G. Van De Hulst

Small footprints — the footprints of a small child — lead across the frozen canal and out into the white winter fields. No one pays much attention to them. Why should they? They aren't important — until Mother discovers that Janie is missing. No one finds the footprints except Janie's foolish little dog Bello. And how can he help? He only comes to play.

978-1-928136-13-2   US$7.90

118

SCL14 Little Tramp *by W.G. Van De Hulst*

It was winter and oh, so bitterly cold. I trotted along the road. My home is gone. My cruel master who kicks me is gone. But where do I go? And, oh, it is so bitterly cold. Then I am spotted and taken into the strange world of people. What do they all mean? And what will happen when my master finds out where I am?
978-1-928136-14-9

US$7.90

SCL15 Three Foolish Sisters
by W.G. Van De Hulst

Three little girls stand before a large iron gate. It is the gate to the Baron's estate, and beyond it are dark, scary woods. The three little girls are Dinah, Suzy, and Joanne, and their faces are streaked with fear. They stare at the padlock and chain that hold the gate shut. Joey, their baby brother, is somewhere on the other side of that gate. And it is their fault! How will they get him out?
978-1-928136-15-6   US$7.90

SCL16 The Secret Hiding Place
by W.G. Van De Hulst

Tom and Davy are missing. They should be in class, but they are not. The village policeman has a mystery, for Mrs. Janssen's big pan is missing too. And so is Farmer Cooper's "Keep Out" sign. When Tom and Davy finally show up, flushed and dirty, they refused to tell their teacher where they have been. It's a secret: so she simply asks them, "Is it a beautiful or an ugly secret?" That's a question only the boys can answer.
978-1-928136-16-3   US$7.90

SCL17 The Secret in the Box
by W.G. Van De Hulst

Catch him! Catch him! The children jump; the teacher screams — and Nick and Neil are in trouble. What are they doing with that frog in school? It's a secret. After school they sneak the frog into their bedroom. Father and Aunt Katie must not see the frog. Mother must not see it either, even though the secret will make her better . . . in the morning. But in the middle of the night — Bump! Crash! Bang! The frog is loose and the boys are in trouble again. Their secret is spoiled. Who will make Mother better now?
978-1-928136-17-0   US$7.90

SCL18 Rockity Rowboat *by W.G. Van De Hulst*

Where was Annalee? When Mother looked in Annalee's special place behind Father's desk in the study, Annalee was gone. She had gone with Peter to play in the pasture. But she left without telling Father and Mother. Out in the pasture Annalee and Peter ran off to play and explore. Together they discovered the rockity rowboat. With each thoughtless step, Annalee was further from the safety of home, more and more lost.
978-1-928136-18-7   US$7.90

SCL19 Herbie, the Runaway Duck
by W.G. Van De Hulst

It was a beautiful spring day, but Herbie couldn't go out. He had to sort beans because he had spilled them and then run away. He felt like running away again. Suddenly he heard a voice outside the window calling his name, but the voice wasn't calling him: it was calling little runaway Herbie. Big Herbie and little Herbie were very much alike. But how could that be? They were a boy and a duck!

978-1-928136-19-4   US$7.90

SCL20 Kittens, Kittens Everywhere
by W.G. Van De Hulst

Penny and Peggy were heartbroken. Their kittens, Feather and Heather, were lost! Then suddenly Dr. Hart, their stern neightbor, was accusing the girls of making all sorts of mischief. And what about those noises behind the tall fence dividing Dr. Hart's yard from theirs? What was happening behind that grouchy doctor's fence?

978-1-928136-20-0   US$7.90

SCL21 Forbidden Path
by W.G. Van De Hulst

The wheatfield was ready to be harvested. The farmer only saw the wheat. But Pam and Polly saw the little poppies that grew between the wheat. Ignoring the "No Trespassing" sign, they followed the path picking poppies left and right. But oh, when the farmer and the policeman notice little footsteps leading into the wheat, what will happen then?

978-1-928136-21-7   US$7.90

SCL22 The Night Before Christmas
by W.G. Van De Hulst

At the Scholten farm, the richest farm in the district, everyone was busy preparing for the great Christinas party. Mr. Scholten prided himself greatly on this annual display of wealth and generosity.
When an old woman came onto the yard begging for firewood, he was too busy to bother with her and chased her away. Everyone was also too busy to answer little Lucas's questions about Christmas. So he went off to find the newborn Baby on his own. When the party began, Lucas was missing.

978-1-77298-008-0   US$8.90y

120

Susanneke by C. J. Van Doornik

Little Susanneke is happy! Tomorrow is Christmas. And Daddy has cleaned the church. But did he forget something? When it is her birthday Mommy always decorates the livingroom. And actually they will celebrate the Lord Jesus' birthday tomorrow. But the church isn't decorated at all. Could the big people have forgotten it? That is sad for the Lord. He loves us so much and now no one has thought about decorating the church for Him. She has to think about that for a moment. What should she do?

Subject: Fiction   Age: 6-8
ISBN 0-921100-61-2   US$7.90

Judy's Own Pet Kitten by An Rook

Fay S. Lapka in *Christian Week*: Judy, presumably seven or eight years of age, is the youngest member of a farm family whose rural setting could be anywhere in Canada. The story of Judy, first losing her own kitten, then taming a wild stray cat with kittens, and finally rescuing the tiniest one from a flood, is well-told and compelling.

Subject: Fiction   Age: 6-10
ISBN 0-921100-34-5   US$7.90

Tekko Series by Alie Vogelaar

. . . You will watch a little African boy do his utmost to save his little sister. You will see his whole village turn against him. And you will see how God works in wondrous ways to help him. I highly recommend this book for parents to read to their young children, some parts are scary, or for older children to read themselves.
— Rebecca Kingswood (*a grade five student*) in *Pioneer*.

Subject: Mission / Fiction   Age: 8-99
1 *Tekko and the White Man*   ISBN 0-921100-47-7 US$8.95
2 *Tekko the Fugitive*   ISBN 0-921100-74-4 US$8.95
3 *Tekko Returns*   ISBN 0-921100-75-2 US$8.95

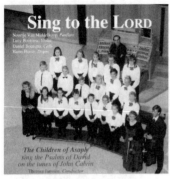

CD Sing to the LORD

The Children of Asaph sing the Psalms of David on the tunes of John Calvin — Noortje Van Middelkoop, Panflute; Lucy Bootsma, Violin; Daniel Bootsma, Cello; Harm Hoeve, Organ; Theresa Janssen, Conductor.

Byron Snapp in *The Counsel of Chalcedon*: . . . There is a richness and depth in these selections that is too often missing in much contemporary music. . . Once again *Church Music & Records* has provided the listener with the opportunity to hear enduring Psalms sung and played with meaning and a quiet, sure confidence. Hopefully this recording will be widely purchased and used in the lives of many for the building up of God's people more and more unto His glory.

Compact Disc CMR 104-2   US$21.99   Cassette CMR 104-4   US$14.99

DVD (with FREE AUDIO CD)
With Joyful Psalm and Song

The Children of Asaph
Sing Anglo-Genevan Psalms
Amy Barendregt, Soprano
Peter De Boer, Baritone
Kent Dykstra, Violin
Joel Bootsma, Viola
Vanessa Smeding, Cello
Harm Hoeve, Organ
Theresa Janssen, Conductor

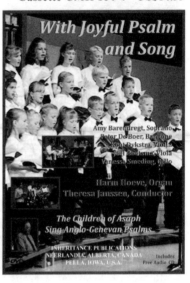

Psalms 76:1, 3, & 5; 93:1-4; 85:1 & 2; 114:1-4; 35:1 & 2; 6:1 & 2 (Soprano Solo); 47:1-3; The Song of Mary; Psalms 33 (Organ Solo); 79:1, 3, & 5; 89:1-3; 119:1, 4, 13, & 40; 24:1, 2, & 5; 144:2 (Strings & Baritone); 84:1-3; 55:1, 2, & 9; 71:1 & 8; 138:1-4.
IPDVD 113-9 (includes free CD)   US$29.95

DVD (with FREE AUDIO CD)
Along the Athabasca River

The Children of Asaph Sing Folksongs From Around the World
Amy Barendregt, Soprano
Kent Dykstra, Violin
Joel Bootsma, Viola
Harm Hoeve, Piano/Organ
Theresa Janssen, Conductor

1. Sing Along; 2. Something to Sing About 3. Hedge Rose; 4. a) Christopher Columbus; b) The Prairie Schooner; c) In the Ropery; 5. My Heart Ever Faithful (Soprano Solo); 6. Along the Athabasca River; 7. The Canadian; 8. Bugle Note; 9. The Spider and the Fly; 10. The Blue Bells of Scotland; 11. The Good Comrade; 12. a) Maple Trees; b) Paul and the Fox; 13. The Londonderry Air (Piano & Violin); 14. The Ashgrove; 15. Ducks on a Pond; 16. Bells; 17. Swing High; 18. This Land is Your Land; 19. William of Nassau; 20. Our Gracious God.
IPDVD 114-9 (includes free CD)   US$29.95

The Escape

The Adventures of Three Huguenot Children Fleeing Persecution
(based on historical facts)

A. Van der Jagt

The Escape
by A. Van der Jagt
The Adventures of Three Huguenot Children
Fleeing Persecution
Huguenot Inheritance Series #1

F. Pronk in *The Messenger*: This book . . . will hold its readers spellbound from beginning to end. The setting is late seventeenth century France. Early in the story the mother dies and the father is banished to be a galley slave for life on a war ship. Yet in spite of threats and punishment, sixteen-year-old John and his ten-year-old sister Manette, refuse to give up the faith they have been taught.

Time: 1685-1695   Age: 12-99
ISBN 0-921100-04-3   US$10.90

The Secret Mission
by A. Van der Jagt
A Huguenot's Dangerous Adventures
in the Land of Persecution
Huguenot Inheritance Series #2

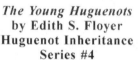

In the sequel to our best-seller, *The Escape,* John returns to France with a secret mission of the Dutch Government. At the same time he attempts to find his father.

Time: 1702-1712   Age: 12-99
ISBN 0-921100-18-3   US$13.90

The Young HUGUENOTS
Edith S. Floyer

The Young Huguenots
by Edith S. Floyer
Huguenot Inheritance
Series #4

It was a happy life at the pretty chateau. Even after that dreadful Sunday evening, when strange men came down and shut the people out of the church, not much changed for the four children. Until the soldiers came . . .

Time: 1686-1687   Age: 11-99
ISBN 0-921100-65-5   US$11.95

RT18 *The King's Service* by Deborah Alcock
A Story of the Thirty Years' War

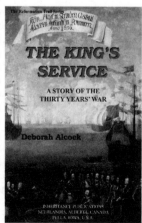

Two motherless children, Jeanie and Hugh, have been in the care of their Uncle Charlie ever since their father left about eight years earlier to fight for the Protestant cause. Uncle Charlie, a restless bachelor, subsequently leaves the bulk of Jeanie and Hugh's upbringing to the Presbyterian minister. He faithfully teaches these orphaned children the beautiful tenets of the Reformed faith. But when Uncle Charlie decides to leave his beloved Scotland to join the army of Gustavus Adolphus in Germany, Hugh wants to go along. Jeanie will go along as companion to Captain Stuart's wife and meets Fraulein Gertrud von Savelburg in Germany. Sifting through the reports and rumours of the times she comes to some disturbing and perplexing conclusions. What has made Uncle Charlie so sad, and why does a Roman Catholic priest regularly visit Hugh?

Time: 1630-1632   Age: 12-99
ISBN 978-1-894666-06-0   US$11.95

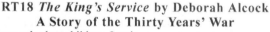

123

Bobby's Friends
by Phia van den Berg
The publisher's most favourite juvenile story

"Lights!" Jessie announced loudly.

Suddenly everyone was awake.

Karachi appeared beneath them on the lefthand side. At first they saw only a narrow strip of tiny lights, but soon it broadened. The plane swung sideways as it turned, gliding above the sea of city lights. The children hadn't paid much attention to the other landings during the trip, but this one became very exciting!

Pakistan! Every year a part of Western Pakistan underwent a drastic flood, washing away all the gardens and homes of the inhabitants. Father Falois, agriculturist, was asked by the government to try to control the floods. But life in Pakistan was so different for Bobby and his siblings. The worst part was understanding the people, that breach between the rich Muslims and the poor Christians. How would Bobby find friends? Would the screaming, proud, millionaire's son, Sadiq, be a friend, or would Jahja, the very poorest of all? Who would be faithful when danger came?

Subject: Fiction   Age: 9-99
ISBN 9780921100515   US$9.95

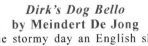

The Big Goose and the Little White Duck
by Meindert De Jong

This story of how the goose became a hero and earned a permanent place on the farm for himself and his friend the duck is full of warmth, humor, and insight.

Subject: Fiction   Age: 7-99
ISBN 0-88815-863-7   US$13.90

Dirk's Dog Bello
by Meindert De Jong

The stormy day an English ship broke up in the terrible waters of Wicked Wife, Dirk rescued the Great Dane, Bello. After that, by the law of the sea, the giant dog belonged to him. But Dirk's family was poor. And Dirk was suddenly faced with the enormous problem of how to feed Bello. A rare and moving book, full of humor and reality.

Subject: Fiction   Age: 10-99
ISBN 0-88815-860-2   US$12.90

Far Out the Long Canal
by Meindert Dejong

When the ice finally came to the ditches and canals, Moonta was afire with enthusiasm, not only to learn how to skate, but to let his skates lead him to adventure. And when he heard of something called the New Church's Pipe, far out the long canal, he was determined to find it at any risk.

Subject: Fiction   Age: 10-99
ISBN 0-88815-861-1   US$10.90

Smoke above the Lane by Meindert De Jong

How could the little baby skunk have known that by falling asleep on the streetcar tracks on Main Street he would cause a traffic jam unequaled in the history of the village?

Subject: Fiction — Age: 9-99
ISBN 0-88815-862-9 — US$8.95

Pierre and his Friends
by W.G. Van De Hulst

Pierre, sick and confined to bed, cannot play with other children. But what about those boys who have come into the quiet canal, shattering Pierre's peaceful routine? A classic from a master storyteller!

Subject: Fiction (World War I) — Age: 9-99
ISBN 0-88815-756-8 — US$11.90

The Mystery of Old Abe by W.G. Van de Hulst

Abe is an angry old man who carries in his heart the secret pain of his daughter's and grandchild's death. The nosy boys are afraid of Old Abe, but they do dare to tease the old man. But why is Abe angry with the boys and what is he going to do with Cindy?

Subject: Fiction — Age: 8-99
ISBN 0-88815-755-X — US$10.90

The Black Phantom of Ravenhurst by Willem G. Van der Hulst Jr.

Was the driver of the cart full of branches really asleep or was he only pretending? How could that black figure vanish from the mill without leaving tracks in the snow?

Subject: Fiction — Age: 8-99
ISBN 0-88815-547-6 — US$10.90

The Black Phantom of Ravenhurst

S.O.S. by K. Norel

A native of Terschelling, a Dutch North Sea island, the boy Dirk dreams of going to sea as his father, a merchant mariner, has done. When he finishes grade school, Dirk signs on as bottle washer aboard the Sea Dog, his uncle's tugboat.

Subject: Fiction — Age: 11-99
ISBN 0-88815-876-9 — US$10.90

Scout

The Secret of the Swamp

Piet Prins

The book that has made thousands of boys into readers

Scout: The Secret of the Swamp
by Piet Prins

One day as Scout was wandering about in the back yard enjoying the sun and exploring, he put his head through the hedge. Suddenly he started. Right beside him were the legs and tattered boots of an evil-smelling man who was standing on the other side of the hedge studying the house.

The man was startled too when the German shepherd's head came poking through the hedge. He aimed a hard kick at the dog's nose, but Scout was too quick for him. Scout wasn't afraid of the man; he bared his teeth and growled.

Then the man suddenly changed his behaviour. He bent forward toward Scout, clucking his tongue and patting his leg. "Here, boy! Come here! Good boy! Look what I've got for you." From his pocket he pulled a chunk of meat and held it out to Scout.ooking for adventure but fighting for his very life.

Subject: Fiction   Age: 9-99
ISBN 0-921100-50-7   US$10.90

The book that made
THOUSANDS OF BOYS INTO READERS

Scout: The Haunted Castle by Piet Prins

Scout
The Haunted Castle
Piet Prins

Tom and Scout are on vacation with Tom's two best friends, Carl and Bert, and his sisters, Ina and Miriam. On their rambles through the woods, the group of young people are stopped one day by customs officials. They are accused of being in league with a gang of criminals who are smuggling goods across the nearby German border. Scout's reputation as a tracking dog has preceded him, and soon the young people are helping both the police and the customs officials. The mystery of the haunted castle, a coded message hidden under a tree, a gang of smugglers that can vanish at will, a burglary without clues — they all come together when Tom and Scout tumble over a four-hundred-year-old secret. Suddenly, however, Tom is no longer looking for adventure but fighting for his very life.

Subject: Fiction   Age: 9-99
ISBN 1-894666-44-5   US$10.90

Scout: The Flying Phantom by Piet Prins

Scout
The Flying Phantom
Piet Prins

When Tom and his friends Bert and Carl set out on an adventure over spring vacation, they are only looking for a good time. But soon a series of baffling events draws them inexorably into another mystery. What connection is there between a dangerous poacher, a police cap on top of a tower, a host of unsolved burglaries, and a mysterious fire? Is the fearsome character who walks on the swamp the ghost of the legendary Flying Phantom? Or is it something or someone else?

Join the boys, Tom's dog, Scout, and their mutual friend Captain Brandenburg as they muster courage, tenacity, and wit to track a very unusual kind of criminal.

Subject: Fiction   Age: 9-99
ISBN 1-894666-45-3   US$10.95

126

Scout: The Sailing Sleuths by Piet Prins

Scout
The Sailing Sleuths
Piet Prins

While Tom and his two friends are making plans for a vacation, Carl's father announces that he has acquired a sailboat, as part of a business deal. The three boys see the chance for a very unusual holiday.

Their peaceful sailing trip is sabotaged when they run into a gang of notorious carnival followers who put on sidewalk shows as a cover for more profitable sidelines. After a confrontation with the gang, the three sailors and Scout find themselves in trouble with the police. Their attempt to clear themselves leads to a wild chase through rivers, canals, and lakes. When at last the boys come face to face with the gang and its ruthless leader, they are stranded on an island in the middle of an isolated lake. In the showdown they are all alone — except for Scout.

Subject: Fiction
ISBN 1-894666-46-1
Age: 9-99
US$10.95

Scout
The Treasure of Rodensteyn Castle
Piet Prins

Scout: The Treasure of Rodensteyn Castle by Piet Prins

When they are invited to spend a few weeks with Uncle Arnie at the seashore, little do Tom, Carl, and Bert realize that they will be staying in the hunting lodge of a medieval castle. Uncle Arnie is quite a storyteller. Soon the boys find their imaginations and the lodge peopled with ghosts from Rodensteyn Castle, a castle long ago buried under the sand. But do ghosts leave tracks, tracks that Scout follows into the sea? Are the legends of the ghost of Sir Isobald and the treasure of Rodensteyn Castle true? Is it a ghost that Tom spots in the dunes at night? Can Scout's nose, no matter how keen, help the boys solve a mystery over 400 years old? Past and present, fact and fiction merge as Tom and his friends search for a treasure that has outlasted the ages.

Subject: Fiction
ISBN 1-894666-47-X
Age: 9-99
US$10.95

Scout: The Mystery of the Abandoned Mill by Piet Prins

Scout
The Mystery of the Abandoned Mill
Piet Prins

Tom, Carl, and Bert are spending the summer on the farm. One day they run into a large, surly man with a black monster of a dog. Scout and the black dog are enemies at first sight. The man arouses the boys' suspicions at once. He is no ordinary vacationer. When Scout pulls a boy from the river, the boys make a friend. From the boy's mother they hear a story about the abandoned mill and a missing treasure. The story draws them into an adventure that sets the boys on a collision course with the dangerous man and his equally dangerous dog. Trying to play the master detective, Tom leads his friends into a desperate situation. Can they stop Scout from clashing with the powerful black dog as he rushes to their aid? After all their hard work, will the boys lose the treasure after all? Worse yet, will the crook decide to kill the only witnesses to his crime?

Subject: Fiction
ISBN 1-894666-48-8
Age: 9-99
US$10.95

Scout's
Distant Journey
Piet Prins

Scout's Distant Journey by Piet Prins

Scout's seventh adventure reacquaints us with his three friends and introduces some new characters. One is Uncle Bob, long absent in North America but now back in the old country where he and his wife settle into a small but honest-to-goodness castle! Naturally Tom and his friends, including Scout, are invited to spend the summer holidays at Uncle Bob's intriguing house. Actually, the invitation is more like a challenge: Uncle Bob pretends to have a low opinion of "modern youth;" he thinks they're soft and over-pampered. To prove him wrong, Tom and his friends decide to travel on foot. But on the journey, little goes right: disasters dog their footsteps and danger is their constant companion . . . Their arrival marks both victory and defeat . . .

Subject: Fiction
ISBN 1-894666-49-6
Age: 9-99
US$10.95

The Curse of Urumbu by Piet Prins

Jack kills a wallaby, not knowing he has thereby violated an aboriginal taboo. The tribe's witch doctor pronounces a curse on Jack and the hunt is on.

Subject: Fiction   Age: 9-99
ISBN 0-88815-807-6   US$10.90
CLOTH ISBN 0-88815-806-8   US$ 11.90

The Search for Sheltie
by Piet Prins

Having shaken the curse of Urumbu, Jack and Sheltie return to the old country. Injured in a traffic accident, Jack is laid up in a Genoa hospital. Sheltie goes on ahead to Rotterdam where he promptly gets lost.

This book gives a fascinating look at the "psychology" of a dog trying to avoid capture as he hunts doggedly for his master. It also tells the story of the extensive, persistent search Jack and his nephews make for Sheltie.

Unaccustomed to civilization, Sheltie faces danger at every turn. Several scrapes with death make this a real nail-biter!

Subject: Fiction   Age: 9-99
ISBN 1-894666-43-7   US$10.95

Who was Piet Prins (pen name for Pieter Jongeling 1909-1985)?

Mr. Jongeling was born in the northern part of The Netherlands and studied to become a teacher. He indeed did teach for some years, but soon became the international correspondent of a Dutch newspaper. In 1942 he was arrested by the Germans and sent to a concentration camp. After the allied victory in 1945 he returned to The Netherlands and became one of the most important journalists and politicians in The Netherlands. For many years he was the editor of a Reformed Christian daily newspaper, in which he wrote most of his children's books as serials under the name Piet Prins. The first thing many people read when the newspaper arrived was these serials. In 1963 Mr. Jongeling became member of the Dutch parliament for the Reformed Political Alliance. One commentator mused: "What makes Jongeling such a remarkable parliamentarian? That's simple. The man works like a horse! He is always fully informed. When Jongeling speaks, the house listens." Both as a journalist and a statesman, Pieter Jongeling knew himself bound by the inspired Word of God and as such his labour has born much fruit.

Did you check page 99 of this catalogue? In **Dispelling the Tyranny** *Piet Prins writes about a dog Sultan, named after the dog the author played with when he was a child. Sultan becomes the best friend of Martin, also in Vol. 3 & 4 of the series.*

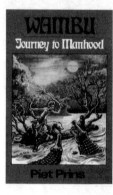

Piet Prins

Wambu Series by Piet Prins

Vol 1: *The Chieftain's Son*

Wambu is a young aborigine whose family is part of a small and slowly shrinking tribe ruled by a witch doctor.

Subject: Mission / Fiction   **Age: 10-99**
ISBN 0-88815-786-X   **US$12.95**

Piet Prins

Vol. 2: *In the Valley of Death*

Hunted by foes, tormented by spirits, and plagued by maleria, Wambu stumbles back to his old village in an effort to reach the white man.

Subject: Mission / Fiction   **Age: 10-99**
ISBN 0-88815-787-8   **US$10.95**

Vol. 3: *Journey to Manhood*

Wambu learns more about Jesus, but the mystery and magic of the old witchcraft die hard in the boy's heart.

Subject: Mission / Fiction   **Age: 10-99**
ISBN 0-88815-788-6   **US$10.95**

We are enjoying the books by Piet Prins so much! Thank you for publishing them . . . Is it possible to get an address of a family member that could give us more information about this dear man? We would especially like to know if he ever lived in Australia & New Guinea or was a missionary there. His books are so vivid & descriptive. My 6-year-old son begs me to read another chapter every day. —D. M. of Athens, Ohio.

The top ten books that will make a reader of your child (age 5 and up):

The Secret Code by Coen Hartman

Hank and Dick are two teenagers who accidentally get mixed up with a narcotics ring. When they intercept a coded message destined for a distributor doubling as a grocer, they become caught in a web of crime and intrigue.

Subject: Fiction	Age: 11-99
Paperback ISBN 0-88815-853-X	US$10.90
Cloth ISBN 0-88815-852-1	US$11.90

The Evil Professor
by Piet Prins
Four Adventurers Series

The Four Adventurers Meet
THE EVIL PROFESSOR

Four high school boys spend their summer vacation touring the country in a horse-drawn carriage. A run-in with a dark, sinister carnival shyster is only the beginning of suspense and adventure.

Subject: Fiction	Age: 10-99
ISBN 0-88815-821-1	US$10.90
Cloth ISBN 0-88815-820-3	US$11.90

The Mystery of the Three-Fingered Villain by Piet Prins
Four Adventurers Series

THE MYSTERY OF THE THREE-FINGERED VILLAIN

The detective work of Paul, Roger, Herb, and Eddie leads to a desperate cross-country chase to rescue their old friend Skippy from the three-fingered villain.

Subject: Fiction	Age: 10-99
ISBN 0-88815-823-8	US$10.90
Cloth ISBN 0-88815-822-X	US$11.90

Run, Kevin, Run! by Piet Prins

RUN, KEVIN, RUN!

Orphaned and feeling shipwrecked, Kevin Robbins ends up with relatives. Unable to make adjustments, Kevin "cops out" by running away to his home town. He is adopted by two crooks who insist on "protecting" him from the police.

Subject: Fiction	Age: 10-99
ISBN 0-88815-837-7	US$10.90
Cloth ISBN 0-88815-836-X	US$11.90

Stefan Derksen's Polar Adventure by Piet Prins

One of the sailors, who was known to be a good shot, decided to try to hit the bear while they were still in the boat. But because his footing was unsteady, he almost missed. The polar bear suffered only a light flesh wound . . . The sailor tried to shoot again, but the gun misfired. It seemed only seconds, and the angry animal had reached the boat. It laid its front paws on the edge and tried to climb in.

Once again Piet Prins has given us an outstanding novel. Follow Stefan's adventure as he runs away from his cruel uncle the cobbler and joins the men aboard the whaling ship the *Sea Dragon*. Hunting whales, encountering ferocious polar bears, storms and fog, dealing with sickness and hunger, floating adrift and shipwreck, all become part of Stefan Derksen's polar adventure. It is an adventure full of distress and surprise. Will Stefan ever return home to his mother?

Time: 1674-1675	Age: 9-99
ISBN 1-894666-67-4	US$11.95

130

Golden Inheritance Series #1
Jessica's First Prayer & Jessica's Mother
by Hesba Stretton

Liz Buist in *Reformed Perspective*: There is much to be learned from this story. It is written primarily for children, but this book is worthwhile reading for adults as well . . . Highly recommended for young and older.

The Sword and Trowel says (about *Jessica's First Prayer*): One of the most tender, touching, and withal gracious stories that we ever remember to have read. A dear little book for our children. We are not ashamed of having shed tears while reading it; in fact, should have been ten times more ashamed if we had not. The sweet portrait of the poor child Jessica is a study, and old Daniel is perfect in his own way.

Subject: Fiction   Age: 9-99
ISBN 0-921100-63-9

US$8.95

Golden Inheritance Series #2
Probable Sons by Amy Le Feuvre

The *Sword and Trowel* says: A lovely story that everybody — man, woman, boy, or girl — ought to read. The heroine is a charming child who, in a most winning way, applies to everyday life the Parable of the Prodigal Son, whom she mis-calls the Probable Son. It is scarcely possible to praise too highly this delightful volume.

Subject: Fiction   Age: 8-99
ISBN 0-921100-81-7   US$8.95

Golden Inheritance Series #3
Pilgrim Street by Hesba Stretton

Little Phil desperately wants to see his brother Tom. He knows Tom isn't guilty. But Phil is afraid of the policeman. Who will help these street urchins?

Subject: Fiction   Age: 9-99
ISBN 0-921100-91-4   US$8.95

Golden Inheritance Series #4
Legend Led by Amy Le Feuvre

Three children, orphaned at an early age and living with a governess, are suddenly sent for by an older step-brother who lives in the country. Steeped in Arthurian legends, Gypsy, the youngest of the three children, is convinced that the Holy Grail, or 'Holy Thing' as she calls it, is hidden somewhere on their brother's estate. When she does actually find the 'Holy Thing', it is not quite what she has expected. Reminiscent of W.G. VandeHulst, this book is sure to endear itself to parents as well as to young children. Most certainly recommended.

Subject: Fiction   Age: 10-99
ISBN 0-921100-82-5   US$8.95

Golden Inheritance Series #5
Little Meg's Children by Hesba Stretton

Christine Farenhorst in *Christian Renewal*: During the Victorian era a family, reduced to penury, lives in a squalid tenement awaiting their seafaring father's return. When the mother dies, the responsibility of caring for her two small brothers devolves to a very young girl. Having been initiated in the rudiments of Christianity through her mother's Bible reading, with child-like faith this little woman keeps her family going.

Reminiscent of W.G. VandeHulst, Stretton manages to pass on to her readers the importance of unquestioning faith in an omniscient God. Excellent reading.

Subject: Fiction Age: 9-99
ISBN 0-921100-92-2 US$8.95

Golden Inheritance Series #6
Teddy's Button by Amy Le Feuvre

The Life of Faith says: Teddy's Button is by the author of *Probable Sons*, and it would be difficult to say which is the better.

Rev. Thomas Spurgeon says: A smile-provoking, tear-compelling, heart-inspiring book. I wish every mother would read it to her children.

The Christian says: A lively little story, telling of a lad whose military spirit found satisfaction in enlisting in Christ's army and fighting God's battles.

Subject: Fiction Age: 8-99
ISBN 0-921100-83-3 US$8.95

Golden Inheritance Series #7
Lost Gip by Hesba Stretton

"Sandy will be a good boy, I know, for he loves to hear me tell him of Jesus Christ, and he's beginning to understand it all better now. Mother," and Johnny put his arm fondly around her neck, "I want you to let Sandy have my Sunday clothes, and let me see him go to chapel with Father.

Subject: Fiction Age: 9-99
ISBN 0-921100-93-0 US$8.95

Golden Inheritance Series #8
Harebell's Friend by Amy Le Feuvre

When her father dies, poor orphaned Harebell is taken from India to England. But Aunt Diana, under whose care Harebell is placed, dislikes children, and would rather send her niece off to a boarding school than keep her at her grand home . . . she again meets Tom Triggs . . .

Subject: Fiction Age: 9-99
ISBN 0-921100-84-1 US$8.95

Golden Inheritance Series #9
Cassy by Hesba Stretton

The dog seemed perfectly to understand the state of affairs, and was somewhat doubtful of the step the girl was about to take. He followed her slowly for a few yards, and then ran back and sniffed about the damp straw by the entrance, where he was used to sleep, and thrust his nose carefully among the smouldering sticks, which were the cause of this sudden flight. But as the girl disappeared among the trees, and whistled softly for him, he made up his mind to follow her, and the next minute the two were running as swiftly as the girl's feet could carry her away from the only home she had.

Subject: Fiction   Age: 9-99
ISBN 0-921100-94-9   US$8.95

Golden Inheritance Series # 10
Andy Man by Amy Le Feuvre

Andy, the orphaned son of a London policeman at the beginning of the twentieth century, becomes John's handy man out in the country. But honest head-strong Andy finds himself in some troubling situations. Will he be allowed to remain with John? And what about the mysterious visitor?

Subject: Fiction   Age: 9-99
ISBN 978-0-921100-95-9   US$8.95

Captains, Pirates and Runaways by Godfried Bomans
Illustrated by Rien Poortvliet

Summer vacation. Fred and Ted and then Ida, their friend and neighbor, leave home for fun and adventure. The boys visit their Uncle Ferdinand, a sea captain, and Ida goes to a girl's camp.

Subject: Fiction   Age: 8-99
ISBN 0-88815-537-9   US$4.95

More about God's Wonderful World by Joanne E. De Jonge

Joanne De Jonge uniquely combines a seeing eye, compassionate heart, schooled mind, and mastery of words to make God's wonderful world come vividly alive for all her readers. She translates the language of creation into words we can all understand.   — Lester De Koster

Subject: Nature   Age: 9-99
ISBN 0-88815-553-0   US$4.95

Nobody's Boy by Hector Malot

Nobody's Boy, published in France under the title *Sans Famille*, has become justly famous as one of the supreme juvenile stories of the world. In the midst of its early popularity, it was crowned by the academy as one of the masterpieces of French literature. A few years later, it was followed by *En Famille*, which was published in English as a companion story under the title *Nobody's Girl*. *Nobody's Boy* is a human document of child experiences that is fascinating reading for young and old. Parents, teachers, and others, who are careful to have children read inspiring books, will welcome this beautiful story of Hector Malot, as among the best for them to recommend.

Such digressions in the original as do not belong to the heart of the story have been eliminated, so that the lost boy's experiences continue as the undisturbed interest, on through to the happy conclusion. Loyal friendship and honest conduct are the vital ideals of this story, and the heart interest is eloquent with noble character.

Subject: Fiction   Age: 10-99
ISBN 1-894666-75-5   US$14.95

Nobody's Girl by Hector Malot

Nobody's Girl, published in France under the title *En Famille*, follows *Nobody's Boy* as a companion juvenile story, and takes place with it as one of the supreme juvenile stories of the world. Like *Nobody's Boy* it was also crowned by the Academy, and that literary judgment has also been verified by the test of time. *Nobody's Girl* is not a human document, such as is *Nobody's Boy*, because it has more story plot, and the adventure is in a more restricted field, but it discloses no less the nobility of a right-minded child, and how loyalty wins the way to noble deeds and life. This is another beautiful literary creation of Hector Malot which every one can recommend as an ennobling book, of interest not only to childhood, page by page to the thrilling conclusion, but to every person who loves romance and character. Only details irrelevant for readers in North America have been eliminated. Little Perrine's loyal ideals, with their inspiring sentiments, are preserved by her through the most discouraging conditions, and are described with the simplicity for which Hector Malot is famous. The building up of a little girl's life is made a fine example for every child. Every reader of this story leaves it inspired for the better way.

Subject: Fiction   Age: 10-99
ISBN 1-894666-76-3   US$14.95

Three Months Under the Snow by J. J. Porchat

This morning when I awoke, I found myself in complete darkness, and at first supposed that my sleep had quitted me at an earlier hour than usual. However, I heard my grandfather feeling his way about, and I rubbed my eyes, but did not see a bit better."Grandfather," said I, "you are up before daylight.""My dear boy," he answered, " if we were to wait for the light of day, we should remain long enough in bed. I fear the snow is above the window."At this I uttered a cry of horror and leaped out of bed. I soon lighted our lamp, and we were then able to perceive that my grandfather's conjecture was well-founded."But the window is low," he added, "besides, it may be that the snow has been heaped up in this part; perhaps we should not see it above two feet deep at some paces from the wall."

ISBN 978-1-894666-19-0 19th Century   US$9.90

No More Singing
by Norman Bomer
with colour illustrations
by G. Carol Bomer

No More Singing is a poignant allegory, beautifully told, that will move many children to an understanding that the aborting of our children is legal [according to the governing authorities]. As parents read this story to their children and explain the sad truth of abortion, conviction will grow in young hearts. As that conviction is strengthened and nurtured, it will draw us nearer to that day when protection is again restored to all children. — Curtis J. Young

Subject: Pro life   **Age: 10-99**
ISBN 0-88815-566-2   **US$5.95**

Songbooks & Compact Disc for Children

Sing About It by S. Van der Ploeg
21 Biblical Songs for Children

Francis M. Elliot in *The Christian Observer*: This well-made little book of music for children will be a nice change for the director of junior choirs or the Sabbath School teacher who thinks he will scream if he hears certain songs one more time. Everything in it is fresh and different.

Subject: Bible Songs   **Age: 5-12**
ISBN 0-921100-03-5   **US$7.95**

All Will Be New — 30 Bible songs
by Hanna Lam and Wim ter Burg

The Song of the Beginning; Creation Song; Noah; The Tower of Babel; The Song of Moses and Miriam; Jericho; David and Goliath; Jonah and the Great Fish; Daniel; Ten Bridesmaids; Zacchaeus; etc.

Subject: Bible Songs   **Age: 4-12**
ISBN 0-88815-592-1   **US$4.95**

Our Hymns of Praise A Children's Songbook

Our Hymns of Praise, a children's songbook formerly published by Herald Press, has been revised and reprinted and is now ready for your classroom. It is comprised of over 200 one, two, and three part children's hymns for grades 1-6, interspersed with over 50 illustrations that children have come to love.

Our Hymns of Praise   **US$15.00**
Teacher's Guide   **US$16.00**

Young Burning Hearts Series

The Young Burning Hearts Series
is a series of fascinating
independent stories
for young and old
of faithfulness in trying times.

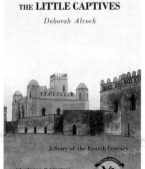

THE **LITTLE CAPTIVES**

Deborah Alcock

A Story of the Fourth Century

Inheritance Publications
Neerlandia, Alberta, Canada
Pella, Iowa, U.S.A.

The Little Captives by Deborah Alcock
A Story of the Fourth Century
The trembling little captives soon found themselves in the presence of the barbarian king. He sat on a raised seat, or throne, conspicuous among the dusky crowd that surrounded him by the rich adornments of his dress, and the staff, or sceptre, which he held in his hand.

Time: about AD 400   Age: 12-99
ISBN 978-1-77298-017-2   US$7.90

A Child's Victory by Deborah Alcock
A Story of the Twelfth Century
On a sultry summer's day, in the twelfth century, a little girl stood at a street door in one of the close, narrow alleys of a Flemish town. Her dress indicated poverty, though not neglect. Other children were playing near; she heard their voices, and looked at them for a few moments with curiosity and interest in her large blue eyes, but apparently with no wish to join their sports. Far more earnestly did she gaze to the right, where the long alley terminated in a broader street, from which a stream of intensely vivid sunlight poured, illuminating a corner of the shaded alley, with the Madonna in her niche, as well as the quaint carvings that adorned the house of rich Master Andreas the weaver. What would little Arlette have given to see one figure that she knew turn from the sunshine into the shadow!

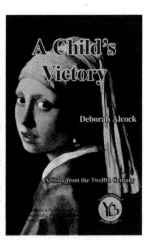

Time: 1100s   Age: 12-99
ISBN 978-1-928136-92-7   US$7.90

The Story of a Poor Scholar by Deborah Alcock
A Story about Germany and Bohemia

"Indeed?" said the old man, his face lighting up with sympathy and interest. "We have heard of the people who are called Brethren of the Unity, or United Brethren, and we own them as brethren indeed, in Christ Jesus our Lord — whose Gospel they knew and honoured, and whom they served and died for, many years before the voice of Dr. Martin Luther was heard in this Saxon land of ours."

"And we also," Wenzel responded, "we honour the name of your great teacher, Dr. Luther, whom God raised up to show His pure Evangel to the people of Germany, even as, one hundred years before, He sent us our dear and venerated Master John Huss. That is why I am going now to Wittenberg, to pursue my studies there."

Time: 1550s   **Age: 12-99**
ISBN 978-1-928136-96-5   **US$7.90**

The Martyr of Kolin by H.O. Ward
A Story of the Bohemian Persecution

When I reached home from afternoon school, I went up to a little upper chamber which Wilma and I had as our own, and there I found my sister — who was at the time a fair young maiden of thirteen — busy with her needle.

"Well, Sister," said I, "so we are to have another of these good gentlemen tonight."

"He has come," she said mysteriously.

"Has he? What is he like?" I asked.

"I have not seen him, for he is closeted with our father in his private chamber."

"Will he sup openly with us tonight?"

"Yes, I think so. Elspeth will keep a careful watch, and there is the door behind the tapestry, you know, in case of a surprise."

Time: 1560-1580   **Age: 12-99**
ISBN   978-1-928136-47-7   **US$12.90**

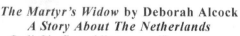

The Martyr's Widow by Deborah Alcock
A Story About The Netherlands

"Flee, Carl! Oh, flee while you can!"

"It is too late! Where should I flee to?"

Another loud impatient knock, and a sound of rough voices outside.

But a thought, sent as she believed from Heaven into her heart, inspired Lisa with sudden hope and courage. She seized her husband by the arm, and drew him toward the little closet, the door of which she had left open.

"There — in there — fear nothing — I will speak to them."

Time: 1570s   **Age: 12-99**
ISBN 978-1-77298-000-4   **US$7.90**

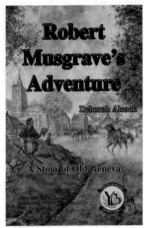

Robert Musgrave's Adventure
by Deborah Alcock
A Story of Old Geneva

"Josef . . . the servant, ye know," said Jeannot, "told us how the soldiers of Captain Brunaulieu's corps, as they came to a halt outside the town, found amongst them a boy who was evidently a Genevan. They seized him, and brought him to the Captain. He said he was an Englishman, which, I suppose, is another kind of heretic . . . oh, I crave pardon of your Worthinesses . . ."

"Never mind our Worthinesses, but go on with thy story," said someone.

"The Captain would have had him run through at once. But the holy Friar who was with them — Friar Alexander the Scotchman, they called him — bade spare him, as he might be of use in the town for a guide. 'Twas just then that Josef, who told us the tale, came up, being sent on a message . . ."

Time: 1602   Age: 12-99
ISBN 978-1-928136-32-3   US$8.90

Sunset in Provence by Deborah Alcock
A Tale of the Albigenses

"My lord, I am your sister's son but not your vassal," the youth replied with perhaps unnecessary pride. "But that is not the question," he added sadly and in a gentler tone. "You counsel me — no, you command me," and he bowed his head slightly at the word, "to submit myself unreservedly to our Holy Father the Pope, in the person of his Legate."

"I do, as you do value life and lands. If your retainers had not infected you with their heresy, why should you hesitate?"

"I — the son of Roger Taillefer — a heretic! None of our race were ever that, thank Heaven. But can the Count ask why I hesitate? Not that I fear the disgrace of a public penance, though I think they might have spared it to the greatest seigneur who speaks the 'Langue d'Oc', and altogether such a submissive and obedient Roman Catholic."

Time: 1200s   Age: 12-99
ISBN 978-1-928136-94-1   US$7.90

SUNSET IN PROVENCE

Deborah Alcock

A Tale of the Albigenses

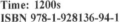

The Cloak in Pledge by Deborah Alcock
A Story About Russia

"If we only had something better for the little one," Ivan added, in a lower tone. "He can't eat that."

"Don't fret, Father," said Michael, a good-humoured lad on the whole. "I'll ask Master to give me a roll for him at dinner-time, and besides, there's Peter —" (the brother next in age, who had just got a place as one of the boy-postillions the wealthy Russians were so fond of having) — "Peter may come and see us, and bring us a kopeck or two for him."

Time: 1800s   Age: 12-99
ISBN 978-1-928136-95-8   US$7.90

138

Archie's Chances by Deborah Alcock
A Story of the Nineteenth Century

This was scarcely as bad as she expected, yet quite bad enough. She flushed hotly. "Uncle has not said anything to you, has he?" she asked.

"Never once. Kate, Uncle Morris is a brick!" There was a wealth of genuine gratitude flung into the boyish word that redeemed it from all trace of vulgarity.

"If Father were alive, what would he say?" questioned Kate. "I think he would be horrified at the very thought."

"Well, I don't know," mused Archie, thrusting his hands into his pockets. "After all, the horrible thing is eating the shop — I mean the bread that's made in it. And since I do that already, and can't help myself, I think it would not make things any worse to earn it before I eat it."

Time: 1880s Age: 12-99
ISBN 978-1-894666-16-9 US$8.90

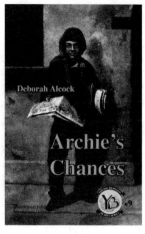

Truth Stranger Than Fiction by Deborah Alcock
The King of Hungary's Blacksmith
and other Stories

"Well, Master Jailer, how goes it? Have you heard anything?" asked the young man in an eager whisper.

The jailer laid his hand compassionately on his shoulder. "Heavy tidings for thee, poor lad," he said. "He will likely die."

The answer was a deep groan, heard distinctly through all the uproar of the crowded room. Then silence; then a broken murmur, "Poor Maida — poor baby!" choked by something very like the suppressed sob of a strong man.

Time: 1570s Age: 12-99
ISBN 978-1-77298-001-1 US$7.90

Etchings from History by Deborah Alcock
Illustrating the Proverbs of Solomon

After a brief though brilliant career (in which he rendered important political services to the cause of Protestantism), Maurice was killed in the battle of Sievershausen, in his thirty-second year. He had enjoyed his electorate about five years. His brother succeeded him, for his only son had died before him. One little daughter, Anna, survived him. She was afterward married, with great pomp and show, to the celebrated William the Silent, Prince of Orange.

Time: 1570s Age: 12-99
ISBN 978-1-928136-97-2 US$7.90

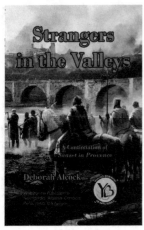

Strangers in the Valleys by Deborah Alcock
A Continuation of Sunset in Provence

"Listen! Someone knocks."

Henri sprang to the door, and hastily unbarred it. A young man, whose fur coat was covered with snow, entered immediately, bringing a current of cold air and a stream of water into the comfortable room.

"You here, Christophe!" cried the pastor, recognizing a member of his flock who lived at a considerable distance. "What errand has brought you so far on such a night?"

"An ill one, Barbe," said the young man. "My poor mother — God help her! — lies since morning speechless, and as far as I can see, at the point of death."

It must be remembered that the barbe was by his calling a physician for the body as well as for the soul. It was not necessary, therefore, for the young peasant even to express a desire that he should accompany him. Without a moment's delay he rose to prepare for the expedition. It was a difficult, toilsome, and even dangerous one. A walk of seven miles at night, and in a snow-storm . . .

Time: 1200s **Age: 12-99**
ISBN 978-1-77298-026-4 **US$9.90**

YBH13 The First Campaign of Arnold Viersen by Ronald Van Reest

"It sure feels good," said Arnold, "driving an old car to start my first campaign. That's how many politicians have done it.""Indeed," said Ronald, thinking of a story about the well-known preacher, Robert Schuller of Crystal Cathedral in California. Apparently, Rev. Schuller and his wife had begun their ministry, travelling in an old Volkswagenbus. They would park it at a street corner and he preached from the roof of the bus. Rev. Schuller was not known for orthodoxy, but his humble beginnings were certainly worthy of admiration. "So this is your first campaign trip?""Yes, apart from going door to door. I have signed up more than two hundred people locally. But several hundred more will be needed in order to win the nomination. Tony Van Pater said that if he had had three hundred more supporters, he would have won his nomination."

Time: 2015 Age: 12-99
ISBN 978-1-77298-034-9 US$7.90

Israel's Hope and Expectation by Rudolf Van Reest

G. Nederveen in *Clarion*: This is one of the best novels I have read of late. I found it captivating and hard to put down. Here is a book that is not time-bound and therefore it will never be outdated.

The story takes place around the time of Jesus' birth. It is written by someone who has done his research about the times between the Old and New Testament period. The author informs you in an easy style about the period of the Maccabees. . . Van Reest is a good storyteller. His love for the Bible and biblical times is evident from the start. He shows a good knowledge of the customs and mannerisms in Israel. Many fine details add to the quality of the book. You will be enriched in your understanding of the ways in the Old Testament.

Time: Inter-Testament Period   Age: 15-99
ISBN 0-921100-22-1   US$19.95

Twice Freed by Patricia St. John

Onesimus is a slave. From early morning until last thing at night he belongs to someone else and has no control over any area of his life. But just for one hour when the sun is at it's highest and everybody else is asleep — Onesimus is free. In the blistering, mid-day sun he climbs the high canyons and escapes his master's rule for a while.

Subject: Fiction   Age: 10-99
ISBN 1-857-92489-4   US$11.99

Quintus by R. Weerstand
A Story About the
Persecution of Christians
at the Time of Emperor Nero

The history of the Church in A.D. 64 is written with blood and tears. This book, based on historical facts, relates what happened in Rome in the summer of that year. It is a gripping chronicle. In the story we meet Quintus, the central character. He is a typical Roman boy, who through a number of ordeals experiences the grace of God.

Time: A.D. 64   Age: 12-99
ISBN 1-894666-70-4   US$10.95

Against the World - The Odyssey of Athanasius by Henry W. Coray

Muriel R. Lippencott in *The Christian Observer*: [it] . . . is a partially fictionalized profile of the life of Athanasius . . . who died in A.D. 373. Much of the historical content is from the writing of reliable historians. Some parts of the book, while the product of the author's imagination, set forth accurately the spirit and the temper of the times, including the proceedings and vigorous debates that took place in Alexandria and Nicea. . . This is the story that Rev. Coray so brilliantly tells.

Time: A.D. 331-373   Age: 16-99
ISBN 0-921100-35-3   US$9.95

RT01 *Hubert Ellerdale* by W. Oak Rhind
A Tale of the Days of Wycliffe

Christine Farenhorst in *Christian Renewal*: Christians often tend to look on the Reformation as the pivotal turning point in history during which the Protestants took off the chains of Rome. This small work of fiction draws back the curtains of history a bit further than Luther's theses. Wycliffe was the morning star of the Reformation and his band of Lollards a band of faithful men who were persecuted because they spoke out against salvation by works. Hubert Ellerdale was such a man and his life (youth, marriage, and death), albeit fiction, is set parallel to Wycliffe's and Purvey's. Rhind writes with pathos and the reader can readily identify with his lead characters. This novel deserves a well-dusted place in a home, school, or church library.

Time: 1380-1420	Age: 13-99
ISBN 0-921100-09-4	US$12.95

RT02 *Crushed Yet Conquering*
by Deborah Alcock
A Story of Constance and Bohemia

A gripping story filled with accurate historical facts about John Huss and the Hussite wars. **Hardly any historical novel can be more captivating and edifying than this book.** Even if Deborah Alcock was not the greatest of nineteenth century authors, certainly she is our most favourite.
— Roelof & Theresa Janssen

Time: 1414-1436	Age: 11-99
ISBN 1-894666-01-1	US$19.95

RT03 *The Roman Students* by Deborah Alcock
A Tale of the Renaissance

Raymond felt the force of the last argument. Besides, he could not contend the point; his schoolfellow had him in his power. A little water

from the crystal flask that lay on the table, a fine white kerchief from the looms of Cambray, and a pair of gentle, firm, skilful hands soon accomplished the task. Theodore's words sometimes missed their aim, and hurt where they meant to heal, his fingers never. Their very form — long, slender, sensitive — evidenced at once fineness of perception and exquisite dexterity.

Meanwhile the schoolfellows talked of the unfair and dastardly conduct of the Nicoloti, and formed plans of revenge. What they said was commonplace enough, but they speedily established a friendly understanding with each other.

"I had not known you were destined to be a physician," said Raymond. "Is not that to sacrifice your genius and your learning?"

Time: 1440s	Age: 15-99
ISBN 978-1-928136-93-4	US$17.90

142

RT04 *The Romance of Protestantism*
by Deborah Alcock

A wonderfully warm and loving book about the beauty of Protestantism. This topic, too often neglected and forgotten, has been revived by the author in a delightful way. Glimpses of our Protestant history are strewn in our path like jewels, whetting our appetite to read on and discover the depth of our history. Too often our role models tend to be found outside of our Christian heritage "to the neglect of the great cloud of witnesses, the magnificent roll of saints, heroes, and martyrs that belong to us as Protestants." This book is not only for adults. Young people and even older children will find riches in its depth which will encourage and build up to carry on the work of God in our own day and age.
— Theresa E. Janssen, home educating mother

Time: 1300-1700	**Age: 12-99**
ISBN 0-921100-88-4	**US$12.95**

RT05 *The Prior's Tithe* by Deborah Alcock
A Tale of the Scottish Reformation

David Stratton stood long at the lancet window — how long he never knew. Strange new thoughts filled his mind, and for the first time for weeks even the Prior of St. Andrews and the Vicar of Ecclescreig were forgotten. For he did not, as might be imagined, amuse and gratify himself by applying the fiery denunciations he had just heard to these his personal enemies. They had indeed impressed and delighted him at the time; but what he afterwards heard almost swept them from his memory. Unaccustomed to abstract thought, though full of practical shrewdness, a mere exposition of doctrine would perhaps hardly have left a clearer impression on him, when delivered in his native tongue, than if it had been couched in Latin; but his mind was quick to grasp and strong to retain the circumstances of a story. Nor did he only retain them passively: he was accustomed to reflect, after a fashion, upon his own doings and those of other men; and to his imagination, the blind man of the gospel was as real, and not more distant, than if he had lived or was living then in Edinburgh or St. Andrews.

Time: 1534	**Age: 14-99**
ISBN 978-1-77298-025-7	**US$9.90**

RT06 *The Dark Year of Dundee*
by Deborah Alcock
An Other Tale of the Scottish Reformation

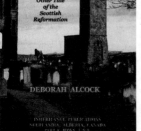

So passed the men of Dundee, in the summer months of that terrible year, step by step from vague apprehension to vivid, actual terror; as the pestilence that walketh in darkness first struck down one, and another, and another; then gradually multiplied its victims until the voice of lamentation filled the city, and no man felt his own life safe from the destroyer for a single hour.

Not very long after the first appearance of the pestilence, Archie Duncan came back one morning in high glee from the grammar-school, to which he had been despatched by the careful Janet only half an hour before.

"Nae mair schule," he cried, flinging his book on the table; "maister's awa', for fear o' the sickness; — and may guid gang wi' him!"

Time: 1544-1546	**Age: 14-99**
ISBN 978-1-894666-08-4	**US$10.90**

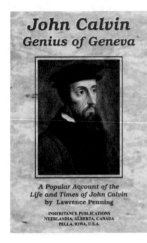

John Calvin
Genius of Geneva

A Popular Account of the
Life and Times of John Calvin
by Lawrence Penning

INHERITANCE PUBLICATIONS
NEERLANDIA, ALBERTA, CANADA
PELLA, IOWA, U.S.A.

RT07 *John Calvin: Genius of Geneva* by Lawrence Penning

A Popular Account of the Life and Times of John Calvin

The publishing of this book is a direct fruit of the reading and publishing of *Under Calvin's Spell* by Deborah Alcock which is a great novel and gives a very good description of life in and around Geneva. However it tells little about Calvin himself. As a result I read Penning's book and was quickly convinced that both books should be published as companion editions, Alcock's book being the introduction and Penning's book the "full" story. Also today the world needs to know it's most important historical facts and since upon the mouth of two witnesses the truth of a matter is to be established we send out in these two books the true story of John Calvin.

Calvin is perhaps the most important person who lived after Biblical times (seconded by Martin Luther, William of Orange, Michael de Ruyter, and William III of Orange). To know and understand how the Lord has used these people in the history of His Church and world will stir in any reader the desire to follow them in their footsteps. — Roelof A. Janssen

Time: 1509-1564   Age:15-99
ISBN 1-894666-77-1   US$19.95

RT08 *Under Calvin's Spell* by Deborah Alcock

A Tale of theHeroic Times in Old Geneva

They had now reached the Forte Neuve, by which they entered the town, with many others who were returning from the Plain-palais. As they walked along the Corratorie they met Berthelier and Gabrielle, taking the air, as the afternoon was very fine for the season of the year. Both the lads saluted; De Marsac with a flush and a beaming smile.

"I did not know you knew them," said Norbert.

"Oh yes; did I not tell you I was going to see them? Master Berthelier's sister, Damoiselle Claudine, and I are fast friends. Some years ago when I came here first, a mere child, I was one day in the market, looking about me and buying cherries or the like, when I saw this poor damoiselle being frightened half out of her senses by a group of angry, scolding fish-women. That was before such good order was put in the market, and in all the town, thanks to Master Calvin. She had told them, quite truly, that they were trying to cheat her. I fought her battle with all my might, which in truth was not great, and at last brought her home in triumph. She was much more grateful than the occasion required, and has been my very good friend ever since. I — they — they are all good to me, though lately, being much occupied with my studies, I have seen them but seldom."

"Do you not think the young damoiselle very pretty?" asked Norbert. "I do."

"She is beautiful," Louis answered quietly; and the subject dropped.

Time: 1542-1564   Age:14-99
ISBN 1-894666-04-6   US$14.95

144

RT09 *Prisoners of Hope* by Deborah Alcock
A Story of the Faith

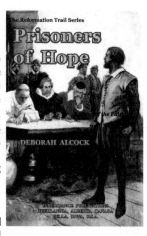

"Not my sister," interposed Will.

"I thought her your sister — but no matter. It makes no difference. You will take my message all the same. Have a care of the lantern, Boy; you will let it fall. Look! The light is out. Well, no harm is done; we will soon be at the clearing now, and in full daylight. I was saying — if you love me, Will, and that I am sure you do — say to Maria that the word we spoke to one another lies ever between us, and God heard it."

Will was silent from amazement, perhaps from something else.

"Do you hear me, Friend?" asked Bilek.

"Yes, I hear," faltered Will.

He felt as if a great stone had fallen on him and crushed him. In his pain he said a thing which perhaps, under all the circumstances, was not wise or generous.

Time: 1548-1562	Age: 14-99
ISBN 978-1-894666-07-7	US$ 9.90

RT10 *The Spanish Brothers* by Deborah Alcock
A Tale of the Sixteenth Century

"He could not die thus for his faith. On the contrary, it cost him but little to conceal it. What, then, had they which he had not? Something that enabled even poor, wild, passionate Gonsalvo to forgive and pray for the murderers of the woman he loved. What was it?"

Time: 1550-1565	Age: 14-99
ISBN 1-894666-02-x	US$14.95

RT11 *Under the Inquisition* by Elizabeth H. Walshe
A Story of the Reformation in Italy

"You have forgotten that you should confess Christ's Name; and do you not remember, O deluded people, that whoever confesses not Christ upon earth, shall be denied by Him before His Father and the holy angels? Certainly you are not alone in this backsliding. There may be some in our valleys of the Alps who carry with them certificates that they are genuine papists, and have their children baptized by priests with all the mummeries of superstition, yes, and go to the so-called sacrifice of the mass, openly bowing the knee to Baal, that they may be seen of men; and they excuse themselves — verily a fancied excuse! — by saying secretly when they enter the mass house, 'Cave of robbers, may God confound you!' I have heard that similar practices extend even here. My brothers, such duplicity is intolerable to the righteous Lord. Do you think that He will not protect the men who range themselves under His banner against Antichrist, in the face of all the world? . . ."

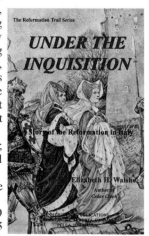

Sobs and moans came from that excitable southern audience; glowing eyes, betokening glowing hearts, met the youthful preacher's every look.

. . . Thus Paschali enunciated the principles which were to guide his ministry.

Time 1554-1563	Age: 14-99
ISBN 978-1-894666-30-5	US$17.95

RT12 *Coronation of Glory* **by Deborah Meroff**
The true story of seventeen-year-old Lady Jane
Grey, Queen of England for nine days.

"Miss Meroff . . . has fictionalized the story of Lady Jane Grey in a thoroughly absorbing manner . . . she has succeeded in making me believe this is what really happened. I kept wanting to read on — the book is full of action and interest."
— Elisabeth Elliot

Time: 1537-1554   Age: 14-99
ISBN 0-921100-78-7   US$17.90

[Note from Inheritance Publications: This book, originally published by Zondervan in 1979, was well received on our visits to schools and churches in the 1980s. Several people had told us that Canadians were not interested in history. And so we used Coronation of Glory and This Was John Calvin by Thea Van Halsema to discover whether this rumour was correct. We thankfully report that it was proven wrong. We sold many copies of the above mentioned books to the great satisfaction of our customers. Since then we began publishing books on our own. God blessed our efforts so that we could publish e.g. the William & Mary Trilogy. It is now our pleasure to again reprint Coronation of Glory.]

RT13 *Doctor Adrian* **by Deborah Alcock**
A Story of Old Holland

Doctor Adrian was a scholar living in quiet seclusion in Antwerp, the Netherlands, until a fugitive Protestant preacher and his daughter Rose sought sanctuary in his rooms. Before he knew it, he became involved with the Protestant cause, and eventually embraced it in theory. When the persecution of the Reformed was stepped up, Doctor Adrian made the dangerous journey to Leyden with his family. They survived the siege of Leyden, along with Adrian's sister Marie. When the siege was lifted by the fleets of William of Orange, they moved to Utrecht. Doctor Adrian's faith in the Reformed religion died when he experienced the loss of some of his loved ones, but a new faith in the Author of that religion took its place.

This is a tale of a doctor and his contact with William, Prince of Orange, and of his spiritual journey.

Time: 1560-1584   Age: 12-99
ISBN 1-894666-05-4   US$15.95

RT14 *Arthur Erskine's Story* **by Deborah Alcock**
A Tale of the Days of Knox

Near the seat she had chosen, beside the window, were the two things that she loved best in the world, and would have found the greatest difficulty in doing without. There stood her embroidery-frame, with a very elaborate piece of work half- finished upon it. During the last few days, this work had necessarily given place to the higher duty of loving ministrations to the dying. But she was bound to complete it within a certain time, and therefore gladly took advantage of the first available moment to return to it. Something else, much more truly and deeply loved, lay on a small table near. It was a moderate-sized book, strongly bound in dark brown leather. Had you opened it, you would have found the Old and New Testaments in the French tongue, and matter enough besides, compressed into a narrow space, to have furnished a small but very useful theological library. There were references, indices, tables of contents, historical summaries.

Time: 1560-1590   Age: 14-99
ISBN 978-1-894666-09-1   US$25.90

RT15 *Not for Crown or Scepter* by Deborah Alcock
A Story of Sweden in the 16th Century

Pastor Sten Nilson, a tall, noble-looking man, stood up to welcome his brother, with a smile on his lips and a glad light in his frank blue eyes. But the next moment he drew back disappointed, and even a little annoyed; for "mine host" was ushering in a stranger, an elderly man in a fur coat, holding by the hand a little boy about seven . . .
[The boy asked] with a half timid, half confiding air, "What book is that?"
Surprised at the question from so young a child, the Pastor answered, "It is the Red Book, my son."
The boy looked up indignantly, all his shyness gone. " 'Tis not red," he said, " 'tis brown, nearly black. I thought pastors always spoke the truth."
ISBN 978-1-928136-28-6   US$25.90

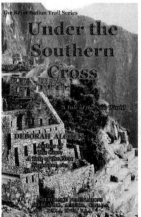

RT16 *Under the Southern Cross* by Deborah Alcock
A Tale of the New World

"A good ending to your story," said the monk, smiling. "It is not quite the end," José answered. "The Auqui came in triumph to the place where his father was. Then the old Inca took from his head the llautu — the sacred crimson fringe — and the black and white wing-feathers of the coraquenque, and he put them on the head of the brave young Auqui; and he bade his captains bear him aloft in the golden chair, and salute him as mighty Inca, Child of the Sun, Friend of the Poor. From then on the Auqui reigned gloriously. He took to himself the name of the bright spirit that appeared to him on the plains of Chita — Viracocha, 'foam of the sea.' He built a beautiful temple in his honour. The work was long, and took many years to finish; but he saw it finished, for he reigned until his hair was white as the snow of the Andes."
ISBN 978-1-894666-14-5   US$21.90

RT17 *The Days of Prince Maurits* by Mary O. Nutting (Mary Barrett)
The Story of the Netherland War from the Death of William the Silent
to its Close 1584-1648

The period during which Maurits of Nassau was the leader of the Netherland people is one which claims attention, not only on account of its exciting and memorable events, but even more because of its intimate connection with the subsequent history of England and of America. The writer has aimed to tell the story so that it shall be neither too long to be easily read, nor so condensed as to seem dry.

Among the works most consulted have been those of Motley, Davies, and Grattan, together with Rogers' "Story of Holland" and Markham's "The Fighting Veres." Some original authorities also have been used, particularly Meteren's "History of the Low Countries," and "Les Lauriers de Nassau," by Orlers and Haestens, a very rare book published at Leyden in 1612, which narrates the victories won while Prince Maurits was commander-in-chief. It is illustrated with many careful representations of battles and sieges, and gives an excellent portrait of the prince, which is reproduced here.
Time: 1584-1648   Age: 13-99
ISBN 978-1-928136-91-0   US$25.90

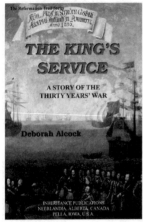

RT18 *The King's Service* by Deborah Alcock
A Story of the Thirty Years' War

Once again Deborah Alcock has delicately woven together an accurate historical novel. This book gives wonderful insights into some of the events surrounding the thirty-years-war in which Gustavus Adolphus of Sweden gives his life for the Protestant cause.

Two motherless children, Jeanie and Hugh, have been in the care of their Uncle Charlie ever since their father left about eight years earlier to fight for the Protestant cause. Uncle Charlie, a restless bachelor, subsequently leaves the bulk of Jeanie and Hugh's upbringing to the Presbyterian minister. He faithfully teaches these orphaned children the beautiful tenets of the Reformed faith. But when Uncle Charlie decides to leave his beloved Scotland to join the army of Gustavus Adolphus in Germany, Hugh wants to go along. Jeanie will go along as companion to Captain Stuart's wife and meets Fraulein Gertrud von Savelburg in Germany. Sifting through the reports and rumours of the times she comes to some disturbing and perplexing conclusions. What has made Uncle Charlie so sad, and why does a Roman Catholic priest regularly visit Hugh?

Time: 1630-1632   Age: 12-99
ISBN 978-1-894666-06-0   US$11.95

RT19 *Martin Luther - The Man and His Work*
by Arthur Cushman McGiffert

Luther's marriage raised a great hue and cry. The union of a renegade monk with an escaped nun, violating as it did their own personal vows, and ecclesiastical and civil law as well, seemed to many to throw a sinister light upon the whole reform movement. Now, they declared, the significance of the Reformation was revealed to all the world, and it was clear what Luther had had in mind from the beginning. Satirical attacks appeared in great numbers. Slanderous tales were spread about him and his bride. Even many of his friends were thrown into consternation, and feared he had dealt a death-blow to the cause.

Time: 1483-1546   Age: 16-99
ISBN 978-1-77298-018-9   US$19.90

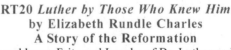

RT20 *Luther by Those Who Knew Him*
by Elizabeth Rundle Charles
A Story of the Reformation

Hours and hours Fritz and I spoke of Dr. Luther and what he had done for us both — more, perhaps, for Fritz than even for me, because he had suffered more. It seems to me as if we, and thousands besides in the world, had been worshipping before an altar picture of our Saviour, which we had been told was painted by a great master after a heavenly pattern. But all we could see was a grim, hard, stern countenance of one sitting on a judgment throne . . . Then suddenly we heard Dr. Luther's voice behind us, saying, in his ringing tones — "Friends, what are you doing? That is not the right painting. These are only the boards that hide the master's picture."

Time: 1483-1546   Age: 14-99
ISBN 978-1-77298-019-6   US$19.90

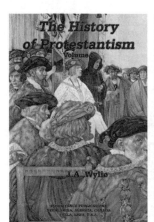

The History of Protestantism
by J.A. Wylie
With hundreds of Original Classic Illustrations

The History of Protestantism is no mere history of dogmas. The teachings of Christ are the seeds; the modern Christendom, with its new life, is the good tree which has sprung from it. The author tells of the seed and also of the tree, small at first, still growing, and destined one day to cover the earth.

How that seed was deposited in the soil; how the tree grew up and flourished despite the furious tempests that warred around it; how, century after century, it lifted its top higher in heaven, and spread its boughs wider around, sheltering liberty, nursing letters, fostering art, and gathering a fraternity of prosperous and powerful nations around it. The author writes that the History of Protestantism is the record of one of the grandest dramas of all time.

It is true, no doubt, that Protestantism, strictly viewed, is simply a principle. It is not a policy. It is not an empire, having its fleets and armies, its officers and tribunals, wherewith to extend its dominion and make its authority be obeyed. It is not even a Church with its hierarchies, and synods and edicts; it is simply a principle. But it is the greatest of all principles. It is a creative power. Its plastic influence is all-embracing. It penetrates into the heart and renews the individual. It goes down to the depths and, by its omnipotent but noiseless energy, vivifies and regenerates society. It thus becomes the creator of all that is true, and lovely, and great; the founder of free kingdoms, and the mother of faithful churches. The globe itself it claims as a stage not too wide for the manifestation of its beneficent action; and the whole domain of terrestrial affairs it deems a sphere not too vast to fill with its spirit, and rule by its law.

—Adapted from the first chapter

Vol. 1 ISBN 978-1-77298-020-2   US$48.90
Vol. 2 ISBN 978-1-77298-021-9   US$48.90
Vol. 3 ISBN 978-1-77298-022-6   US$48.90

Set of Three Large Hardbound Volumes US$124.90

IN INDIVIDUAL BOOKS

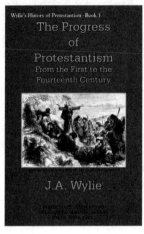

WHP 1 *The Progress from the First to the Fourteenth Century* by J.A. Wylie

In A.D. 653, a deacon returning from captivity in Syria rested a night in the house of an Armenian named Constantine, who lived in the neighbourhood of Samosata. On the morrow, before taking his departure, he presented his host with a copy of the New Testament. Constantine studied the sacred volume. A new light broke upon his mind: the errors of the Greek Church stood clearly revealed, and he instantly resolved to separate himself from so corrupt a communion. He drew others to the study of the Scriptures, and the same light shone into their minds which had irradiated his. Sharing his views, they shared with him his secession from the established Church of the Empire. It was the boast of this new party, now grown to considerable numbers, that they adhered to the Scriptures, and especially to the writings of Paul. "I am Sylvanus," said Constantine, "and you are Macedonians," intimating thereby that the Gospel which he would teach, and they should learn, was that of Paul; hence the name of Paulicians, a designation they would not have been ambitious to wear had their doctrine been Manichean.

Time: AD33-1300   Age: 13-99
ISBN 978-1-77298-038-7   US$18.90

WHP 2 *Wycliffe and His Times* by J.A. Wylie

England is the first of the European communities to flee from that prison-house in which the Crowned Priest of the Seven Hills had shut up the nations. That cruel taskmaster had decreed an utter and eternal extinction of all national independence and of all human rights. But He who "opens the eyes of the blind," and "raises them that are bowed down," had pity on those whom

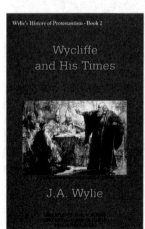

their oppressor had destined to endless captivity, and opened their prison-doors. We celebrate in songs the Exodus of early times. We magnify the might of that Hand and the strength of that Arm which broke the power of Pharaoh; which "opened the gates of brass, and cut the bars of iron in sunder;" which divided the sea, and led the marshalled hosts of the Hebrews out of bondage. Here is the reality of which the other was but the figure. England comes forth, the first of the nations, led on by Wycliffe, and giving assurance to the world by her reappearance that all the captive nationalities which have shared her bondage shall, each in its appointed season, share her deliverance.

Time: AD1324-1384   Age: 13-99
ISBN 978-1-77298-039-4   US$19.90

WHP 3 *John Huss and the Hussite War* by J.A. Wylie

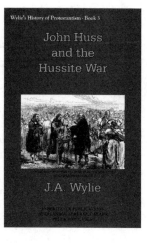

It is the year 1413. Sigismund — a name destined to go down to posterity along with that of Huss, though not with like fame — had a little before mounted the throne of the Empire. Wherever he cast his eyes the new emperor saw only spectacles that distressed him. Christendom was afflicted with a grievous schism. There, were three Popes, whose personal profligacies and official crimes were the scandal of that Christianity of which each claimed to be the chief teacher, and the scourge of that Church of which each claimed to be the supreme pastor. The most sacred things were put up to sale, and were the subject of simoniacal bargaining. The bonds of charity were disrupted, and nation was going to war with nation; everywhere strife raged and blood was flowing. The Poles and the knights of the Teutonic order were waging a war which raged only with the greater fury inasmuch as religion was its pretext. Bohemia seemed on the point of being rent in pieces by intestine commotions; Germany was convulsed; Italy had as many tyrants as princes; France was distracted by its factions, and Spain was embroiled by the machinations of Benedict XIII, whose pretensions that country had espoused. To complete the confusion the Mussulman hordes, encouraged by these dissensions, were gathering on the frontier of Europe and threatening to break in and repress all disorders, in a common subjugation of Christendom to the yoke of the Prophet.

Time: AD863-1471   Age: 13-99
ISBN 978-1-77298-040-0   US$21.90

WHP 4 *Christendom at the Opening of the Sixteenth Century* by J.A. Wylie

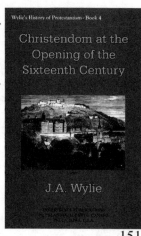

The monarch of Spain, though master of so much, was laying schemes for extending the limits of his already overgrown dominions, and making himself absolute and universal lord. Since the noon of the Roman power, the liberties of the world had at no time been in so great peril as now. The shadow of a universal despotism was persistently projecting itself farther and yet farther upon the kingdoms and peoples of Western Europe. There was no principle known to the men of that age that seemed capable of doing battle with this colossus, and staying its advance. This despotism, into whose hands as it seemed the nations of Christendom had been delivered, claimed a Divine right . . . .

Time: AD364-1500   Age: 13-99
ISBN 978-1-77298-041-7   US$8.90

WYLIE'S HISTORY OF PROTESTANTISM

IN INDIVIDUAL BOOKS

All 24 books of

WYLIE'S HISTORY OF PROTESTANTISM
are already available in the Three Volume Series on page 149!

Thomas Skyler: Foothills Preacher by Ralph Connor

Another compelling tale of the Canadian West in the late 19th century by Ralph Connor. Meet Bronco Bill . . . Hi Kendal . . . the Duke . . . the Old Timer . . . and of course Gwen . . . and discover why the impact of "the Sky Pilot" was far different than any would have expected.

Subject: Fiction	Age: 12-99
ISBN 0-940652-07-2	US$9.99

Jim Craig's Battle for Black Rock by Ralph Connor

The moving drama of life in a rough 1880s mining town and lumber community. A compelling tale of the Canadian West in the late 19th century by one of Canada's most popular authors of the beginning of the 20th century (the author was a Presbyterian minister/missionary who has been there!).

Subject: Fiction	Age: 12-99
ISBN 0-940652-06-4	US$12.99

St. Elmo by Augusta Jane Evans

The third most popular novel of the 19th and early 20th centuries, *St. Elmo* captivated millions of readers and generations of schoolgirls but lost popularity as Americans strayed toward the 1960s. Nowadays readers keep telling us that once started, nothing else gets done until they reach the end. Hundreds of grateful readers wrote Miss Evans that the book led them to see their need for salvation. Few books are both sensational and Christian; Augusta Jane Evans succeeded on both counts. Ideal as gifts to daughters and mothers.

Subject: Fiction	Age: 13-99
ISBN 0-9661426-0-8	US$17.90

Winterflight A novel by Joseph Bayly

A disturbing, unsettling vision (some would call it nightmare) of the future. A chilling story that will rivet your interest, leave you with questions about moral and political trends in American life today.

Time: Future	Age: 18-99
ISBN 0-8499-0297-5	US$8.95

Least of All Saints by Grace Irwin

In this novel Grace Irwin has brought into vital focus the kind of religious conflict that anyone concerned with both reason and faith cannot long avoid. Her main concern is with a human being — Andrew Connington — and the human problem — belief and unbelief. "Perhaps the most outstanding Christian novel I have read," wrote Dr. Frank E. Gaebelein.

Subject: Fiction	Age: 14-99
ISBN 0-8028-6015-X	US$11.95

Tales & Tellings by Paulina M. Rustenburg-Bootsma

J. Tangelder in *Christian Renewal*: This book begins with the story of Polle and Henderkien Eijsinga, great-grandparents of the author. The author also tells about her own experiences growing up in a new country, the people she came to know, as well as the tales and happenings she heard or read about. Each story is inspirational and Christ-centered and shows how God guides and sustains His people in times of joy, dangers, and sorrow. The poems which precede each chapter show the work of a God-fearing craftsman. A welcome addition to one's personal or church library.

Time: 1870 - 1997	Age: 11-99
IP0000005790	US$12.95

153

Prince and Heretic
by Marjorie Bowen
A Novel on William the Silent vol. 1

"The mind and the soul are not in the keeping of king nor priest — no man has a lordship over another man's conscience. All history has proved that." —William of Orange

Here is a fascinating historical novel for teenagers and adults about one of the greatest heroes of all time. William of Orange, considered today the father of Europe (and who can also fittingly be called the step-father of North America and the whole free western world) sets the stage as stadtholder of the Roman Catholic King of Spain, Philip II. William, though a nominal Roman Catholic at the time, determines to help the persecuted Protestants and in the process marries the Protestant Princess Anne of Saxony. But will Anne truly be a helpmeet for her husband? When he is pressed to take up the sword against King Philip he does not hesitate. In his struggles, William not only finds the God of his mother but grows in courage and the conviction that God has chosen him to be a faithful instrument to gain freedom for Christ's Church. William sacrifices all his possessions to pay the hired soldiers, but is it of any use? His brothers, Lodewyk, John, Adolphus, and Henry, also give all they have for the cause of freedom of a country which can hardly be called their own. Behind these heroes, a faithful praying mother, Juliana of Stolberg, waits for news at the German castle of Dillenburg.

Time: 1560-1568   Age: 13-99
ISBN 978-0-921100-56-0   US$17.95

William by the Grace of God
by Marjorie Bowen
A Novel on William the Silent vol. 2

The sequel to *Prince and Heretic*, by Marjorie Bowen.

King Philip II of Spain is prepared to make any concession to the lowlands, except freedom of conscience and worship and thus William of Orange continues in the struggle for true liberty. More important noblemen and personal friends

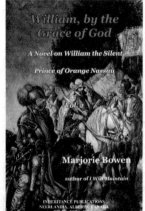

sacrifice their lives, leaving few of William's original friends alive. But Charlotte de Bourbon is ready to encourage her hero despite all the crises he must endure. When Leyden is under siege William becomes ill. Will the cause have to be given up?

King Philip, in the meantime, is furious because he cannot get rid of William. Everyone on his black list is dead but not the most important one: William of Orange. In a fury he writes the Ban and publishes it abroad. With this permission to dispose of his enemy in any way, the King is sure someone will kill William for him. After all, they will receive a great reward: a high position and name, wealth, fame . . . Will King Philip's plan succeed?

Time: 1569-1584   Age: 13-99
ISBN 978-0-921100-57-7   US$17.95

This Was John Calvin by Thea Van Halsema

Roger Nicole: "The most lively and readable biography of Calvin available in English."

J.H. Kromminga: "Though it reads as smoothly as a well written novel, it is crammed with important facts. It is scholarly and popular at the same time. The book will hold the interest of the young but will also bring new information to the well informed. . . . This book recognizes the true greatness of the man without falling into distortions of the truth to protect that greatness."

This Was John Calvin has been translated into Spanish, Portuguese, Korean, Chinese, Indonesian, and Japanese. This is its fifth printing in English.

Time:1509-1564   Age: 12-99
ISBN 978-1-894666-90-9   US$11.95

Thea B. Van Halsema
INHERITANCE PUBLICATIONS
NEERLANDIA, ALBERTA, CANADA
PELLA, IOWA, U.S.A.

Thea B. Van Halsema

Three Men Came to Heidelberg &
Glorious Heretic: the Story
of Guido de Brès

by Thea Van Halsema

From the sixteenth-century Protestant Reformation came two outstanding statements of faith: The Heidelberg Catechism (1563) and the Belgic Confession (1561). The stories behind these two historic documents are in this small book.

Time: 1556-1587   Age: 12-99
ISBN 978-1-894666-89-3   US$9.95

Trust God, Keep the Faith
by Bartha Hill - de Bres

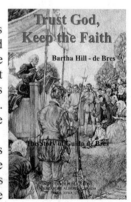

During the late sixteenth century the Reformation was sweeping across Europe. As the Bible became a loved book by the common man, many people questioned the beliefs and practices of the Roman Catholic Church at the perils of their lives. By torture and cruel deaths the priests attempted to return these "rebels" to the church. In the midst of this battle Guido de Bres lived as he died — trusting God and keeping the faith.

Nearly five hundred years have passed since he was born, but the confession of faith written by Guido de Bres — a wonderful summary of God's Word — continues to live on in the lives of Reformed people around the world.

This book, written by one of his descendants, is about Guido de Bres. It describes the time in which he lived, and the confession of faith God allowed him to write.

Though intended for older children it also will be enjoyed by adults.

Time: 1522-1567   Age: 12-99
ISBN 978-0-921100-10-2   US$9.95

Love in Times of Reformation
by William P. Balkenende

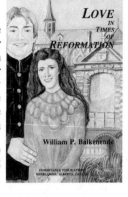

N.N. in *The Trumpet*: This historical novel plays in The Netherlands during the rise of the protestant Churches, under the persecution of Spain, in the latter half of the sixteenth century. Breaking with the Roman Catholic Church in favor of the new faith is for many an intense struggle. Anthony Tharret, the baker's apprentice, faces his choice before the R.C. Church's influenced Baker's Guild. His love for Jeanne la Solitude, the French Huguenot refugee, gives a fresh dimension to the story. Recommended! Especially for young people.

Time: 1560-1585   Age: 14-99
ISBN 0-921100-32-9   US$8.95

The TowerClock Stopped
by J. DeHaan
A Story during the time of the Reformation

An amazingly true story about a surprise attack by the Spanish army on Sluis, a small city in a southern coastal province of The Low Countries, now known as The Netherlands. The Dutch fought for their freedom from Spain in an eighty-year war, from 1568 to 1648. The surprise attack on Sluis is part of that war.

"As soon as I finished reading this book, I had to check Motley's *United Netherlands* to see if these amazing facts really happened! Yes, the Towerclock truly stopped!"   — Roelof A. Janssen

Time: 1606   Age: 10-99
IP0000008516   US$9.95

The Governor of England by Marjorie Bowen
A Novel on Oliver Cromwell

An historical novel in which the whole story of Cromwell's dealings with Parliament and the King is played out. It is written with dignity and conviction, and with the author's characteristic power of grasping the essential details needed to supply colour and atmosphere for the reader of the standard histories.

Time: 1645-1660   Age: 14-99
ISBN 0-921100-58-2   US$19.95

William III and the Revolution of 1688 and Gustavus Adolphus II
2 Historical Essays
by Marjorie Bowen

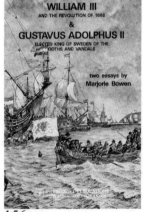

F.G. Oosterhoff in Reformed Perspective: I recommend this book without any hesitation. The two biographies make excellent reading, and the times the essays describe are of considerable interest and importance in the history of our civilization. Moreover, although Bowen obviously is not one in faith with Gustavus Adolphus and William of Orange, her essays relate incidents that are testimonials to God's mercies in preserving His Church. Remembering these mercies, we may take courage for the present and for the future.

Time: 1630-1689   Age: 14-99
ISBN 0-921100-06-X   US$9.95

The William & Mary Trilogy
by Marjorie Bowen

The life of William III, Prince of Orange, Stadtholder of the United Netherlands, and King of England (with Queen Mary II) is one of the most fascinating in all of history. Both the author and the publisher of these books have been interested in this subject for many years. Although the stories as told in these books are partly fictional, all the main events are faithful to history.

F. Pronk wrote in *The Messenger* about Volume 1: The author is well-known for her well-researched fiction based on the lives of famous historical characters. The religious convictions of the main characters are portrayed with authenticity and integrity. This book is sure to enrich one's understanding of Protestant Holland and will hold the reader spell-bound.

D.J. Engelsma wrote in *The Standard Bearer* about Volume 1: This is great reading for all ages, high school and older. *I Will Maintain* is well written historical fiction with a solid, significant, moving historical base . . . No small part of the appeal and worth of the book is the lively account of the important history of one of the world's greatest nations, the Dutch. This history was bound up with the Reformed faith and had implications for

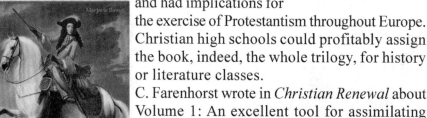

the exercise of Protestantism throughout Europe. Christian high schools could profitably assign the book, indeed, the whole trilogy, for history or literature classes.

C. Farenhorst wrote in *Christian Renewal* about Volume 1: An excellent tool for assimilating historical knowledge without being pained in the process, *I Will Maintain* is a very good read. Take it along on your holidays. Its sequel *Defender of the Faith*, is much looked forward to.

Time: 1670-1702   Age: 14-99
Volume 1 - *I Will Maintain*   ISBN 0-921100-42-6   US$19.95
Volume 2 - *Defender of the Faith*   ISBN 0-921100-43-4   US$19.95
Volume 3 - *For God and the King*   ISBN 0-921100-44-2   US$19.95

The Escape
by A. Van der Jagt
The Adventures of Three Huguenot Children
Fleeing Persecution
Huguenot Inheritance Series #1

F. Pronk in *The Messenger*: This book . . . will hold its readers spellbound from beginning to end. The setting is late seventeenth century France. Early in the story the mother dies and the father is banished to be a galley slave for life on a war ship. Yet in spite of threats and punishment, sixteen-year-old John and his ten-year-old sister Manette, refuse to give up the faith they have been taught.

Time: 1685-1695　　　　　　　　　　　　Age: 12-99
ISBN 0-921100-04-3　　　　　　　　　　US$10.90

The Secret Mission
by A. Van der Jagt
A Huguenot's Dangerous Adventures
in the Land of Persecution
Huguenot Inheritance Series #2

In the sequel to our best-seller, *The Escape,* John returns to France with a secret mission of the Dutch Government. At the same time he attempts to find his father.

Time: 1702-1712　　　　　　　　Age: 12-99
ISBN 0-921100-18-3　　　　　　　US$13.90

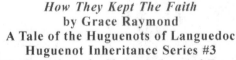

How They Kept The Faith
by Grace Raymond
A Tale of the Huguenots of Languedoc
Huguenot Inheritance Series #3

Christine Farenhorst in *Christian Renewal*: Presenting a moving account of the weals and woes of two Huguenot families during the heavy waves of persecution in seventeenth century France, this book, although its onset is a bit slow, is fascinating and moving reading. Covering all aspects of Huguenot life during this difficult time period, this goodsized paperback volume is a well-spring of encouragement for Christians today and highly recommended as reading for all those age twelve and over.

Time: 1676-1686　　　　　　　　　　　　Age: 13-99
ISBN 0-921100-64-7　　　　　　　　　　US$14.90

The Young Huguenots
by Edith S. Floyer
Huguenot Inheritance Series #4

It was a happy life at the pretty chateau. Even after that dreadful Sunday evening, when strange men came down and shut the people out of the church, not much changed for the four children. Until the soldiers came . . .

Time: 1686-1687
ISBN 0-921100-65-5

Age: 11-99
US$11.95

Driven into Exile
by Charlotte Maria Tucker
A Story of the Huguenots
Huguenot Inheritance Series #5

Christine Farenhorst in *Christian Renewal*: "Set in the days following the Revocation of the Edict of Nantes, (an edict in effect from 1598-1685 providing religious freedom for the French Protestants), this story follows the lives of two Huguenot families. Losing all to remain constant, the La Force family flees to Britain, while the Duval family remains in France. Suspenseful, the unfolding panorama of persecution and intrigue is well-suited for twenty-first century church goers who take freedom of religion for granted."

Time: 1685-1695
ISBN 0-921100-66-3

Age: 13-99
US$9.95

The Refugees
by A. Conan Doyle
A Tale of Two Continents
Huguenot Inheritance Series #6

The Refugees is a fast-paced exciting historical novel filled with daring and adventure. It depicts the escape of Louis De Catinat and his cousin from France after the revocation of the Edict of Nantes in 1685. Fleeing aboard a merchant vessel they attempt to reach America but find themselves stranded on an iceberg. The result is a hazardous trek through Canadian forests, avoiding both Roman Catholic Frenchmen and savage Indians. Follow the adventures of well to do people, bereft of all convenience and fleeing for their lives to seek refuge in a country where freedom of religion returns stability to their lives.

Time: 1685-1686
ISBN 0-921100-67-1

Age: 12-99
US$19.90

Done and Dared in Old France
by Deborah Alcock
Huguenot Inheritance Series #7

Christine Farenhorst wrote in *Christian Renewal*: Ten-year-old Gaspard, accidentally separated from his parents, is raised by a group of outlaw salt runners who fear neither God nor man. . . . Through the providence of God, Gaspard's heart turns to Him in faith and after a series of adventures is able to flee France to the safer Protestant shores of England. Fine and absorbing reading. Deborah Alcock has wonderful vocabulary, is a marvelous story-teller, and brings out the amazing hand of God's almighty power in every chapter. Highly recommended.

Time: 1685-1697   Age: 11-99
ISBN 1-894666-03-8   US$14.95

About the Huguenot Inheritance Series:

When speaking about the Huguenots, one often hears the exclamation, "I am also a descendant of the Huguenots!" Considering the fact that thousands of Huguenots were dispersed over the whole world, especially to Canada, England, The Netherlands, Switzerland, South Africa, and the U.S.A., it is very likely that 30% of the North American population has some Huguenot blood running through their veins. Of the Protestants it may well be the majority that has some connection with those who were martyred and exiled for their faith. Eight generations back our forefathers number approximately 132. One of these ancestors may very well have been a Huguenot. But, aside from the family connection, all descendants of the Reformation, who maintain the Faith of the fathers, will realize the kinship we have with these brothers and sisters in Christ. This kinship, and the example of their faith, has moved the publisher to launch this series of books.

A Loyal Huguenot Maid by Margaret S. Comrie
Huguenot Inheritance Series #8

Azerole, a young fugitive, was serving at Castle Brianza at Piedmont as governess to Madame de Rohan's crippled and plaintive foster son Christophe. But Azerole was a Huguenot maid, and Castle Brianza was ardently Roman Catholic. Madame's son Gaston, who was serving in the French army, was said to be a fiery Roman Catholic and tolerated no Protestants. What would happen to Azerole when he came home?

Azerole and her brother Léon struggle amid many troubles to keep their faith alive. When Michel unexpectedly comes on the scene a new unforseen danger lurks in the shadows. Would these two young Huguenots remain safe under the roof and shadow of Castle Brianza?

Time: 1686-1690   Age: 12-99
ISBN 978-0-921100-68-3   US$15.95

The Baron of Salgas
A True Huguenot Story by Sabine Malplach
and
The Cross and the Crown
& The Carpenter of Nîmes
Two Huguenot Stories by Deborah Alcock
Huguenot Inheritance Series #9

The Cross and the Crown tells about a man by the name of Gabriel Vaur. After the Revocation of the Edict of Nantes (1685), life once again became very dangerous for the Huguenots in France. When the Dragonnades came, Gabriel tried to get help, leaving his father, sister, and brother behind. Would he ever see them again? Would he ever be able to flee France and reach England?

The Baron of Salgas is the true story of the Baron and Baroness de Salgas. Even though her husband forbids her to be an open Huguenot, the Baroness knows that her Saviour had said that whoever would deny Him would be denied by Him. So one night she made her escape to Geneva. Would her husband follow? Would he recant? What would happen to their sons who were taken to the convents?

The Carpenter of Nîmes goes back more than a century to the year 1569 and tells about a man named Jacques Maderon. When the pastor tells him that Christ had said, "Son, go work today in My vineyard," he knows it is time to do something. Then the father of his friend was imprisoned. Would he succeed to cut the bars of the gate and so make way for the Huguenots to enter the city and deliver it?

Time: 1568-1715   Age: 13-99
ISBN 978-0-921100-69-0   US$14.95

The Well in the Orchard
by Deborah Alcock
A Story of France in the 18th Century
Huguenot Inheritance Series #10

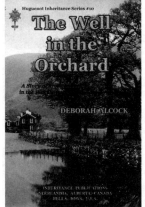

"Father!" Eugène burst forth, unable to withhold his tidings. "Father, the king is dead! The wicked rebels in Paris have slain him, slain him on the scaffold. Think of that! The king, the Lord's anointed, Louis of France!"

A flush overspread the old man's face, a tremor passed through his frame. Had he been able, he would have sprung from his seat, but he could not; one of his lower limbs was paralysed. So he lifted up his white and trembling hands to heaven, and said with deep feeling, — "God is just. His holy will be done."

Eugène was amazed. This way of taking a hideous crime, a terrible calamity, seemed to him incomprehensible. But then, as he reminded himself,

161

The Friends of Pascal by Deborah Alcock
or, *The Children of Port Royal*
Huguenot Inheritance Series #11

Geneviève looked up quickly. "Then you think I ought to take the veil?" In truth it is from among the young hearts that bleed and suffer, like Geneviève's, that convents gain their best and most willing recruits. "Willingly, most willingly. But not until Mademoiselle has need of me no longer."

"My need must yield to higher claims. And I own that it would be a joy to me to give back to God the best and dearest gift He has given me in these sad later years. But we will do nothing rashly or in haste. Meanwhile believe me, dear child, that I can feel for thy sorrow. Renunciation, however clearly we may see the duty of it, can never be anything but pain, bitter pain. Yet it is in such pain that Christ draws near to us, and gives us the foretaste of His joy."

"I know it, Mademoiselle," whispered the pale lips of Geneviève. "And now go and pray for thyself and for me. I also will pray for thee. Kiss me, dear child. So — once more — lip to lip and heart to heart. God bless thee! God make thee in very truth the saint I dreamed of being, but am not, and shall never be."

Time: 1650--1670   Age: 13-99
ISBN 978-1-894666-15-2   US$18.90

In the Desert by Deborah Alcock
A Story of the Church under the Cross
Huguenot Inheritance Series #12

IN the pages of this book fiction has only been employed for the purpose of illustrating fact. All that has been told of the sufferings, the faith, and the patience of the Church in the Desert — or, as her children loved to call her, "The Church under the Cross" — is true, and within the truth. Especially the character and the history of Majal-Désubas owes nothing to the pencil of fancy. It is a portrait, carefully drawn from contemporary sources, from the memoirs, narratives, and popular songs, in which grateful hearts have embalmed a beloved and fragrant memory.

Time: 1745-1760   Age: 16-99
ISBN 978-1-894666-13-8   US$13.90

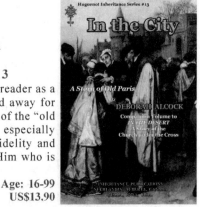

In the City by Deborah Alcock
A Story of Old Paris
Huguenot Inheritance Series #13

The narrative here presented is offered to the reader as a picture of a state of society which has passed away for ever. It aims at reflecting the men and women of the "old régime" as they acted, thought, and suffered; especially taking note of those who, in that age of infidelity and corruption, yet lived and walked "as seeing Him who is invisible."

Time: 1760s   Age: 16-99
ISBN 978-1-894666-12-1   US$13.90

162

Must I Give Him Up
by Deborah Alcock
A Story of France in the 18th Century
Huguenot Inheritance Series #14

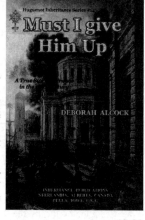

Among those who could not get away was an aged man, who had almost fulfilled his fourscore years of life. Him the soldiers took, and were leading him away to prison. His son, who was in another part of the Assembly, knew nothing of it until, having reached a place of safety, he sought everywhere for his father, and could not find him. His young active feet soon retraced their steps. He met the soldiers with their captive on their way to the town. Madly Fabre threw himself into their midst, and made a wild despairing effort to tear their prisoner from their grasp. Vain — vain of course! What could one man, alone and unarmed, do against a band?

Time: 1760s
ISBN 978-1-77298-005-9

Age: 12-99
US$8.90

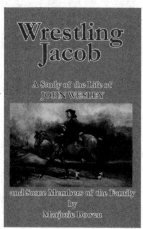

How Sleep the Brave
by James H. Hunter
A Novel of 17th Century Scotland
"Hush ye, hush ye, little pet ye,
Hush ye, hush ye, do not fret ye,
The Black Avenger shall not get ye."

Even though the Scottish covenanters endured harsh persecutions by the King's Inquisition the mysterious name of the Black Avenger sent thrills of hope and courage to many a tormented soul. Yet the captains and dragoons feared this elusive figure while at the same time determining to place his head on the Netherbow. Many faithful Presbyterians were murdered on the spot or threatened with a touch of the thumbscrew or a place on the rack if they did not disclose the hiding place of some sought-out Covenanters.

Lady Marion Kennedy, the beautiful daughter of the Lord of Culzean Castle, was also threatened with similar reprisals if she refused to marry Luis Salvador de Ferrari, the usurper of Fenwick Ha', and supporter of the Inquisition. Yet her heart longed for Duncan Fenwick, the rightful lord of Fenwick Ha'.

An exciting, fast-paced historical novel regarding the events of Scottish history in 1688.

Time: 1685-1688
ISBN 978-1-894666-41-1

Age: 12-99
US$15.95

Wrestling Jacob by Marjorie Bowen
A Study of the Life of JOHN WESLEY
and Some Members of the Family

MARJORIE BOWEN has come neither to judge nor to explain. Religious controversy and theology she avoids, being content to give her readers the fullest portrait of the man to be attempted in our time, and leave the rest to them. HERE, then, stands John Wesley, a titan with the message that set England afire. HERE also is the "Holy Club" at Oxford, that first step towards his real destiny. THEN comes the adventure in Georgia, where he knew love, only to turn away for religion's sake.IMPOSSIBLE to imagine our quiet England stirred to such depths.

Time: 1703-1791
ISBN 978-1-928136-86-6

Age: 15-99
US$24.90

The Great Escape by Christine Farenhorst
40 Faith-building Lessons From History

"Poignant vignettes from history are captured in fascinating word pictures. Chapters open with Scripture that is fleshed out in the lives of historical figures. The impact is more in the story told, not in the lives lived, which point either to or away from Christ."
— John Van Dyk, Christian Renewal.

Subject: Short Biographies   Age: 14-99
ISBN 0-87552-729-9   US$9.99

With Wolfe in Canada
Or, The Winning of a
Continent by G.A. Henty

With Wolfe in Canada

Or the Winning of a Continent
by
G. A. Henty

Through misadventure the hero of the story, James Walsham, becomes involved in the historic struggle between Britain and France for supremacy on the North American continent. The issue of this war determined not only the destinies of North America, but to a large extent those of the mother countries themselves. *With Wolfe in Canada* will take the reader through many battles of this conflict. Meet a young George Washington and General Braddock as they fight the French and Indians, join up with Rogers' Rangers, and learn of the legendary generals Wolfe and Montcalm. *With Wolfe in Canada* is a model of what a children's book should be with its moving tale of military exploit and thrilling adventure. This classic provides a lesson in history instructively and graphically, whilst infusing into the dead facts of history new life. Mr. Henty's classic *With Wolfe in Canada* is a useful aid to study as well as amusement.

Time: 1755-1760   Age: 14-99

Cloth ISBN 0-921100-86-8   US$17.95
Paperback ISBN 0-921100-87-6   US$14.95

The Soldier of Virginia by Marjorie Bowen
A Novel on George Washington

"Mr. Washington — and who is Mr. Washington?"

"It is the Governor of Virginia's envoy, Monsieur — bearing a letter from his Excellency."

St. Pierre gave his inferior officer a quick glance; two things occurred to him: the first was that Dinwiddie must be serious if he had sent a messenger in such weather; the second was that it would have been more courteous if the envoy had been a man of some rank; he remarked on neither of these things, but quietly requested that Mr. Washington should be brought into his presence. The scene was St. Pierre's room in the newly erected Fort le Bœuf; December cold filled the apartment despite the huge fire of logs that roared on the hearth; and the view from the window was of a frozen lake, great trees against a drab sky, and the steady falling of snowflakes.

Originally published in 1912, this is a fictionalized biography on America's first President by one of the best authors of historical fiction.

Time: 1755-1775   Age: 14-99
ISBN 0-921100-99-X   US$14.95

Servant of Slaves by Grace Irwin
A Biographical Novel of John Newton

This is Grace Irwin's best novel to date. She recounts the exciting adventures of John Newton's life both as profane and immoral slave trader and later as a devoted servant of Christ. And is there anywhere a more beautiful love story than that of John Newton and Mary Catlett? — Clyde S. Kilby

Time: 1725-1807   Age: 14-99
ISBN 0-88815-908-0   US$19.90

Roger the Ranger by Eliza F. Pollard
A Story of Border Life Among the Indians

Indians, Frenchmen, Englishmen, wars, strained friendships, and romance are all interwoven in Eliza Pollard's fast paced historical novel.

When Charles Langlade deserted his birth place in upper Canada to marry an Indian squaw and then to fight with his Indian tribe for the French against the English, he also lost his best friend, Roger Boscowen, who led his rangers for the English against the French.

Meanwhile the historically famous General Louis de Montcalm entered Canada on behalf of the French and things took a turn in favour for the French due to the help of Langlade. But would the jealous government of French Canada succeed in using De Montcalm's daughter Mercedes — who had come with her father from France with the intention to enter a Canadian convent — to destroy Montcalm's fame?

And would Charles and Roger indeed fight each other? Would their friendship ever be restored?

Time: 1754-1760   Age: 12-99
ISBN 978-1-894666-31-2   US$14.95

The Czar by Deborah Alcock
A Tale of the Time of the First Napoleon

As, with a hand still trembling, Clémence poured out the tea, she remembered the stories she had heard of such evening visits made by the Czar, "to talk at his ease," and recalled the words of De Maistre when someone criticised this habit in his presence: "It is a touching thing to me to see the ruler of a great empire, in the age of all the passions, find his recreation in taking a cup of tea with an honest man and his wife."

Ivan Ivanovitch Pojarsky, an orphaned Russian Prince, adopted by loyal people in the village of Nicolofsky meets the great Czar Alexander of Russia while the Czar does his best to bring back to life a seemingly dead carpenter. This historical fact, and many others related in this captivating story, gives a very accurate picture of the life in Russia during the time of Napoleon.

Time: 1795-1825   Age: 14-99
ISBN 978-1-894666-11-4   US$19.90

Three Months Under the Snow by J. J. Porchat

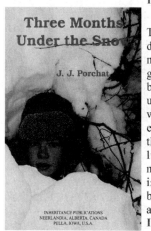

This morning when I awoke, I found myself in complete darkness, and at first supposed that my sleep had quitted me at an earlier hour than usual. However, I heard my grandfather feeling his way about, and I rubbed my eyes, but did not see a bit better. "Grandfather," said I, "you are up before daylight." "My dear boy," he answered, " if we were to wait for the light of day, we should remain long enough in bed. I fear the snow is above the window." At this I uttered a cry of horror and leaped out of bed. I soon lighted our lamp, and we were then able to perceive that my grandfather's conjecture was well-founded. "But the window is low," he added, "besides, it may be that the snow has been heaped up in this part; perhaps we should not see it above two feet deep at some paces from the wall."

ISBN 978-1-894666-19-0 19th Century   US$9.90

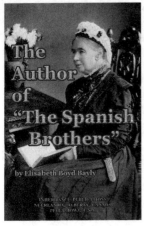

The Author of The Spanish Brothers (Deborah Alcock) Her Life and Works by Elisabeth Boyd Bayly

"ONLY remembered by what I have done."

That will never be true of Deborah Alcock. Partly because the unknown cannot be remembered, and year after year her books came out — the first by "D. A.," the next "By the Author of" the one or more before it, until the wide success of The Spanish Brothers stamped its name, without her own, on all she wrote; and for twenty years longer she went on writing stories which left their impress on innumerable lives, while the writer's identity remained strangely unknown outside the quiet little city in the South of Ireland where her best years were spent. In 1890 The Story of Constance came out in serial form, and was afterwards continued and published under the title of Crushed yet Conquering, "by Deborah Alcock." In 1891, at the age of fifty-six — a lone woman, deeply bereaved — Miss Alcock came to England, and to her astonishment "found herself famous." And still her new friends, like the old ones, said, "She is greater than her books — though we loved them so well." More than by her writings or her gracious acts — by what she was will she be remembered, in life and in eternity, by those whose privilege it was to know her.

Time: 1835-1913   Age: 14-99
ISBN 978-1-77298-024-0   US$19.90

Walking with God by Deborah Alcock
The Life of the Venerable John Alcock (Late Archdeacon of Waterford)

"John," said his father, calling him one day to his side, "what would you like to be?"

"A doctor, Sir," was the prompt reply of the doctor's son, who shared the family esprit de corps to the uttermost. "I was born a doctor, of a family of doctors," he often said afterward.

"Well, Ben and Nat are going to be doctors; I think you had better be a clergyman," was the disappointing answer.

Time: 1804-1886   Age: 16-99
ISBN 978-1-77298-023-3   US$21.90

A Dictionary of Lowland Scotch by Charles Mackay
With an Introductory Chapter on the Poetry, Humour, and Literary History of the Scottish Language and an Appendix of Scottish Proverbs

"Broad Scotch," says Dr. Adolphus Wagner, the erudite and sympathetic editor of the Poems of Robert Burns, published in Leipzig, in 1835, "is literally broadened, — i.e., a language or dialect very worn off, and blotted, whose original stamp often is unknowable, because the idea is not always to be guessed at." This strange mistake is not confined to the Germans, but prevails to a large extent among Englishmen, who are of opinion that Scotch is a provincial dialect ofthe English, — like that of Lancashire or Yorkshire, — and not entitled to be called a language. The truth is, that English and Lowland Scotch were originally the same, but that the literary and social influences of London as the real metropolis of both countries, especially after the transfer of the royal family of Stuart from Edinburgh to London, at the commencement of the seventeenth century, favoured the infusion of a Latin element into current English, which the Scotch were slow to adopt.

ISBN 978-1-77298-028-8   US$22.90

Simon Gieke 1: The Heretic of the Swamps
by Mevahor

Simon Gieke was a man in the prime of his life. His father and mother had died when he was very young: he had never known them. An uncle had taken him in when Simon was just a boy. He hadnot enjoyed any kind of upbringing. He got food, drink, and clothing. Nothing else. There was no education of any kind. What good would that do? Even his uncle had been unable to read or write. The uncle had been a rough, fearsome fellow who wandered about in the huge commons, trying to make his living by hunting, fishing, and poaching. He would steal whatever he could get. Whoever could, avoided him. When he had money, he spent it in the tavern with other rowdy characters. Then he was a dangerous man who picked fights and pulled out his knife for the smallest things. In reality, he terrorized the whole village and its surroundings. Whenever something seemed to be missing and people were certain that he had taken it, no one dared to report him. What a relief it was for Scherpenisse when they heard that the uncle had died. No one really knew how he had come to his end. Most assumed that he had suffocated in the water and mud. One January morning, he had gone into the commons. It had been freezing for several days and during the night there had been a heavy snowfall. He must have gone through the ice. No one had heard any more about him until a haymaker had found him in a deep slough the following summer. They had recognized him because of his vaulting poleand musket.

Simon had been eighteen years old at the time andhad not shed many tears for the uncle whom he succeeded. And what kind of successor? In churlishness and godlessness, he exceeded even his uncle. He wanted nothing to do with religion but ranted and raved at the parish priest and never performed a single religious duty. He was a total heathen, who cursed and drank even more than his uncle had done. Everyone avoided him as much as they could. Many crossed themselves when they had to pass his house. However, in one thing he differed favourably from his uncle: he never stole. No one had ever complained that he had stolen from them.

Time: 1566

Age: 14-99

ISBN 978-1-77298-084-4

US$16.90

Hunted and Harried by R.M. Ballantyne
A Tale of the Scottish Covenanters

It was in 1662 that the celebrated Act was passed by Middleton and his colleagues in Glasgow College. It provided that all ministers must either submit to the bishops or remove themselves and families out of their manses, churches, and parishes within a month. It was known as the "Drunken Act of Glasgow," owing to the condition of the legislators. Four hundred brave and true men left their earthly all at that time, rather than violate conscience and forsake God. Their example ultimately saved the nation from despotism. The Archbishop of Saint Andrews was chief in arrogance and cruelty among his brethren. He afterwards obtained permission to establish a High Commission Court in Scotland — in other words, an Inquisition — for summarily executing all laws, acts, and orders in favour of Episcopacy and against recusants, clergy, and laity. It was under this authority that all the evil deeds up to now described were done, and of this Commission Sharp was constant president.

Time: 1660-1688

Age: 14-99

ISBN 978-1-77298-090-5

US$12.90

Ann of the Prairie Series

A compelling story of the indomitable pioneer spirit of women — the unsung heroines of the American West. "Heartwarming and heartrending . . . a reminder of what life was really like." — Janette Oke

In the tradition of *Little House on the Prairie*
Time: 1874-1900 Age: 14-99

This Rough New Land
by Kenneth Sollitt
ISBN 0-940652-03-X
US$9.99

Our Changing Lives
by Kenneth Sollitt
ISBN 0-940652-04-8
US$9.99

These Years of Promise
by Kenneth Sollitt
& Nick Harrison
ISBN 0-940652-05-6
US$9.99

Ann of the Prairie: A Family History by Kenneth Sollitt & Lucy Bullard
ISBN 0-940652-10-2
US$9.99

The Seventh Earl by Grace Irwin

A dramatized biography on Anthony Ashley Cooper, the Seventh Earl of Shaftesbury, who is most widely remembered as a 19th-century British philanthropist and factory reformer. "This is Grace Irwin's strongest and most poignant book . . . I have been moved and enriched by my hours with *The Seventh Earl*," wrote V.R. Mollenkott.
Time: 1801-1885   Age: 14-99
ISBN 0-8028-6059-1   US$11.95

A Stranger in a Strange Land by Leonora Scholte

John E. Marshall in *The Banner of Truth*: This is a delightful book. It tells the story of H.P. Scholte, a preacher in The Netherlands, who being persecuted for his faith in his own country, emigrated to the U.S.A., and there established a settlement in Pella, Iowa, in the midst of the vast undeveloped prairie. . . The greater part of the book is taken up in telling the stories of the immense hardships known after emigration. Interwoven with this story is an account of Scholte's marriage and family life. . . It is a most heartwarming and instructive story.
Time: 1825-1880   Age: 14-99
ISBN 0-921100-01-9   US$9.95

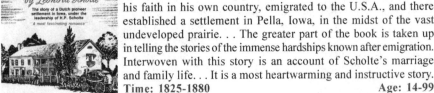

168

Captain My Captain by Deborah Meroff
Author of *Coronation of Glory*

Willy-Jane VanDyken in *The Trumpet*: This romantic novel is so filled with excitement and drama, it is difficult to put it down once one has begun it. Its pages reflect the struggle between choosing Satan's ways or God's ways. Mary's struggles with materialism, being a submissive wife, coping with the criticism of others, learning how to deal with sickness and death of loved ones, trusting in God and overcoming the fear of death forces the reader to reflect on his own struggles in life.

This story of Mary Ann Patten (remembered for being the first woman to take full command of a merchant sailing ship) is one that any teen or adult reader will enjoy. It will perhaps cause you to shed a few tears but it is bound to touch your heart and encourage you in your faith.

Time: 1837-1861	Age: 14-99
ISBN 0-921100-79-5	US$14.95
ISBN 0-921100-79-Cloth	US$24.95

By Far Euphrates by Deborah Alcock
A Tale on Armenia in the 19th century

Alcock has provided sufficient graphics describing the atrocities committed against the Armenian Christians to make the reader emotionally moved by the intense suffering these Christians endured at the hands of Muslim Turks and Kurds. At the same time, the author herself has confessed to not wanting to provide full detail, which would take away from the focus on how those facing death did so with peace, being confident they would go to see their LORD, and so enjoy eternal peace. **As such it is not only an enjoyable novel, but also encouraging reading.** These Christians were determined to remain faithful to their God, regardless of the consequences.

Time: 1887-1895	Age: 11-99
ISBN 1-894666-00-3	US$14.95

The Mystery of Mar Saba by J.H. Hunter

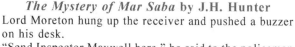

Lord Moreton hung up the receiver and pushed a buzzer on his desk.

"Send Inspector Maxwell here," he said to the policeman who came in.

A moment later, Maxwell entered. He was heavy-eyed from lack of sleep and, if anything, looked more melancholy than ever.

"Sit down, Max."

The inspector seated himself.

"Well, it is heavy going," said Lord Moreton.

The other nodded. "The ship of state is going to founder, sir, mark my words, unless there is some change within the next forty-eight hours. We had one hundred and three suicides last night and eighteen murders within the Metropolitan area. We cannot stand this for long. No word from Jerusalem yet?"

Time: 1930s-1940s (historical fiction)	Age: 12-99
ISBN 978-1-928136-88-0	US$21.90

Thine is The Kingdom by J.H. Hunter
A Story of the Cold War

Tresham looked at the picture accompanying the article and might have been gazing into a mirror, so startling was the resemblance. "Of course, it is my brother," he said slowly. "So he went to Canada to work for a capitalistic state and help to start another war. What do you want me to do, since I suppose my coming here has something to do with that item in the newspaper?"

The Russian nodded and handed him a cutting from a newspaper pasted on a piece of stiff cardboard. "Read that also," he said. It was a report of a later address given by Tresham's brother in Washington to an organization affiliated with the United Nations and called "The Society for the Promotion of World Peace and Good Will." "The first two paragraphs are all that you need read at present," said Vasiloff. The report was in English with a Russian translation beside it.

Time: 1950s-1960s (fiction)   Age: 12-99
ISBN 978-1-928136-87-3   US$16.90

They Looked for a City by Lydia Buksbazen
A True Story of World War I & II
WWII Memorial Series 1

They Looked for a City is the saga of a Hebrew Christian family tossed by all kinds of national and personal storms, yet always emerging on the crest of each menacing wave, as if carried by the hand of a merciful God and the force of their faith. It is a pilgrim story of real people whose lives were marked by a two-fold stigma and a two-fold privilege — that of being Jews as well as believers in the Messiah of Israel, Jesus.

The center of this family chronicle is occupied by my beloved mother Yente, because to me she personifies something that is so precious and peculiar — the heart of a Jewish mother, and the impact of her faith upon her family and all those who came in touch with her.

ISBN 978-1-77298-013-4   US$17.90

No Price for Freedom by Philip Gibbs
A Story of Poland in World War II
WWII Memorial Series 2

In *No Price for Freedom* a colourful story of one Polish family is told. We follow their tragic experiences under changing enemy occupations from 1939 to 1945. We witness their exploits during the amazing epic of the Warsaw Rising, and follow them in France, Italy, Russia, and England - to which some of them escape with the hope that in the West they will still be able to continue their fight for freedom and liberation of their country.

No Price for Freedom, a vivid and exciting novel, is based on authentic facts. Through its pages move real persons, who played an important and glorious part in the last chapters of the history of the Polish nation, such as General Anders, General Bor-Komorowski, the late Mayor of Warsaw, Mr. S. Starzynski, Father Paul, and others.

ISBN 978-1-928136-29-3   US$24.90

The Tartan Pimpernel by Donald Caskie
A Story of France in World War II
WWII Memorial Series 3

"As exciting and eventful as the novel from which its title drives. It is an inspiring story, a testament of the power of goodness in the conflict with evil." —Scotsman

"Dr. Caskie recounts his adventures racily and well, without rancour and with constant humour." —Glasgow Herald

The Rev. Dr. Donald Currie Caskie (1902-1983) was a minister in the Church of Scotland, best known for his exploits in France during World War II, during which he helped an estimated 2,000 Allied sailors, soldiers, and airmen to escape from occupied France (mainly through Spain).

ISBN 978-1-928136-30-9   US$15.90

A Theatre in Dachau by
Hermanus Knoop
WWII Memorial Series 4

In the concentration camp of Dachau the God of all grace did wonders of grace by His Word and Spirit every day. Oh, it was indeed a dreadful time for me that I spent there, and yet it is not at all a hollow phrase when I say that I would for no amount of money have missed this time of my life, since it was so unspeakably rich in grace. I saw God there. The LORD was in this place. It was a house of God and a gate of heaven.

Time: 1940-1943   Age: 14-99
ISBN 0-921100-20-5   US$14.95

In This Hour by Rudolf Van Reest
A Story of World War II and the Floods of 1953
WWII Memorial Series 5

"That's a rather rough expression, brother Melse — 'traitor.' How could you call someone a traitor if he's simply obeying the government? I would rather not hear such language from the mouth of an elder."

"I maintain that such work as building bunkers is treason against our land," repeated David Melse. "The bunkers have a definite purpose: when armies come to liberate us from the power of the Germans, the bunkers are supposed to hold them back. Each

bunker could help sink one of the naval vessels approaching our coast. And on those vessels are our friends — perhaps even our own soldiers. Reverend, you should think carefully what those bunkers represent."

Rev. Verhulst shook his head. "You people have completely the wrong idea about those bunkers. Do you really believe that Germany will one day sink to its knees before England? If you do, you're completely mistaken, brother Melse. Germany will take control of all of Europe and will never let itself be overthrown. Germany is much too powerful to be defeated. Moreover, if you had listened carefully to last Sunday's sermon, you would know full well how I think about these matters. The apostate covenant people spent seventy years in the grip of Babylon, and I'm sure that our time under foreign domination will not be any less.

Time: 1942-1953   Age: 15-99
ISBN 0-894666-68-2   US$15.95

A Mighty Fortress in the Storm
by Paulina M. Rustenburg Bootsma
WWII Memorial Series 6

Fay S. Lapka in Christian Week: [This book] . . . is the fictionalized historical account of the actual village of Never Thought Of (literal translation of *Nooitgedacht*) in the Netherlands, and the efforts of the tiny, two-farm town to aid the resistance. This is a thoroughly interesting, at times warmly-amusing story, that will be enjoyed by adults. The photographs reproduced throughout the text add realism to the amazing story.

Time: 1940-45   Age: 14-99
ISBN 0-921100-37-X   US$12.90

Schilder's Struggle for the Unity of the Church
by Rudolf Van Reest

Klaas Schilder is remembered both for his courageous stand in opposition to Nazism, which led to his imprisonment three months after the Nazis overran The Netherlands in 1940, and for his role in the Church struggle in The Netherlands, which culminated in 1944 with the suspension of scores of office-bearers and the formation of the liberated Reformed Churches.

Thomas Vanden Heuvel in *The Outlook*: I strongly recommend this book for everyone interested in the preservation of and propagation of the Reformed faith.

Time: 1890-1952   Age: 16-99
ISBN 1-894666-79-8   US$19.95

My Path to Liberation
by Douwe Van Dijk
Reflections on My Life in the Ministry of the Word of God

J. Bruning in *Una Sancta* of August 7, 2004: . . . In short, Rev van Dijk provides you with a realistic picture of the Church and its struggles, and encouragement to deal with current issues in a Scriptural and Church orderly manner. . .

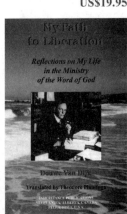

. . I learned much from this book. Although written in a personal and easy style, it is a treasure for (future) office bearers and very educational for all who love the church. From time to time we hear the phrase "we have a rich Reformed heritage". This book definitely conveys some aspects of this heritage and will enrich you; it will also arm you.

Time: 1890-1960   Age: 16-99
ISBN 0-921100-26-4   US$19.95

And We Escaped
by G. Van Dooren

A story of the Kingship of the Lord Jesus Christ in a local church in the 1940s.

IP11979   US$17.95

The Best of our Library Series

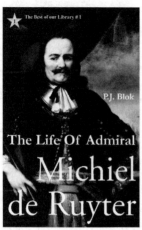

BL01 - *The Life Of Admiral De Ruyter*
by P.J. Blok

The Dutch people remember Michiel Adriaansz De Ruyter not only as a great naval hero, one of the very greatest of all times, praised as imrriensi tremor Oceani, a "terror of the ocean," "Hercules of the Seas," as he was called in those days of grandiloquence, it prefers to think of him in the affectionate spirit which is so well conveyed by the name Bestevaer, "Dear Father," given to him by his own sailors, as it had also been given to his glorious predecessor, Marten Harpertsz Tromp. He was not only a model of pure patriotism, of devotion to duty, of unflinching courage, an incomparably balanced mixture of audacity and prudence, a perfect hero, a great sailor, and a born leader in battle. He was also a noble man, a character without blemish, honest and direct, faithful and just, upon whom everybody, low or exalted, could rely implicitly. He was simple, humble, pious as well as frank, and all those who knew him praise him as a model father not only to his own family but to the men of the fleets he commanded. He was indeed a model of those middle-class virtues and personal characteristics which the Dutch have always valued so highly.

Subject: Biography 1801-1876   Age: 14-99
ISBN 978-1-928136-62-0   Regular Edition US$21.90   Large Print US$39.90

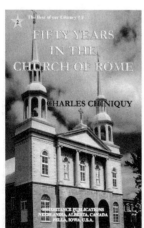

BL02 - *Fifty Years in the Church Of Rome*
by Charles Chiniquy

The Unabridged Reprint of the Revised and Complete Edition of 1914.

WITH AN APPENDIX (also from the 1914 edition) CONTAINING AN ACCOUNT OF THE LAST DAYS AND DEATH OF PASTOR CHINIQUY; ALSO A DECLARATION OF HIS FAITH.

Subject: Biography 1809-1899   Age: 16-99
ISBN 978-1-928136-70-5   Regular Edition US$26.90
                               Large Print US$44.90

BL03 - *James Chalmers: His Autobiography and Letters* by Richard Lovet

An unabridged reprint of the Fifth Edition of 1903

James Chalmers, the missionary, was a remarkable man from every point of view. His personality attracted every one who met him. The mere narrative of his actions and experiences reads like a romance. Hence it is not surprising that in the course of a few months three large editions should have been exhausted.

One gratifying feature has been the hearty welcome accorded to the book by all sections of the Protestant Church, and by all kinds of papers in the press of Great Britain, the Colonies, and the United States. Papers that rarely devote a line to missionary intelligence have exhorted their readers to get this book 'because it is more interesting than any novel ' and the official organs of bodies as widely sundered in some respects as the Society for the Propagation of the Gospel, the Church Missionary Society, the United Free Church of Scotland, and the Baptist Missionary Society, have urged their readers to study this volume, and from it refresh their missionary knowledge and missionary enthusiasm.

Subject: Biography 1841-1901   Age: 14-99
ISBN 978-1-928136-80-4   Regular Edition US$26.90   Large Print US$44.90

The Best of our Library Series is a selection of our personal books that I would like each of my children, grandchildren, great-grandchildren, etc.to read and to own.
— Roelof A. Janssen

BL04 - *Abraham Kuyper* by Frank Vanden Berg
A Biography

Abraham Kuyper was one of Holland's foremost leaders in politics, education, and the church from 1865 to 1917, a period of over 50 years. His influence is still felt today in his native land and in many other countries.

Kuyper is unique in that he carried on parallel careers in separate major fields, both as a thinker and as a doer. He carried a sword in one hand and a trowel in the other, for he was both a builder and a battler. His followers loved him with warm, undying devotion, while his enemies hated him as they hated no one else.

This biography, which is aimed at the general reader, gives us a running account of Kuyper's 83 years on earth. It outlines his personal history and sketches the background whenever the scene shifts to a new phase in Kuyper's many-sided career.

Subject: Biography 1837-1920   Age: 14-99
ISBN 978-1-928136-77-4   Regular Edition US$16.90
                       Large Print US$44.90

BL05 - *Jan Smuts - A Biography*
by F.S. Crafford

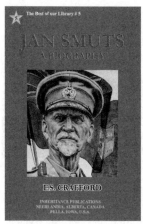

Jan Smuts was lauded as the first successful general of the Allies in the war; as "the general in whom the whole Empire has most confidence"; as "the destroyer of the German power in Africa"; as "the most conspicuous figure in greater Britain"; and as "a remarkable combination of talents not usually found in the same person, unless, indeed, that person belongs to the small and select class of which the Caesars, the Cromwells, and the Napoleons are the outstanding types." His character was described as "too spacious and complex to be read offhand." In an article in the press Mr. Winston Churchill wrote: "At this moment there arrives in England from the outer marches of the Empire a new and altogether extraordinary man . . . The stormy and hazardous roads he has travelled by would fill all the acts and scenes of a drama. He has warred against us — well we know it. He has quelled rebellion against our own flag with unswerving loyalty and unfailing shrewdness. He has led raids at desperate odds and conquered provinces by scientific strategy . . . His astonishing career and his versatile achievements are only the index of a profound sagacity and a cool, far-reaching comprehension . . ." And while introducing him to the Imperial War Cabinet, Mr. Lloyd George referred to him as "one of the most brilliant generals in this war."

Subject: Biography 1870-1950   Age: 14-99
ISBN 978-1-77298-027-1   US$23.90

BL06 - *The Persecutor*
by Sergei Kourdakov

His job in the Russian police was to inflict pain and terror on Christians . . . and he did it well.

Sergei Kourdakov, who led attack raids for Russia's secret police, points to the place off British Columbia, Canada where he escaped from a Russian naval ship to begin his search for the faith of those he once persecuted.

Subject: Biography 1951-1973   Age: 13-99
ISBN 978-1-77298-027-1   US$14.90

7000 Shall Remain by A. Van der Jagt
Some important topics of early Christian history

Nearly all chapters in this book deal with the less known aspects and contradictory issues of particular events, which happened prior to the Reformation of 1517. Hopefully, this will lead to exciting discussions in study groups and, maybe, even within family circles.

Time: about 4000 B.C. - A.D. 1500   Age: 12-99
ISBN 978-1-928136-84-2   US$14.90

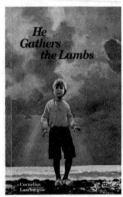

Church History by P.K. Keizer

Mary Pride in *The Big Book of Home Learning, vol. 3*: [Keizer] . . . neither overloads the student nor skips over anything important . . . The writing is interesting and pious — from a solidly Reformed Protestant viewpoint — and does the teenager the great service of distilling the lives and teachings of many important people in a form he can remember . . . An excellent resource.

Time: A.D. 33-1970   Age: 13-99
ISBN 0-921100-02-7   US$12.95

Fiction for Teenagers and Adults

He Gathers the Lambs by Cornelius Lambregtse

A moving book, written not only with deep insight into the ecclesiastical, religious, social, and historical situation in which the story takes place, but also with a warm, rich understanding of a child's soul. Every page of the book carries proof that it was eked out of the author's own experience. It is written from the inside out, and the people who appear in it are flesh-and-blood people as they walked the streets of southeastern Zeeland. Zeelanders with a mystical character . . . who had great difficulty appropriating in faith the redemptive deeds of the covenant God. Also beautiful in this story are the descriptions of the natural beauty of the island on which it takes place. The author views nature with a loving but also with a knowledgeable eye. The landscape through all the seasons. . . But what is most striking is his knowledge of the soul of a child, a knowledge born out of love. — Rudolf Van Reest

Subject: Fiction   Age: 14-99
ISBN 0-921100-77-9   US$14.95

The Crown of Honour by L. Erkelens

Rachel Manesajian in *Chalcedon Report*: This book is about an illegitimate girl whose mother died when she was born, and no one knows who her father is. She grows up in an orphanage, and she goes through many hardships and is treated poorly because she is illegitimate. The few people she loves are taken away from her. Because of all her trials, she thinks God is against her, and so, in rebellion, she refuses to go to church or pray. However, the prayers of an old man who loves and prays for her are answered and she realizes . . . a wonderful story.

Fiction   Age: 14-99
ISBN 0-921100-14-0   US$14.95

while. You know what you have to do. Posing as a member of the local underground, you tell them you know a way to bypass our defenses. This dark area marks the swamps, and these are the two small ponds. This is the trail that leads through the swamp, as you well know. They won't be able to take their tanks and heavy artillery across this soft ground, but their infantry won't have any problem. You tell them that we've left this route undefended because we don't expect them to advance along this trail. Talk them into sending as many soldiers as they can spare for this outflanking manoeuvre. You'll head them through the swamp, and over here you'll reach high ground. That's where the woods start. Take them down this path, and the first chance you get make a run for it. As you know, the woods will be full of machine-gun nests. Once they're in the trap, not a single one of them will get out alive."

"It's a splendid plan, Captain." said Van der Nat.

"Yes, I think so," responded the officer. "If you carry out your part. So before nightfall you'll sneak to the Canadian lines and pass yourself off as a friend of the Allies. Your job will be to persuade them to try their out-flanking manoeuvre tonight."

"Yes, Sir Captain. But . . .," Van der Nat whined, "but I won't be able to do it myself."

"What!" screamed the German. "What do you mean, you won't be able to do it yourself? You're not running out on us, are you?"

"No, no! Certainly not, Captain!" answered the Dutch traitor hastily. "But no matter how badly I would like to go myself, it would be very unwise. Everyone around here knows I belong to the Nazi party, including many people in the next village. If they see me talking to the Canadian brass, they'll certainly warn them. Then I'll probably be shot."

"Hmm, I guess you're right," grunted the German, "but why didn't you say so before? What's in that head of yours anyhow?"

"Well, you see, Sir," said Van der Nat, "I know just the man for the job. He's a young fellow who grew up around here and knows the area like the palm of his hand. No one will recognize him, because he moved away from here when he was a boy, and now he's a man. He's with the National Guard."

"You're sure he can be trusted?" the officer asked sourly.

"Certainly, Captain! You have my word on that."

"Hump! The word of a . . ." The German stopped mid-sentence, but Van der Nat knew what he had started to say. He flushed with anger, but he kept his mouth shut.

"Okay," said the officer, after having thought it over, "but then I want to meet this man immediately. I want to sound him out first, and then we'll have to rehearse the plan with him. There's no time to lose."

His footsteps moved toward the trapdoor and "Van der Nazi" followed him. It was high time the two men were leaving, for the two boys in the crate were in a bad way. The holes in the ends of the box didn't let in enough fresh air, so they were gasping for breath. Moreover, they were lying almost on top of each other and hadn't dared to stir while the men were there.

When they could no longer hear the sounds of the men descending the ladder, Carl carefully lifted the lid of the box a little ways. They both breathed deeply as fresh air came pouring into the stuffy crate. They had been at the point of passing out. Painfully they raised themselves, listening carefully. They heard nothing further. Tiptoeing to the little window, Tom saw the German officer and "Van der Nazi" striding away from the windmill. "There they go," he said to Carl, who hurried over beside him. Together they watched the two men go.

"Filthy scum!" scolded Carl. "They took my dad away. Maybe they'll kill him."

"If only the Canadians get here in time to set him free!" said Tom. "But they're going to walk right into a trap. There should be some way to warn the Canadian commander."

Carl nodded. The boys discussed several plans, but both of them knew it would be very difficult and dangerous to sneak through the German lines. "Come on," said Carl, "let's go down. Mother will be very anxious."

They quickly descended and ran to the house, where they met Carl's mother. She had seen the German officer leave and was just coming to the windmill to find Carl and Tom. The boys could tell she had been weeping, but now she was very calm. "Father was very brave," she said, "and now we must be brave, too. His life is in God's hands. If only we're liberated soon! Thank God the Germans didn't find you two. What happened in the windmill?"

Carl told her how they had hidden in the crate, but he didn't tell her what they had overheard. Meanwhile, Tom had been looking around the yard.

"Where is Scout?" he asked.

"I don't know," said Carl's mother. "I haven't seen him for quite a while."

The boys called and whistled, but the German shepherd didn't show up. Suddenly Linus came out of the sawmill. He grinned at Tom and Carl and beckoned to them.

"You boys looking for a dog?" he asked.

"Yes," said Tom. "The Germans didn't take him along, did they?"

"Not a chance," said Linus. "I saw to that. He was standing beside me when the Germans came marching around the side of the house all of a sudden. I just managed to grab him by the collar and drag him inside. Just follow me."

They followed Linus through the sawmill to a tiny office in the rear. He opened the door and out leaped Scout, barking happily. He was overjoyed to see Tom and to be released from the small cubicle. Tom was no less glad to see that his dog was safe.

Together they went back outside, but the boys were in no mood to play. All they could think of was the awful secret they had overheard in the mill. Soon they were again discussing the German plot.

"We just have to think of something!" said Carl. "We know exactly where the Germans have set up their trap. Hey, I think we've got a map of this area in the house. Wait a minute; I'll go get it."

He hurried into the house and returned a few minutes later with the map. When he started unfolding it, Tom said, "Couldn't we better go up into the windmill? From there we can see all the German defenses and outposts. I've got a pencil in my pocket, so we can mark the German and Canadian positions on the map."

They climbed back up the ladder while Scout watched them from below, obviously disappointed. He couldn't understand why the boys wouldn't play with him today.

Up in the crown of the windmill, it was already becoming dark, but the small windows still gave them a good view of the battlefield.

"Okay," said Carl. "Let's begin by marking the places where the Germans are dug in and where they have put outposts."

Continually studying the terrain below through the window, and making use of everything they had heard and seen during the past week, the two boys soon had a fairly detailed map of the German positions. They were surprised themselves at how much they knew.

The Canadian positions were much harder. They could indicate a few landmarks that had been seized by the Allies, but very few details.

When their handiwork was finished, the two boys studied it once more. The German line had few weak points. The only place the Canadians could outflank the Germans was through the swamp, but then they had to go through the woods where the Germans lay in ambush.

"We've got to warn them!" said Tom. "If they walk into that trap, they won't stand a chance."

"Yes," said Carl, "and then it will be that much longer before we're liberated. In the meantime, who knows what might happen to my dad."

Again they bent over the map. It was a hiker's map that marked every creek, gully, hill, and forest. But they didn't really need it, for both boys knew this area like their own backyards. One thing was sure: they would never reach the liberated village if they took the shortest route. There were too many German outposts. They'd be spotted for sure.

"I've got it!" Carl cried excitedly. "We'll go through here," he said, pointing to the swamp.

Tom looked at him, puzzled. "How do you expect us to get through there, Carl? There's only one trail through the swamp, and we'd have to go through the woods where the Germans are hiding."

"No, we wouldn't," said Carl. "There's another trail. It's very narrow and hard to find, and almost no one knows about it. A couple of years ago I went out duck hunting with old Klaas Van den Brink. That's right, the one who died last year. He knew those swamps like nobody else, and he took me through here. Look." Carl traced a line on the map with his finger. "It's not much of a trail; here and there you have to jump from one dry spot to another, but it skirts the woods around the northern end, and cuts the main trail somewhere around here. Then all we have to do is turn left to reach the Canadian lines."

"Do you think you could find it again?" Tom asked him.

Carl's enthusiasm ebbed a little. He thought a moment, frowning. "It was a long time ago," he said doubtfully, "and I haven't tried the trail since then. Besides, I wasn't paying a lot of attention when I went with Van den Brink. I just followed the old man. But I do remember where the trail starts: it starts in this small gully."

Both boys sat quietly staring at the map.

"Let's try it," said Tom. "We'll take Scout with us. Maybe we can find our way through. We've got to try; a lot of lives depend on it."

"Our own too," said Carl. "If we miss that trail and bump into the Germans, we'll be shot for sure."

Again they both hesitated. Outside, dusk was turning into darkness. The small attic in the top of the windmill was almost completely dark now. The boys' faces stood out from the surrounding shadows, pale with the seriousness of what they were about to do.

"Then let's go!" they both said at the same time.

Chapter 18

In the Swamp

Now that they had decided, they suddenly felt relieved.

"When should we leave?" asked Carl. "I'd like to be back by tonight. I don't want to tell my mom about this. Not that she would stop us; she might agree that we have no choice. But with my dad and me both gone she would worry herself sick. Do you think it's dark enough to leave now? Then we could be back before bedtime."

He walked to the window and yelped in surprise. "Look, Tom! It's getting foggy outside. You can hardly see a thing."

Tom, too, hurried to the window. Carl was right. Not only was darkness coming on, but a white mist was also creeping over the countryside from the direction of the Canadian lines and was covering the whole front with a gray blanket.

"In another ten minutes it will be completely dark," said Tom. "Let's get ready to leave right now."

They quickly climbed down the ladder, receiving a happy welcome from Scout.

"Just a minute," Carl said softly. "We'd better take along something to eat."

He sneaked into the house and emerged a minute later with a lunch-kit that hung from his shoulder by a leather strap. "I put in a few of the rolls that my mother made at noon," he whispered. "We can't wait for supper, so we'll probably get hungry on the way. Let's take the binoculars along too. I know it's dark, but you never know how they'll come in handy."

"And the map," said Tom. "We better not forget the map."

Carl found a long piece of rope to tie to Scout's collar. Scout was always very obedient, but since they were going into the swamp, the boys thought it would be better to have him on a leash.

"Have we got everything?" asked Carl.

"No," said Tom. "Let's both cut ourselves a good walking stick to test the ground ahead of us when we get into the swamp. It will save us some wet feet."

Close to the mill stood a row of willow trees. Tom shinnied up into the top of one of them and cut off a couple of straight branches with his jack-knife. Then they were ready to go.

Carl hesitated. "I hate to go without saying something to my mother," he said. "But I'm also afraid to tell her where we're going."

The boys looked at one another in silence.

Then Tom said, "What we're doing can't be wrong. God would want us to try to save the lives of all those soldiers."

"And if we're killed . . ." began Carl. He stopped and began again. "Lots of others have risked their lives, too, and been killed. We shouldn't be afraid to take a risk to save so many others."

Resolutely Carl turned away from the farmhouse and headed in the direction of the swamp. Tom fell in beside him. At first they had thought of it as a great adventure, but now there wasn't a trace of the adventurer left in either one of them. Only Scout bounded ahead eagerly, unaware of the danger that lay ahead. Even he, however, kept his ears alertly pricked up, because Tom had forbidden him to bark and had added the warning, "Watch out for Germans, Scout!"

First they followed a narrow cinder trail, but soon they struck out to the right, climbed a wire fence, and then headed across the fields.

The fog was quite thick here, and with darkness coming on, there was little chance of their being seen. They trod on in silence. Now and then Carl would give directions in a very low voice.

After about twenty minutes, they were in the danger zone. Now the trick was to slip through a double ring of sentries. They stopped behind a clump of shrubs in the middle of the field, and Carl took out the map. In the deepening dusk they could hardly make out the lines, but they almost knew it by heart.

"There should be a path about a hundred metres from here," whispered Tom. "That's where we run into the first German positions. We have to try to cross the path about halfway between two sentries. They should be just about here and here, about a hundred metres apart."

He pointed to two *Xs* on the map which marked the location of the German posts. The sentries had camouflaged themselves, but from the windmill they had been clearly visible.

After carefully estimating where they were in relation to the two German positions, the boys made a beeline for the spot where they wanted to cross the path, keeping as low as they could. They had almost reached the path, when Scout suddenly stopped and uttered a low growl. If this weren't enough to frighten the wits out of them, at the same moment a light flashed on about twenty metres to their left.

They dropped to the ground, Tom hissing a whispered command to Scout to "play dead." Heavy footsteps approached. The beam of light flitted across the fields, passed just over their heads, and then returned to the path. Tom's heart pounded in his temples. They were goners if they were found here, especially with the map marking all the German positions.

They heard voices now. It sounded like two German soldiers coming down the path. "Lousy weather in this lousy country. I'll be glad to get back to Germany," said one of them.

"It's not all that great at home either," answered the other. "I wish this war was over."

The voices moved away out of earshot. The boys stayed where they were for another full minute. They could hardly believe they hadn't been seen. Then they raised their heads to look. They could still see the glow of the flashlight bobbing away across the field.

"That was a close call!" breathed Carl, his voice trembling.

"That's for sure! I don't understand how they missed us. They must be a patrol going from post to post. If they hadn't switched on their light when they did, we would have bumped right into them. I think God was watching over us."

"You're right," Carl answered quietly. "But now we better move on and get out of this area as fast as we can."

Again they went on in silence. Their legs still felt weak from the sudden fright they had undergone and all their nerves were taut and tingling. On the other side of the path, the ground began to slope downward. Here and there the ground was soft and wet. They avoided these spots as much as possible because their feet made sucking sounds when they tried to walk across the soggy terrain.

Finally they reached the barbed wire fence at the end of the field. Helping each other through, they got to the other side without any snags. Fences posed no problem to Scout; he could easily jump much higher obstacles.

Now they were on the outskirts of an old peat bog, where turfmen still came to dig peat for fuel. A few hundred metres beyond was the swamp they had to cross. Although it hardly seemed necessary, the Germans had placed several sentries along the swamp too, but they were few and far between, so this line wasn't nearly as dangerous as the one they had just crossed. The experience with the patrol, however, had made the boys doubly cautious. They also had to be very careful because the terrain was so rough here. Scattered all about the area were deep holes, many of which were full of water. Both boys were good swimmers, but neither relished an unexpected bath. Besides, the splash might draw the attention of the sentries, so they proceeded with great care. Carl led the way because only he knew where they were going.

Just before they reached the swamp, they passed a large bowl-shaped pool fringed with reeds. As they skirted the reeds, suddenly, with a loud flutter of wings, a wild duck rose from the reeds. Tom and Carl started with fright. Scout growled but, fortunately, did not bark.

The boys immediately crouched down in the reeds. They waited for five minutes, hardly daring to breathe, expecting soldiers to appear any second, but nothing happened. They were getting cold. A wind had arisen which chilled them as they sat still.

"Come on, let's move," whispered Carl.

They crept out of the rustling reeds. They were now less than one hundred metres from the edge of the swamp. But as they looked ahead to where they had to go, they saw that the wind was blowing away most of the fog, at least between them and the swamp. Tom and Carl cast worried looks at each other. With the fog lifting and with darkness not yet complete, visibility had improved markedly. They discussed what to do next.

"We'll have to crawl," Tom said softly.

Carl nodded. That was the only thing to do, and even that would be dangerous with German sentries about two hundred metres away. They squirmed ahead like snakes across the dark peat ground. Scout, too, crawled forward on his belly, right behind the two boys.

These last hundred metres were not very pleasant. The ground was wet, and here and there they had to make their way through shallow puddles, so they were soon wet and filthy, but they were making good progress.

The field was very quiet. The boys heard nothing but the whistling of the wind and their own ragged breathing.

As Carl pushed himself forward, suddenly his right hand slid out from under him. The slippery ground dropped away in front of him and two big clods of dirt went splashing into a deep hole filled with water. Carl himself also lurched forward and almost followed the clods into the hole, but Tom, who was right behind him, grabbed his legs and held him on the edge. Carefully he pulled his friend back.

They lay side by side throbbing with fear. Carl had been saved from a dangerous plunge, but the splash made by the clods must have carried a long way across the quiet fields. Again they hugged the earth for several minutes, not daring to move a muscle. Then, very softly, Carl breathed into Tom's ear, "I don't think anyone heard. The wind's blowing away from the sentries."

They began crawling again, but after a few metres Carl stopped and whispered, "I'm not sure we're going in the right direction. I'm afraid I lost my bearings at that hole."

They both looked around and tried to remember exactly how they had fixed their bearings.

"I think we have to go a little to the right," Tom said softly.

Uneasily they edged forward on their stomachs. Carl hesitated a couple of times, but each time he went on again. Finally he stopped and whispered, "I'm afraid we're crawling in a circle. What if we're heading straight for one of the German posts?"

"Scout will warn us," Tom whispered back. "I don't think we're that far off, though."

The fog had closed in again. They stared hard into the deepening gloom. Tom pointed to a dark shape a few metres in front of them.

"What's that?" he whispered.

Carl studied it very closely. Then suddenly he hissed happily, "I know! It's that old willow tree with a clump of bushes around it. It marks the edge of the swamp. The path that we're looking for begins about ten metres to the left of it."

Both boys breathed easier. Quickly they crawled ahead to the dark clump of bushes, where they sat and rested for a few minutes. Now they knew they were a relatively safe distance from the nearest sentries. From here the path should be easy to find. In the shelter of the bushes they felt quite safe. The front of their clothes was drenched and caked with mud. They tried to scrape it off a bit, but didn't have much success. The darkness of the night surrounded them — a darkness filled with mysterious muted sounds.

"We're in no-man's-land here," Tom said quietly. The Germans are behind us and the Canadian lines should be about two kilometres ahead of us."

Carl opened his lunch-kit. "Let's eat something," he proposed. "I'm hungry."

For the first time Tom, too, felt how hungry he was. They divided half the rolls among them, Scout getting his share. They didn't want to eat everything now, because they had no idea how long their mission might take. The food and the rest did them good. It also gave them a chance to unwind and relax after the scares of the last hour, so that they were ready to continue with renewed strength and spirit.

Growing along the edge of the swamp was a border of bulrushes and reeds. The boys stalked ahead in a deep crouch so that they could not be seen above the dense stalks. They, thus, covered the last few metres to the swamp in relative safety.

"It should be somewhere around here," whispered Carl.

With his long stick he probed beyond the swaying wall of reeds for solid ground. When they were crawling, the sticks had been a nuisance, but now the boys saw that the sticks would come in very handy. After poking around for a minute or so, Carl found the beginning of the trail. He pushed forward through the reeds, followed closely by Tom and Scout, still on his leash.

They advanced very slowly. The trail was very narrow and full of twists and turns, but by constantly probing ahead with his long stick, Carl had no trouble following it. He himself hadn't expected it to be so easy. After passing through the broad strip of reeds surrounding the swamp, they were now in a more open area. Here and there heather and large clumps of willow bushes grew up out of the swamp, but the boys were no longer greatly worried about being discovered, because they had put a good distance between themselves and the German lines.

Suddenly, about a hundred metres ahead Tom saw the glow of a light. It bobbed up and down. He poked Carl. "Look," he whispered, hoarse with fear. "There's someone ahead of us."

Carl, too, stopped and stared. Just as quickly as it had appeared it was gone, but immediately it came on again farther ahead. Then suddenly a second one appeared to the left of the first.

Tom laughed with relief. "You know what those are?" he whispered to Carl. "They're swamp ghosts. Long ago people used to think they were evil spirits trying to lure men into the swamps. Our biology teacher says they're gases that escape from the swamp and catch fire somehow or other."

Their fears allayed, they continued on. They were slowly approaching the most dangerous part of the swamp. Again they began to run into tall reeds, and here and there they skirted deep waterholes. Carl kept probing ahead for the path with his stick, but he began hesitating more and more often. Their was very little progress.

By now the night had become very black, and although the boys didn't admit it to each other, the fear began to grow in their hearts that they would never find their way out of the treacherous swamp. They had been betrayed by what seemed like solid ground a few times already and their feet had sunk through. Finally Carl stopped.

"I don't know which way to go anymore," he said, barely stifling a sob. "I'm afraid we've been following a false trail for the last couple of minutes. I think it runs dead. See if you can find solid ground."

Carefully Tom edged forward to stand beside him. The path was very narrow here. He pried and poked with his stick, but he could find nothing that would bear their weight. Then he had an idea. Bending forward very carefully, he probed farther ahead, and there, less than two metres ahead of them, his stick struck something solid.

"I think part of the trail has sunk away, but it seems to begin again over there," he told Carl. "We can easily jump it." He handed Carl the rope that was tied to Scout's collar. Stepping back a little, he took a deep breath and leaped forward into the darkness. Immediately he sank into the swamp up to his waist.

Frantically he groped around for the solid ground that he had found, but it turned out to be nothing more than a muddy clump of swamp grass. Tom tried to wade back to Carl, but the mud was sucking him down farther and farther and his legs wouldn't move.

"Help!" he cried to Carl. "I'm stuck in the swamp!" Carl reached forward, but couldn't find him. Then he held out his stick, and Tom quickly seized it with both hands. But no matter how hard Carl pulled and Tom struggled to free himself from the mud, Tom stayed where he was.

The impenetrable darkness and oppressive stillness made their fight against the swamp even more frightening. Tom felt as if monstrous hands were holding him by the legs and were slowly but surely pulling him downward to suffocate in the slime. Suddenly Scout launched himself into the swamp, landing right beside Tom. He sank his teeth into Tom's jacket and tried to pull him loose, but the dog's heroic attempt was in vain. Scout himself could find no foothold, and he too began to sink away into the bottomless mire. Carl had difficulty pulling the big dog back out by the rope.

However, the rope gave him an idea. "Here, grab this!" he told Tom. "I'll throw you the other end of the rope we tied on Scout. Tie it around your waist, and Scout and I will both try to pull you out."

He threw the rope to Tom. By this time the darkness was so total, Tom had to find the rope by groping around in the mud, but he quickly found it and tied it around his waist. "Ready!" he panted.

Carl and Scout pulled as hard as they could, and Tom, too, threw every last ounce of his strength into wrestling himself loose from the swamp's hold. The muck seemed to try to suck him back. They were all sobbing with strain, but Tom was starting to move. Slowly his legs were twisting free from the grip of the hungry swamp. One of his legs broke loose, and with a last frantic lunge, the other leg, too, came shooting free. He slid forward over the slime, pulled by the rope, his hands finding the edge of the trail. Carl was sent tumbling backwards by the sudden surge.

They both scrambled back to their feet, winded with exertion, but filled with gladness at the success of the rescue, "Thanks," gasped Tom. "I thought I was a goner!"

"Boy, if Scout hadn't been here to help, I'd never have gotten you out," said Carl, patting the dog.

But their situation was far from happy. They were swallowed up by a deep blackness and had no idea which way the trail went. Yet they were not without hope. For although the boys said nothing about it, they were both very much aware that God had saved Tom, and they also trusted Him to bring them through the swamp.

"We have to go back," said Carl. "I'm sure we got sidetracked. When Van den Brink took me down this trail, I remember him going off on a dead-end spur a few times to stalk ducks."

Still probing with their sticks, they made their way back along the trail. They were going slower than ever, for now they were also looking for a turn-off.

After a few minutes Carl said, "This feels like it. We came from the left a while ago, but there's also a trail to the right here. It seems wider than the one we're on now. It has to be the right one!"

He started to turn into the new path, but then he stopped. "Should we go on like this?" he asked Tom. "You're wet up to your waist and we're not even halfway through the swamp yet. Maybe we'll run into more dead-ends. If we turn back now, we know the path, and in this darkness we shouldn't have any trouble sneaking back through the German lines."

"Are you kidding?" said Tom. "We can't give up now! So what if I catch a cold. The lives of hundreds of soldiers depend on us getting through. I'll tell you what: why don't we let Scout lead the way. He's a better trailblazer than either one of us. Just wait and see; he'll lead us out of here."

They continued down the trail with new resolve, following Scout. Tom's trust in the dog was not misplaced. Even in the dense blackness, he kept them on solid ground. Tom and Carl still tested the trail with their sticks, but they moved ahead with ever greater confidence.

It was not a pleasure hike, however. Tom was wet up to his waist and couldn't stop shivering. Carl was in better shape, although both his shoes squelched with water at every step. Both boys were beginning to feel the drag of exhaustion. The fear and tension and the effort of Tom's rescue had drained a lot out of them, but with grim determination they pushed on, metre by metre.

Their legs grew heavier and heavier, for the trail was quite muddy here, and large clods clung to their shoes. The boys, however, entertained no more thoughts of turning back.

After another twenty minutes of slogging along the trail, Carl suddenly hissed, "Look! Over there. Over to our right."

They had come to a spot where the fog had lifted almost completely. Through the cloud cover overhead they could see a few stars twinkling comfortingly. By the faint light of the stars Tom could see what had caught Carl's eye. About twenty metres ahead of them was an area that gleamed lighter than the rest. Tom stopped, mystified. What could that be?

"That must be one of the two ponds in the middle of the swamp," Carl said, his voice filled with relief. "It's somewhere close to the first pond that our trail is supposed to cut the main one, the one on which the Germans are hoping to trap the Canadians."

Tom, too, breathed a deep sigh of relief. If Carl was right, the worst was behind them. And, sure enough, a few minutes later they found themselves on a broader trail.

"Now we're about in the middle of the swamp," observed Carl. "We have to go left here."

On the main trail the boys could walk much faster. The ground was still marshy, but the path was wide enough for them to walk side by side. Although the path was rough, they didn't have to be afraid of falling into any deep waterholes. They were now making good time, and along with new hope, new strength seemed to flow into them.

All of a sudden, however, Tom blurted, "What if we got here too late? It took us a long time to get here. What if those Canadian soldiers already passed this way?"

Carl wasn't sure how much time they had spent on the small trail either; but after talking it over, the two boys decided the Canadians couldn't have passed by yet. The path would have been torn up by the soldiers' boots, and they would have reached the woods where the Germans were hiding. Then the boys would have heard shooting by now.

The ground was gradually becoming more solid underfoot. A few minutes later they reached the other end of the swamp. Their awful journey was almost at an end, but the suspense was far from over for the boys. Were they in time? Could they convince anyone of their story?

Chapter 19

Disappointment

After a five-minute walk they were coming to the outskirts of the liberated village. "Funny that we haven't seen anybody," Carl said to Tom. "Do you think they didn't put out any sentries?"

No sooner had he spoken, than a bright beam of light fell on them, and a voice ordered them to stop. Blinking timidly into the bright light, they obeyed.

"Where did you come from?" demanded one of the two guards, examining the two boys, who were covered with mud from head to foot.

At first Tom had trouble understanding the man's English. He spoke so fast; it sounded much different from what he had learned at school, but when the man repeated the question, Tom understood. He motioned to the swamp and said, "We come from the next village. The one still held by the Germans. We know something about the German plans. We've got to speak to the commander."

Tom spoke in stops and starts, searching for the right words. Nevertheless, the guard who was doing the talking seemed to have understood him, for he shook his head and answered, "Impossible!"

Tom's heart plummeted. Were the guards not going to let them through? But they simply had to deliver their message! Nervously he began telling the two soldiers about the German plan to lead the Canadians into a trap, but Tom became all tangled up in the English sentences. It was such a long and complex story to tell in a strange language. Carl would help him out occasionally, but Carl knew even less English than he did.

The soldiers seemed to understand only part of their story. The two men spoke to each other in short, broken phrases. Then the one man turned back to them and said once more, "You can't pass here. Go back to your own village."

With difficulty Tom swallowed back his rage and frustration. Had they risked their lives only to be sent back by a couple of stubborn sentries? Then Tom had an idea. From his pocket he took the map on which they had marked the German positions and fortifications. He opened the map to explain again, but the soldier took the sheet out of his hands and studied it by the light of his flashlight. His face immediately came alive with interest, and he looked at the boys with a much friendlier attitude.

"What is this?" he asked Tom.

"We marked all the German defenses on the map," explained Tom.

The two guards carefully studied the markings on the map once more. They held a brief, whispered conference, and then the soldier who did all the talking pointed to the other man and said, "Just follow him."

A load seemed to fall off their hearts. They were going to see the commander after all. Leading Scout by the rope, Tom and Carl followed the Canadian soldier, who seemed to have forgotten all his earlier suspicion. Soon they were in the village.

Outwardly the village looked much as it always had. Here and there light glowed through small cracks around the blacked-out windows of houses. Apparently many of the people were so excited by their liberation, they were staying up late tonight.

At the school, a lot of soldiers were walking around. The school seemed to have been turned into a barracks. Several army tents had been pitched in the town square.

Still led by the soldier, they crossed the square. The boys wished it were lighter so they could see some of the Canadian war machinery.

Overhead they heard the flutter of a Dutch flag, and their hearts were filled with excitement at the thought that they were now in liberated territory.

The guard stopped in front of a large mansion. Tom knew the house. This was where the Nazi mayor had been living during the German occupation. He must have fled when the Canadians arrived.

Their guide said a few words to the guard at the door. Again they were examined under a bright flashlight beam that traveled over their dirty clothes and the big German shepherd beside them. Then the first man shook hands with them and turned back to his post. The new sentry opened the door of the big house and led them down a long, wide hallway. He knocked on a door and went in. The boys stayed in the hall.

There was a light in the hall, so for the first time the two adventurers could see what they looked like. They were caked with mud from their shoes to their hair, and Scout too was filthy. They looked behind them in embarrassment at the dirty tracks they had left on the fine carpet in the hall.

"We look like a couple of street urchins," whispered Carl. "No wonder those soldiers looked at us so strangely."

Tom nodded. He felt chilled and clammy in his wet clothes. The boys were told to enter, and the guard went back to the front door.

They stepped into a spacious, brightly lit room where two Canadian officers sat at a large table. The older one, who was graying at the temples, seemed to be the commander. On a chair on the opposite side of the table sat a young man in civilian clothes. He had a pale, intense look about him. Tom and Carl did not know him, but by his clothing they could tell he was a Dutchman. The two officers had a large military map spread in front of them. They were busy putting various markings on it according to information that the Dutchman was providing in fluent English. Carl and Tom, the latter still leading Scout, bashfully stayed by the door which the guard had closed behind them. Awed, they stared at the two officers. So these were the leaders of the army that had come to liberate them from the Germans.

After a moment, however, Tom began to pay attention to what the young civilian was saying. The man spoke English fluently, much better than Tom, but Tom could understand him quite well. Tom listened with increasing amazement. He nudged Carl.

"That man knows more about the German positions than we do," he whispered.

Carl nodded. He too understood most of the conversation. "Our map isn't worth much anymore," he said softly, a note of disappointment in his voice.

"No," answered Tom. "But we know about the trap the Germans are setting in the woods, and that's much more important."

He turned his attention back to what the young man was saying. Maybe it wasn't polite to listen in, but he couldn't resist. Was he hearing right? Now the man was describing German positions Tom had been able to view very clearly from his vantage point in the windmill. As he sketched their location, he gave detailed information about the kind of artillery stationed there. Tom's mouth dropped open. What the man was saying couldn't possibly be right. He had to be mistaken, for not only did the lines run differently from the way he described them, his estimate of the numbers of guns and troops was far too high.

Again Tom nudged Carl. "Do you hear that? The information that he's giving them now is all wrong."

Carl shrugged his shoulders. "I don't understand it. He talks as if he's sure, but he can't be right."

Now they listened very closely. Repeatedly they heard things that didn't fit. The Dutchman was usually far too high in his reporting of German troop strength and in general described the German positions as almost impregnable.

The Canadian commander's face took on a stubborn look. "There's no such thing as an impregnable position," he said. "We'll drive them out of there."

The young man leaned forward over the map. "It will be a lot easier if you follow the plan I outlined a few minutes ago. The trail through the swamp will pose no problems for the infantry. The Germans don't expect an attack from that side at all. They don't even have sentries along the swamp and are not at all prepared to defend against an attack from there, at least, not yet. We should take advantage of this hole in their defenses tonight, before they catch their mistake and correct it. If we take this path and muster an attack from these woods . . ."

"He's lying! He's a traitor!" Tom's voice suddenly shrilled through the room.

He had been listening with increasing wonderment until the man began talking about the trail through the swamp, and then the truth hit him like a lightning bolt. This was the Judas goat who was supposed to lead the Canadians into the trap!

When this dawned on him, he couldn't restrain himself and the warning burst from his lips before he had time to think. The two officers were now looking at him with obvious irritation. They hadn't understood Tom's words because, in his indignation, he had spoken Dutch.

"What's the matter?" the commander demanded to know. He did not look very happy at the interruption. Hurriedly and nervously Tom stammered out his story in badly broken English. In his agitation, he had trouble thinking of the right words. The commanding officer frowned darkly. "Come here!" he ordered, pointing to a spot right in front of the table.

The boys and the dog approached the two Canadian officers.

Upon hearing Tom's outcry, the man in civilian clothes, already pale, turned even paler. Momentarily his eyes had the look of a trapped animal. When he noted the boy's nervousness and his trouble with the English language, however, he quickly recovered. He looked at the boys with a mocking smile. Meanwhile, Tom had calmed down a little, although his head was still throbbing and pounding. He pulled the map from his pocket and laid it on the table in front of the commander.

"The information that this man gave you is wrong," he said. "This map gives the true strength of the German positions and where they are. Above all, don't go through the swamp! It's a trap! The woods at the end of the trail are full of German soldiers."

It took Tom every last ounce of emotional energy to find the right words, but when he was finished, the Dutchman burst into scornful laughter.

"I hope, Commander, you're not going to put any stock in the fantasies of a couple of boys playing at being spies," he said. "They're obviously trying to get a little attention, but this is no time to humour children with overactive imaginations. They've read too many westerns. How could a couple of boys get their hands on secret military information?"

The man spoke so glibly and confidently, the Canadian commander seemed to be swayed by his words. He looked at the boys' map. To a

military man, the marks and lines drawn by the boys must have looked rather childish and certainly didn't give the impression of being very reliable.

Standing up, the Dutchman brazenly pulled the map toward himself and began picking it apart. He started spouting numbers and other details so adroitly, he quickly made a convincing case that the markings made by Tom and Carl were just amateurish jottings.

The commander, however, didn't seem to be completely convinced. "How did you boys find out about the German defenses?" he asked them.

"We could see everything from the top of a big windmill. That's also where we overheard the plans to lure you into an ambush," said Tom.

The officer shrugged. That sounded awfully farfetched to him. The Dutchman began talking again. "You see, Commander?" he said, laughing. "I told you these boys have been reading too many westerns! My information comes from the underground. We've worked hard for weeks to gather all this information. Surely you're not going to toss it all out just because of a couple of boys trying to play hero!"

Tom had reached the limits of his endurance. The exhausting journey, the hours of fear and suspense, and the discouragement at the way his story was being received — all had taken their toll on him. He burst into tears.

"This man is a dirty spy, a Nazi collaborator," sobbed Tom, pointing at the civilian.

He had lapsed into Dutch again, however, so the officer didn't understand him. The commander shook his head and pushed a button. The door opened and a soldier entered the room.

"Take these boys somewhere where they can wash up, and find them a bed," he ordered.

Shattered and sickened at their failure, the two friends followed the soldier, Scout trotting along behind. All their determination and hope had evaporated. The door of the officers' room closed behind them. They walked back down the long hallway, moving as if in a nightmare. Tom rubbed his hands in his eyes. He didn't notice that his hands were so dirty; he now had two black eyes. He was past noticing anything. Just as they were approaching the front door, it suddenly opened in front of them. It was the guard who had escorted them in, followed by two other men.

Tom wasn't looking, but Carl yelped in surprise and Scout leaped forward, barking happily. Now Tom looked up too.

"Haaksma! Bert!" he exclaimed.

No less surprised, the two newcomers stared at the two mud-caked boys in amazement.

Chapter 20

A Surprise Encounter

"How did you get here?" asked Haaksma.

"We crawled through the German lines," said Tom, and then we came through the swamp. We came to warn the Canadian commander about a trap set up by the Germans, but . . ." Tom swallowed back the tears and his voice trembled. "But he didn't believe us. There's a man in there with him feeding him false information."

Tears of anger and frustration sprang to his eyes. Haaksma's face took on a grim, intense look, but his voice sounded cheerful as he said, "Well, then I arrived in the nick of time. Let's see if we can't pluck the bird's feathers. Follow me."

Tom and Carl looked questioningly at the soldier who had been escorting them out. He had been standing by waiting impatiently for the end of the conversation, and now he moved in to coax the boys outside.

Haaksma spoke to him in fluent English. "I'm taking these boys back inside," he said. "They have important information, and I can back up their story."

The soldier hesitated. He looked Haaksma over and asked, "But who are you?"

"Captain Brandenburg, officer in the Dutch army, working for British intelligence since 1940," was his terse reply.

The boys looked at each other in astonishment, but they could tell by Haaksma's face that he was telling the truth. Although they had long suspected that Haaksma was not a farmhand, it had never entered their minds he might be working for British intelligence.

The soldier exchanged a few words with the guard who was leading Haaksma and Bert inside, and then he said, "Follow me, please."

Tom and Carl had a strange sensation as they approached the commander's door for the second time: they weren't sure whether they were awake or dreaming. The soldier reached for the doorknob, but Haaksma, as the boys continued to call him, said, "Wait a minute."

He took out a small notebook, wrote something down, tore out the page and handed it to the soldier, saying, "Please be so kind as to deliver this to the commander."

The man disappeared, and the foursome was left alone in the hall.

"How did you get here?" Carl whispered to Bert.

"Oh," he replied, "we had quite a trip. We took a boat across the river and then waded up a creek for a ways." He pointed to the high wading boots the two men were wearing. "But by the looks of you two, what we went through is nothing compared to your adventure."

The door opened and the soldier asked them to come in. The foursome trooped into the room, Haaksma taking the lead.

The two officers were still sitting at the big table. Now the Dutchman was standing beside them. The map in front of them had been marked in red. Apparently the three men were making plans for the attack through the swamp. The boys could tell that this new interruption was not at all welcomed by the Dutchman. The Canadian commander, however, studied Haaksma from head to foot with keen interest. His first impression seemed to be favourable. At least, he asked the group to approach the table in a civil enough voice, without making any comments about the reappearance of the two boys.

A rapid exchange followed between Haaksma and the commanding officer. The Canadian posed a number of short, pointed questions, which Haaksma answered calmly and without hesitation. The boys didn't understand much of the conversation. It didn't seem to make much sense to them, but they did understand that Haaksma was being grilled to see if he really was who he claimed to be. Gradually, the officer's face began to relax. He stood up from his chair and, bending forward across the table, extended his hand to Haaksma.

"Well, Captain Brandenburg," he said, "your answers jibe. I'm very eager to hear what you have to tell us."

Haaksma reached into an inside pocket of his jacket and produced a small package. It was wrapped in oilcloth. The men behind the table, and also the boys, looked on in suspense as he unwrapped the package. A couple pieces of lead rolled out onto the table, and Haaksma pushed them aside. "That was just to weigh down the package in case the Germans stopped us. Then I would have dropped it into the river."

Besides the pieces of lead, there was a second oilcloth package, wrapped even more carefully than the first. When Haaksma opened it, a number of very small micro-photos and several graphs, drawings, and charts spilled out onto the table. "These provide detailed information about the German positions. Not only for the next village, but for the entire front in this sector. The micro-photos were taken by men who were helping to build the German fortifications."

The officers' interest in the material was written all over their faces. The commander spoke a few words to his orderly, who went to a cabinet and returned with a powerful magnifying glass. The two Canadians examined several photos through the magnifying glass.

"This is excellent work," said the commander. His voice was filled with open admiration.

Haaksma nodded. "I had some good men helping me," he said. "They all risked their lives, but it came off without a hitch. That isn't all. Here are charts showing the strength and deployment of the German troops. We've put all the information on this map. If necessary, I can supply more details personally."

The commander bent forward over the map and the lists of numbers. "Well, I'll be . . ." he said in surprise. "These numbers agree pretty closely with those given by these two lads. If they're right, then this man's information is all wet!" He looked at the Dutchman standing beside him.

The man's face had turned ashen. His eyes flared with fear and anger. "This so-called Captain Brandenburg is a German agent!" he cried hoarsely. "He and these two brats are in on a plot to discredit me. Don't believe a word of what they say!"

Haaksma, or Captain Brandenburg, faced the man squarely. "Is it all right if I ask this man a few questions, Commander?" he asked the Canadian officer.

"Be my guest," said the commander, sitting down.

Haaksma began a question-and-answer contest with the man. The fellow claimed that he had obtained his information from the underground, so Haaksma bore in on this claim. He began asking the young man for all kinds of information and details about the underground, and although the spy was clever, Haaksma soon had him trapped on several counts. The man tried to save himself by inventing more and more lies, some of them outright challenges to his interrogator, but Haaksma kept after him with an icy calmness, stalking him like a hunter cornering his prey.

The conversation was conducted in English, for both men had a good command of the language, so that the two officers could follow the exchange from A to Z. Finally Haaksma turned to the commander.

At that moment, the German spy, seeing that the jig was up, kicked over the table. He leaped forward and, dashing for the door, yanked it open.

The heavy table tumbled against Haaksma and the two boys, almost bowling them over. The two officers had jumped up, but they had to go around the table to go after the fleeing man. By that time he was already through the door. He raced down the hall and was almost at the front door. If he could surprise the sentry and make it out into the night, he had a good chance of getting away.

He might have succeeded, except for Scout. While the men in the room were still disentangling themselves, Scout was already bounding after the man. Tom had dropped the rope when he had been knocked over by the table. Scout went flying after the traitor in a blur of speed. Tom saw him disappear around the corner of the door. This also brought him into action. He sprinted after his dog, but everyone else arrived at the door at the same time, so that a sudden traffic jam resulted as everyone blocked everyone else.

From the hall came a terrified scream, followed by furious barking. Then a shot rang out. Tom was the first one into the hall, on his heels came Haaksma and the commander.

The traitor lay on the floor frantically trying to ward off the German shepherd. He had a small pistol in his hand and was trying to aim it at the attacking dog. But Scout had been trained to avoid the barrel of a gun. He had seized the man by the wrist of his gun hand and kept pulling the man off balance as he struggled to get to his feet.

Again the pistol fired. This time the bullet creased Scout's back, taking a pluck of hair with it. Before the man could shoot again, however, Tom was on him and grabbed his gun hand.

Wild with desperation, the man flung Tom against the wall and made a lunge for the door. But this time he was seized by Haaksma, and no matter how fiercely he fought, he was no match for the powerful Captain Brandenburg.

Within a few seconds the others also arrived. The Canadian commander called a couple of soldiers and ordered them to take the traitor away and lock him up. He would decide what to do with the prisoner later.

Haaksma, Bert, the two boys, and Scout returned to the big room with the two Canadian officers. The commander had remained very cool during the commotion, but now he looked at the dog with respect and admiration. "That's quite a dog!" he said to Tom, patting Scout on the head.

Then he ordered chairs to be brought in so that everyone could sit down around the table, which the orderly had righted. Tom was very glad for the chair, because he was so tired, his knees were threatening to buckle. Carl, too, looked exhausted. Both boys, however, were also glowing with delight at the turn of events. Their story had been proven true.

Now the two officers questioned Tom very closely about the trap laid for the Canadians in the woods. He told them everything he had heard. Haaksma could provide no further information concerning the woods. All he knew was that for the last four days German sentries had kept all Dutchmen away from the area.

When the commander heard this, he nodded. It was clear that something sinister was being organized in the woods, and he no longer doubted the truth of Tom's story. Now he asked the boys to describe, in as much detail as possible, how they had stolen through the German lines. The little-known trail through the swamp especially interested him. Not even Haaksma knew about the path.

"Do you think you could find it again in the dark?" the commander asked them.

Tom shuddered. He hated to think of repeating the terrifying journey through the darkness. When he saw the urgency in the faces of the two officers, however, he summoned up all his courage and resolve. "I think we can. Scout knows the way; he won't let us get lost."

The commander nodded thoughtfully. He exchanged a few whispered words with his fellow officer and then turned back to the boys. "I'm very grateful for what you boys have done. You have risked your lives to save those of my men. That we'll never forget. We may need you fellows again, but first we have to show you a little better hospitality."

He pushed a button. A door which Tom and Carl hadn't noticed before opened and in came another Canadian soldier.

"Take these three lads and their dog," said the commander, "and see they get something to eat and a place to wash up and sleep. We may need them later."

The soldier led Tom, Carl, Bert, and Scout through an adjoining room down a short hall and then up a flight of stairs. Upstairs was a large bedroom with two beds, a table and two chairs. The soldier motioned to them to have a seat and then hurried off.

"Are we going to sleep here?" asked Carl. "But we're wet and filthy. Even my underwear is muddy. I can't crawl into bed like this!"

"Let's wait a minute," advised Bert. "I think that soldier is coming back."

He turned out to be right. A few minutes later the door opened and the soldier was back with another uniformed man. Both were carrying a pile of clothes: underwear, socks, boots, and three uniforms.

The boys eyed the clothes, finding it hard to believe they were meant for them, but the soldier smiled and said, "Sorry, but we don't have any civilian clothes here. We'll just draft the three of you into the Canadian army. All of you are a pretty good size, and I dug up the smallest outfits we have. Try them on. Oh, first you'd better take a shower."

He opened a side door in the bedroom; behind it was a bathroom and a shower. Then the soldiers left, leaving the boys marvelling at everything that had happened.

"A real uniform," gloated Bert. "Won't Haaksma be surprised when he sees us! And won't the boys in town be jealous when we come marching into town with the Canadian army!"

They quickly stripped off their mud-soaked outer-wear and took turns in the shower. They stood under the warm, clear water letting it rinse away all the dirt and tension. The soldier had also supplied a big bar of soap and a stack of towels. They each took their time, splashing and scrubbing until they tingled with cleanliness.

Then they began trying on clothes. The clothes, it turned out, fit pretty well. Carl was given the smallest set of clothes, which were still somewhat large for him, but he didn't mind. He beamed with pride. They admired one another and examined themselves in the mirror over the dresser. They were still preening themselves when the door opened again.

Again the soldier came in. This time he was carrying a tray stacked high with egg sandwiches and a big pitcher of milk.

The boys whooped when they saw the food. Suddenly they realized how hungry they were. In a flash they were all sitting around the table enjoying the sandwiches. The soldier hadn't forgotten Scout, and he also fell to hungrily. They didn't stop eating until the last sandwich was gone.

"And now let's hit the sack," suggested Tom, who was having trouble keeping his eyes open. They carefully took off their prized uniforms and crawled into bed — Tom and Carl into one, and Bert into the other. Scout curled up on the floor beside Tom.

Bert, who was the closest to the switch, turned off the light.

"You still haven't told us what happened to you and Haaksma," Carl said, yawning.

"Oh," answered Bert, "after dark, Haaksma and I took the boat and then very, very quietly we rowed to the creek. You know, the one that comes into the river just a couple of kilometres downstream? Well, we had put on our wading boots and then . . ."

He yawned. His thoughts were becoming jumbled.

From the bed occupied by his two friends came a soft snoring.

"I'll . . . I'll tell . . . tomorrow . . ." mumbled Bert. Then he too was asleep.

Chapter 21

The Surprise Attack

When a hand rudely shook him awake, Tom felt as if he had only just crawled into bed. He turned over and tried to go back to sleep, but the hand wouldn't leave him alone. Then the voice of Haaksma was hollering, "Wake up, boys! Great things are happening!" Tom opened his eyes. He blinked in the glare of the ceiling light. It still seemed to be dark outside.

Haaksma was standing beside the bed. At first Tom didn't recognize him because he too was dressed in a Canadian uniform. Groaning, Tom sat up. He had a dull headache and was far from rested.

"You mean we have to get up already?" he grumbled groggily.

Bert was already sitting up in the other bed, but Carl was still asleep beside Tom. Haaksma shook him too until he opened his eyes with a start. "Sorry, fellows, but that's the way it is in the army," he said, grinning. "You've had two hours rest. That's not near enough, I know, but the troops are ready to go, and they're waiting for their guides. That's you."

Now the three boys were wide awake. They jumped out of bed and hurriedly pulled on their new clothes, firing scores of questions at Haaksma as they did so. Where were they going? What was going to happen?

Haaksma smiled mysteriously. "The Canadians are going to make a bold play," he said. "Those two officers and I have spent the last two hours working out the plan. I can't tell you all the details, but it amounts to this. We're going to take fifty men through the swamp along the trail you fellows took to get here. We have to be in the village before daylight to stage a surprise attack on German headquarters. The rest you'll see for yourselves. We need you boys, and Scout here, to show us the way. We don't have time to go searching around in the dark, because it will start getting light within two hours."

The boys were still terribly tired, especially Tom and Carl, but when they heard Haaksma's story, they forgot their tiredness, and their eyes brightened in anticipation. They were going to become the liberators of their own village!

Hurriedly they finished dressing and shortly they were trooping down the stairs. Scout, too, seemed to sense that something special was about to happen. Strong as he was, he appeared to be rested and raring to go as he bounded along beside Tom.

In the square in front of the house stood a large squad of soldiers. It was still very dark outside, but Haaksma was carrying a powerful flashlight with him. By its light Tom recognized the Canadian officer who had been sitting next to the commander. He was the officer in charge of the special strike force.

Haaksma exchanged a few words with him. Then the officer hissed an order and the squad started moving. Haaksma, the three boys, and Scout led the way. Behind them came the Canadians.

They crossed the town square. By now Tom's eyes had adjusted to the darkness. He noticed that there was movement everywhere. Soldiers were running back and forth between the tents, and the playground beside the school was bustling with activity. Although the soldiers were careful to make as little noise as possible, it was quite a commotion. Obviously preparations were being made for a full-scale attack.

On they went, between the black houses, down the unlit streets until they reached the outskirts of the village. They passed several sentries, who seemed to know what was going on, for they let them through without a challenge.

Soon they arrived at the edge of the swamp. Now the soldiers walked two abreast in a long column. One of the soldiers produced a long rope which was passed down the column so that everyone could hold onto it. It would prevent them from losing contact with one another in the dense darkness of the swamp.

Tom and Carl and Scout took the lead. Right behind them were Haaksma and Bert. They could see very little, so they had to walk with extreme care. Time was precious, however, so they could not move too slowly. The boys were impatient to see how the Canadians would carry out the surprise attack, but Haaksma told them they would find out soon enough.

"Isn't this squad way too small to take the whole town?" asked Tom. "There are only about fifty men."

"True," said Haaksma, "but these aren't just any old soldiers. The commander asked for volunteers for a very dangerous mission. About a hundred of the best men volunteered, and these fifty were selected. These soldiers have fought all over Europe and have proven themselves again and again. Besides, we're counting on catching the Germans completely by surprise."

"What if it turns out differently?" asked Carl.

Haaksma paused before answering. "That's always possible, of course," he said, "but what we're doing now is no more dangerous than what you boys already did earlier last night. We're all risking our lives for the sake of freedom. But we'd better not talk any more unless it's necessary. You never know, the Germans may have posted spies along the trail. After all, they are expecting us to pass by here on our way to the woods."

The boys knew Haaksma was right. Quietly the long column advanced along the narrow trail. Ahead was the dull gleam of one of the two ponds that marked the middle of the swamp.

"The other trail branches off somewhere along here," whispered Tom.

Haaksma passed the message on to the commander of the troop. A whispered command passed down the trail, and the column came to a halt. Tom and Carl were again armed with long sticks. They carefully probed for the turnoff.

"It's a good thing we took Scout along," said Tom. "Otherwise we would never have made it through the swamp the first time, and now he'll keep us from getting lost on the way back."

The Canadian officer again spoke to his men, giving them additional instructions. The rope was uncoiled even farther, for now they would have to travel single file.

With Tom and Scout in the lead, moving along very cautiously, step by step, the column turned off onto the narrower path. Now it became especially clear how important Scout was to the plan. Without his nose and alertness, the long line of soldiers would have had tremendous difficulty navigating the scant, winding little trail. Every time the boys hesitated, Scout confidently went ahead, and every time he was unerring in his choice of direction. In this way, the column was making much better time than Tom had expected. They were spurred on by Haaksma, who followed right on Carl and Tom's heels. On the eastern horizon, a faint glimmer of light was already beginning to tint the sky.

"Even a few minutes can make all the difference," Haaksma whispered. "If we're just a little late, the Germans might see us coming, and then we won't stand a chance."

With the help of the rope, the soldiers seemed to be having no trouble following. Now and then someone would stumble or slip off the trail, but not badly enough to hold them up. The end of their plodding journey through the swamp was in sight, for ahead of them rose the tall reeds that formed the border of the swamp. The reeds swayed and rustled in the early morning breeze. The officer signaled the men to keep low and not to make a sound, for they were now approaching the first real danger point — the first line of sentries.

They advanced another thirty metres, and then, in response to a whispered command from the officer, the troop crouched down on their haunches. The officer hissed the names of two men, who came to the front and crept forward with him to the edge of the reeds. Tom, Carl, Haaksma, and Scout also followed.

The dark marshland, where the boys had experienced so much fear a few hours earlier, stretched out ahead of them. Tom shuddered. It was cold just before sunrise, but he didn't shudder only because of the cold.

Someone was whispering in his ear, so softly he could hardly hear it at first. It was the officer: he was holding his mouth right by Tom's ear. "Where are the nearest sentries?" he asked.

The darkness was beginning to lift a little, but Tom couldn't make out anything. He pointed in the direction where he estimated the man to be. "He should be somewhere over there. A few metres to the right of us is an old willow tree surrounded by bushes. If we go there, we can see much better."

They crawled to the tree on hands and knees, reaching it without any problems. Hidden in the bushes, the small group scanned the field in front of them.

Carl was the first to see something. He pointed to a dark, indistinct figure about twenty metres from where they were hiding. It had to be the sentry. He seemed to be standing with his back toward them, otherwise they could have been able to make out the pale outline of his face.

The Canadian officer put his head beside those of the two soldiers. They nodded at his instructions. Lying flat on their bellies, noiselessly they squirmed forward. Tom was surprised to see how quickly they could move without making a single sound. He had often crawled like that while playing cowboys and Indians with his friends, but he had to admit that these soldiers were much faster.

In the first faint glimmers of dawn, which was slowly beginning to dissolve the darkness, the men on the ground looked like a couple of shadows. Soon Tom couldn't see them at all anymore. He listened very closely, but heard nothing — nothing but the rustling of the wind in the reeds. A couple of minutes went by. The German hadn't moved. He seemed to be watching the growing ribbon of light on the horizon. He was probably looking forward to being relieved.

Suddenly Tom and the others saw the sentry turn around. He must have heard something, but in the same moment two other shadows rose from the ground and merged with his. The German soldier disappeared without uttering a sound. What happened after that, Tom couldn't see. It only took a few seconds. He guessed that the men had tied and gagged him.

The two soldiers were back almost immediately. They were now moving in a crouch, dragging their prisoner. They grinned with pride when the officer congratulated them on their good work. The German was trussed up in the bushes. The Canadians carried off all his weapons, including his pocket knife. Then the small group returned to the spot where the rest of the column was still waiting.

"Are there any other sentries nearby?" the officer asked Tom and Carl.

"Not as far as we know," whispered Tom. "The next guard is far enough away so he won't hear us if we move quickly and quietly."

That was enough for the officer. Again a whispered command was passed along among the men, and they got to their feet. Keeping low, they advanced across the dark marshland. They reached the meadows beyond without being challenged and began moving faster. The grass fields were wet with dew.

Haaksma, who had been talking softly with the officer, now joined the boys. "I can tell you more about the plan now," he said. "We're going to try to seize the German headquarters — that big mansion with the outbuildings which were converted into barracks. You know the building I'm talking about? We have to have total surprise on our side, so everything depends on us not running into any sentries before we get there. Not that we couldn't overpower them, but one shot would be enough to raise the alarm and mess up our plan. Now, it seems to me, that if we circle around the village, we should be able to reach the back of that mansion without running into anybody. Right?"

"Sure," said Tom, "but there are also guards at the back of the building. I've seen them often enough."

Haaksma smiled. "We'll worry about them when we get there. Now the important thing is to avoid the sentries watching the roads into town."

With the help of his three young companions, Haaksma sketched out a route for the squad. They made a wide sweep through the meadows bordering the village, moving as swiftly as they could. They had no time to lose. With growing uneasiness the officer saw the sky becoming lighter and lighter.

It was dawn when they turned from the grassland onto a small road lined with trees. They couldn't risk staying in the open fields any longer; they would have been spotted for sure.

Warily they stalked down the road. The dirt road took a few turns and then ran into the street that passed behind the mansion where the Germans were quartered. Just before they reached the intersection of the two roads, Haaksma waved to Tom.

"Will you and Scout sneak ahead and check out the rear of the house for us?" he asked Tom. "When you come to the end of this road, you should have a good view of the back yard. Keep your eyes open for anything unusual."

Tom trembled with excitement. Very cautiously he crept forward with Scout beside him. The dog had already sensed the nearness of his old enemy, for he bared his teeth and uttered a low growl deep in his throat.

They reached the intersection in about two minutes. Carefully Tom peered across to the big house. Two sentries were on duty. They were clearly visible in the early dawn. Lights were already on in the mansion and in one of the outbuildings, but Tom saw nothing out of the ordinary. Moving very deliberately, he made his way back to where Haaksma and the others were waiting in the cover of some bushes.

He told them what he had seen, and the officer nodded his head in satisfaction. He glanced at his watch and then sat back to wait. Tom eyed him, puzzled. All during the march here, the officer had constantly hounded them to move faster. What was he waiting for now?

First Tom didn't dare say anything, but as the minutes ticked away and daylight began to spread across the sky, he whispered to Haaksma, "Why don't we attack?"

"It's too early," Haaksma whispered back.

Too early? Tom could hardly believe his ears. His face must have shown his astonishment, for Haaksma grinned at him and said softly, "Our attack has to be launched so that the German soldiers around the village don't notice a thing. If there's shooting, we don't want them to hear it."

"But how can you prevent that?" Tom asked, even more puzzled. "They'll be sure to hear any shots."

Haaksma held up his hand. "Just wait a minute. Then you'll see how."

Again the officer looked at his watch. There was tension in his jaw.

Then, suddenly — BOOM!

The stillness of the morning was shattered by the deafening roar of artillery. It frightened Tom. A whole string of explosions followed. A thundering barrage of artillery fire sounded from outside the village.

"Those are our guns in the next village," said Haaksma. "They're shelling the German positions outside the town. This is our signal."

Carefully Tom peeked between the bushes. The Canadian soldiers were so well hidden, he saw nothing.

Then a whistle shrilled and fifty men jumped up and raced across the street toward the mansion. Both sentries were disarmed before they realized what was happening. Onward the soldiers stormed, through the garden and the back yard to the house and the outbuildings.

Everything seemed to have been well rehearsed. The troop divided into several squads, each of which surrounded a different building. The attack took the Germans so by surprise that they put up almost no resistance. The Canadian soldiers immediately occupied all doorways and posted themselves at the windows.

The astonished Germans, who were in the middle of getting dressed, had no chance to fight back. Here and there a few shots rang out, and two of the Canadians were wounded. The great majority of the Germans, however, saw that resistance was useless and quickly surrendered.

At the express command of Haaksma, the three boys had hung back. They would have loved to take part in the attack, but they themselves understood that this was impossible, for they were untrained and unarmed.

Haaksma, the Canadian officer, and two other soldiers entered the large mansion. Several other soldiers watched the doors and windows. The boys hesitated a moment. What should they do? Should they follow Haaksma inside? Still undecided, they circled the house. As they rounded a corner, a shot rang out. A Canadian soldier guarding one of the windows slumped to the ground. Then the window was thrown open and a German leaped outside. He wore an officer's uniform and high boots. He was making a run for it.

"Get him!" shouted Bert. "It's the German Commandant!"

The officer had quite a lead already, and he was waving the pistol with which he had shot the Canadian soldier. He seemed determined to resist to the end.

Even before the boys could move, however, Scout had torn himself loose and was springing after the escaping German. He caught up to the man in a few seconds and leaped at his throat. The sudden weight of the big German shepherd sent the man sprawling forward on his face. His pistol flew from his hand. He tried to scramble back to his feet, but Scout gave him no chance.

The boys came racing up as fast as they could. They had never before seen Scout so ferocious. He seemed to have recognized the officer. It was a good thing for the man that Tom arrived to call his dog off, otherwise he would have come out of it in very sad shape indeed.

The officer lay on his back protecting his throat with his arm, which had already been badly mauled by Scout's teeth. He stared at the dog with fear-filled eyes.

"That's . . . that's the dog . . . But I shot that dog!" he gasped dazedly.

When Tom heard his words, suddenly he understood. This must be the man who had shot Scout! By now several Canadian soldiers had also come running up. The fugitive was pulled to his feet and led away under close guard.

Haaksma and the Canadian officer also came running outside. They had taken a few prisoners in the mansion, but the commandant had escaped through the window. They breathed a huge sigh of relief when they saw that Scout had captured the man.

"Now do you see how we could stage the attack without the soldiers around the town hearing anything?" Haaksma asked Tom, smiling. "Thanks to you fellows, no one got away to sound the alarm. If that commandant had gotten away, our operation might still have been undone."

Chapter 22

The Missing Prisoner

The prisoners were all herded into one of the outbuildings, locked up and put under close guard.

Haaksma and the Canadian officer went back into the big house to study the papers on the commandant's desk. The three boys and Scout strolled around looking at the other buildings, which were being searched by some of the Canadians.

"Look," said Tom, "what's that low concrete building over there? It must have been built not long ago. I've never noticed it before."

Curious, they went to examine it. The door was equipped with heavy iron latches and sliding bars, but it was standing ajar. When they opened it all the way, the boys looked down a long, narrow corridor lined with doors on both sides. Above each door was a number. A row of bare light bulbs lit the gray hallway. It looked as if someone had just run out of the door.

"Hold it," said Bert, as he closed the outside door behind him. "There's a little room off to the side here. That must be for the doorkeeper."

"Or maybe for the guard," suggested Carl. "This looks more like a prison to me. I'm sure there are cells behind all those closed doors."

The door to the small room was also unlocked. The lights were on there too. Inside stood a table, two straight chairs and a cot. Tom walked to a wall cabinet and opened it. The first thing he saw was a large ring of keys.

He seized them eagerly. "Now we'll see what's behind those doors," he said. "See, there's a number attached to each key, so we know which key fits which door. The guard must have made a run for it. I hope our boys caught him. They said no one got away, didn't they?"

They hurried back into the hall and went to the nearest cell door. As Tom fit the matching key into the lock, their hearts pounded with excitement. He had to pull hard to get the door open, but it moved.

With a grinding noise, the heavy door swung open. They were met by a draft of cold air. It was too dark in the cell to see anything. There was a small, barred window high in the wall, but the faint morning light did not yet penetrate into the cell.

Hesitantly the three boys stood in front of the open door. They were still a little wary. Was that the creaking of a mattress?

"You can come out," Tom said in his deepest voice, but he noticed that it trembled just a little.

They heard a cry of surprise from inside. In the dark cell someone jumped off a cot and came staggering out into the light, blinking in the bright hallway lights.

Then it was the boys' turn to look surprised. "Mr. Bouwman!" they all cried. Bouwman was one of the men from the village who had been arrested by the Germans several days ago. Since then no one had heard anything of him or his fellow victims.

Thin and haggard, the man stared at them in confusion. Then suddenly he recognized the three "Canadian" soldiers standing in front of him. A huge smile spread over his face. "Well, isn't this something! I'm being liberated by our own boys. I can't believe it! Has the whole town been liberated already?"

"No, Mr. Bouwman, I'm afraid not. We're here with a special commando that took the German headquarters by surprise. Who are in the other cells?"

"As far as I know, they're all political prisoners like myself. At least, I know there are several others from our village in here, men who were arrested at the same time I was. Yesterday the guard told me we were all going to be moved to Germany because the Allies were so close. You fellows arrived just in the nick of time. Wait a minute, I'll tell the others."

He cupped his hands around his mouth and bellowed as loudly as he could: "Listen, mates! We're free! The Canadians have arrived! Long live the Queen!"

Suddenly from behind all the doors erupted a muffled chorus of cheering and banging. The prisoners had already been awakened by the shelling. Now they set up a joyful clamour to be released.

Tom hurried down the hall, unlocking one cell after another with the big bundle of keys. Every cell held men from the village. Some were weeping with joy and others loudly praised God for their rescue.

Carl followed on Tom's heels, pale with suspense. Surely his father would be in one of the cells! Here was the last cell door. Again a man emerged whom they all knew, but it wasn't Carl's father. Carl looked at his friends, his face deathly pale. "My dad's not here!" he gasped as if he'd lost his breath. "Maybe they've shot him." And then he burst into tears.

Tom looked at the keys in his hand. "There's one key left," he said. "Look, this one. It doesn't have a number, but it's marked with a K."

The man who had been locked in the last cell, approached them. "I think there's a trapdoor at the end of the hall," he told them. "I could hear the guard opening it and going down some stairs. I'm sure there's a basement under here."

The boys studied the floor. Here, at the end of the hall, the light wasn't very good. Suddenly Carl yelped, "Over here! This isn't cement; it's wood. You can't see it because it's painted gray, but I don't see any keyhole."

Tom dropped to his knees. "It's a trapdoor all right," he said. "Here's a ring. It's cut into the wood; I can't get a hold of it. Wait a minute, I'll pry it up with my jackknife."

He lifted the ring and pulled up on it. The wooden trapdoor came up. Underneath it, iron steps came into view leading into the darkness below. The boys stared down into the black opening. The men who had just been released also gathered around the open trapdoor.

"Look, over there by the stairs," said one of the men, pointing down. "Isn't that a light switch?"

Tom flicked the knob and immediately the hole was flooded with light. They saw a storage cellar with pails, brooms, mops, and other equipment for cleaning the prison standing along the walls.

Tom descended the metal stairs, followed by Carl, Bert, and two of the freed men. The others stayed upstairs. As soon as he reached the bottom of the stairs and turned around, Tom cried, "There it is! At the other end of the cellar — a door with a K over it. That's where our last key fits."

He ran to the door. His hand shook so badly, he could hardly get the key in the lock. Carl stood behind him trembling with suspense.

The lock clicked. Slowly the door opened. They stared into the black space beyond. Nothing happened for a few seconds. Then a man came shuffling forward, slowly, hesitantly, blinking in the bright light that shone into the cell.

"Thank you for . . ." he began.

He was cut off by a loud whoop from his youngest liberator. "Father!" cried Carl, throwing his arms around his father's neck. Van Doorn looked stunned. Then he realized who this young soldier was that was hugging him. The emotions of the moment completely overpowered him. He wept and laughed at the same time.

"My boy, my boy! Is it really you? My own son comes to liberate me! I can't believe it. Are the Germans really gone?"

The onlookers all had tears in their eyes too. Van Doorn went upstairs with his young liberators and shook hands with everyone. Carl stuck to his father as if he were afraid he would suddenly disappear again. He beamed with pride and happiness.

Mr. Van Doorn told them that he had been tossed into the special punishment cell probably because the cells upstairs were all filled and also because the commandant had been so angry at him. He had spent all this time in total darkness, for there was no window in the cell.

At that moment, the outside door of the prison opened. Haaksma and the Canadian officer stepped inside. They stared at the men in the hall in complete surprise. Then with a big smile Haaksma began shaking hands.

He knew most of the men, and in recent months he had worked closely with some of them. "We just came to see what the Germans had stashed away in here," he said. "If we'd known, we would have come right away, but I'm happy to see that our brave young friends took care of things for us here."

The boys blushed with pride at Haaksma's remark, especially because they now knew he was Captain Brandenburg. The whole group crowded outdoors. During the time the boys had been in the prison, many things had changed in the yard. The Canadians had been busy. Several German army trucks had been found on the grounds and were standing ready to go. They had been loaded with machine guns and other weapons. Haaksma was talking with the Canadian officer. Then he turned to the released prisoners.

"We're about to begin the second stage of our operation," he told them. "Our plan is to attack the German defenses outside town from the rear. Anyone who wants to join us is welcome, but don't feel that you're being pressured. It's entirely up to you. You men have suffered enough, and if you don't feel up to it, I advise you to go home."

All the men insisted on volunteering to help in the liberation of their village.

"All right," said Haaksma. "Because we don't have any extra uniforms, every volunteer will be issued a bright orange armband. We've got plenty of rifles and other weapons, so help yourselves."

The three boys immediately volunteered too, their faces filled with anticipation, but Haaksma laughed and shook his head. "Sorry, boys," he said, "I didn't mean you. You boys are too young, and you don't know how to use a weapon. Almost all the other men have been involved in military service, or have learned to shoot. Your parents would never forgive me if I let you join us and if something happened to you. Besides," he went on with a mysterious look, "you three will be helping me elsewhere."

The boys were burning with curiosity, but Haaksma wouldn't answer any of their questions. He laughed and turned to Van Doorn. "I'd like to talk to you a moment," he said. "I also have a special job for you."

He took Carl's father aside a few steps and spoke with him briefly. Van Doorn listened attentively, nodding now and then. Finally he said, "You can count on me. I'll take care of it and I'll time it just right."

"Okay, boys," said Haaksma coming back to them. "We're going to take a walk into the village. We have a little chore to take care of there."

The four, with Scout, struck out along the road. Captain Brandenburg now walked with the military stride that he had carefully avoided for the last few years, and the boys, proud of their uniforms, did their best to match his step. Off they marched toward the village.

Chapter 23

In the Tower

The mansion that had served as German headquarters actually lay on the outskirts of the village. They followed a path that led into the village without taking them close to any German guard posts.

Soon the four, with Scout still faithfully tagging along, were walking through the village streets. Artillery fire continued to thunder away at the German positions, but the German guns were hammering back with equal ferocity; they didn't seem about to give up.

Although it was still early in the morning, it was now full daylight. There was no one in the streets, however. This was no wonder, for, expecting an attack, the Germans had issued orders last night that no one was to leave home. The boys did glimpse an occasional face risking a quick peek from behind the curtains. Their curiosity must have been whetted even more by seeing four soldiers in strange uniforms strolling down the street. Nevertheless, they didn't dare to come outside.

In the middle of the town stood a huge tower, rising high above all the other buildings. Beside it stood a small house. It looked like a frightened child cowering at the feet of a giant. The tower was very old. People who are supposed to know about such things said it had been built during the Middle Ages. It must have seen quite a few battles during its lifetime. In the little house lived Old Gerrit, the keeper of the tower.

Haaksma stepped up to the little wooden door and rattled the doorknocker. Everything remained quiet inside. Once again Haaksma swung the knocker, and when there was still no response, he pounded his fist on the door.

A wrinkled, bearded face appeared in a little window. It stared at the four soldiers with large, frightened eyes. The old man's eyes opened even wider when he saw that they weren't Germans. Haaksma didn't notice the face at first, but then Tom nudged him and pointed to the window.

"Hey, Gerrit, open up! We're friends. I've got to talk to you," called Haaksma.

The face disappeared and soon shuffling footsteps sounded in the hall. The door opened a small crack.

"Who are you? What do you want?" asked the old man hoarsely. He eyed them suspiciously.

Then suddenly a light of recognition dawned in his eyes. He took another good look at Haaksma and then threw the door wide open. All of a sudden the old man looked much younger. Even his stooped back seemed to straighten a little.

"I didn't recognize you right away," he said to Haaksma. "You look so different in that uniform."

Haaksma laughed. "I know, Gerrit. I came to ask for your help one more time. Do you have a big Dutch flag?"

Old Gerrit nodded. "I still have the big flag that I used to hang from the tower on national holidays. I hoped I'd be able to see it hoisted up again one day," he said, beaming.

He opened the living room door and ushered them in. Then he went to an old cabinet, opened a large drawer, and from underneath a pile of sheets, he produced a beautiful flag. He showed it to them very proudly.

"Perfect!" said Haaksma. "Just what I had in mind."

The wrinkled old man looked at Haaksma in puzzlement. Worried, he shook his head. "But we're not liberated yet," he pointed out. "I know the Canadians are very close, but the Germans are strong here. You know that!"

Haaksma laughed. "I know, Gerrit! I know, but, God willing, today will be the day. This flag is going to serve not just after we're liberated, but it's going to help speed up our liberation, and I'll need your help too."

He motioned to the old man, and they retreated into the hall, where they talked quietly.

When they came back inside, all the worry had disappeared from Old Gerrit's face. "We'll do our best," he said. "Man, won't that be something — if it works!"

The old tower-keeper rolled up the big flag and hid it under his coat. Then together they went back outside.

The boys still had no idea what was going on, but Haaksma and Old Gerrit seemed to know what they were doing. They stepped next door to the huge, metal-plated doors of the old tower. Old Gerrit produced a big key and put it in the lock. The old door opened, squeaking and grinding on its hinges. Quickly they all squeezed inside, and the old man carefully closed the heavy door behind them.

Inside, the old tower was quite dark. A little light came in through two small windows high in the wall. A thick length of rope dangled down out of the gloom. That was the rope to the big bell, the boys knew. Before the war they had sometimes peeked in on Old Gerrit as he was ringing the big bell. The sound would carry through the whole village and far into the surrounding countryside. There were also a few old crates to be seen and a stone staircase that wound to the top of the tower.

"Okay," Haaksma said to Gerrit, "the boys are going up with me. Scout will stay down here to keep you company. He's a good watchdog and he'll let you know if any Germans are coming, but I don't think there's much danger of that."

He took the big flag from the tower-keeper and started up the spiralling staircase. The boys followed him, filled with anticipation and suspense.

The staircase was very narrow and steep, so they had to be careful not to slip. Here and there they had to claw their way through huge cobwebs. Suddenly Haaksma stopped. Above him was a trapdoor that he pushed upward. The foursome climbed through and found themselves on a stone floor. In it was a slot through which the bell-rope passed to the bell farther overhead. A wooden ladder rose to a small attic a few metres higher up. Now they were right under the big bell.

Another ladder took them past the big bell, hanging still and ponderous in its heavy frame. For a moment they stopped and looked at the magnificent metal dome. It was so old and unique that even the Germans, who had melted down most bells into bullets, had bypassed this one.

Tired of their long climb, they finally reached the top of the tower. There was barely enough room here for all four of them. They could see in all directions through the large portholes, but for the time being the boys had their eyes fixed on Haaksma, who was carefully unfurling the big flag and fastening it to a long rope. Now all he had to do was to pull the rope, and the flag would be waving from the flagpole at the top of the tower. However, the time was not yet right. After fastening the flag to the rope, Haaksma neatly put the flag in a corner of the small space and said, "Okay, that's all set! Now let's have a look — see what's happening outside."

They looked down through the portholes. Far underneath lay the village. The houses looked very small from so high up — like dollhouses. Tom could clearly see his own house. "Maybe they're still sleeping," he thought. "Or they're afraid to show themselves. I don't see a thing." He kept looking. Were they very worried about him? Yes, he imagined they would be. They didn't even know whether he had reached the windmill safely. Mother must have shed quite a few tears when he didn't return.

Then his attention was diverted by an excited cry from Bert, "Look! A direct hit! Those Canadians are doing some fancy shooting!"

A dull explosion rocked the village. The Canadian artillery had blown up a German bunker.

The light was excellent now. Behind them, the sun was well over the horizon, shining in full splendour. From their raised vantage point, the boys could see everything very clearly. Tom and Carl still had Van Doorn's binoculars with them. They and Bert took turns scanning the battlefield. Haaksma had his own binoculars.

"Brother!" said Haaksma after a while. "Our artillery has already done quite a bit of damage to the German positions. They're making good use of the maps and information we provided. I'm sure the Germans are wondering how come the Allies are shooting so accurately."

Suddenly from the neighbouring village the boys saw several tanks moving toward the German lines. Now it really became clear how hard the Germans had been hit, for although they fired back, the barrage was not nearly as fierce as it had once been.

The foursome in the tower followed the battle with extreme suspense. Haaksma, however, paid little attention to the tanks; instead, he focused his binoculars closer to their own village. Then he stretched out his hand and pointed excitedly to something moving in the distance. "There they are, boys!" he cried. "This is when the show really starts!"

Looking through their binoculars, the boys saw four German trucks leaving their own village. For a moment they looked puzzled. Where did they come from?

Then it dawned on them: of course, it was the Canadian strike force and the freed prisoners!

The return fire of the Germans suddenly picked up a little, encouraged by what they thought were the arrival of reinforcements. After that, everything went with astounding speed. More Canadian tanks and trucks came out of the liberated village. At the same time, the German trucks approaching from the opposite direction suddenly displayed Dutch and Canadian flags. They stopped, and the soldiers and volunteers spilled out and deployed themselves behind the German positions. Then they opened up on the unprotected German flank with rifle and machine gun fire and also with some light artillery.

"Now it's our turn!" said Haaksma triumphantly. He seized the long rope to which he had fastened the flag and pulled on it. In a few seconds the red, white, and blue flag was fluttering from the top of the tower. The boys were almost bouncing up and down in excitement. "Ring the bell, Gerrit!" Haaksma shouted down to the old man. "Your day of liberation is here!"

A few seconds later, the rich tones of the old bell rang out over the village rooftops, almost drowning out the sounds of battle.

Looking out over the countryside, Carl suddenly shouted, "Look! There's a flag flying from our windmill too."

"Right!" Haaksma shouted back over the sound of the bell. "Your father is in on the plan. As soon as he saw our flag, he was supposed to hang out his. That way the Germans will think we have control of the whole village. We hope!"

Again they studied the German lines, which were now caught in a crossfire. The return fire from the Germans had almost ceased altogether. Apparently, the Germans had been caught completely by surprise and were stunned by the sudden turn of events. They heard the triumphant pealing of the big bell and saw Dutch flags flying from the tower, the windmill and, to their great consternation, even from their own headquarters.

The boys were jumping and hooting exuberantly, but Haaksma was still watching tensely. He knew they were playing a dangerous game. If the Germans discovered that the force behind them was relatively small and that the village was not really occupied by the Allies . . .

Laying down a steady barrage of fire, the Canadian tanks rolled closer and closer to the German positions. Then, suddenly, Haaksma, too, let out a whoop of joy. From one of the German positions rose a dirty white flag.

"A white flag! They're surrendering!" shouted Haaksma.

The boys fought for the binoculars to get a better look at what was happening. Yes, now they saw it too. Elsewhere another white flag went up, and fifty metres farther down the line another, and another!

The shooting had now stopped completely. Trooping forth out of the bunkers and trenches came the German soldiers, their hands held high. Whole squadrons were laying down their weapons.

"This is it, boys! This is the real thing! Now we're really liberated. That earlier show was just a pretence to fool the Germans. But now we can be pretty sure this flag won't come down again," said Haaksma. There was a strange tremble in his voice.

Chapter 24

Flags and Bells

Meanwhile, the village streets below were coming alive with people. First there were only a few who had seen the flag fluttering from the tower. Everyone was hesitant about coming out, because the previous night the commandant had threatened that anyone caught out on the street would be shot. But when the shooting had stopped, followed by a strange silence broken only by the festive pealing of the big bell, here and there a brave soul ventured outdoors. They saw no Germans, but they also saw no Canadians. Nevertheless, the old tri-colour was flying from the tower, and the bell was ringing triumphantly.

More people ventured out into the street. They looked up at the top of the tower and saw figures moving in the large portholes. They looked like soldiers in uniform. What was going on?

Up in the tower the boys were still watching the exciting drama on the battlefield. They saw another German squadron surrendering. The German defenses were being overrun and occupied by the Canadians. Several tanks and trucks had already penetrated the German lines and were headed toward the village. The strike force that had attacked the Germans from the rear, creating great confusion among the Germans, was also heading back to the village.

Finally they looked down into the village and saw that the street below was crowded with people. They waved and shouted down at the villagers, but the jubilant voice of the bell drowned out everything, and no one seemed to recognize them.

Tom had again taken up the binoculars. He suddenly flushed and then paled. "There's my dad!" he exclaimed. "And there's Mother too. And Miriam and Ina. They're coming into town." The binoculars trembled in his hands and he blinked rapidly.

The boys didn't have eyes enough to see everything. Only now were the people beginning to believe that their village was really liberated. Here and there flags were beginning to appear in the village. Several children came running into the street wearing orange, the colour of the House of Orange, the Dutch royal family. Many were still wary because they saw no Canadian soldiers. The optimists, however, were already cheering and singing. With a few last, powerful chimes the bell-ringing ceased. Old Gerrit, who had been pulling the bell-rope for some time, was tuckered out.

In the crowded streets down below Tom had lost sight of his father and mother. They ought to be somewhere close to the tower by now, he thought. "Should we go down now?" he asked Haaksma impatiently.

The latter nodded. "Our job is done," he said. "The first Canadian tanks are already on the outskirts of town and all German resistance seems to be broken. Let's go see how Gerrit and Scout are doing."

As quickly as they dared, they descended the steep, narrow stairs. Haaksma hollered at the boys several times, telling them to watch their step. In their jubilation, they tried to rush down the dangerous steps much faster than was safe.

When they reached the last landing before the bottom floor, they heard a loud babble of voices. Gerrit must have opened the big door and let the people in. Quickly the boys lowered themselves through the last trapdoor to take the last flight of steps.

They were greeted by a loud cheer as they came into view.

"Hurrah for the Canadians!"

"Welcome, boys!"

"Three cheers!"

Haaksma burst into laughter. "Sorry folks!" he shouted down. "But we're all Dutchmen!"

The crowd subsided in surprise. "We gave the Canadians a little help to confuse the Germans, and it worked. The Germans have surrendered, and the first Canadian tanks are already coming into town."

Another loud hurrah went up. The people didn't really understand what had happened, but they realized that the four friends, whom they now finally recognized, had helped liberate their village. When Haaksma and the boys reached the last steps, they were seized by the exuberant crowd, hoisted up on their shoulders, and carried out into the street. Scout barked happily and jumped around in excitement as if he understood what was going on.

The street outside was packed with people, who all began cheering when they saw the four "Canadians" emerging from the tower. Haaksma and the boys wanted to get down, but the men carrying them wouldn't let them go. They were carried down the street through the celebrating crowd.

Suddenly, at a corner of the main street, Tom spied his mother and father. He felt himself flushing with eagerness, and again he tried to get down to the ground, but without success. From where they were standing, his parents apparently could not see who these "Canadians" really were. They didn't look nearly as happy as the rest of the crowd, however. Tom knew that they must be terribly worried about him. "Dad! Mom!" he shouted.

The singing and clamour of the celebrating crowd, however, overwhelmed the sound of his voice. But then Scout went bounding ahead. He, too, had spied Mr. Sanders, and he ran toward him barking happily. Tom's parents stared at the dog in astonishment. Mr. Sanders grabbed Scout and, petting him, asked, "Where's Tom, boy? Take us to Tom!"

Scout barked impatiently and darted a few steps in Tom's direction and then came prancing back, as if telling Mr. Sanders to follow.

Anxiously Mr. and Mrs. Sanders followed their son's dog. They frantically searched the crowd to see if their boy was among the celebrating people. But they didn't give the four "Canadian" soldiers a second look. They were interested only in finding their son.

Tom saw his parents coming closer, scanning the crowd for him. Again he shouted, "Dad! Mom! Over here!"

Haaksma, who also saw them looking, bellowed in his powerful voice: "Mr. Sanders! Over here!" He pointed to Tom. "Here's Tom! He's okay!"

Haaksma's voice penetrated to the anxious parents. They stared up at the soldiers, nonplussed. At first they couldn't believe their eyes. Then they came flying through the crowd.

The men lowered Tom to the ground. His parents threw their arms around him. "My boy, my boy! Where have you been? Are you all right? Oh, thank God! Thank God!"

Tom's mother wept, and Tom, too, couldn't blink back the tears. His father stood by, swallowing and pulling strange faces. The scene brought a momentary stillness to the crowd.

Suddenly, fifty metres down the street, a new cheer went up. Two large tanks and a German truck decorated with flags appeared around the corner, heading toward the centre of the village. Everyone went running toward the tanks. Tom's parents, Haaksma, and the boys were swept along, will or no.

Then Tom's eyes fell on Ina and Miriam standing on the sidewalk, pressing themselves against the side of a building to keep from being caught in the crush. They had come with Mother and Father, but had lost them in the crowd. Tom pushed through the people toward the two girls and suddenly seized them both by the hand. First they looked up startled and frightened by the bold "Canadian," but then they saw who it was. Overjoyed, they threw themselves at Tom, who pulled them along with the stream of people.

The streets were now crammed with elated people, so that the tanks could no longer move. The villagers surrounded the laughing soldiers, and when they discovered who was riding in the German truck, the celebration became even more jubilant. The truck was loaded with men from the village who had been arrested during the last few weeks of the German occupation. The men leaped from the back of the truck and joined their celebrating friends and relatives. Emotional scenes took place as wives were reunited with husbands, and parents with sons. There was weeping and rejoicing. Never before had the village known such gladness.

When the Dutch volunteers saw Haaksma and his three young companions, they cried, "There they are! They set us free and they made the plan to liberate the village!" Once again Haaksma and the boys were hoisted up; this time they were put up on the truck and so was Scout.

Slowly the procession moved ahead. The two Canadian tanks led the way, followed by the German truck carrying the four heroes. Around them swarmed the jubilant mob. On the street, in doorways, in windows — everywhere there were faces filled with joy. Slowly they moved into the village square and stopped in front of the town hall.

The entire population of the village gathered in the square. A man came forward out of the crowd and, accompanied by the cheers of the people, climbed the high steps of the town hall. It was the former mayor; he had been dismissed by the Germans, but the villagers still considered him to be the real leader of the community.

In the best English he could muster, the mayor welcomed the Canadian liberators. Then he turned to Haaksma and his three companions and praised them for the brave part they had played in the liberation of the village. Although he didn't know all the details, said the mayor, he had found out that the boys had sneaked through the German lines to pass valuable information to the Canadians, and that with Haaksma they had served as guides for the Canadian strike force that had taken the German headquarters.

The boys flushed at the words of praise directed to them and squirmed under the admiration of the villagers. Haaksma too wished the ceremonies were over and done with. But when mention was made of Scout's role in the affair, Tom beamed with pride at his faithful dog, who stood beside him wagging his tail happily.

Then the mayor advised the people to calm down and go home for now. There would be time for celebrating later. The war wasn't over yet and a large section of the country was still waiting to be liberated. Soon the crowd began to trickle away to their homes.

Tom joined his parents and the two young girls. His friends had already left. Together they walked back home to *Heathview*.

With everything behind him, Tom felt how terribly tired he was. His head was pounding and he seemed to be moving in a dream. As they walked home, many people stared at him in admiration, but he was completely unaware of them. When some of his schoolmates shouted, "Hi, Tom!" he gave them a little wave. He found it hard to believe how exhausted he suddenly felt. His parents, too, noticed how tired he looked and anxiously kept a close eye on him. The intense effort and excitement of the last twenty-four hours had made excessive demands on his strength.

When they reached home, Coby and the gardener were waiting for them in the front yard. They, too, gave Tom a joyful welcome. A flag was draped from an upstairs window and the front door stood wide open. Mother insisted that he lie down on the sofa in the living room. But Tom didn't want to seem like a weakling, so he insisted on sitting up even though his head was spinning. Mother fetched her last bit of real tea, which she had been saving for some time already, and they all celebrated his return with a cup of tea. Father and Mother told him how worried they had been when he hadn't come home. Then Tom had to tell them everything that had happened since he had left to go to Van Doorn's windmill yesterday.

Everyone gathered around to listen to the story; the two girls listened in growing wonder, awed by his daring. Scout sat beside Tom as if he too were listening to the story. Every time Tom mentioned his name, he wagged his tail and gave Tom an eager look.

Suddenly he was interrupted by the sound of the doorbell. Coby went to answer the door, and a moment later Van Doorn was ushered into the living room. He was carrying a big bag.

"Tom didn't finish his errand," the miller said, grinning. "He stopped by yesterday morning to pick up a bag of flour, and now I end up delivering it myself." Everyone laughed as Van Doorn shook hands all around. Tom could barely believe that it was only yesterday he had left for the mill. So much had happened in the meantime!

"I came on Tom's bike," said Van Doorn. "He left it at our place. But, seriously, Sanders, your boy behaved with real courage. I'm proud of Carl too, but Tom was definitely the leader. I gathered that much from what Carl told me."

Tom blushed. Father looked at him affectionately and said, "We're all thankful to God for bringing Tom and Carl home safely through great dangers."

Van Doorn sat down. "Carl is already in bed," he said. "He was sick with exhaustion."

"It's time for Tom to go to bed too," Mother said anxiously. "I know he's not feeling very well either, even though he doesn't want to show it."

Tom had to admit that Mother was right. He let her send him up to bed. When Mother looked in on him a little while later, he was having chills, and she knew he was running a fever.

Chapter 25

Healing and Wholeness

The next day the town was again bustling with people, all in a festive mood. More Canadian troops arrived, and everyone went out to welcome them. But Tom wasn't among them. He lay sick in bed. His parents had called in the doctor, who told them that, not only had Tom been over-exhausted by the physical and emotional strain of his adventure, he had also caught a bad cold.

The first few days Tom ran quite a high temperature, and Mother spent most of the day at his bedside. But soon he was on the road to recovery.

On the third day the commander of the Canadian troops dropped in to see how his young hero was doing. He was delighted to hear that Tom's fever had broken. To show his appreciation for Tom's help, he presented Tom with a beautiful watch. Tom, of course, was immensely proud of his gift. His two friends, Carl and Bert, also received similar watches.

Tom beamed with pleasure and was ready to come bounding out of bed, but wiser heads prevailed. For Scout the commander brought a beautifully decorated collar. He petted the dog and told Tom he would love to have him as an army dog, but he knew that Tom would never part with his four-footed friend.

The Canadian troops had already advanced well beyond the village. When the strong German defenses around the village had collapsed so suddenly, the Germans had quickly retreated to other positions. So the Canadian commander and his staff also had to move on. He shook hands once more and said goodbye to Tom.

Haaksma, or Captain Brandenburg, also dropped in to say goodbye. By this time Tom was already up and around. Haaksma was still wearing a Canadian uniform, for he had joined the Allies. The front lines had advanced quite a ways beyond the village, but he had managed to get a ride back to make a brief visit.

He told Tom about the time he had spent hiding at the farm, and about gathering information for the Allies. He had been a soldier long before the war had broken out. And for several years he had been a dog trainer for the army. That was why he had been able to teach Scout so much in a very short period of time.

Haaksma had to cut his visit short, for he had been given only a few hours leave. But he promised to come back again soon.

A few weeks later, the village was again celebrating. The Germans had surrendered. The whole country was liberated.

Tom was back to his old self. So he joined in the celebrations with his two friends, Carl and Bert. The two girls joined them, and, of course, Scout tagged along. All over the village flags were flying. People streamed into town to watch the big parade, and afterwards there were games in the town square. Old Gerrit rang the tower bell as it had never been rung before.

The five children thought the noise and festivities were wonderful. They kept running into people they knew. In fact, Tom and his friends were now so well known, they were greeted by almost everyone. And Scout, strutting about in his new collar, attracted great admiration.

To his pleasant surprise, Tom suddenly saw Jeremiah Sap, the farmer who had been hiding Miriam and her grandparents, strolling about in the crowded street. Tom nudged Miriam and pointed. "Look who's here!" he said.

Miriam suddenly turned pale. Once again she remembered that horrible afternoon when she and her grandparents had been found by the Germans. They pushed their way through the crowd toward the farmer. There were so many people in the streets, it took the children some time to catch up with him, but finally Tom was able to grab him by the sleeve.

Jeremiah Sap turned around. "Hi there, Tom!" he said jovially as he recognized Tom.

Then he saw Miriam and his mouth dropped open in astonishment. He bent forward and put his hands on her shoulders. "Is it really you?" he cried. "Did the Germans let you go?"

"I ran away, just like you," said Miriam, "and Tom helped me escape. I've been living with the Sanders family."

"And your grandparents?" Jeremiah asked hesitantly, almost afraid to ask.

Tears came to Miriam's eyes. "They were taken away and I never heard from them again," she said softly. "I'm afraid they're dead, like Dad and Mom." She wept quietly. Ina too couldn't keep back the tears.

But Miriam quickly got hold of herself again. She wiped away her tears and said, "But I'm not sad; I may stay with Tom and Ina, and I've learned all kinds of things I never knew before."

Tom and Ina knew what she was talking about. Miriam had learned to know and love the Lord Jesus.

When the children came home later that day, they had many stories to tell Father and Mother. They were all excited about what they had seen and heard. Tom sat on the floor with his arm around Scout's neck.

"Now the bad times are over," he said. "Now that the Germans are gone, won't everything be wonderful!"

Father looked at him with such a strange, serious look, he fell silent.

For a moment everyone was still. Then Mr. Sanders said quietly, "Yes, Tom, we must thank God for liberating us. But things won't really be wonderful if people keep drifting farther away from God and if they turn away from His church."

Tom nodded. Even though he didn't understand everything, he knew Father was right.

Later, he often thought of his father's words.

Are you looking for a good devotional Bible for your teenager?

The Dort Study Bible is one of the best tools to study the Word of God. Its greatest strength is that it constantly leads one back to the Word. Though it has been used for nearly four hundred years by thousands of ministers, it is first of all intended for the common people. When we were proofreading *The Dort Study Bible* our seven year old son, Hinne, said, "I think I understand it much better now."

In an Afrikaans sermon on Lord's Day 21 (dealing with the communion of saints) Dr. C. Van der Waal said, "By what was the communion of Saints strengthened in the days of Luther? By 95 theses, scientific theses, which were printed and copied from hand to hand. By what did Calvin strengthen the communion of Saints from Poland to Hungary, from France to the Netherlands? By publishing his commentaries and dedicating them to princes and those in authority. That was a use of gifts for the benefit of the communion of saints with the help of his brother Antoine who had a printing press. How did the seceders (of 1834)[1] in all their helplessness and perhaps also in their narrow-mindedness and weakness also serve the communion of Saints? By publishing a correct version of the States Bible (which is the Dutch edition of *The Dort Study Bible*) and the (three) Forms of Unity, and by publishing a new translation of the Canons of Dort, especially made by the immigrants of 1847 (Van Raalte, etc.) in America."

"The whole States Translation bears the mark of conscious, pious, and necessary resistance against any Arminianism."

— Dr. Klaas Schilder

(in *Extra-Scriptural Binding — A New Danger*)

"The importance is that we see how ecclesiastical awareness runs throughout Scripture, and that we use this to teach us what church consciousness really is. The men who gave us the States Bible had an eye for that. This is clear from the annotations which are still worth while to consider."

— Rev. H.H.J. Feenstra

(in *Was Abraham Reformed?*)

"Fathers and mothers who fear God and desire to serve Him according to His Word find in the States Bible a precious tool."

— Prof. L. Lindeboom

(in *a Preface to several reprints of the States Bible*)

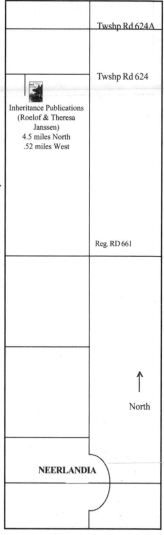

Inheritance Publications
(Roelof & Theresa Janssen)
4.5 miles North
.52 miles West

Twshp Rd 624A

Twshp Rd 624

Reg. RD 661

↑
North

NEERLANDIA

---

[1] The words within the brackets have been inserted by the translator, Roelof A. Janssen.